More than one way
to skin a cat

"I'm telling you, Charlie, the answer isn't in the records. Don't you think I looked?"

"My methods aren't quite the same as yours," said Charlie, recognizing the despair that Mickey was attempting to keep from overwhelming him. "I have other resources, other means of gaining information. Let me have the victim's map, his files, and something that belonged to him, please. I'll return them to you before he is buried, you have my word on it. I won't disgrace his memory, and I'll do everything I can to find his murderers."

Mickey folded his arms, but a glimmer of hope was in his eyes, a hope that he strove relentlessly to subdue. "What the hell do you think you can do?"

"If I'm lucky, I can find out what happened," said Charlie deliberately.

"What are you?" Mickey scoffed. "Some kind of medicine man?"

Charlie did not laugh with him. "Yes," he said. "That's exactly what I am."

"A fun series."—*Scars*

Jove Books by C.Q. Yarbro

BAD MEDICINE
FALSE NOTES
POISON FRUIT

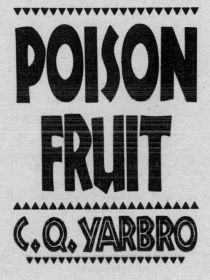

POISON FRUIT

C. Q. YARBRO

JOVE BOOKS, NEW YORK

POISON FRUIT

A Jove Book / published by arrangement with
the author

PRINTING HISTORY
Jove edition / September 1991

ISBN: 0-515-10666-6

Jove Books are published by The Berkley Publishing Group,
200 Madison Avenue, New York, New York 10016.
The name "JOVE" and the "J" logo
are trademarks belonging to Jove Publications, Inc.

PRINTED IN THE UNITED STATES OF AMERICA

10 9 8 7 6 5 4 3 2 1

A decade ago I dedicated Ariosto *to the conductor whose recordings have accompanied more of my working hours than any other. Since it is still true—*

this is for
MAESTRO COLIN DAVIS
encore!

ACKNOWLEDGMENTS

The writer would like to thank the following people for their generous assistance in the preparation of this book:

Robin A. Dubner, attorney-at-law
David Nee, continuing intrepid researcher
William R. Allen, psychological consultant

In law, evidence improperly obtained is inadmissible; any additional evidence obtained and/or devolved as a result of improperly obtained evidence is by extension inadmissible and is known as *the fruit of the poisonous tree*.

ONE

Tuesday afternoon

CHARLIE KNEW FROM the sound of the ring his wife was calling; that puzzled him for she rarely interrupted his work, or hers. Briefly he wondered why court was in recess. He pinched the bridge of his nose as he reached for the receiver. "Charles Moon," he said instead of her name, knowing how much she was unnerved by his sense of her.

"How much time will I get if I strangle a cop?" Morgan asked without any preamble, her voice tight.

"You tell me: you're the judge," he answered, hearing the anger and frustration in her voice and knowing she was depending on him to help her get beyond them.

"I'll plead justifiable homicide," she said to him, her words coming faster than usual.

So she felt guilty as well as angry. He did not let his worry for her color his answer. "Sounds serious. What did the poor blighter do to deserve this?" Charlie asked, taking a pencil from a mug filled with them. He started to doodle as he listened.

"Damned hotdog cop! He reinterpreted a search warrant," said Morgan, sounding very tired along with the rest. "I have to exclude the evidence, and all the rest of the material he got from it."

"At this stage?" Charlie said, surprised at the development.

"That's the worst of it. We're in front of a jury. The whole thing is blown. The defense has been insisting all along that the evidence was not covered in the search warrant, and now it turns out that he was right. But you know how Towne likes to grandstand. He uses every delaying trick in the book. He files

1538.5s on a' nost all the evidence, all the time. Everyone thought this was more of the same." She sounded as if she wanted to bite something. "We didn't know—why should we?—that the police report was false."

"They lied," said Charlie.

"They certainly fibbed," Morgan countered, trying to make light of it.

"So Towne did file a motion to suppress? In spite of what the police report said?" Charlie inquired.

"Sure did. With all the usual bells and whistles, saying that the search was not legal. He said the cops prevaricated. Nice choice of words. But the D.A.'s office said it was correct. Grainger ruled on it the week before his heart attack." She gave a quick, impatient sigh. "I like to think that if I'd had the case from the beginning this might never have happened. I tell myself I would have asked the cops about their report, just in case."

"And if they lied to you? If they filed a false report knowing it was false, they probably wouldn't admit it because you ask them to. You're not the conscience of the whole world, Morgan."

"I am a judge, and there are obligations that go with being a judge," she said, stubbornness apparent in her voice.

"You're a stickler for due process," said Charlie. "Is the evidence likely to make that much of a difference?"

"Oh, yeah," she said with weary scorn. "It's crucial. The D.A.'s been itching to get something on Scooter Ferrand, and all the cops know it; Ed Massie's just a little more zealous than most of them. He's got a young yahoo partner, too. They're on a vendetta against Ferrand. Let me tell you, they got material! That's the worst of it. Properly obtained and Ferrand would go away for a long long time. But the cops did it wrong. And that wrecks the D.A.'s case. Lovejoy's got all his eggs in one basket again." She hesitated, and he had enough understanding not to interrupt. "We can't touch Ferrand now, no matter what he did. This is a bad man, Charlie, a very bad man. You should see the videotapes they found." Her voice dropped. "Or maybe you shouldn't; they made me feel sick."

"Does it really wreck the case?" Charlie asked.

"Right down the line." She drew a long, pinched breath. "The search warrant said residence. Residence, not property. The cops added a detached greenhouse—*detached!* way at the back of the lot—so long as they were there. They had no reason to assume that they could extend the terms of the search warrant. There was no suggestion of imminent danger or the possibility of flight. So it's useless. And Lovejoy's playing the wounded innocent, saying he had no idea the cops had acted improperly."

"Give him a break," Charlie recommended, turning one of his doodles into a frolicking dolphin. "He probably didn't know. The cops don't always tell the D.A. everything, and he might not have asked, if the evidence found was that good. I can't see Lovejoy looking a gift horse in the mouth. He doesn't want to have his case thrown out of court on that kind of technicality, not if the evidence is the convicting kind. It looks bad."

A bit more tension was gone from her voice. "You should have been here: good old Victor Lovejoy storming around my chambers like a wounded hog."

"What an image," said Charlie, and could not keep from chuckling

Morgan faltered. "Well, maybe not a hog, maybe a prize bull." There was the first hint of amusement in her voice now.

"I think I like hog better," said Charlie, as if giving the matter due consideration. "More his style."

"Yeah," said Morgan, now sounding almost like herself. "Not that I blame him this time—if he's telling the truth, that is, and he really didn't know that his case was compromised." She was not ready to laugh, but her next words caught once, as if she were making her best attempt. "I don't know who I wanted to brain more—Lovejoy or that cop Ed Massie, who made the mistake, or that despicable—" Her voice was rising again and Charlie interrupted her.

"Well, you'd be up for assault no matter who you hit, so it's probably just as well you didn't." He waited for her to speak again, and when she remained silent, he said, "What about going somewhere decadent for dinner tonight? You got other plans?"

"I'd love it," she said without enthusiasm. "I would, really. But I don't think I'll be out of here until seven-thirty. That's pretty late."

"It's very fashionable," Charlie corrected her, though he was used to having dinner before seven. "I'll make reservations for eight, if you think that'll give you time enough. What about Modesto Lanzone's at Opera Plaza?"

This time there was a tiny-but-real laugh. "Not in the middle of the presymphony rush. Somewhere away from City Hall. Less . . . I ought to suggest something sensible like Japanese or salads, but . . . what the hell. Anything you choose is fine.

Curry or Hunan or Russian or Greek or Italian or Scandinavian or Peruvian—or any of the rest." She took a deep breath. "Thanks, Charlie. I wish I knew how you do it."

"How I do what?" he wondered aloud.

"Get me out of . . . everything."

"I thought that's why we got married," he said, doing his best to keep the serious note out of his voice.

"Yeah," she said slowly. For Morgan this was a major concession.

"I'll make the reservations. And I'll pick you up at seven-thirty." At that time of evening it would take him roughly fifteen minutes to reach her, but he allowed a little extra. "I'll think of a good place."

"You always do," she said, her manner nearly normal. Her voice was softer. "I look forward to it. Really."

"See you then." He heard her hang up, and put the receiver back in the cradle. Then he sat for more than five minutes staring at the window, his face supremely blank. What had happened? and what could he do about it?

His reverie was ended when there was a sharp knock on the door and Nathaniel Wong came in without further announcement. "I have to talk to you about this Hoopermier case. You got a minute?" Nathaniel had a way of pretending to make requests when he was actually giving orders.

"Sure," said Charlie, knowing it was the only acceptable answer to give any of his three partners. "You start the trial next week?"

"One week. Tuesday morning sharp." Nathaniel was almost a decade younger than Charlie, but his grave demeanor made him appear nearly the same age. He wore large tortoiseshell glasses, though his vision was perfect; he wanted to give an impression of thoughtfulness, and glasses were one of the best props at an attorney's command.

"Who's the judge again?"

"Mawson," Nathaniel said flatly.

"Fearless Freddie? I'd forgot." Charlie leaned back. "Well, be careful how you use shrinks as expert witnesses. Mawson's mother must have been frightened by a volume of Freud, the way he reacts to psychological testimony."

"I know that," said Nathaniel mildly. "I think I've got Mawson covered on that score. What worries me is that we've got a prosecutor I don't know much about, that new guy. I've been trying to get a line on him, but so far, nothing much."

Charlie tapped his desk with the eraser end of his pencil. "I'll make a couple of calls," he promised, deciding to tend to it that afternoon: his next appointment was over an hour away. "Anything you want to know other than general information?"

"I'd like to talk to someone who's been against him. If you can find someone, I'd appreciate it." He had the good fortune to possess a beautiful speaking voice, and he wielded it expertly. He also used throat lozenges the way some people used cigarettes. He took out a small case of them and selected one. The sharp scent of eucalyptus filled the room.

"I'll do what I can. It might take a day or so." Charlie knew Nathaniel well enough to accept his reticence to make the sort of calls he was asking Charlie to place for him.

"Fine. Whatever you can get. Thanks," said Nathaniel, adding belatedly "I hope I didn't interrupt anything?"

"Nothing that can't wait a few minutes," said Charlie.

Nathaniel looked chagrined, aware that he had intruded. "Oh, shit. Sorry."

Charlie dismissed the apology with a small shake of his head.

Dinner was superb, California-Mediterranean, experimental enough to be interesting but not unfamiliar. Through appetizers and entrees, Morgan discussed everything from repapering the guest room to taking time on the weekend to get into the country with their two malamutes to one of the parks, perhaps Point Reyes. She commented on the next opera season, the trouble her secretary was having with the computer, suggested which vegetables they might want to plant in the back, gave her reasons for thinking that sports were given an exaggerated importance on network television, remarked on the Miami-pink-and-blue the neighbors across the street had painted their house, guessed how much more she would have to pay in taxes come the middle of the next month. Over a dessert of raspberry tarts topped with bittersweet chocolate, Morgan finally settled down and discussed the case.

"I know it isn't quite proper to do this, but . . . Well, the case is being dismissed. Without those tapes, there isn't sufficient evidence. I had a call from George Wycliff about it already."

"I'll bet you did," said Charlie, who thought the recently elected District Attorney was too much of a politician and not enough of a prosecutor. "Probably wanted a damage assessment for his public image."

She raised her brows, indicating how accurate his supposition was. "I told him if he thought the case was as important as he kept saying it was, he should have tried it himself instead of leaving it to Victor Lovejoy." There was heightened color in her face now, and it was not from the two glasses of wine that accompanied dinner.

"He won't do that. Pornography is too hot an issue, all tangled up in First Amendment questions and community pressure. He won't go near it," said Charlie with certainty. "You know how difficult pornography trials are."

"But this isn't any old pornography, it's child pornography! I don't think we have any right to stop people looking at dirty pictures or reading whatever they want to read, but to do things like that to kids, that's clear sexual abuse of the worst kind and you'd think that—" She made a gesture dismissing her own protestations. "Don't tell me. Wycliff won't take it on. He'll give it to his strongest person on staff, but he won't touch it himself."

"That's right; and if the case succeeds, he'll take credit for it, and if it fails, he can wash his hands of it. He's done it before." Charlie sipped at the strong tea he preferred to coffee. "Lovejoy's lucky to have such a good track record with his cases. He's the one Wycliff has to blame. He might get his ears pinned back, but he won't get fired."

"Wycliff wouldn't dare fire Victor Lovejoy," said Charlie. "There's all sorts of reasons, including his family connections."

"Elizabeth," said Morgan with great satisfaction.

"Well, it doesn't hurt she's his aunt," said Charlie, thinking fondly and with exasperation of his favorite client.

"I was also thinking of Horatio Cronin," said Morgan; Cronin had been the District Attorney in San Francisco for twenty-eight years, and though he was retired now, he still swung tremendous legal and political weight. "Lovejoy's some kind of cousin."

"Good connections," said Charlie with a single-shoulder shrug. "And Victor's a strong prosecutor—a little too rigid, but prosecutors can get that way."

"It's the tunnel vision that bothers me," said Morgan, taking a small, lingering sip of espresso. "If he just hadn't depended so much on those tapes." She put her demitasse down.

"Tell me," said Charlie.

For a moment Morgan's temper flared. "Don't talk to me like a client, Charlie. I don't deserve that."

Charlie held up his hands in mock surrender. "I was just curious, that's all." He reached out and took one of her hands in his. "I have a vested interest in you, Morgan Studevant. Part of that 'till death do us part' contract, remember?"

She relented. "There are times I don't know how you stand me."

"Well," he said, smiling a little. "One of us has to, and since you're angry with yourself, I figure I'll put in a good word for you."

It took her a little while to respond to him. She looked away from him, then directly into his flint-dark eyes. "I'm sorry I'm such a difficult woman," she said quietly.

"I'm not," he said at once. "Not that I think you're difficult: you're complex, I'll grant you that."

"Charlie," she said ruefully. "You're not entering a plea."

"No." He released her hand. "Finish your coffee and let's go home." He reached for his wallet and picked up the check that had appeared at his elbow as if by sleight-of-hand.

As Charlie held her coat for her, Morgan said, "They'll have to find one of those kids, or more than one. Then they'll have to be willing to testify, and they'll have to do it well enough to convince the jury." She looked over her shoulder at Charlie. "Even then, who's to say a jury would believe kids over Scooter Ferrand?"

"That's up to the prosecutor," said Charlie in a neutral tone as he opened the door for her.

"Is it? Kids are tricky witnesses, and where sexual abuse is concerned, juries are skittish as deer." She huddled down into her coat. A fog that was more than mist and less than rain hung over the city, clammy and clinging.

"Fine night," said Charlie sarcastically. The eight-year-old bullet scar on his shoulder ached as it always did in this weather, but he gave no sign of it. Later he would rub it with herbs and soak in a hot bath to ease it.

"What about Caesar and Pompei?" asked Morgan, referring to their dogs.

"They can come in tonight," said Charlie, but could not resist adding as he did so often when a question of their pets came up, "How can you be so tough a judge and then such a sucker for those dogs? They're malamutes, they're used to hard weather, they're bred for it. San Francisco is mild for them."

"And those big blue eyes don't get to you at all," said Morgan, knowing that Charlie was as susceptible to the dogs' blandishments as she was. "You treated Rufus better than most of us treat our families," she said, very gently, for Charlie still missed his old dog who had been killed in traffic five years ago.

"It's different for me: I'm Ojibwa," said Charlie, as if that answered all questions.

Morgan shook her head, finally laughing outright. "And I'm Dutch and Danish and French and Russian, and what of it?"

He put his arm around her. "You're Morgan, that's what counts. The rest is frosting on the cake."

They chuckled as they walked down California toward their Camry.

Wednesday

HARDING TOWNE SAT across from Morgan, both his wardrobe and an hour of his time running well into four figures. He indicated the documents in question a second time. "The search warrant is specific. It says residence. A greenhouse at the rear of the property is not and cannot be construed as a residence, except for plants, and they cannot be brought into court, can they? There was no probable cause excuse for what they did, and no way the evidence devolved can be ruled admissible."

"Mister Towne, being facetious isn't very wise. Right now you have the advantage, but if you come into my court again, I won't forget your conduct," said Morgan, her smile tight.

"You like being a tough judge, don't you, Your Honor?" Towne replied. "You're going to prove you're the best of all of them."

A few years ago Morgan might have risen to that bait, but she had become much more discreet. "If I have a reputation for being tough, I don't mind, so long as it means I enforce the law fairly," she said. "And little as I want to do it, I am obliged to dismiss all charges because of illegal search and seizure." She let out a long breath. "Your client will be free to go as soon as the paperwork is complete."

"And how long is that going to take?" Towne asked, suspicious. "I'm prepared to file suit for malicious prosecution."

Morgan gave him a long, steady look. "Let me give you a little advice, counselor: don't push your luck. Your client is guilty, and we both know it. The only reason he isn't going to prison is that a cop got carried away and then lied about it."

"And the cops?" Towne inquired with his famous nasty smile.

"They've been given a month's suspension without pay and there is going to be a departmental hearing. What happens next will depend on what the hearing recommends. They could be tried for perjury, among other things; you don't need to point that out." Morgan took her reading glasses out of her purse. "I didn't have to tell you that, but you would have learned of it through the news media."

"Sergeant Maccio is still a sergeant?" Towne asked as he watched Morgan review the papers she had to sign.

"For the time being. The hearing may change that. His partner has already attempted to resign, but his resignation won't be accepted until after the hearing." She picked up her pen and scribbled her angular signature at the bottom of the page. "You can meet your client about four. The prosecutor on his case has asked for the chance to speak with him then, so you will want to be present, won't you?" She did not wait for an answer. "Let me remind you of what was on those videotapes we could not admit into evidence—you were given copies during discovery, weren't you. Think about what you saw. Scooter Ferrand has made a fortune with tapes like that. He might think that he's free to continue making tapes of children being sexually abused, but that is not going to happen. I urge you to encourage Mister Ferrand to change his line of work. He might have walked this time, but you can bet that he's not going to do that next time. When the cops make this kind of mistake they only do it once; that's my experience." She put her pen away. "You know, Mister Towne, I have a lot of respect for your skill as an attorney. But I deplore your . . . showmanship."

"I win cases, Your Honor," he said, taking the documents and slipping them into the Cross briefcase he carried.

"Yes, you win them," she said. "But this wasn't a win—it was a fluke."

"A fluke is as good as a win any day," Towne said, his manner polished and slick. "I appreciate your concern for Mister Ferrand, Your Honor; perhaps while you're handing out good advice, you might remind the D.A. and the cops about double jeopardy? My client cannot be tried for this crime again, and I will not tolerate any harassment from official or unofficial quarters. Is that quite clear?"

"Very clear," said Morgan.

"Good," said Towne, rising and holding out his hand. "We'll give the justice system another run for its money one of these days, Your Honor."

Morgan took his hand reluctantly. "I didn't know it was a horse race, Mister Towne."

"Everything's a horse race," Towne said with the greatest sincerity Morgan had ever seen him evince. With a jaunty wave he left her chambers, leaving the door ajar.

As Morgan went to close the door, she found herself hoping that the day would come when she could—just once—prove Harding Towne wrong.

Lydia Wong Lemmini motioned her five-year-old son back to his chair, confiding in Charlie, "I'm always amazed when he behaves. You should see him at home."

"Nathaniel says he's a holy terror," said Charlie, looking at the angelic boy. "I understand he likes to spread papers all over the living room floor, especially his father's papers."

"There are times," said Lydia, unable and unwilling to disguise her enormous pride in her oldest child.

Charlie smiled at Eric and then addressed Lydia. "And what is it you want to talk to me about that you can't discuss with your brother?"

She did not answer at once. "Years ago I thought you'd learn to be less brusque, but you didn't," she said, referring to the years Charlie had been in partnership with Willis Ogilvie and J. Alexander Tallant, when she had been their receptionist and secretary. She had married less than a year after Charlie had left the partnership, and Willis Ogilvie was still miffed about her defection. "You were the only one at Ogilvie, Tallant & Moon who gave straight answers. It's not common among attorneys, is it?"

"Why waste time? And money?" He knew that the latter was no real concern to her now that she was the wife of Anthony

Lemmini, the maverick of the formidable clan of San Francisco Florentines.

"This is very awkward for me," Lydia said, then fell silent.

"I can't help you if all you do is pussyfoot around, Lydia," said Charlie, his demeanor calm. "You know that."

"Oh, yes," she said. "But it is one of those cases . . ."

"This is about a legal case?" Charlie asked, more surprised than ever that Lydia had not gone to her brother Nathaniel for advice. "I thought it was—"

"It's not my case. It's . . . a friend." She straightened in her chair. "Now, don't look at me like that, Charlie Moon. It *is* for a friend; I'm not disguising myself, okay?"

"Okay," said Charlie. "Who is this friend and why does he need an attorney?"

"He needs one because he's about to be charged with a crime," said Lydia.

"That's an excellent reason," said Charlie, deliberately cautious. "Does he know what crime he'll be charged with, or is this just general apprehension?"

"Don't be sarcastic, Charlie," said Lydia, and glanced nervously at her boy. "Eric, why don't you go see Uncle Nathaniel?"

Charlie shook his head. "Uncle Nathaniel is in court right now. But Brian's here." Brian MacCurrey was recognized as the office softie where children were concerned. "He's got a deposition in half an hour. Will this take much longer than that?"

Lydia shook her head in answer to Charlie's question. "I don't think so," she said as she pointed Eric in the direction of the door. "This isn't the kind of thing I want him to hear," said Lydia, adding dangerously, "and if you tell me I'm an overprotective mother, I'll scratch yours eyes out, Charlie."

"Wouldn't dream of it," said Charlie, doing his best to keep from smiling, which would infuriate Lydia.

Lydia sat down once more. "I don't really know how to describe this, except to say that I am certain that Frank Girouard has been accused unjustly. I wouldn't be speaking to you if I didn't believe that most sincerely." She folded her hands. "The whole thing is so repellent."

Charlie looked at her, trying to keep his face expressionless. "What is he supposed to have done?"

"Oh, dear," said Lydia, catching her lower lip between her teeth to gain a little time. "Anthony is as convinced as I am that Frank is innocent. I'm not the only one who thinks so, and you know how cautious people are where H.P. programs are concerned."

"H.P.?" Charlie repeated.

"Oh, you know. The Board of Education is always being pressured about them one way and another. You know the classes and special schools for the kids with high I.Q.s—you remember all the accusations of de facto segregation and racism because not all kids test over 120 on their I.Q. tests. The most recent protest called for a change of standards to achieve a more representative ethnic balance." She nodded. "I see you do know."

"Not very much," Charlie warned her.

Lydia stared at the bookcases without seeing them. "He teaches at Sutro Glen Junior High—that's one of two H.P. junior highs in the city. They didn't put the H.P. schools into the middle school program." She hesitated, then went on. "He's very popular with the students there, one of the teachers who gets regular high reports himself. His reputation is . . . was impeccable."

"And what happened?" asked Charlie in a tone that allowed no caviling. "What changed?"

"It's his students, and that's what makes it so bad," said Lydia.

"What have they said and why is it bad?" Charlie persisted. "You know better than to carry on like this, Lydia." As he said it, he realized that Lydia was more upset than she appeared, and he let up. "Tell me however you want, but . . . but get to the point eventually, okay?"

She laughed a little, the sound forced but her eyes grateful. "He's not the kind of man you'd expect to be charged this way. He's popular and respected, as I've said. You know how high the standards are for H.P. teachers. They have tough requirements for their licensing and there are very high expectations on them."

"I remember the accusation that the H.P. schools were nothing more than prep schools being paid for by a public unable to make use of them, and that they were taking all the good teachers away from the regular schools where they were needed the most," said Charlie.

"Yes. The kids are bright and most of them are ambitious, or their parents are. They're also . . . oh, more naive, a little socially unsure; you know how that can happen to bright kids." She made herself come back to her subject. "The thing that is so upsetting about Frank is that there has never been so much as a whiff of anything . . . wrong about him."

"If he's been fired because he's gay and the parents are afraid of AIDS," Charlie began, thinking back to a case he had won last year, "it's a pretty simple matter."

"No," said Lydia with a decided shake of her head. "No, it's not that. He's healthy so far as I know, and he's straight. In this instance, that's no help." She coughed once, as if that might jar the words loose. "A few of his students . . . Oh, God, this is hard to say, even though it's not true . . . his female students have said . . . well, they've said that he abused them." Now that she had said it, her face paled.

"Abused them?" Charlie repeated. "You mean sexually?"

"Yes." Lydia nodded twice for emphasis.

"When did this happen? The accusation, that is, not the alleged abuse?" He had his pencil at the ready over his notepad.

"Friday night one of the students went to the Dean of Girls and said she had a problem. That was the beginning. Monday morning, two more girls did the same thing. They said they had wanted to complain before, but were too scared to try. They said Frank threatened them. Frank! It's . . . just absurd. Frank wouldn't do . . . those things to them. He surely wouldn't threaten them. But they were scared of something, Charlie. Someone hurt them. They were all very distressed." She stared down at the carpet, frowning intently.

"Is that it?" Charlie asked when Lydia did not go on.

Lydia raised her head. "Of course not. That was the beginning. There were recriminations and scenes and all the rest of it. You see, no one thought that Frank would ever do anything to hurt his students, not even the kids who didn't like him. They had trouble at the school that almost became a riot." She turned toward the window as if she thought there might be answers scribbled on the glass. "In the end five girls said that he'd forced them to . . . to do all kinds of things with him, so they could get good grades. I can't tell you how distressing this is. Frank left voluntarily that day, so that things could get back under control."

"That might not have been a good idea," said Charlie absently as he continued to write on his pad. "What happened then?"

"Then they called the school psychologist and she called the cops and now it looks like Frank's going to be arrested." This came out fast, as if saying it quickly would not make it so bad.

"Un-huh," said Charlie, continuing to write.

Lydia was put off a trifle at Charlie's lack of response. "Well?" she inquired.

"Well." Charlie looked up from his notes. "Well, your friend

Frank needs a lawyer, no doubt about that. But these cases are tricky—you remember, don't you?—and he'd better know going in that innocence is not always the most important factor. If the jury once gets an idea that he's capable of doing it, they're apt to suppose the worst, no matter what the evidence supports." He paused. "These cases can be very costly, and not in money alone. There are always subsidiary troubles in sexual abuse cases, no matter what; he'll need to prepare himself for a long haul. No matter how the case turns out, there will be those who think the worst of him, just as there will be those who will think the best."

"I've told him about Doctor Prince. He said he understands," Lydia said, referring to the last client Charlie defended at Ogilvie, Tallant and Moon. "He remembers the trial. He said at the time he thought you'd got Prince off."

"I wouldn't want to think Prince really did those things. I don't want to think that your friend Frank could, either. Still. Guilty or innocent, he's entitled to the best defense he can get. But for my own conscience, I hope he's not guilty."

Lydia made a quick gesture. "I told him that."

"Good," said Charlie, about to go on when Eric hurtled, laughing, back into the room, then came quickly to order.

"It's time we left," Lydia said as much to her son as to Charlie. She hesitated. "When can I tell Frank to call you?"

"Immediately," said Charlie. "The sooner the better. If he decides he wants me to represent him, we'll figure out how we're going to handle it." He rose, looking down at Eric. "You've got a good-looking boy there, Lydia."

This time her smile was wide and pleased. "Half Chinese and half Italian: he ought to be the greatest cook in the world when he grows up."

"Or bicycle rider. Or artist." Charlie grinned, but it faded as soon as Lydia was out the door. He read over his notes, and did his best to reserve judgment.

TWO

Thursday

THERE WAS A traffic snarl on Hyde Street that slowed progress to a walking pace. If it had not been sprinkling, Charlie would have found a parking place—no mean feat in itself—and walked the last half mile. As it was, he rubbed once at his stiff shoulder and let himself think.

Yesterday evening while he and Morgan had watched a performance of Prokofiev's *Romeo and Juliet,* he had tried to make up his mind if he had been right to take on Frank Girouard's case. With Morgan's recent disappointment in the Ferrand case, perhaps it was too loaded an issue with her and might be disruptive between them. She had insisted that was not the case, but the doubts lingered. Morgan told him with asperity that she knew the difference between Scooter Ferrand and Frank Girouard, that she could keep the two men separate in her mind. "Besides," she had said shortly before they went up to bed, "I won't be involved in your case. Where's the problem?" At the time he had had no answer for her, but had felt he owed her one, and the belief was still with him.

Up ahead the light turned green and the cars inched their way forward around the crew gathered at a manhole cover.

When he reached Green Street, Charlie turned left and signaled for the right turn into the basement garage the building tenants shared. As he pulled into his parking place, he found himself wondering, as he did every few days, what would happen to the cars if there was a really serious quake, that dreaded and quasi-mythical Big One San Franciscans joked about with apprehension in their eyes. What would happen to the building, as well. It had survived the quake and the more destructive fire of '06, but would it do it again? He continued to speculate as he rode the elevator to the fifth floor where MacCurrey, Moon, Nelson and Wong had their offices.

Drisa Gaya was at her station, her long black hair pulled back and confined at her neck in an elaborate bun. "Good morning, Mister Moon," she said, hardly looking up from the calendar spread in front of her showing what the appointments were for the four partners and seven associates of the firm. "Ms. Nelson would appreciate a word with you, if you can spare the time. She has to be in court in an hour. Your first appointment is not until eleven."

"Wrong," said Charlie with a quick smile to show that he was not blaming her. "My new client will be here in about fifteen minutes. Maybe a little longer if the traffic stays the way it is." He glanced toward Jocelyn Nelson's door. "Is she in?"

"I'll signal her," said Drisa, who was very sensitive to protocol.

"Fine," said Charlie, who had decided over a year ago that it was useless to expect her to relent. As Drisa gave her signal, Charlie went and rapped on the door.

"Good," called Jocelyn. "Come in."

Charlie stepped into the room and closed the door, though he did not move further into the office. "Good morning, Joss," he said.

"I hope so." She was a strapping woman, big-framed and strong-featured, with an urgency about her that was present in everything she did. Almost as old as Charlie, she had one child still at home, the last reminder of a marriage that had failed more than a decade ago. She dressed with great care, always choosing simple, clean lines in her clothes. Her blonde hair was cut short in a tailored style. Charlie had never seen her without perfectly applied makeup. "I've convinced Parsons to plead. The D.A. said they'll make every allowance for first offense and all the rest of it. What do you think?"

"Sounds good to me. Have you asked Nathaniel and Brian?"

"Not yet. Nathaniel will go along with you because his sister will cut him in two if he doesn't. Who knows what Brian will think? If the Glending-Smith thing is going well, he'll think it's fine, and if it isn't . . ." She sat at her antique oak desk, reaching for her Styrofoam cup of caffe latte. "I hear you've got a new client."

"He's coming in this morning," said Charlie, keeping his tone light.

"Something about the sexual abuse of school kids?" Jocelyn pursued.

"Spare me your cross-examination, Joss," said Charlie, not moving from his place by the door. "The man teaches junior high school. Five of his female students claim he has required them to perform certain sexual acts with him. They say they were afraid not to because he'd give them bad grades." He waited; when Jocelyn said nothing, he went on. "Frank says he's innocent."

"What did you expect?" Jocelyn countered.

"I'm not going to argue merits with you, Joss," Charlie said. "I haven't had more than a cursory interview with him, and that was—"

"At the jail, I know," said Jocelyn. "Well, I only wanted to say that cases like this can tarnish a firm's image if things go badly."

Charlie knew better than to wrangle with Jocelyn. "One case, Joss, and Lydia brought it to me. Did you want me to tell Nathaniel's sister no?"

Jocelyn pounced. "Nathaniel's sister! Nathaniel's! Why did she bring the case to you?"

"Because I've handled one before," said Charlie. "While I was still with Willis and Alex. Lydia watched the whole thing. And since Nathaniel hasn't had a case like this before, she came to me. You'd do the same thing, and you know it." He reached back for the knob. "Anything else?"

To Jocelyn's credit she laughed. "No, go ahead. I ought to know better than to try to corner you before you want to be cornered."

"That's right," said Charlie. "You ought."

As he came into Charlie's office, Frank Girouard fussed nervously with his rust-colored knit tie. Away from the hectic and depressing atmosphere of the jail he regained some of the self-possession Charlie supposed he must have in teaching. "I'm sorry I'm late," was the first thing he said.

"Parking's a bitch in this part of town," Charlie agreed. "There's a lot three blocks away, but that's the closest."

"I found a place up the hill, on the third try," said Frank, coming to shake Charlie's hand. "I can't tell you how relieved I am that you agreed to take my case." He was dressed for teaching, in brown slacks, a tweed jacket and a cream-colored cotton shirt. There was a little bandage on his chin where he'd cut himself shaving.

"Say that when it's over," Charlie recommended, and indicated one of the three chairs opposite his desk. "Please. Sit down. Let's get started."

"Okay," Frank said, his nervousness increasing. He caught the ends of his knit tie between his blunt fingers.

As Charlie picked up a pencil, he said, "You tell me there's no basis whatsoever for the accusations of your students. If that's not the absolute truth, you'd better tell me now."

Frank blinked. "What do you mean? Shit, Moon, I don't go around getting it on with thirteen-year-olds. I *teach* kids, I don't fuck them." He stopped very quickly. "I . . . I didn't mean to say—"

"That's all right," said Charlie. "But you'd better get used to questions like this, and moderate your answers, or you'll get into more trouble." He watched Frank take this in. "Let's try again. Is there any reason, no matter how remote, why one or more of your students might think you had abused her sexually, or intended to abuse her sexually. And think about your answer."

It took Frank more than thirty seconds to make his response. "I've been up most of the night trying to figure that out. My students like me, Mister Moon. They talk to me about things that bother them. You know what English classes are like—little essays all the time—and that tends to make them less nervous about talking to me. You can check my file, if you want to. Year before last, one of my kids came to me because he said his father was hitting his mother, and we were able to get some help for all of them. Would I turn around and force those girls to be sex slaves, the way they've claimed?"

"I don't know," said Charlie, not looking up from the notes he was taking. "Did you?"

"NO," Frank answered vehemently.

"The complaint says that you had vaginal, oral and anal intercourse with these girls, not just once but on several occasions, that you threatened to tell their parents—"

"That's the most outlandish threat—" Frank interrupted.

"Not to these girls. They were ashamed of what had happened, and according to what they've said, you had convinced them their parents would believe the girls seduced you." Charlie studied Frank's expression. "Did you do any of those things."

"No, no. No!" He slipped down in the chair and propped his left ankle on his right knee. "Jesus, if you think I could do that, why'd you agree to represent me?"

"First, I didn't say you did these things. I am saying the girls say you did these things. Second, you and everyone else in this country are entitled to defense to the full extent of the law." Charlie resisted the urge to doodle in the margin of his legal pad. "From the report here, from the primary evaluation, the psychologist seems pretty certain that those five girls have been victims of some kind of sexual abuse. The question seems to be whether or not you did it." Before Frank could protest again, Charlie held up two fingers to silence him. "I will make no attempt to say they were not abused unless subsequent reports indicate otherwise."

Frank nodded. "That's okay with me," he said, sounding a little short of breath.

"So: why you? It keeps coming back to that, Mister Girouard." He held his pencil poised.

"I don't know," said Frank, attempting to put a knot in the end of his tie. "That's the truth. I don't know. Not much help, am I?"

Charlie chose to ignore the last; he did not want to discourage Frank. "These five girls—Emma Westford, Diane Twayn, Wendy Maple, Ruth Camberwell, and Michelle Hawkins—were all students of yours."

"Diane was in the remedial reading section—she's as bright as the others but dyslexic and needs extra instruction to deal with it. The other four have been in my regular classes, yes," said Frank. "Emma and Michelle are very good students, both of them really excel; Wendy and Ruth are about average."

"For H.P.," Charlie added.

"Yes, for H.P. In regular classes, they'd be at the top. Straight As. And Emma and Michelle might well have dropped out because of boredom by now." He saw skepticism in Charlie's eyes. "It's happened more than most of us want to admit."

Charlie did not question this. "Are these girls all part of the same crowd? Do they socialize?"

"Not that I know of, but . . . I don't keep much track of who's in with who." He tilted his head back so that he looked at the ceiling instead of Charlie. "I think they all came from the same grammar school, though."

Charlie underlined the note he made. "So they live in the same part of town?"

"I think so."

"We'll check that out," said Charlie as he made a note on his pad.

"Let's see: Michelle's parents are getting a divorce. Her mother has a court order to keep the father from visiting Michelle at school. Apparently she's worried about kidnapping. Ruth Camberwell's father was in a drug-abuse program two or three years ago; her older sister Thirza was in my class then. I don't know very much about the other three girls." He rubbed his forehead. "The trouble is, there are always so many kids, and you do what you can for them, but it isn't very much, not really. The ones that are going to read are reading by the time they get to Sutro Glen, and the rest have put their attention somewhere else. So the ones who will read, you try to get them to read a lot and you hope they get something out of it. But what does a kid in this day and age get out of reading Hawthorne? Most of them ask why Hester doesn't leave. And Dimsdale! They all think he's a wimp and a nerd, and I can't say I disagree." He stopped quickly. "Sorry. We're not talking reading plans, are we?"

"No," said Charlie, then added, "What about Diane Twayn? You said she's dyslexic?"

"Yes. And so far as she's concerned, there's no reason to read. Her family doesn't read. Her father does something in TV, and Diane's very visually oriented; she does sketches and drawings all the time. She's got a couple prizes for her work in school displays. But reading things other than comic books—no. She doesn't know why she should bother." He relaxed a little as he talked, being on familiar ground.

"She's not angry or disappointed with schoolwork, is she?"

"I don't think so," Frank replied, looking startled.

This wasn't promising. Charlie tried another tack. "What about amusements and entertainment? Do you know if the girls had the same hobbies or sports, or went places together?"

"I don't know," said Frank, and defeat was on him once more.

Charlie abandoned that line as well. "Who at school might be able to tell me?"

"Leda Dawson, maybe," said Frank, considering. "She's in charge of girls' P.E. and most of the girls like her. Talk to Leda."

Charlie wrote down the name. "Good. That's for starters. Now think of someone who might be able to tell me about them in classes."

Frank shrugged. "Their other teachers, I suppose. Jorge Esteban has them all in either algebra or geometry. Diane's very good at geometry and trig, he tells me. Bob Nettles has four of them in his biology classes. Emma's in the advanced science program, so she takes chemistry." He shifted in his chair, and changed knees and ankles. "I don't know about the others. Truly. Until now, I haven't had any reason to."

"How many students in your school?" Charlie asked.

"Just under three hundred. That's too many, if you ask me." He placed the palms of his hands together. "But there are just two H.P. junior highs in San Francisco, so . . . The first few years I tried so hard to keep them all straight. All of them, not just the ones in my classes. But then it got too hard, and there were always new ones and, well, I didn't bother as much. I did my best to learn who was in my classes. That's about the best I can do." He dropped his hands and cleared his throat. "Well, where do we go from here, Moon?"

Charlie looked at his notepad. "First off, we're going to do as much damage control as we can. We don't want this to turn into a full-blown scandal, not for you or those girls. That means downplaying this so the press doesn't have you for breakfast. Some of this is going to get expensive. I'm sorry about that, Mister Girouard, but any reputable attorney would tell you the same thing, and recommend the same measures. If we're going to defend you properly, we'll need a solid investigation, and I use people who know how to earn their money. I'm telling you this right now so you can get used to the idea." He paused. "It would be a cliché to tell you that your freedom and exoneration are worth whatever it costs. That's not the way it's going to feel while the case is on-going. So, if you really are guilty, now is a good time to admit it, while the costs are still manageable, and while the District Attorney is inclined to accept a lesser plea. Once we get into gear, it'll be a lot more difficult to get you a reasonable deal."

"By a lesser plea, you mean I would say I'm guilty to something not quite as bad as what I've been accused of doing?" Frank's face darkened and he looked away as if trying to keep hold of his temper. "Mister Moon, I guess this is part of your job. But I want you to know"—he looked squarely at Charlie—"I didn't do anything to those girls except teach them English. I swear it on the graves of my parents, if it makes it more acceptable to you. I never touched those girls. I never . . . made them do sexual things. And if someone else did, then I want to make sure the bastard gets caught and locked up for good. Next to that, money isn't too important. Is that clear enough for you?"

"Yes," said Charlie quietly. "That's fine."

Ten minutes after Frank Girouard left, Charlie began his first phase of damage control; he placed a call to Arthur Bartram at the Board of Education.

"Charlie," said Bartram with guarded enthusiasm. "How are you? I'm not being sued again, am I?"

"No," said Charlie, pleased that Bartram still remembered the case he had won for him three years before. "But there's a teacher in trouble."

The guarded sound increased. "You mean that business about the Balboa—"

"No, I don't, and you know it," Charlie countered, unwilling to fence. "I mean an accusation made against a teacher at Sutro Glen Junior High."

"Sexual abuse of female students," Bartram said.

"That's the one," Charlie replied. "I am representing him, and I'm calling to ask you to leave the press and the rest of the news media out of this for the time being."

"For your client," said Bartram.

"For the girls," said Charlie bluntly. "They're the ones who need protection. My client needs to have his rights protected, and I'm prepared to do that, but not at the cost of the reputation of the girls. They've been through enough, no matter who has taken advantage of them."

"Such as your client," said Bartram stubbornly.

"It has been alleged that he did, but he denies it."

"Which you have to believe, since you represent him," said Bartram. He sighed. "But I understand what you're saying. All right. I'll do what I can to downplay the events. I'll make sure the office hedges everything they say and we'll do what we can to keep names and specifics out of the papers and off the tube." He was silent for a couple of seconds. "Who else are you going to pressure?"

"Sorry, that's a trade secret," said Charlie.

Bartram could not keep from chuckling, though the sound had little humor to it. "I suppose I ought to be upset, but you kept the lid on the case during the suit, and I know it made a difference. Now the shoe's on the other foot, isn't it?"

"Something like that, yes," said Charlie.

"Okay. We'll stonewall as best we can." He was about to hang up, then he asked, "How bad is it, really?"

"If someone abused those girls, it isn't good," said Charlie.

Morgan was already at home by the time Charlie put their Camry behind her new Acura. As he climbed the stairs to the kitchen he could hear the welcoming yelps from Caesar and Pompei, who were waiting for their evening walk. "Hi," Charlie called out as the two dogs converged on him, Pompei from the breakfast nook, Caesar from the hall.

"Hi yourself," Morgan answered from the dining room. "How's it going?"

"Traffic was awful both ways," said Charlie as he bent to mock-wrestle the two malamutes. "It's the rain."

"Well, spring's here and the rain will be over before you can say drought." She came through the swinging door, her hands filled with the cut stems of flowers. "I got something for the table," she explained.

"Good," said Charlie. He was on one knee with Caesar lolling at his feet and Pompei trying to crawl under his arm. "Any occasion or just for the hell of it."

"For cheering," said Morgan. "I've had three meetings today all aimed at trying to blame someone for the illegal seizure. Everyone wants to point the finger at everyone else. You can't imagine the polite way they're all calling each other names. I give it another day before they get down to the mudslinging." She dropped the stems into the garbage can.

"Who's going to get stuck with it?" Charlie asked. "I don't mean who's responsible, but who's going to get stuck?"

"Well, if it were me, I'd make Wycliff responsible because he let the thing go to trial with faulty evidence. He permitted the evidence to be introduced because he didn't find out about that illegal seizure. That should never have happened, no matter what Wycliff would like us to believe. Someone was lax, or thought they could get away with faking it. I think it means one of Lovejoy's team more or less deliberately ignored important information, as well as accepting a report that was fallacious. We wouldn't have found out about it if Massie hadn't got carried away with his testimony." She sighed as she rinsed her hands. "That's the worst part; the trial was under way. We went round and round about how to get the goods on Ferrand, and the trouble is, there's not a lot we can do. Double jeopardy protects him, and the courts are stranded. We can't try him for this case, and we have insufficient probable cause we can use for another case unless we assume the evidence we have now points to illegal activities, but that evidence has to be suppressed as the fruit of the poisonous tree, and there you are without a case." She dried her hands and looked around at Charlie. "Are you going to play on the floor until dinner or are we taking the boys out for a walk?"

Charlie got to his feet. "Walk. Definitely walk."

"All right," she said. "But dinner'll be ready in forty-five minutes."

"That sounds reasonable for a walk." He held out his arms to Morgan. "Come here first."

She gestured in fond exasperation, then went to him, glad for his embrace. "You are the most perplexing man, Charles Spotted Moon," she said as she kissed the corner of his eye.

"Now why would you think that?" Charlie asked, and kissed her before she could answer.

"You put up with me. I never seem to get to you." She shoved a few loose strands of hair off his brow. "Why is that?"

"The only getting to me you do is the good kind," Charlie said, and his mouth this time was more insistent. "You can get to me before dinner if you like—just as soon as we get back from the walk."

When she stepped back, Morgan laughed once. "I rest my case."

Friday

SEEN TOGETHER, GAIL Harris and Mickey Trang did not look like private investigators, which was a tremendous advantage to both of them. Gail Harris was just thirty but was so fresh-faced and perky that she could easily pass for a college student, a disguise that often stood her in excellent stead. Her partner, Mickey Trang, was what he called Vietnamese soup: some Vietnamese, some French, some American—whatever that meant—and a little Chinese. He was slight and angular and tough as wire.

"None of us like this kind of case," Charlie concurred when Gail had objected to defending Frank Girouard. "Sexual abuse of children is about the worst thing short of terrorism you can do to wreck a person's life. But Frank Girouard claims he is innocent. We'll have to try to find something to support that claim."

Mickey folded his arms and slung his weight onto one hip. "Trying to prove five schoolgirls liars isn't very attractive, Charlie."

"Probably not," said Charlie at once. "He's the client, though, and he says he didn't do it. We have to go on the supposition that someone must have done something, and then find out as much as we can about who did what and to whom, or cast enough doubt that the establishment of reasonable doubt can be used with the jury."

"And what if there's nothing?" Gail asked. She had been a champion fencer for her university and Charlie knew she still practiced every other day; it showed in the way she moved and how she watched people.

"Let's wait until that happens," said Charlie.

"I hope we don't end up helping bad guys," Gail said, her tone making it a warning as well as a wish.

Charlie regarded her levelly. "Everyone wants to wear a white hat; it's easy to do when you know you're on the side of the angels. Most of the time everyone's in a shade of grey, and you have to do your job as best you can, and settle for that. It's harder with very bad crimes—you haven't had to do one of those for me yet, and now is your chance—because you don't want to make it possible for it to happen again. Do you think that doesn't trouble me? It does, I promise you. If he's guilty, he ought to be convicted no matter how well I defend him. But if it turns out he really didn't do it, and you didn't help him, what then?"

"You've made your point," said Mickey. "And don't get onto that old whatever-he's-done-he-deserves-the-best-defense thing, okay?" He pulled up one of the least-comfortable chairs in the office and dropped onto it in reverse, his arms folded over the back. "We'll do what we can. You have that oath binding you, but we don't, and if we don't turn up anything, you'll let us off the hook, all right?"

"All right," said Charlie, not willing to argue about it. "In the meantime, I want a thorough investigation. You know how to do it, and you can find out what's been going on." He tapped his desk with nervous fingers. "I don't want anything by halves, because you can be damned certain that the D.A.'s office is going for maximum penalty for this. There aren't many things this city agrees on, but the sexual abuse of children is one exception: no one advocates it publicly, no matter what kinks they have."

"What about psychological testimony?" asked Mickey. "I suppose that's an angle you're going to work?"

"Yes, as a matter of fact," said Charlie. "Starting with Frank Girouard. I'm arranging for a whole battery of tests; I'm hoping to show that he isn't the right type to do this. That won't prove anything, of course, but it will show parameters. It will also help line up expert testimony, and I know we're going to need it in this case. You can bet the prosecution's going to have a long parade of shrinks to impeach anything Girouard says. And I want to know if there is any reason to think he might be capable of doing . . . abusing girls."

"Does that mean you'd suggest he plead guilty if you find out that he is?" Mickey asked with cynical doubt.

"Of course," said Charlie. "Especially in a case like this. I never want to help a guilty person avoid the consequences of his or her act. I have to be able to live with myself, too. Some attorneys think that if you can get away with it, that's all that matters, but I don't." The previous four cases Gail Harris and Mickey Trang had worked on for Charlie had been far less serious, and he realized that their demand for his response was not out of line. "If you think I'm off-track on any of this, tell me."

"Sounds okay," said Gail after a brief silence.

Charlie indicated the windows as the light rain and morning traffic provided a diversion. "It's settled then. How long before you want to give me your first report? Two days? Three?"

"Let us have until Tuesday. We have a new operative who just joined us: Cadao Talbot. He's very sharp. He can get started on the case this afternoon. Besides, I want to wait until you see the tests, and then we'll coordinate our work, when we know more of what we're looking for." She paced around the office. "Can I get a cup of coffee?"

Charlie picked up his phone. "Drisa, ask Merek to bring in a small pot of coffee and a pot of tea. Three cups, no sugars."

"Yes, Mister Moon," said Drisa crisply. "Right away."

"Thanks, Charlie," said Gail.

Charlie nodded, hating the process of thanks and acknowledgment. "I've written down the names of the students making the accusations and I have a few notes about them. It's not very much to go on, but it's a start. Girouard doesn't know what the girls might have in common other than he teaches them all and they all have I. Q.s over 120. I leave it to you and your new operative to find out if there's more to it than that. I'll also want to know if there are any indications of previous complaints from any one of the girls having to do with abuse—emotional, physical or sexual, or any history of family violence. You might check if there have been any recent traumatic changes in any of the families: deaths, divorces, marriages, moves, you know the list."

"Oh, yeah," said Mickey, taking the copy Charlie offered him.

"I also want the other teachers in the school checked, especially those who teach or have taught all five girls. Again, Girouard had no impression about any misconduct, so I leave the whole mess to you. Be very, very discreet. You have to be careful about this, because it's such a delicate problem, and the whole H.P. program is such a tricky issue. There may be rumors about other students having similar problems, and if there are, I want you to find out as much as you can, no matter how far-fetched it might seem." He had been ticking off the notes he had made to himself the night before. "One last thing. I don't want to exacerbate the situation. We've been able to hold the news media off, but that could change quickly. If that happens, the whole case could turn explosive on us very easily, and we would have a lot of trouble."

"Sexual abuse of teenagers seems pretty exacerbated to start with," said Mickey. "What did you have in mind for worse."

"Media. Invasion of privacy. Headlines. Reporters and cameras and TV crews crawling all over the school and the court." Charlie made a gesture of helplessness. "Tabloids—print and screen—thrive on things like this."

Gail nodded twice, decisively. "We'll keep it in mind." She looked around as Merek Rzeszow came in with a tray.

"Please put it on the desk," Charlie said to the young Pole. "I appreciate it." He gestured dismissal and was grateful when Merek put down the tray and left. As Charlie poured coffee for Gail and then tea for Mickey and himself, he remarked, "If anything catches your attention, call me. You can call me at home if you think it's necessary. I'll put my machine on when I'm out and I'll check with the office service from time to time, but I'm relying on you to decide what the best way to deal with this is."

Mickey handed the cup of coffee to Gail, then reached for his tea. "You sound afraid of a leak."

"I am," said Charlie. "Sexual child abuse is . . . is upsetting for everyone. Few things make adults feel more vulnerable than harm done to their children. Things can get out of hand very fast."

He lowered his head briefly. "Use good sense and circumspection, that's all I can ask."

"Fine," said Gail. "Fine. We'll be careful."

Morgan was still in her robe when George Wycliff came into her chambers. She looked up, startled to see him. "Good afternoon, Mister District Attorney," she said formally.

"Not very, Your Honor," answered Wycliff. He had just come from the Hall of Justice and was on his way to the Board of Supervisors; he was dressed for power and stability. His haircut emphasized the determined thrust of his jaw and minimized his receding hairline. "And why the title."

"Because I assume this isn't a social call," said Morgan as she went to the utility closet where there was a microwave and tiny refrigerator as well as bottled water and packets for tea, soup, coffee and snacks. She poured powder into a cup, added the water and popped it into the microwave. "Are you going to tell me what's on your mind, or shall I guess?"

Wycliff put his hands on her desk and loomed forward. "You refused to issue that search warrant."

"Yes," said Morgan. "And until you come by a probable cause that isn't tainted, I won't be willing to issue one. Find another judge and let him take the flak. And stop leaning that way; you won't threaten me like that." She made herself smile to disarm his tactic still more.

Wycliff stood up, brushing his hands together as if to get dust off them. "I wasn't trying to threaten you," he said, sulking.

"Does intimidate sound better? It's what you do to defense witnesses all the time, so don't pretend you don't know what I'm talking about." She opened the microwave as it buzzed, and took out a cup of spicy chicken broth. "You've been pushing Victor Lovejoy and you've been putting pressure on me. I don't like that. Judges are not supposed to be pressured by anyone." She went to her desk and sat down. "Who are you trying to impress, George, or is this an attempt to make it look as if the case wasn't bungled by the police?"

"Not bungled," he muttered.

"My, we are splitting hairs today, aren't we?" she said brightly. "All right, the case wasn't bungled. What would you say happened?" She leaned back, watching him closely. "Well, George?"

"They were too eager," said Wycliff as if reading from

prepared notes. "They took too much upon themselves. They over-reacted. But where child pornography is involved, cops are no different than every other decent adult in the world—they get caught up."

Although she had said much the same thing to Harding Towne, Morgan told him, "They aren't supposed to. They're supposed to observe due process and the rights of the accused, which didn't happen to Mister Ferrand, more's the pity, because now we've got a monster back on the street, and he's warned you're onto him. Scooter Ferrand isn't stupid and he has a vindictive streak." She put her hand to her cup. "Listen, George, I've been over this ground so many times there's nothing left to find on it. Let it go. Mount a new investigation from the other end of the business, so you can get a handle on Ferrand that way. I warn you, I am not going to be party to harassment, no matter how justified you may think it is. Harding Towne is ready to slap suits on all of us if his client is made the object of what he likes to call a witch-hunt. He'll do it, too, and in the full glare of every bit of publicity he can get. I have a letter to that effect from him, if you'd care to read it?"

George Wycliff heard her out with an expression of baffled rage marring his features. "I can't let him get away with it."

"You already have. You let a falsified report get through, you didn't oversee the investigation the way you know you should have because you were afraid of the repercussions, and now you've got them whether you want them or not." She took a first, careful sip of her broth. "I want it ended."

"Just like that?" Wycliff switched to a different ploy. "You're going to let him out, so he can go on making videos of big guys raping kids? Is that it? You've decided your hands are tied?"

"They *are* tied," said Morgan firmly. "And you are the one who tied them." She put her cup down and got to her feet. "Find me probable cause that does not come from the poisonous tree and I will happily issue a warrant, a very specific warrant. I will instruct the cops myself on the particulars so you can let yourself off the hook. But I will not do anything more to prejudice the case; we've done quite enough already." She met his eyes squarely. "Is there anything else, or were you going to leave?"

"All right," said Wycliff, half backing toward the door. "We'll discuss this next week, when you've had a chance to calm down and think it over."

"*George,*" she warned quietly.

"I'm going," he assured her as he opened the door.

THREE

Sunday afternoon and evening

THERE WERE NOT many people at the beach; the rain kept them away. A few hardy joggers ran along the waterline, and on the roadway above, half a dozen cyclists were fighting the stiff, blustery wind out of the southwest. For two thirty, it was unusually dark. Charlie and Morgan, both in rainwear, followed Caesar and Pompei north on the wet sands, laughing at the dogs' antics.

"God, I've missed getting out," said Morgan as they came to a halt near where the Great Highway rose up to the Cliff House. "I didn't recognize how claustrophobic I was becoming until now. We should make more of an effort to do this." She held Charlie's arm, grinning at him. Under her anorak and sweater and shirt, his talisman lay against her side, the wood feeling warm.

"No argument from me," said Charlie, wiping the rain off her face with the back of his fingers. "You still look tired, love."

"After lolling about all morning reading the paper and doing crossword puzzles and you bringing me breakfast in bed?" she scoffed fondly. "I'm being hopelessly spoiled by you, Charlie."

"Not a chance," said Charlie, resuming his stroll, and resumed their general conversation. "Brian's taking on a case, a filing against fishermen who've been shooting seals for raiding their nets." He looked ahead toward the rocks where seals and sea lions often gathered. "He's very good at these cases. He knows where to go for the right information. One or two of the environmentalists he's interviewed have been the hysterical sort, but most of the material he's got it solid."

"Good for him," said Morgan, her gaze on the middle distance.

After a brief silence, she said, "I don't mind talking about it, you know."

He looked at her, pretending confusion. "Talking about what?"

"About the case you've taken," she said patiently, matching her stride to his exactly. "You can tell me what your partners are up to—they aren't going to plead before me—but you don't have to avoid your own work."

"I wasn't," he protested unsuccessfully.

Morgan shook her head once. "You don't want me to be worried that you are handling a sexual abuse case. You're afraid that after what I've gone through with Scooter Ferrand I will disapprove of what you're doing."

Charlie peered at the beach ahead as if scouting for dangerous traps. "Something like that," he allowed.

"Well, I don't," she said decisively. "Not now, at least. Last week I might have been less . . . sensible." Her eyes were rueful as she stopped and looked directly at him. "Your case isn't my case, and what Scooter Ferrand did isn't what your client is accused of doing."

"Both sexual exploitation of minors," said Charlie. "I don't want you to be bothered."

"I'm bothered that we had to let Ferrand go because a cop screwed up. I'm bothered because Towne can't wait to slap a suit on the D.A. for harassment. I'm bothered because I know that Ferrand is going to do this again and keep doing it until he's caught in the act. He isn't just a cynical voyeur who's pandering to a sick market, he's someone who has to have proof of what he's masterminded. He'd make the videotapes if he had to pay for them instead of sell them. I wish they'd drop the videotape angle altogether and concentrate on kidnapping and abuse—no First Amendment confusion there. I don't want to give the bigots and Bible-thumpers any more leverage than they already have about the First Amendment, and not over this case." She leaned her head to the side so that her hood brushed his shoulder. "You're going to have a hard time with Girouard without having to worry about what I think."

"Probably," said Charlie. "No matter what we do, Girouard is probably going to be stigmatized for a long time. People are very paranoid about what gets done to their children."

Morgan stopped again, and squinted out at the waves. "Any regrets about that, Charlie?"

"You mean because we don't have any?" he asked, thinking

how often they went over the same ground; about twice a year the subject came up between them, and was once again put to rest. "If I do, it's my own damn fault. What about you?"

"Once in a while; not often enough to make a real difference." Her grip on his arm tightened. "I don't like it when my family gets on my case about it. But that has nothing to do with you."

"Do you want me to have a talk with them?" Charlie offered, as he always did, and hoped in vain she would agree.

"I'll handle them, don't worry." A few strands of brown hair had blown out from under her hood and were clinging to her face. "I just wish Uncle Ned would shut up about his genetic theories."

"He still can't stand you being married to an Indian, can he?" Charlie asked gently. "We ought to get him and Harry Foxhollow together; they'd agree on just about everything. The last time I was back for a tribal council, Harry wanted to have me excluded because you, being white, have compromised my magic. His ethnic purity line sounds just like the shit the Nazis preached, only saying Indian where they said Aryan." He pulled his arm free of her hold, but only to wrap it around her shoulder. "He thinks it's magic that ought to keep us apart, and I think it's magic that keeps us together."

She kissed him lightly, as if she did not trust herself to reveal more of her emotions. They started walking again, Morgan permitting herself to lean against him a little. "I wish I could think of some way to get Scooter Ferrand. Bad conduct for a judge, but . . ."

He turned his head to kiss her cheek. "I'd worry if you felt any other way."

They went a little further in silence, then Charlie lifted his head. "It's about a mile and a half back to the car, and into the wind. We're supposed to be at Elizabeth's in an hour. What do you think?"

"I think we'd better call Caesar and Pompei," said Morgan, and without waiting shouted for the dogs.

In response, the two malamutes came hurtling back along the beach, tongues lolling. They bounced around Charlie and Morgan, then launched themselves southward, toward the parked car.

Moving more slowly, Charlie and Morgan followed after.

It took a moment for Charlie to recall the new houseman's name. "Good afternoon, Clifford," he said, glad he got it right.

The midd'-aged man gave Charlie and Morgan a long hard stare. "Yes?"

"We just came from the beach," said Morgan. "Will you tell Elizabeth we're here?" She pulled her hood back and shook out her hair. "We're about ten minutes late."

Clifford hesitated, as if weighing his options; he made no move to open the door to admit them.

"Is that you, Charlie? Morgan?" Elizabeth's authoritative voice came from the floor above, and was accompanied by her firm tread as she started down the stairs. "For heaven's sake, Clifford, show them into the back parlor, and make sure the fire will last."

Charlie and Morgan stepped into the foyer just as Elizabeth reached the landing half a floor above. "Afternoon, Elizabeth," Charlie called, waving before he removed his waterproofed anorak.

"You two are a sight. Where on earth have you been?" she asked.

"Out for a walk," said Charlie, adding, "Caesar and Pompeii are in the car. Do you mind if I turn them out in the side garden? They won't wreck anything. At least, they haven't before."

"Oh, yes, I know that," said Elizabeth as she reached the bottom of the stairs. In her mid-seventies, she had been Charlie's client for fourteen years and had come to regard him as part of her family. The two words her family used most for her when they were in charity with her were *incorrigible* and *indefatigable:* the rest of the time they called her *infuriating,* which she preferred. She held out her hands to Morgan and gave her a resounding kiss on the cheek. "Goodness, you're cold. Clifford, take care of that fire." Next she rounded on Charlie, exchanged pecks and said, "By all means, turn the dogs loose. There's shelter by the gardener's shed." She reached to open the door, then lowered her voice, saying, "I can't tell you how much I miss Henry. It isn't the same with him gone. Clifford is the fourth houseman I've had in three years, and I don't think I want to keep him on."

Charlie put his hand on her shoulder. "I'm sorry, Elizabeth."

Elizabeth accepted this without saying thank you, respecting Charlie's Ojibwa traditions. "I hope we didn't prolong the end unnecessarily," she said. "That's what I can't be certain of, that he didn't suffer more than he had to." Then she shoved Charlie's arm. "Go attend to those dogs before I indulge in bathos. Go, go," she shooed, turning to Morgan as Charlie went to get the dogs. "I've been following this Ferrand situation. It's very distressing."

She indicated the hall. "Come on. I'm certain there'll be a place by the fire. I'll take your . . . jacket?"

"Anorak," said Morgan.

"Whatever-it-is," Elizabeth compromised. "Once you're warm enough. Keep it with you until then." As she opened the door to the back parlor, she went on, "I never know why people are always snatching wraps just when you want them the most. There you are, standing in the foyer, with the door open likely as not, and the first thing they will do is take away your coat while there's still goose flesh on your arms."

The room never failed to impress Morgan: the walls were all wood-paneled. The carved molding and wainscoting were glossy with wax and buffing. The fireplace was not large enough to roast an ox, but might have taken a goat easily, and just at present there was a well-laid blaze going in its depths. Its hearthstones were ornamented with low-relief Tudor roses. Morgan went to the high-backed chair which had become her favorite. She looked around at Elizabeth. "You know me too well."

"At my age," Elizabeth declared, "I'd better, or I've wasted the last seventy-six years." Her own chair was a low-slung thing upholstered in heavy brocade. The frame was flexible, creaking as she sat down. "Well, don't stand there, make yourself comfortable," she ordered Morgan.

With a faint smile, Morgan went to the fireplace and raised her arm to rest it on the mantel. "I'll warm up soon."

"You look tired," said Elizabeth as she put her feet on the hassock at the foot of her chair.

"I am, a little," she said, staring down at her short boots, vaguely curious about how long it would take them to dry. "It's been a rough week."

"Because of the Ferrand case," said Elizabeth in her version of easy inquiry. "According to Victor, it was mishandled from the beginning and he has been made a patsy. What do you think?"

"I think that he shouldn't be telling stories out of school, relative or no relative," said Morgan.

"Oh, agreed, but you mustn't fault Victor for that: I was very persistent." Elizabeth's smile was jolly and predatory. "Eventually he told me the lot. He's feeling very ill-used. I suppose I sympathize with him, but not as much as he'd like. He thinks George Wycliff wanted to embarrass him, but I told him that having to release Ferrand looks as bad or worse for Wycliff as it does for him."

"There's some truth in that. Not that I'd expect Victor to believe you," said Morgan. The heat from the fire was working its way into her with great speed. Her hands were no longer gelid and her face felt less as if cold plastic had been stretched over it.

"He will, in time. His pride is smarting now. Give him a month or two and he'll have a better perspective on what has happened to him." She watched Morgan with bright eyes. "It bothers you, doesn't it?"

"Yes," said Morgan. "I know it's irrational, but I feel responsible. I was the one who said the charges had to be dismissed. The search warrant didn't give them the right to look in the greenhouse, and they did. Since the whole case depended on evidence found as a result of that search, I stopped the trial. Victor told you what they found because of that search, the keys and the Polaroid shots of the filming? That led them to the storage unit and all the rest. The cameras were there, and some of the props used, and a couple boxes of make-up and things like that. I've seen the videotapes, and they sicken me, but they were not taken legally, and the trial cannot—" She broke off.

"I understand the law enough to appreciate your dilemma," said Elizabeth. "Well, has the fat lady sung yet? that's the important question. As long as she hasn't, there's a chance to make Ferrand answer for his crimes."

Before Morgan could answer, the door was opened and Charlie came into the room. "They're in the side yard, and the rain is getting worse."

"What have you been up to?" Elizabeth asked him with keen attention.

It was an indication of the depth of Charlie's affection for Elizabeth that he was not offended by her banter. In almost anyone else, he would have given a short answer or none at all. As it was, he chuckled. "You can't make me responsible for this, Elizabeth. For one thing, Ojibwa don't go in much for rain dances, and for another, it's too much work."

Clifford came into the room with the cocktail cart and a tea tray. "There are hot stuffed mushrooms and scallops broiled in mustard sauce," he said, indicating the two covered trays. "Dinner will be served in one hour."

Once he was gone, Elizabeth got up and marched up to the cart. "He's a weasel, but he's a wonderful cook." She took a bottle of Charbono from the tray and reached for the corkscrew. "It's old enough to be civilized," she recommended.

"Yes, please," said Morgan, who had learned to share Elizabeth's enthusiasm for Italian varietals.

"Tea now, wine with dinner, if you will," said Charlie, knowing better than to offer to open the wine for her. He tugged his anorak over his head and looked about for a place to hang it.

"Put it over there, on the parsons bench," said Elizabeth as she busied herself with the corkscrew. "I'll tell Clifford to take care of it while we eat." As she skillfully drew the cork from the bottle, she gave a single, slow sigh. "It isn't fair, I know, to judge him against Henry. Poor Clifford hasn't a prayer, conscientious though he is. Henry was my houseman for a quarter of a century, and this poor young man has been here only four months. But Henry was so perfect; we were so used to each other and this kid—"

"No one will replace Henry," said Charlie seriously, remembering the last four months of Henry's life when Henry had refused to go to the hospital, so Elizabeth had diligently cared for him while AIDS leached the life out of his body. Elizabeth had pulled strings and called in favors to obtain the use of every experimental drug she could, but still Henry died. "Don't resent Clifford for wanting to do his job. He isn't trying to sully Henry's memory."

"I know," said Elizabeth. She sniffed at the extracted cork before pouring a little into her glass, swirling the wine in the glass and then holding it up to the light. "The legs are good."

"You're a wine snob, Elizabeth," Morgan chided her affectionately. "God, what an effort you make."

"It's not an effort, it's the practice of a skill. And you've never had a bad bottle here, have you?" Elizabeth asked as she poured Morgan's glass, then topped off her own. "Nose and finish are very nice."

"Thanks," said Morgan as she took the glass.

Charlie helped himself to tea and remarked, "I know it's none of my business, but I'd feel better about your situation here, Elizabeth, if you had someone you liked and trusted working for you again."

"I did," she said at once. "But he's dead. I don't know if I have it in me to develop another . . ." She sipped at her wine, not finding a word to describe her feeling.

"But you won't try," Charlie objected, his flint-dark eyes kindly. "That's what bothers me. You act as if no one in the world could be your houseman. All right, no one in the world could be another Henry Tsukamato. Granted. But you can find someone else, someone different who can work for you and with you without letting you intimidate him so much he cannot do anything."

"I'm not intimidating. Only ninnies think I am," said Elizabeth in a tone that could etch brass.

Charlie laughed. "You're absolutely terrifying, and you know it."

"Charles, I am five-foot-three and over seventy; how could anyone be terrified of me?" Elizabeth looked to Morgan for help and saw that Charlie's wife was grinning at her. "I think you're both ridiculous," said Elizabeth with hauteur worthy of royalty. "But if you have this absurd view of me, why don't you find me a houseman and see if I decide he's suitable?"

"Flinging down the gauntlet, are you?" Charlie asked. "All right, challenge accepted. But you will have to give whomever I select a reasonable time to prove his worth. None of this three-months trial, you'll have to allow at least six months."

She cast him a scorching look. "You will find me a houseman, someone with the experience necessary for what I require, who is willing to live here and be in my employ. You want a period for full evaluation, and I agree that's a reasonable request. Six months: done." She lifted her wineglass and drank to the deal.

By the time Charlie and Morgan reached home it was ten-thirty. "I'll take care of the dogs," said Charlie as Morgan lowered the garage door from the inside. At this hour the basement seemed more still, with less light than other parts of the house, as if the darkness had sunk to the lowest parts of the house.

"Good. Thanks," said Morgan as she started toward the stairs to the kitchen. "I'll get a bath going."

Caesar and Pompei, after their hours of playful freedom, had been content to huddle in the back of the car, half-asleep, until they were sent to their part of the basement where they could reach the backyard quickly through their own gate.

"Use the tincture in the green jar, will you?" Charlie called after her as he secured the small gate that kept the dogs out of the rest of the garage.

"What?" she yelled down.

"The tincture!" he shouted back. "In the green jar. In the bath!"

"Okay!" she returned, and he heard her walking over his head on the floor above. As she made her way from kitchen to hall, her steps passed directly over Charlie, and he had a brief and intense sensation of her nearness.

Satisfied the dogs had dried food and water, Charlie turned off the two rear lights and went upstairs to the main floor. "Morgan?"

"Upstairs," she called, revealing she had been climbing upward at the same time he had. "I'm turning on the heater. And I've got the green jar."

Charlie grinned as he followed her, knowing that their bathing together would be welcomed by both of them. As he reached the top of the stairs, he paused. "Want me to bring towels?"

"Not necessary. I've got them already." There was a rush and splash of water as their oversized tub began to fill. "The heater's on, too."

"Good," said Charlie as he stepped into the bathroom. It was one of the three rooms he had had renovated shortly after he moved into the house, before he married Morgan. The changes to the room had included annexing a small storage closet for a place for the tub and extending the floor out beyond the house, so that there was an upper deck beyond the bathroom, and filtered light beneath in the garden, where ferns and rhododendrons grew. The predominant color in the room was sage green. He lowered the lights to a soft glow like twilight.

"Don't expect too much of me, Charlie. I haven't done much of this and I still don't have the hang of it." Morgan was taking off her clothes, nothing flirtatious in her manner. She moved efficiently, without coyness or tantalizing glimpses; Charlie found it more arousing than the most artful, provocative striptease could have been. He started to toss his clothes into a pile. When Morgan saw the growing heap, she protested.

"But it's nothing," said Charlie. "Everything's going into the washing machine, anyway. Why take the time to fold it?"

"I can't imagine," said Morgan, indicating the somewhat neater pile of her own clothes. "What are we doing, other than getting clean and smelling good?" she asked as she stepped to the edge of the tub.

"Well, there are a number of things the tincture can help," said Charlie, considering her question carefully. "First, it will help reduce depression and clean up the psyche. Then it will help ease you so you can get the rest you need. After that, it will bring understanding of your dreams." He was naked now. "I asked my grandfather once about using the tincture this way—for two—but he had no answer because all the lore in the tribe forbade it. He wasn't so rigid in his thought that he automatically rejected all questions like that, but he was strict in his teaching, and said that if it was possible, it would have to be out of the tribe because no one in the tribe would accept it." He climbed into the bath and turned down the cool water so that the temperature would be higher than what she had set.

"Are we going to be parboiled?" Morgan asked, putting the lid back on the tincture jar.

"Not quite," said Charlie as he eased back into the bath. "But it has to be hot."

"Doing fine so far," Morgan said, then touched the small, dark piece of carved wood that hung around her neck on a gold chain. "Should I take this off?"

"No reason to," said Charlie at once. "Leave it on. This will help recharge it." He leaned back, letting the hot water rise up his chest. "Come on in," he offered, reaching out a hand to her.

She took it and stepped into the tub, wincing a little at how hot it was. "Do you have to make it—"

"So hot? Yes." He splashed her legs gently. "You'll get used to it more quickly if you just sit down. If it's too cool, the magic doesn't work."

"Okay," she said, not as accepting as she wanted to be. "If you were with the tribe, would you make it this hot?"

"Hotter," he assured her. "But I'd have to do it alone. We don't have women in these rituals." He stretched out more, pleased that the tub was large enough for this. At the time he had put it in, he had feared it was an extravagance, but now he was certain it had been a wise decision. "Come on, sit down."

She moved very carefully, not comfortable in the hot water. "Is it true? If you were with the tribe, you couldn't do this with me?"

"Yes, it's true." He slid to the side so there would be room for her. "Lie back. It feels great; really."

"Why are you different?" she asked, then answered her own question. "Because you were born here and went back there as a child? Did it make that much of a difference?"

"It seems to have," said Charlie, letting his mind drift.

She stretched out very carefully, turning a little so she could watch him. She never quite knew what to make of these times with him, when he was a shaman instead of an attorney. No matter how often he assured her that there was no difference between the two, that they were only aspects of himself, not divergent personalities, she always had a lingering suspicion that it was more complicated than that. At one time she had thought it was one of those left-brain-right-brain shifts, but she was no longer certain of it. "Is there anything I ought to do?"

"You can start by relaxing," he said, smiling. "Then let your thoughts drift. Don't try to think about anything."

"That's not easy for me," she warned him.

"Nor for me. But do it. Make it a game." He stared up at the ceiling, at where the light fixtures cast faint, curving shadows. If he had not needed to turn off the water, he would not have moved at all.

"What do you look for?" Morgan asked.

Charlie leaned back again. "Nothing. You let it come to you, you don't try to go to it. You . . . let it take shape, whatever it is."

She sighed. "That's where I get hung up. I don't know how to let something come, without knowing what it is." Dutifully she stared at the ceiling. "I wish there were more stuff to do."

"Waiting is the stuff to do," said Charlie quietly. "Watching for what is coming." He reached over and took her hand. "Make it easy, Morgan. That's the trick to it. You don't have to do anything to make it work. No abracadabra or chants, or—"

"You chant sometimes," she said.

"Not while I'm doing this," he said, refusing to be distracted by her challenge. "If something comes, fine; if something doesn't, what's wrong with lying here in hot water with me?"

She smiled a little guiltily. "Nothing wrong with that."

"Well, then." He settled back, still holding her hand, and watched the ceiling.

Morgan wanted to think of something to add, but the right words eluded her. The heat and the water were beginning to work the tension out of her, and the worries which had continued to gnaw at her throughout the evening were fading. It was almost sinful to spend so much time on nothing more than a bath, she admonished herself, and at the same time decided that she liked it; another half hour would be pleasant. Satisfied, she resigned herself to waiting for whatever was coming.

Tuesday

"I UNDERSTAND THAT this is *not* a deposition, and that I will not be under oath?" said Melissa Budge with an engaging and slightly condescending smile. She was comfortably plump and dressed in attractive and unremarkable clothes. Her short-cropped hair was almost white, and Charlie could tell from the hair on her arms and her eyebrows that the color was natural. She had been a psychologist with the San Francisco school system for fourteen years, and for the last five had specialized in abuse cases.

"Well, since depositions are taken in civil, not criminal, cases, this isn't a deposition at all. I believe I requested a statement from you, and as I read your answer, you agreed to this interview." He motioned to where John Carroll, their youngest associate, sat in the least comfortable chair in the office. "I've provided a witness, since you haven't brought an attorney with you."

"Should I have?" Melissa Budge asked.

"Not that I am aware of," Charlie replied. "But in instances of this sort, it helps both of us to have a third party present."

"I was told you were willing to accept my patients' confidentiality. I don't know how you can do this with this . . . witness."

"He isn't here to expose anyone or anything, merely to act as an impartial observer. He isn't working on this case and does not deal directly with me in most things; he's one of my partners' kids, and he knows what is required of him," said Charlie. "It isn't smart to rely entirely on memory for interviews of this sort. I will want to consult with John to find out if I have misread anything you have told me, or anything I have asked you. I may need more than this statement later, and I might want to call you as an expert witness." He indicated the chair opposite his desk. "Would you like coffee or tea?"

"Tea would be very nice." She sat down, her wariness well

concealed. She adjusted her glasses on her nose and looked once at John Carroll. "I think I had better tell you that it might not be wise to call me as a witness."

"Why?" asked Charlie as he ordered tea for both of them, and coffee for John. "Milk and sugar?"

"No, thank you," she said a little wistfully, then answered his first question. "I'm afraid I am certain that the girls were abused. I could not say anything else."

"That would be most helpful," said Charlie, noticing how surprised she was at his answer. "I have no desire to have such information blocked or underrated, or dismissed in any other way. You see, Ms. Budge, I think it is evident that the girls were abused, too, and I want it to be well-established that we are not disputing that fact. I have no intention of making light of their ordeal, and I give you my word that I will not call their experiences overstated or anything else. My question is who did it." He held up his hands. "I know what they say, but you have to admit it is possible they are not telling the   whole truth."

Her expression was dubious. "Girls don't make up these kinds of stories; not very often."

"Exactly," said Charlie, and had the satisfaction of seeing Melissa Budge look more confused than before. "Everything I've learned about this case indicates that something happened to them: I am going on the assumption that they are telling the truth about the abuse and are deliberately lying about who did it to them."

"Mister Moon!" exclaimed Melissa Budge. "If you sensationalize—"

"No, nothing like that." He was preparing to go on when Merek Rzeszow brought in the tea tray.

"Good morning," he said as he set the tray on Charlie's desk. He nodded to Melissa. "Beautiful weather."

It was still raining and the wind was blustery, so Charlie replied, "If you say so."

"I am practicing irony," Merek explained as he left the room. Melissa watched as Charlie poured the tea. "What an . . ."

Charlie glanced at her. "What an odd young man? Yes, he is, isn't he? Very enterprising. He came here eight years ago with his older sister. They've invented lives for themselves." He handed a cup to her and took his own, indicating with a sign to John Carroll that he could pick up his coffee. "About the girls?"

"Yes," said Melissa, getting down to business. "They are . . . well, they are teenagers, and that creates some curious problems.

They are caught up in their experience, self-involved in a way few of us experience except at that time of life. Most of them are fascinated with their sexuality and even more terrified of it. These girls are no exception. For the first time they have encountered the difference between the social myths about women and the realities, and it is very confusing for them." She took a sip of tea. "For all of us, in fact. Luckily, most of them come from fairly stable homes, and have had few major traumatic experiences until this one."

Charlie thought of the reports Gail and Mickey had provided so far, but decided not to challenge Melissa. He wanted her cooperation, not her resistance. "I don't want you to compromise the confidentiality of these girls, but, in your opinion, how long had the abuse been going on, and what form did it take?"

"I'll answer the first part, Mister Moon, but not the second," she said primly. "I gather that the abuse began with Wendy and Michelle about five months ago."

"In other words, shortly after the fall semester began?" Charlie suggested as the tea began to cool.

"Yes," she said. Her face hardened. "It is despicable, using a position of trust to do such things to these children!"

"Most certainly it is, if that's what happened," said Charlie at his most reasonable.

Melissa drank half her tea. "I don't know if I should mention this, but I had been seeing one of those girls already. Her advisor had recommended she talk with me. She was having some difficulties at home."

"Oh," said Charlie, knowing that to learn more he would have to present complete neutrality. He wondered what girl Melissa Budge was talking about, and what the problems were.

"The girl is having more than the usual . . . problems with adjustment to her sexuality. She's definitely sexually attracted to females—has been for most of her life, though she didn't recognize what it meant until very recently—and so this abuse has created a crisis for her that is . . ." She took a last sip of tea. "I won't say that it is worse for her, but the nature of the trauma is not the same as for the others."

"I can understand that," said Charlie.

"In the Bay Area she's not under quite the same pressures she might be in other places—"

"Like the Bible Belt?" Charlie suggested.

"Well, yes. Here there are counselors who know how to help,

and there are hot lines and other services to make the transitions easier." She hesitated. "May I have some more tea?"

"Of course," said Charlie, and stood to pour it.

Melissa looked around the office. "I don't know if I can explain this adequately, but this one girl has less conflicts about what happened to her and more conflicts about what to do now. She is tempted to withdraw completely, shutting away both the abuse and the conflicts about her sexuality." She frowned. "I'm talking about her because she said something that troubled me, and I can't stop thinking about it. She said that if she had to do anything like that with anyone, Mister Girouard would be the man she'd do it with." Her expression was flustered. "You must be aware that there are a variety of responses to abuse of this sort, and many forms of avoidance and denial. But that remark, coming from the girl it did, weighs on me. It's really why I'm here."

As Charlie sat down, he picked up his teacup. "You mean you might agree with me: the girls were abused but not by Frank Girouard."

Grudgingly Melissa Budge nodded. "All right. Let's say that I think it may be possible."

Charlie accepted this. "Well," he said, having gained more than he had hoped for, "it's a start."

Between the rain and road repair, traffic was crawling on Union Street. "I'm sorry it's like this," said Gail Harris, most of her attention on the cars ahead. Her 4Runner gave her a slight edge because of its size and she took full advantage of it. "I should have suggested another place. Sorry. I didn't think."

"We'll get there, don't worry," said Charlie, who rode beside her. "You're right about meeting somewhere we're not known. And I've been meaning to try this place for months."

"Sounds good," said Gail dubiously as she slapped the horn in warning to a BMW trying to nose in ahead of her.

"So how is the snooping going?" Charlie asked, content to settle back while Gail tended to the driving.

"Better than expected. Talbot's turning out to be very, very good." A hint of color touched her cheek but faded quickly.

"You're impressed with him," said Charlie.

Gail considered her answer. "Yes," she said as she inched the car forward again, "yes, I'm impressed with Cadao Talbot."

Charlie nodded. "I have to say that your work so far has been great. I appreciate all you've done."

"Well, you might not feel the same way after lunch. We dug up something troubling. But you better know—" She pounced on the brakes and swore. "Yuppies. I thought they were on the way out."

"It's the BMW?" said Charlie without looking.

"Yeah. God, I *hate* it when they drive like that, when they come scootching along in a bus stop or loading zone and then force you to let them in." She moved another foot forward. "Anyway, like I said, thanks to Cadao Talbot, we've found something buried in the school records, and it might go against you."

"How do you mean?" Charlie asked, his mind suddenly alerted. "What is it? What did you find?"

Gail made a rude gesture at someone beyond the window. "It seems about two years ago there was a scandal hushed up at that school. One of the teachers was rumored to be taking photographs of his students in the nude. Apparently that was as far as it went, and the whole thing was privately settled and swept under the rug. Trouble is, your guy was teaching there at the time, so he must have known about it."

"Frank was implicated?" Charlie asked, trying not to anticipate any answer, welcome or unwelcome.

"I wasn't able to find out which teacher it was—those records are sealed. But you know about things like that, they never really die, do they?" Gail did not take her eyes off the street, but she managed to wiggle her fingers in such a way that she seemed to draw Charlie into her anxiety.

"Un-huh," said Charlie slowly. "And? Is there something more?"

"Well, he wasn't the one implicated, according to three of the teachers we checked with, if that's what you're asking about, but he did defend the guy, saying that it was the students' word against their teacher's, and all the students in question were getting bad grades in the teacher's class." Gail pointed. "Look. Almost there."

"Good," said Charlie, anxious to get the rest of this information. "Tell me what happened then?"

"Well, the teacher in question resigned with the understanding that his resignation was not an admission of responsibility or any misconduct, and two of the students were transferred to other schools. Of the two that remained, one of them died a year later—last year, in fact—under suspicious circumstances: his motorcycle went out of control on Highway 1. He was on drugs at the time according to the autopsy report." She signaled to turn. "There's the garage."

"I hope it isn't full yet," said Charlie, knowing how scarce parking places were in this part of the city.

"Mickey said he'd arranged everything." She maneuvered her 4Runner across traffic and pulled up at the ticket booth. "Hi," she called as she opened the door. "Mickey Trang sent me."

The man in the booth was Vietnamese. He indicated a space in the corner. "Put it over there."

As she jockeyed the car into position, she said, "See? I told you."

"Great," said Charlie, and unfastened his seat belt.

Mickey was waiting at their table by the window. He cocked his head toward the heavy rain and fitfully blowing wind. "Don't you love this place?" he asked as Gail and Charlie walked up to him.

"So long as you don't get seasick," said Charlie, and sat down in the chair that faced the room, knowing that the storm could be far more engrossing to him than to most people; today he would not welcome the distraction. "What do you recommend?"

"All the pasta's fresh," said Mickey. "The rest is a matter of taste." He smiled at his partner. "So, did you tell him about the photos?"

"Yes, a little," said Gail. She was finding her way through the menu. "Homemade fish sausage. I wonder what that's like?"

"Order some and find out," Charlie suggested, anxious to get the rest of their report. "What about the teacher who resigned. Is he still in the area? Is there any way we can find out what really happened?"

Mickey grinned. "His name is Wilson Harness. He's running a supply store in Angel's Camp."

"What kind of supplies?" Charlie asked.

"You know, the usual rural things: feed, hardware, fuel oil, seeds, shavings, lumber, bait." He had a Coach briefbag over his shoulder and he opened it, selecting a file folder. "Have a look."

"Wilson Harness," said Charlie, reading the name. "Any direct contact?"

"Not yet," said Gail. "We didn't know what you wanted us to do. It's nice in the Gold Country this time of year. What do you think? Should we go up there, or leave it be for now?"

"Let me think about it while we eat," said Charlie as a waiter approached.

* * *

At one-thirty Sergeant Ed Massie knocked on the door of Morgan Studevant's chambers, grinding his teeth in anticipation of the coming interview. He hated being summoned by the judge in so uncompromising a fashion, the more so because he knew that she had reason to be upset with him.

"Please come in, Sergeant," said Morgan, not rising as the policeman entered. "Thank you for coming. I think you and I need to have a little discussion. Off the record."

"I've been having a lot of those," said Massie in a surly undervoice, adding, "You're the judge, Ms. Studevant." He never trusted women who called themselves Ms.; you never knew where you stood with them.

"No doubt you have been having discussions," she said, making it clear she had heard him. "And no doubt you're afraid of what your Review Board will recommend." She motioned him to a chair. "Which is why I wanted to speak to you before you have their final decision."

He glared down at the floor. "Look, I know we fucked up, okay? The greenhouse wasn't part of the house and wasn't a residence. It wasn't even on the lot the residence occupied, but in one adjacent. Everyone's drilled that into us, that we can't extend over a property line. But Ferrand was renting the lot and the greenhouse! Hell, he rented four of those vacant lots. It wasn't like he had no link to it. It was his greenhouse, he said so himself." He sat down, his arms braced and his legs spread as if he expected a direct attack.

"And you were aware that you had not executed the search warrant properly because you falsified your report," Morgan said sternly. "You claimed that you found the key and the journal in the house itself, not out in the greenhouse on the adjacent lot. That means you were aware that you exceeded your authority, and you admit—admit!—that the seizure was illegal." She waited a moment for him to respond and when he did not, she went on. "Because of your actions, all that evidence is tainted. We will not be able to use it in any way again, even if legitimately obtained, because your deception has made it . . . unacceptable. You try to enter any complaint on that evidence and you know that Harding Towne will be all over you. The whole question of those videotapes could be considered prejudicial, because of what you did. Thanks to you, I have to declare a mistrial and dismiss the charges. I have no discretionary privilege here: this is illegal seizure. No judge would hesitate to suppress evidence linked to this seizure, no matter how much they might wish to do otherwise. Do you see that?"

"You're assuming that Towne is going to keep on with his old tricks. Well, when he moved to suppress, you didn't go along with it because everyone thought it was his usual shit. You had sworn statements to show the seizure was okay."

"The statements were lies," Morgan reminded him.

"Just about where we found the key. You can't doubt what's on those tapes, can you? All that has to happen is that we're allowed to show the tapes, because they make it crystal clear Ferrand's guilty. Ask anyone on that jury. They'll think the same thing, won't they? You're making too much of this. I admit we blew this case, but we'll get him one of these times, and we'll make it stick, no matter what we did wrong on this. So I think you're doing a worst-possible scenario, Your Honor," said Ed Massie. "No offense."

"Of course I am," she said. "It's necessary I do a worst-possible scenario because of—"

"I told you we know we fucked up, okay?" he burst out.

"No. Not okay," she said with feeling. "Not okay at all." She brought her temper under control and gave Massie a steady look. "You know the law. You know how to observe due process, and you set it all aside because you were too angry to think straight. That's . . . irresponsible."

"I'm not going to resign, if that's what you're leading up to; they won't let us until after the review," Massie growled. "Your Honor."

"Resignation is the least of it, Sergeant." She watched as he fidgeted in his chair. "What about the rest of the department?"

"There are only eight of us doing Juvenile Vice," said Massie defensively. "Hey, there's a major kiddie-porn ring out there, taking kids out of schools and off the streets, making them think that they owe something to Ferrand and the rest of them. You saw what was on the tapes, and that isn't the worst of it by a long shot. Some of those kids get as hooked on that shit as they do on ice. Those kiddie-porn kings are turning them into . . . things no kids should have to be. We don't have nearly enough men to handle the job."

"I understand that. I also understand how much of a burden your work can be. How do the other six feel about what you and your partner did?" asked Morgan, her face blank with sudden concentration.

Massie shrugged. "They're cops. Working Juvenile Vice isn't easy. They've all been finding kids turned into hookers and drug mules and all the rest of it. That's what I'm trying to tell you. It gets to them, you know? Someone like Ferrand, he's scum, he's slime. You saw."

"Yes," said Morgan, her eyes hardening.

"Yeah." Massie shifted in his chair again. "Look, Your Honor, we wanted to get that turd off the streets. We did it the wrong way, I grant you that. We should have tried for the second warrant, though you know as well as I do that he'd have moved everything to another location, and it might have taken months to get a lead on him again. But what the fuck, that's the letter of the law, right? He knew we were onto him, and he's no fool. But you're right. We didn't observe due process. We shouldn't have tried so hard. He's got the same rights as the kids he's been using and destroying, hasn't he? That's what the law says, doesn't it? But if you saw what we see every night, you wouldn't be so quick to judge us."

"That's where you're wrong," said Morgan with strong feeling. "Because getting them off the streets is just the beginning. *Keeping* them off the streets is what we're supposed to be doing, the cops and the courts together. We can't hold up our end if you don't hold up yours. In your hurry to *get* Ferrand off the streets, you've put him back on them, with guarantees and protections that will make it much, much harder to *keep* him off. And why did you limit the warrant to Scooter Ferrand? There are two other names on that tenants' agreement: who are Ryffial Malkuros and P.A.K.O. Hambai? You can't single out Ferrand and ignore the other two, can you." She looked Sergeant Massie in the eye, not letting him turn away from her.

"We have enough on Ferrand to make it logical, Your Honor," said Massie heavily. "The other guys are probably aliases in any case, or they don't exist."

"And if they are real, what then?" Morgan paused, then went on. "I've been asked by the Review Board for my recommendation in your case. The D.A.'s office is suggesting that you be asked to resign, but without having perjury charges filed against you. Do you want me to go along with them."

Massie's face was shocked but he made himself sound resigned and sullen. "Sure. Why not. Throw us to the wolves. Fine with me."

"Really? Just like that?" Morgan asked sarcastically. "Do you think your ex-wife and kids will agree?" She studied him as he tried to frame an answer. "I intend to suggest suspension with compulsory attendance at certain classes in law, because your regard for due process appears to be in question. If you are not willing to attend the classes and accept the suspension, then I will join with the others—reluctantly, I assure you—and support your resignation or dismissal, and I will further recommend that you be bound over for trial on charges of perjury."

While Morgan spoke Massie had grown steadily more pale. "Where do you get off making conditions like—"

"I get off on the side of the law, the same as you do, Sergeant." She indicated the door. "Let me know what you decide by this evening, will you? I have to tender my recommendation by tomorrow morning."

FOUR

Wednesday night and Thursday morning

ASIDE FROM CHARLIE the only person left in the offices of MacCurrey, Moon, Nelson and Wong was Jocelyn Nelson; it was almost eight. The sounds from the street were less intrusive now that the evening commute was all but over, and residual slams and conversation in the building had faded.

Charlie was making his third pot of tea for the afternoon and evening when he saw Jocelyn emerge from her office, her coat over her arm and her keys in her hand. "Finished?"

"No, but tomorrow is deposition time again, and I have to be in Sacramento before nine. At least it's supposed to be clear. There might still be a little frost, but no blowing rain, thank God. I should be there in under two hours, if the bridges are clear. So I need some food and sleep before I tackle Piesleigh and his crowd. What about you?"

"I'm going over the latest from Mickey and Gail. I reckon it'll go another hour or hour-and-a-half." Charlie poured boiling water into his preheated pot, sniffing as the first scent of the tea came with the steam.

"The Girouard case," said Jocelyn with less enthusiasm.

"Yes." He deliberately changed the subject to less disputed cases. "We'll be getting a directed verdict in the Stoner case; Judge Cleuytens said so this afternoon. You remember those depositions last October? they paid off. And you'll be glad to know that we've finally negotiated a reasonable settlement on the Durkheim case—both sides are at long last listening to reason, and no one wants any more adverse publicity." He put the lid on the pot and smiled at Jocelyn. "I don't know if the counteroffer we made to Nially on Park's behalf will be acceptable, but I decided we might as well give it a try, and Park said he would go along with it. Everything else is in flux, though we're looking for a break in the Wallingham suit, if the tests show contaminants in the ground samples."

Jocelyn offered thumbs-up for encouragement but her attitude shifted almost at once. "I'm starting penalty phase on the Willard case next week. Judge Magnussen set Monday morning for it so he can have a long weekend. Poor guy looks worn out." She pursed her lips critically before going on. "You're still determined about Girouard, aren't you? How is it going?" She sounded resigned, as if she were tired of protesting. "If you still think the case has merit, I suppose we might as well carry through."

"Thanks," said Charlie, preparing to take his tea back into his office. "You and Brian may be right, and I might not be able to find enough material for a reasonable doubt, but I believe that this man did not hurt those children, either in the way he's accused or any other." He knew that his certainty did not banish Jocelyn's continuing reluctance to believe. "If you want to review the material I've got?"

"No," she said at once. "I haven't got the time even if I had the inclination. If you insist that he might be wrongfully accused, then I'll still stand by your decision to defend him. It's just that the whole thing is so . . . *repugnant* to me."

"I know what you mean," said Charlie, watching as she walked to the stairs. "The elevator's still running."

"I need the exercise," said Jocelyn before she gave him a final wave. "I haven't gone to the gym in a month."

Back in his office Charlie opened the largest of the folders, the one that was dedicated to the school records of the five girls. He had been over the material before, but he wanted to review it, hoping that this time he might trip over a fact that he had not noticed previously. He read the comments Gail Harris had made very closely, for he felt that the chances were good that Gail would be particularly sensitive to what the girls said. It was just after nine when he stumbled across a remark: *Emma Westford and Michelle Hawkins have both referred to accused as "handsome", "terrific", "real special", "gorgeous", "nice" and "wonderful". Wendy Maple reports that the accused is "understanding" and "helpful". These statements were made after their accusations were filed and Girouard arrested; they were given separately to separate officers. Unless they are suffering from hostage syn-*

*drome, this is strange language to use to describe a man who has
abused them the way they claim he has.* Charlie stared down at the
page, frowning at the implications of what he saw there. What
would prompt those girls to say such complimentary things about
Girouard after his arrest, when according to their sworn statement
both had been bound, whipped and sodomized by him less than a
week before? One girl, he thought, might try to protect herself
from facing the extent of her abuse, but three? He ticked the box
at the top of the page and set the document aside, pouring the last
of his lukewarm tea into his cup and drinking it down slowly. Why
would they all do that? What reason could they have? He resolved
to find out.

Frank Girouard stared at his interlaced fingers. "Is it really
necessary? I know what you said, but—"

"Yes," said Charlie. "You know the opposition will bring in
every big gun they can, and we have to counter with the best we
can get. Those tests will be very hard to dispute, and they have
been regarded as indicative in other cases. I warned you about the
tests when we talked at the first of the week, and you said fine, no
objections. I thought you understood what the tests could mean."
He saw Girouard's depression as if he had wrapped himself in a
dark shroud. "You agreed, Frank."

"Yes, I suppose I did," he replied lethargically. "My wife . . .
you've got to understand. I didn't talk it over with Angelique. I
should have told her what was involved, what it would mean. I
should have, I really should have. I didn't think it through; I'm too
upset. It wasn't fair to her."

"How is a battery of psychosexual tests given to you unfair to
her?" Charlie asked with genuine confusion. "We can't use other
methods because we have no tissue samples from any of the girls.
We'd do a chromosome type if we had the chance, and that would
be that. But we can't. The purpose of this battery of tests is to
determine some degree of the likelihood that you are capable of
such abuses. Unless you have abusive fantasies about the kids you
teach, I doubt the tests will be to your disadvantage. It's crucial to
your defense, Frank. You'd think she'd want answers as much as
anyone."

Frank shook his head, still looking at his tangle of fingers. "She
isn't as . . . sophisticated as some women are. She comes from a
little town up in Trinity County, very conservative, very religious,
and she isn't . . . very accepting of tests like these. She doesn't

agree with what the tests are supposed to do, and she . . . well, she thinks they're harmful." He looked at Charlie and tried again to explain. "First off, she doesn't believe in them, says that they're designed to obscure, not to reveal. I tried to tell her otherwise, but . . . She said she didn't want . . . any part of them." He had not touched the coffee prepared for him, and his heavy eyes indicated long nights with little or no sleep. "When you asked me about them, I said the first thing that came into my head, and I shouldn't have; I hadn't thought about her when I said yes."

"Did you explain how serious this is and what a difference it could make in your case?" Charlie was becoming concerned, for he did not want to contribute to any divisiveness in his client's family. "Did you tell her that without these tests, there are those who would think that you had something to hide? In theory the defense is not required to present a psychological or psychiatric evaluation, and in certain instances cannot be specific to the case for expert testimony, but if there is no psychological testimony at all in your defense, it might go against you by its absence."

"She tells me it's between us and God," said Frank quietly. "She said that no one ought to discuss these things outside the home, and then only before God." He opened his hands. "The thing is, it's never been an issue between us until the last two or three years. We . . . well, we had a couple problems, the way couples do, and I suggested we get some help. She wouldn't allow it. She was willing to talk things over with her pastor, in private, but she wouldn't ask for assistance from anyone who wasn't a practicing Christian, and fairly Fundamentalist in orientation. She turned down a Quaker because she doesn't trust them because they have no clergy."

This complication was as unwelcome as it was unexpected. Charlie framed his next question with great care. "I don't want to make a difficult situation worse, but I'm convinced it is in your best interest to have these tests. I doubt if the testimony of her pastor would be considered a suitable substitute."

"I realize that, and I've tried to explain things to her," Frank murmured. "But I don't want things to get like they were. You don't know how important her religion is to her."

"If this is the case, wasn't it a problem for you when you first married?" He did his best to put very little emphasis on the question, so that he would not inadvertently weight it and distort his client's reaction. "Religion is the sort of thing most couples discuss early."

"No, we didn't talk about it, not that way; I didn't see it that way," said Frank after a short silence. "She told me that she had faith enough for us both and that if I had doubts she would help me end them. I . . . I thought her devotion was touching. You know how it can be. Then I realized shortly after we met that she needed my . . . protection. Protecting her made me very happy, and Angelique as well. I didn't see the downside of it until we had . . . that trouble. Then I began to notice how little chance I had to help her beyond the protection. She had retreated and she liked it just fine that way. So I was . . . upset. She kept telling me that she was married to me for better or worse, and that nothing would change that. I thought that if we had a little therapy, she might be able to get along better; she wouldn't find things she disagreed with so frightening." At last he gulped down the coffee.

"I see. And she disagrees with these tests, even though they might mean the difference between your imprisonment or release?" Charlie waited for the answer, knowing that whatever Frank Girouard said, it would be crucial to how he managed the case.

"She says that if I deserve punishment, God will see that I have it. She says that if I doubt that, then I've fallen from grace." He put his cup down hard. "She won't change her mind."

Charlie folded his arms. "Would you like me to talk to her? Because, Frank, any attorney you engage is going to want tests like these run if they intend to make any kind of defense. You can fire me and go through the same thing with someone else."

"She says," Frank muttered, "that if I do this, she'll leave me. Not divorce me, because she believes that marriage is forever. She will leave me and not let me go. She means it. There are certain things she's very inflexible about, and this is one of them. She's angry that I even considered the tests. She says that I would be turning to the Devil for my protection, and—" He stared away. "She'll do it, I know her. She'll head back to Trinity County and I'll never see her. She's pregnant."

There was a brief silence. "You have rights, Frank," said Charlie, very much to the point. "If you are convinced that these tests will harm you, that's one thing, but if you're refusing them to placate your wife, that's another." He hesitated as he weighed up the various permutations of Frank's wife's decision. "I think you'd do best to inform her you have taken the tests after you've done it."

"But she'll leave," protested Frank.

"Possibly. It's a risk. But prison is a risk as well, and you don't seem confident that she will be accepting of that, either. She may leave no matter what you do," said Charlie. "But you have some rights as husband and father, and you have my word that I will do everything to see they are protected." He watched Frank. "I need your cooperation, Frank. I wouldn't ask you to do something like this if I didn't think it was necessary."

"I'm scared to death. I've been counting on her." He looked toward the clock on the wall. "You have an appointment in five minutes."

"You've still got a couple more. If we go over a little, so be it." He handed Frank a sheet of paper. "There's the address, the time of your appointment and the name of the psychiatrist doing the test. I really do urge you in the strongest possible way to do this. If you don't, we'll be at a tremendous disadvantage; I won't kid you about that."

"How will it look if Angelique leaves me?" Frank asked, his mouth turning down at the corners.

Charlie considered his answer and spoke more casually than he felt. "With a little care, it shouldn't be too damaging. There's no reason for her departure to look like more condemnation. Since your wife is pregnant and you're both under such a strain, it probably fits right in with the other aspects of your relationship if you try to minimize her stress. You might want to arrange for her to be out of the city for a while in any case, to take the pressure off. You can say it is for the health of your baby, and you won't be lying." How easily he said it! Charlie was amazed and disgusted with himself, thinking that a decade ago such a ruse would be unacceptable to him. But that was before he had seen cases won and lost on such minor points, before he had come to realize that his scruples might well cost a client his freedom.

"Do you think they'll buy it?" Frank asked, looking slightly ill.

"Unless your wife decides to open up to the tabloids, I think you're safe enough," said Charlie, then relented, seeing how distressed Frank was becoming. "It *is* pretty unsavory, isn't it? But it is one way to keep the press from hounding your wife; an appeal to the sensibilities of a pregnant woman facing such an ordeal as this one could save her a lot of media unpleasantness."

"She's not going to like any of this," said Frank unhappily.

"Who does?" Charlie responded. "Take the tests. And remember to set up a meeting for early next week. Drisa will take care of it for you. And in the meantime, call me if you need to talk to me. And whatever you do *don't* talk to the news media about anything, even the weather or the sports scores." He had risen and offered Frank his hand. "I know this is very difficult for you, and I'm sorry."

"Things just keep getting worse. It was bad enough when the girls said I'd . . . Angelique made me pray with her all night before she was willing to hear my side of it. Then she said it was all over and we'd never talk about it again. After the police came, she was truly distraught. She didn't like having to borrow money on the house to make bail," sighed Frank. "She hasn't . . ."

Charlie shook his head. "One thing at a time. Do the tests and we'll proceed from there."

"All right." He started away to the door, then stopped and turned. "The worst part of it is doing nothing. I want to teach, but the school won't permit it, and . . . sitting around the house all day is driving me nuts. I'd get a part-time job, to bring in a little money and . . ."

"I'll see if there's anything I can do to help," said Charlie, hoping that Oliver Kenwydd would not be too upset in the short delay for his appointment. Since Kenwydd was often a few minutes late, this turning of the tables might be a good notion.

Frank nodded, his expression abashed. "It's not your job. You're doing your job already. Never mind."

"Hey," Charlie said with a lightheartedness he did not feel, "I do want to get paid when all this is over, and I don't want to clean you out doing it. So by all means, let me see what I can come up with." He held the door for Frank Girouard and did not permit himself to frown until Frank turned down the hall and was out of sight.

About eleven Mickey Trang dropped by with more folders and printouts. He met Charlie in the hall outside his office. "Sorry to take you away from your client," he said as he held out the folders, "but I figured you'd want these before the end of the day, and I won't have extra time until late tonight."

Charlie took the folders. "What are these about?"

"More information on the girls. Family histories fleshed out, medical records for three of them, general comments. I think you're going to want to talk to some of the other teachers at the school. Teenagers are all a little odd, but two of those girls are out-and-out strange. Check the files."

"Drugs?" Charlie asked.

"One of them for sure, the other"—he shrugged—"your guess is as good as mine. If she's on something, there's nothing on paper about it."

"Is that all?" Charlie asked as he weighed the files with his hand. "They feel pretty heavy."

"They're not too bad," said Mickey. "We can get you lots more." He started away, then stopped. "You know, that Camberwell girl, there's something in her records from fifth grade you might want to look at. I might be reading between the lines, but . . ." He made himself stop. "Well, you read it and you let me know what you get out of it."

Charlie frowned. "All right," he said cautiously.

"I'm going to spend part of the afternoon checking out Missus Angelique Girouard, as requested an hour ago. I'll have preliminaries for you in the next three days." He pulled his motorcycle gloves from the helmet he carried under his arm. "That's it for the time being, boss."

"Keep on it," Charlie recommended.

"Anything you say," said Mickey as he slipped into the elevator.

On his way back to his office, Charlie kept wishing he had a free hour that afternoon when he could get started on reviewing the files. He would have to start putting his case together pretty soon, and though he would ask for a continuance, he doubted he could get the trial postponed much more than three weeks.

The client waiting for him, a bent and crabbed old man with the burden of the name Reginald Wolverton Parmalee III, glowered at Charlie as he returned to the office. "I will deduct the cost of your absence from my payment of your bill."

Charlie made a gesture of resignation. "I wasn't planning on including them in the bill."

"So you say!" scoffed the angry old man. "And what about this fence, then? What about it?"

"They're within their property lines, and the fence is designed to have minimal interruption of the view. The Planning Commission of San Mateo County approved it, and the public hearing did not result in any reason not to allow the fence to be built. I'm a little at a loss for what you expect me to do."

"I want you to force that snake to pull the fence down!" Parmalee declared ferociously. "Sue the pants off the son-of-a-bitch!"

Usually Parmalee wanted to sue someone about three times a year. This year he was running a little ahead of himself, Charlie thought. "A suit isn't in your best interests. I would be failing in my obligation as your attorney if I did that, Mister Parmalee."

"You do what I want, or someone else can have the outrageous fees I give to you!" He stamped his foot for emphasis.

Charlie pinched the bridge of his nose. "Mister Parmalee, let me try to explain this to you. We've discussed the problem before, as you recall. There were opportunities all during the building of that house and the completion of the landscaping for you or anyone else to express their objections. You did not come forward, though this house is behind yours. Both lots are five-acre lots, and there is an access easement between each of the lots that is fourteen feet wide, for rescue and emergency vehicles and for the use of those living in that particular development. You were notified of all the hearings and all the reviews of that property, and you did nothing. It isn't as if you were in Europe for a year and returned to find that the neighbors had behaved irresponsibly: you were in your house and you saw the house go up and the garden being planted, and the fence-post holes being dug. You said nothing at all. You did not attend the hearings although you were notified of them. Now you shriek like a scalded cat because you don't like the type of fencing they're using, and you want the whole thing taken down. You're not being reasonable."

Sitting still to listen to this summing-up was almost more than Parmalee could bear. He lurched to his feet. "I tell you, ignorant savage! you're fired!" He shoved his beaky nose in Charlie's direction. "I'll send you a registered letter for your files tomorrow. And be damned to you."

"If that's what you want," said Charlie, his tone more resigned than his thoughts; he wished Parmalee would fire him—in spite of frequently repeated threats, it never actually happened.

"I want an attorney who will protect my interests!" he raged, striding around the office, his elbows working at every step.

"I would not be protecting your interests if I filed this suit, and any competent attorney would tell you the same thing. Mister Parmalee, you've been warned from the bench about frivolous suits before, and that should put you on your mettle." Charlie studied the rambunctious old man, thinking that another generation would have called him a geezer. "If you want to fire me for that, go right ahead." He indicated the door. "We'll send you a closing bill and that will be that."

"Oh, no you don't! I want something for my money." He

stopped in his tracks and pointed at Charlie. "You're asking for a malpractice suit yourself."

Charlie sighed. "Go ahead and try it. But, Mister Parmalee, I put you on notice now that if you make such an attempt I will make the process as expensive, drawn-out and unpleasant as possible."

The light of battle came into Parmalee's wrinkle-wrapped eyes. "You wouldn't dare," he exclaimed hopefully.

"I would. And it would be a shame to both of us." He indicated the door. "Go home, Mister Parmalee, and make peace with your neighbors. If in twenty-four hours you still want to fire me, call the office and say so. Otherwise, this conversation, and the lawsuit against your neighbors, are forgotten."

"And the charge for this visit?" demanded Parmalee.

"If you fire me, the charge will be at the maximum rate. If you continue, it will be part of your annual retainer." It was only two hundred dollars, but Charlie was no longer inclined to fight with Parmalee. He wanted his energy and wits for more important matters.

"I'll let you know," Parmalee declared, and slammed out of the office.

Does he do this for recreation, Charlie asked himself when Parmalee had gone. Does he want attention, or some reassurance that people know he's still alive? Is he hungry for adventure? He shook his head and picked up his briefcase. Parmalee was for later: he had to concentrate on Frank Girouard for now.

FIVE

Friday, Saturday and Sunday

GEORGE WYCLIFF ARRIVED at Morgan's chambers five minutes after she did. He knocked perfunctorily once, then strode in. "I said I'd give you a week, Your Honor," he reminded her. "The week's up."

"I haven't changed my mind. Sorry," said Morgan, fastening her robes over her neat suit. "You know," she said reflectively, "years ago Charlie took me to the Magic Cellar—it was a magic nightclub; it's been closed for years—and we saw a young magician named Harry Anderson perform. He put a knitting needle through his arm at the end of the show. And now I see him playing a funny judge on *Night Court*."

"What does that have to do with—" Wycliff began, thrown off by her recollection.

"Nothing. It is my way of telling you, George, since you insist, that I am not going to discuss this with you again. Given what has happened, a search warrant is improper. And what are you going to do about the cops who perjured themselves?" She enjoyed turning the tables on him, watching him try to keep up with her.

"They haven't had their review hearing yet." He said it warily, expecting a trap. "The perjury is still alleged."

"They're guilty, and you know it. They knew the search was illegal and they took pains to conceal the illegality. They *lied* about it, George, deliberately and with full intent to deceive. They wanted the court to believe that they had found that key legally, and so they falsified their reports and they lied under oath. That is perjury, the more so because they are policemen, sworn to uphold the law." She stepped behind her desk. "I have a full calendar today, so why not get to your point?"

George Wycliff scowled. "I was hoping you had reconsidered your position."

"I certainly have," she said affably. "And I am more determined than ever to see that those two cops answer for what they did, like any other citizen caught committing perjury. We don't bend the law for ordinary people and I, for one, will not bend it for cops." She paused so he could speak. When he said nothing, she went on, "Is there anything else?"

"What are you going to recommend to the Review Board?" His voice was flat and for once he made no commanding gesture.

"I am going to recommend they be fired, of course, and then charged," she said. "The issues are very clear, George. There are no grey areas. They knew their search was illegal, they deliberately lied about it: that's against the law."

"They're good cops, Morgan." It was a plea more than a statement.

"Not any more," she replied. "They stopped being good cops when they broke the law."

Wycliff flung up his hands in baffled incredulity. "I don't understand it. You're being stubborn and unreasonable."

"Careful, George; you're treading on very thin ice," Morgan said, her amiable veneer wearing down. "I have to go, George; the bailiff just signaled me." She nodded toward the outer door. "You know the way."

"You can't leave yet. We haven't settled this." Wycliff loomed toward her, radiating well-groomed menace.

Morgan smiled. "Watch me."

"We have the first discovery material from the D.A. on the Girouard case," said Merek Rzeszow as Charlie came into the office from a meeting with his longtime client Terry Banning of Spinnaker Press. It was shortly after ten and the office was busy.

"Good," said Charlie, taking the package. "Who've they assigned to it?"

"Isolde Aldred," said Merek.

"Sally? She's a pretty big gun in the D.A.'s office." He clicked his tongue. "Sally. She's tenacious as a badger. It's going to be quite a fight if Sally's prosecuting." He decided he needed to talk to Jocelyn about facing Sally Aldred, since she was the last member of the firm to take on the formidable Assistant D.A.

"There's half a dozen calls for you, as well," said Merek. "I put the slips in your office. Oh, and the fax machine isn't working right."

Charlie suppressed a smile—he had never learned to trust fax machines and computer mail—and thanked Merek for his information, then headed to his office.

The first call he made was to Mickey Trang. "How was Angel's Camp?" he asked when the investigator came on the line.

"Quaint," said Mickey. "Mark Twain would be proud. Still, it's pretty at this time of year." His manner became more businesslike. "I've got a report I'll send over. Do you want me to go over the basics?"

"Sure," said Charlie, reaching for a legal pad and a pencil. "Give me the highlights."

"Well," said Mickey, his voice turning colorless, "Wilson Harness, former schoolteacher, does indeed run a supply store. He is moderately successful at it and said he wouldn't go back to teaching for all the gold in the Mother Lode. When I asked him about the scandal, he said he had taken pictures of some of his students—clothed, not naked—for a class project. The kids who turned him in were getting poor grades in his class and wanted a way to compromise him so they would not have Ds on their report cards. The school was waffling about the accusation. I asked him why not fight it, if that was the case, and he said he did not want it coming out that he was gay, which would have made things much worse. If that came out, he said, they'd assume the worst and it wouldn't matter if he won in court. So he quit."

"Do you think he is gay? Or is that just an acceptable ploy to divert attention from the real issues?" Charlie asked, doodling on the yellow pad.

"I think he probably is. Not the swishy kind, but the jockey kind, all very hail-fellow-well-met, let's-do-sports and palsy, but not going as far as leather. I suspect he has some kind of arrangement with someone up there, but that's only a hunch." He paused. "He's angry about what happened, but more at the administration than the students. He said if the administration had been doing its job properly the students could not have got away with the smear. He said they'd been unwilling to support their teachers—the administrators, he meant. He might have something there."

"Check that out, will you?" Charlie said. "I'd like to know how much tap da cing the school is doing. It'll make a difference in court."

"You got it," said Mickey, and hung up.

His next call was a courtesy call to the District Attorney's office to thank them for speedily processing their discovery material. He made a point of saying he looked forward to more of the same.

"Your ten-thirty appointment is here," said Drisa Gaya over the intercom.

"Thanks; send him in," said Charlie, putting the Frank Girouard case aside for the time being.

It was three-thirty when Leda Dawson arrived at Charlie's office. She apologized for being late, saying, "We have trampoline on Tuesday and Friday afternoons and some of the girls don't like to quit." She was of medium height, in her middle-thirties, with short light-brown hair and steady light-brown eyes. She was dressed in stylish sports gear in a soft apricot color, with expensive running shoes on her feet.

Charlie motioned to the chairs on the other side of his desk. "Thank you for coming; at the end of the week you must have better things to do than interviews like this one, but I do appreciate your help. It can make a difference. Please sit down, Ms. Dawson."

"It's Missus Dawson, actually," she said. "Bert and I've been married for fifteen years this month." She held up her left hand to show an attractive but modest wedding ring. "It's been quite a ride."

"Congratulations," said Charlie. "I can offer you coffee or tea; and I'll send for one of my colleagues to join us, if you don't mind."

"Isn't this supposed to be confidential?" she inquired with some surprise. She selected one of the sling chairs, the one nearest the desk, and slipped into it.

"It's privileged, if that's your concern. But in this case, this is for Frank Girouard's protection, in case there's some question about what was said here." He did not want to say that he was auditioning her as a witness and wanted to be able to impeach her testimony if she changed it in court.

"Well, if that's how it's done," she said a little uncertainly. "I'd love a cup of coffee. Decaff, if you have it."

When Charlie had ordered, he buzzed Lyle Hammond's office;

John Carroll was in court this afternoon. "Just come and sit in," said Charlie. "It's the case I told you about."

"Right away," said Lyle, who was showing great promise in the thorny field of domestic law.

"I hope I've done the right thing in coming here," said Leda Dawson, shifting in her chair. "What's happened to Frank is so . . . so unfair. I thought I ought to help him."

"That's what I hope you'll do," said Charlie, soothing her. "I believe both of us are anxious to see him free of these charges."

"Yes," she said promptly, continuing. "It's every teacher's nightmare, you know—that your students will accuse you of something like this. Once it happens, you're hooked. It follows you all the rest of your career, if you can keep a career, even if you're cleared of all charges. Something like this always sticks, and there's always doubt in the minds of some parents . . ." Her words trailed off. "Look what they did to poor Wilson Harness."

"I've checked that out. It's most unfortunate," said Charlie, looking up as Drisa brought in the tray.

"Lyle will be right in with you. He's on his way." She smiled at Leda Dawson and then at Charlie. "Shall I hold your calls?"

"Not necessarily," said Charlie. "Use your judgment. If the call is urgent, connect it."

"All right," said Drisa, and left the office, nearly running into Lyle Hammond as he came through the door.

"Sorry," said Lyle in a kind of blanket excuse. He was tall, his rumpled face as comfortable as an unmade bed. "What's the deal here?"

"Missus Dawson is helping me out on the Girouard case. I'd like you to be around for it." He indicated another chair. "If you don't mind."

"My pleasure." He turned to Leda Dawson. "I'm Lyle Hammond; glad to meet you." He held out his hand and took hers.

"I'm glad to meet you, too; I'm Leda Dawson." That done, coffee and tea were poured and the reason for their meeting got under way.

"Tell me about Frank Girouard. How do you feel about him? What kind of a teacher is he?" Charlie held his pen over his legal pad.

"Frank's a very good teacher, very conscientious. Students like him, for the most part. His classes are interesting. He pays attention to his students; I've told him once or twice that he was getting too involved for his own good, though he did make a difference for one student, as I recall." She stared into the middle distance. "Teachers suffer a high rate of burnout, you know? Like nurses and air traffic controllers. They . . . we have the trouble that we're dealing with kids all the time, trying to teach them something, give them something without draining ourselves so much that we have nothing left to give."

"Perhaps the kids ought to give something back?" Lyle suggested. "Sorry," he added to Charlie.

"It's okay," said Charlie.

"Well, that's what the story is, and sometimes it happens. You get the rare student who almost makes the rest worthwhile. But then you have to keep from piling all that on top of the special student. That's the hard thing, not to load the kid up with all the other disappointments and require that you get some compensation. I've seen that happen all too often." Her face had grown somber. "We had a music teacher like that, two years ago. She got her one brilliant student, and she pushed him and pushed him and pushed him, and he couldn't take it.

"What happened?" Charlie asked, wondering what bearing this might have on Frank Girouard.

"The boy committed suicide. Oh, there were other reasons for it—he came from a broken home, he had a lot of stress with his stepfather, his oldest brother was in prison for dealing cocaine, his grandfather had Alzheimer's—but what Nancy did was the final straw, and we all knew it. So did she." She stared into her coffee as if looking for answers. "We don't talk about it much. Most of the time teachers gossip about everything, but we don't about this."

"Do you think that could make a difference in the way the teachers respond to Frank's case?" Charlie asked, approaching the question as directly as possible.

"Yes," she said candidly. "We're all jumpy. Between Nancy and Wilson Harness, we're all pretty keyed up. It's as if we're all there on sufferance. We don't say so; that's how we know that we're upset." She drank most of her coffee. "This is very good."

"Thank you. Do you want some more?" Charlie offered, indicating the little pot on the tray.

"Not yet." She set the cup aside. "I don't know how I got off on that. It's got little to do with Frank."

"But it has a lot to do with how the teachers sense the case. What's your take on it?" Charlie asked it casually enough but there was tension at the back of his eyes.

"I don't know," she answered slowly. "I don't like to think that Frank could do anything like that. He's not the kind of man I'd expect to do that. But you hear all the time of men who are not that kind of man and who have done heinous things. So maybe he did do it. I like Frank and I can't imagine him using his students that way. But suppose he did? I don't know." She smiled uncertainly. "I guess I'm as jumpy as the rest of us."

"Would you say it's with cause?" Charlie asked.

"You mean being jumpy or having doubts about Frank?" Leda countered.

"Both, if you're willing," Charlie told her.

Leda reached out for the pot and poured more coffee into her cup, though she did not drink it. "I guess we don't need a cause to be jumpy. On the surface everything's fine and we're all doing our jobs and teaching up a storm, but I think most of us want to be sure that we keep our heads down. Poor old Frank."

"How do you mean that?" Charlie inquired. He was outlining a figure playing a guitar.

"He can't keep his head down." She put her cup down.

"Tell me about the girls—you've had them all in gym, haven't you?"

"Yes." She fidgeted in her chair. "Well, Wendy is good at team sports, things like volleyball and basketball. She's not so good at track or swimming—or trampoline, for that matter. She's better with other people around her. She gets on really well with the other girls on the team in a rah-rah kind of way. Ruth is hard to reach; she's a remote kid, all inside herself. We put her into the modern dance group for her gym class, but it doesn't seem to have changed her much. She doesn't like gym; she'd rather be reading. She's good at tennis when she puts her mind to it. She's horsey, but many girls her age are. She's sponsoring a horse at a stable in Colma. She's won ribbons for gymkhana. Michelle is another matter; she's extremely competitive. She's very active in swimming and diving. That girl has a lot of drive, though I think most of it comes from anger. She's not as popular as Wendy because she's always pushing to be first. Emma has trouble. Many of the girls are suspicious of her—she's very bright and they all know it. She joined the fencing club last year and did quite well, but she hadn't done any épée this year. Her parents have enrolled her in an aikido course, but that isn't taught at school. Diane is a very good gymnast; in fact, she's done some competition in various school meets. Last year she took up figure skating. She's very good at ballet; she's been taking it for ten years and it really shows. She's a graceful child, very controlled."

"Would you say these girls are friends?" Charlie asked.

"Wendy, Ruth and Michelle are, I guess, but Diane and Emma, probably less so. They all know each other, of course, but girls that age—" She broke off, shaking her head.

"I see," said Charlie, thinking over what he was hearing. "Are these girls likely to cook up a story between them?"

"You mean without cause? Their story about Frank?" She saw Charlie nod. "No, I don't think so, not those five. They see things too differently."

"Excuse me," said Lyle, "but I have a question."

"Go ahead," said Charlie, curious about what Lyle might have noticed.

"Well, they have all accused the same teacher of molesting them, isn't that right? They're all students of his, aren't they? Well, they might not get along together as such, but maybe they all have the same idea about him. Maybe that's the commonality here, that they all feel the same way about Frank Girouard."

"How does that help Frank?" asked Leda, confused by the question.

"Don't you see? If Frank didn't do it, but these five girls could agree on accusing him instead of whoever actually harmed them, it might explain why Frank and not someone else." He looked at Charlie. "It makes some kind of sense, doesn't it?"

"It could," said Charlie, remembering what Melissa Budge had told him.

"Why would they blame Frank for something like this?" Leda stared at Charlie. "What would that accomplish?"

"I don't know," said Charlie, "but do you think it's possible?"

She thought it over. "I suppose so," she said at last. "I suppose they could . . . fabricate that way."

"Would you be willing to say so on the stand?" Charlie asked. "It might not come to that, but if I called you, would you be a witness for Frank?"

"I don't think I'd do you much good," Leda warned.

"Let me worry about that," Charlie recommended. "The question is, will you do it? I'm going to be speaking to two of your colleagues who also have all five girls in their classes. With any luck, each of you will have something useful to contribute."

She looked uncertain. "What makes you think so? It's one thing to talk to you this way, informally, but appear in court, under oath . . ." With a sudden, smooth movement she rose from the chair. "Why should we do this for Frank?"

"Because he would do it for you, if the situation were reversed," said Charlie, certain this was true. "And possibly for yourself, so you can stop being so frightened of the school administrators." He hoped this last would do the trick.

Leda wandered over to the window. "I feel sorry for those girls. They've been through a nightmare, and now things at school are even worse for them. I want whoever did those things to them to suffer for it. But if that person isn't Frank, then . . ." She looked back at Charlie. "I'm in a quandary, Mister Moon."

"It's not an easy decision to make, is it?" Lyle said, taking over for a moment. "These questions are always the hardest to answer because there are so many unknowns. How can you justify defending Frank if he really did abuse the girls? It would be bad for you personally and professionally, and you're concerned what it could do to your continued employment. But at the same time, you know that he's legally innocent until the prosecution proves he's guilty and that hasn't happened yet. So you have to choose sides while it's all up in the air." He rose and walked over to her. "Think about the girls first, Missus Dawson. If they're accusing the right man, then they deserve to have their accusation supported. But if they are accusing the wrong man, whatever their reason, they will have to live with that for the rest of their lives, and that false accusation can be more damaging than the abuse they have suffered already. Think about them, and make your decision that way." He glanced at Charlie. "I didn't mean to—"

"You did fine," said Charlie, meaning every word of it.

Leda Dawson folded her hands. "I'll have to think about this. If you don't mind?"

"Certainly," said Charlie, annoyed that she could not or would not give him an answer. "I'll give you a call next week and we can discuss this again, if you like?"

"Thank you," she said. "I really do want to help Frank, but testifying in court . . ."

"I do understand," said Charlie, for whom it was only too true.

Morgan leaned back against the pillow and stretched, relishing the lateness of the hour and the warmth of their bed. "Saturday is probably sinful," she said, wiggling a little closer to Charlie.

"We could make it more so," he said, waking up quickly.

"What time is it." He was lying prone, his face against the mattress.

"After ten. The dogs are hungry," said Morgan, grinning.

"They have extra food, and they won't starve in an hour or so." He lifted his head. "God, I miss snuggling you during the week."

"Me, too," she said, her voice much softer. "Maybe we can forget about the dogs after all."

"Good idea," he approved, nuzzling her neck. He slid his arm across her, underneath the oversized tee-shirt she wore to bed. "Come closer. And get rid of this thing."

Obligingly she wriggled out of the tee-shirt and tossed it away from the bed, then turned close against him. "Better?"

"Much better," he said as he kissed her. It was a leisurely kiss, thorough and friendly; his arms went around her and pulled her atop him.

"I'm squashing you," said Morgan when she could speak.

"Lucky me," Charlie agreed. His hands moved over her back and hips. "You are so beautiful."

There was a little color in her cheeks. "You always say that."

"Because I mean it," he assured her, and knew she would never entirely believe him. "In the eye of the beholder, remember?" His hands were more audacious, roving over her flesh eagerly, knowing where to touch, and how.

"Un-hum," she said, bending to kiss him so that they would not have to talk any more.

It was close to noon when they finally got up, showered and dressed. By that time Caesar and Pompei had started to bark their protest.

"We better let them in before someone calls the pound," said Morgan as she pulled on a loose sweater in a soft amber color that set off her brown hair to advantage.

"I'll do it," said Charlie, who was already dressed. He started out of the bathroom, then stopped and looked at her. "What's up for you today. Other than that," he added as he caught her smirk.

"I've got some cases to review and I ought to look up a couple precedents, but other than that, nothing much." She pulled on her camel-hair slacks as she stood up.

He watched her with approval. "What say we go rent two or three videotapes and watch old horror movies tonight? We could order a pizza and pretend we're twenty-two again."

"I didn't know you when I was twenty-two," she said.

"All the more reason to order the pizza," he said, perilously close to laughing. "Say yes. That way I won't have to worry about dinner."

"Is that what this is about? You don't want to cook?" She tried to look shocked and ended up giggling.

"Well, I certainly don't want you to cook," he said.

"Very true; neither of us is that desperate," she agreed. "All right, I'll knock off at five and we'll regress all over the living room rug. So you suppose anyone has a copy of *Fire Maidens from Outer Space* to rent? That's dreadful enough for pizza." She motioned toward the door. "Now go let the dogs in, won't you?"

"I guess I'd better." He left her alone in the bathroom and went downstairs, not quite whistling. He had just let the dogs into the kitchen and was being greeted with frantic yelps of relief when the phone rang. Disengaging himself from Caesar and Pompei, he went to answer.

"Mister Moon? I'm sorry to call you at home. I wouldn't have . . . but I've . . . I've got to talk to you. It's urgent . . . I'm sorry . . . This is Frank Girouard. I need to . . . it's important."

The playfulness that had taken all Charlie's attention evaporated. He paid no heed as his dog put his front paws on the chair by the phone. "Frank? What is it? Are you all right?" He patted Caesar's head, making him get down.

"It's my wife . . . she . . . Oh, God, she's left me. We had a big fight yesterday evening, and this morning she . . . she left." He broke off, choking back sobs. "She's . . . gone."

The Girouard house was small, located in a cul-de-sac off Parnassus in the shadow of Sutro Tower. Proximity to the University of California at San Francisco Hospital made parking difficult, but Charlie finally found a place three blocks away and hiked back at a brisk pace. He knocked twice before he heard the dead bolt snick open.

Frank Girouard was red-eyed and pale, wearing sweats and no shoes. He motioned Charlie into the house, then closed the door, leaning on it as if to keep the full weight of his troubles out. "Thanks. For coming," he said.

Charlie stood in the tiny entry hall, his attention on his client. He had a vague impression of inexpensive maple furniture with chintz pillows and dust ruffles everywhere. "You want to tell me what happened?"

"We had a fight. I didn't think . . ." he said softly. "It was my fault. I know that. I forced it on her. I should never have brought the case up." He flung himself away from the door and lurched toward the living room, to the right of the entry.

Charlie followed after him, wondering if Frank might be drunk or high. There was no smell of liquor, but that could be disguised; there was nothing that hinted at drugs. He watched closely. "How did it happen, this fight?"

Frank had thrown himself on the sofa and was crushing one of the cross-stitched cushions under him. "It was stupid, stupid, stupid." He pounded his fist into the cushion. "I should never have said anything."

"What did you say?" Charlie asked reasonably.

"I should never have told her about the case, about the teachers being asked to testify." He huddled on the sofa, eyes squeezed shut, legs drawn up, the cushion tight against him.

"Whyever not?" Charlie asked, taking care to keep his voice even and disinterested.

"She's pregnant! She's in no condition to . . . She doesn't need to have . . . I promised her I would not let the case taint our marriage. She insisted on that, and I agreed." He opened his eyes and looked directly at Charlie. "But I didn't understand, not really, that she meant every aspect of the case. I didn't know she would not tolerate any mention of it. Truly, I didn't." He shuddered with his effort not to weep. "Oh, God, God, I'm so sorry."

Charlie felt an irrational desire to find Frank's wife and deliver a stiff lecture on her responsibilities and the realities of a criminal trial, especially one dealing with so reprehensible a crime, but he stifled the urge. "I'm sorry, too, Frank."

"I wanted her to know that something was being done, don't you see? That it wasn't hopeless as she thought," he said to Charlie, beseeching him for understanding, perhaps absolution. "I thought she'd want to know about that. But she was so . . . so upset. She said I'd broken my promise and that I was threatening our marriage. But I hadn't meant it that way. I'd only thought she'd want to know that some of the teachers are on my side. I didn't think telling her about that was wrong. I really didn't." There were tears on his face now, and he wiped them away impatiently. "Shit. I shouldn't do this. Not in front of you."

"Who better?" Charlie asked, though he thought that Frank ought to have been able to reveal all his feelings to his wife. "I'd rather you do it here and now than on the stand, of course. Juries are unpredictable when a man cries; it's too bad." He came and laid a hand on Frank's shoulder. "Get it out. You can't afford to keep it all inside."

It was all the permission he needed: Frank gave himself over to deep, quiet sobs. He kept his face averted, embarrassed by the emotions that overwhelmed and confused him. At last he stopped, making himself breathe normally while he wiped his swollen face with his sleeve. "I didn't mean to do that," he said, ashamed now that he had control of himself once more.

"It's all right," said Charlie, drawing up a fake Colonial-style chair. "Look, Frank, this is going to be a long and grueling business, no matter how it turns out. Don't kid yourself about it, okay? You're going to have to have some way to release your tension or you'll never make it through in one piece. I don't want you ending up in the hospital, because that will only draw the process out more."

"Jesus," Frank whispered.

The next bit was going to be tricky, Charlie knew, and he approached it with caution. "If the pressure's getting too hard for you to handle, then maybe you need to have a few changes. I think it could be helpful. Since your wife doesn't want to deal with your case, it might not be a bad thing if she keeps away for a while. I told you we can give the press a plausible story about her absence, and we will. No man wants his pregnant wife to endure stress like this, does he?"

Frank blinked as if he did not recognize the language Charlie spoke. "What? What do you mean?"

"I've explained it before: we'll say that you are concerned for your wife's welfare during her pregnancy and have arranged for her to stay with relatives until the trial is over. Now, tell me why she was angry with you for talking about the other teachers."

Frank was almost sitting up. He pulled the cushion higher up his chest as if to protect himself from attack. "She . . . she thought I had no business bringing them into the matter. She said that this was between my conscience and—"

"Now, that's her first mistake—this is not about conscience unless you're guilty. It's about a crime that someone has committed. If you did not molest those girls, then your innocence has to be established so that the real criminal can be apprehended." He kept his tone matter-of-fact, level and businesslike for Frank's benefit.

"Who could have done it? I try to figure it out but . . ." His words trailed off. "It's all such a mess."

"And it's going to get messier," said Charlie, deliberately blunt. " You might as well know that right now."

Frank's grip on the cushion loosened. "Can't you stop it? Isn't there something we can do to put an end to it?"

"Other than plead guilty?" Charlie asked. "You wouldn't have to stand trail then, but that would not do much good, either. It would result in your unjust imprisonment and would leave other girls exposed to the same abuse the five girls have suffered. And keep that in mind, Frank. You don't want to contribute to—"

"Stop! Just stop!" Frank thrust his hands out as if to keep the world at bay. "I don't want any more of this. Not now."

Charlie sighed, recognizing the emotional exhaustion that possessed Frank. "All right, not now. But Tuesday morning, nine-thirty, in my office. Just the way we set it up."

Frank shook his head slowly and repeatedly. "I don't think I can go through with it."

"Through is the only way there is," said Charlie. He got to his feet and went to stare out the window. "Do you know for certain where your wife has gone? Did she tell you?"

"No." His voice dropped to a whisper. "She didn't say in her note, just that she had to leave. But she doesn't know anyone, really, not here. She's said that she'd go back to her family. Or to her aunt in Auburn. I hope that's where she is, in Auburn. If she goes to her aunt . . . she might come back to me when this is all over."

"But not if she goes back to Trinity County? Where in Trinity County?" Charlie asked, trying to picture the remote northern California county in his mind, between Mount Lassen and the Pacific Ocean.

"Lewiston," said Frank. "That's where her family is. If she goes to Auburn, it'll be different, less cut off. Her aunt's more . . . sensible than . . ." He faltered and stopped.

"Okay; we'll get someone to work on it right away. But we're going to have to keep a very low profile on this. The news media have been nosing around already and if they think there's been a major defection, it could make things a lot more difficult for us." Charlie sensed Frank's increasing distress. "We're going to need to make sure you have a buffer zone. Is there anyone who can house-sit for you for a month or two?"

"What?" Frank asked.

"I don't think it would be wise for you to stay here by yourself. You're too obvious here, and the press could show up any time. Think about it, Frank. You're a suspect in a trial that has every chance of turning sensationalistic, and now your wife has gone. That could be turned into . . . well, we don't need anyone reporting that your wife is gone because she thinks you harmed those girls."

"She never said that," said Frank.

"She never denied it, either," Charlie pointed out. "You admit that she doesn't believe you, and that would be enough for the press. More than enough. The trouble is, too many people know where you live, and you're not in any condition to handle them by yourself." He paced down the rose-pattern rug. "I'm going to try to arrange something for you. I want you to get someone in here to take care of the place for you, and leave the rest to me. I think I know a place where you can stay while the case is . . . in process." He glanced toward Frank to see how he was taking all this. "Is that acceptable to you?"

"I . . . But . . . How will Angelique know how to reach me? How will anyone know? Wouldn't it look bad if they can't find me?" His expression was confused and upset, but Charlie paid little heed.

"We can make arrangements about that. In the meantime, get yourself an answering machine and screen all your calls. Don't talk to the press, don't talk to the news media, don't talk to anyone who is not directly involved with the case. If there are any questions, refer them to me. We'll take care of them for you." He noticed that Frank looked a little less bewildered. "I'll handle the D.A. and the police about the move."

"Is it necessary? I mean, I should be here in . . . in case Angelique changes her mind." He shuddered and clutched at the cushion once more.

"We'll handle that when the time comes," said Charlie, being evasive. He wondered how Mickey Trang would feel about searching for Frank's wife. "I'm going to make a few calls after I leave here. I want you to pack for a week. One of my associates will pick you up this evening, after you've arranged for a house sitter." He knew better than to smile or to appear too confident. "This isn't going to be any fun, Frank."

"No," said Frank heavily.

"So help me out, will you? Don't take on more than you have to." He patted his shoulder again. "I'll go so you can make your arrangements, and I'll give you a call in a couple hours, so we can set up your move."

Frank's eyes were wet again. "I really don't want to leave here."

"It won't be forever, Frank," Charlie said, making the words as gentle as he could.

"Still . . ." He put the cushion aside. "Okay. Whatever you say."

Charlie wished he felt more relieved than he did. "Good for you," he told Frank, already trying to think of what he would tell Elizabeth.

"I suppose I could have him catalogue the library—I haven't had it updated in years. That ought to distract him," Elizabeth Kendrie said as she peered at Charlie through wraiths of steam rising from her coffee.

"He's going to need something to keep his mind occupied other than the case," said Charlie, secretly relieved that Elizabeth had consented so quickly to having Frank in her house.

"You believe he's innocent, don't you," she stated, watching him narrowly.

"Yes, and I think we'll be able to prove it." He took a long sip of coffee and scalded his tongue.

Elizabeth shook her head at him. "Don't fib, Charlie; it doesn't become you. What you mean is you hope you'll be able to convince the jury that there are grounds for a reasonable doubt."

Charlie shrugged. "If that's what it takes," he said.

"Even though you believe he's innocent," she persisted, offering him a plate of hot scones. "Do have some. Poor Clifford made them specially. They're not bad, considering." She selected one and bit the end off. "Does this Frank Girouard know how to cook?"

"I haven't any idea," said Charlie, accepting a scone. The room where they sat faced the garden where the rhododendrons were just starting to show promise of blooming; right now it was chilly but Elizabeth did not seem to mind.

"I'll ask him," said Elizabeth, then had more of her coffee. "Suppose he's convicted?"

"We appeal," Charlie answered flatly.

"Naturally, but because you think it's right or pro forma?" She watched him closely, her eyes bright.

"Because innocent men do not belong in prison," said Charlie, refusing to let Elizabeth goad him into a hasty response. "What's the reason for all these questions?"

Elizabeth did her best to look inscrutable and succeeded in looking crafty. "I want to know what kind of man you're putting into my house, and I want to know what I am to do with him while he's here." She poured more coffee into her cup. "Under the circumstances you cannot blame me, can you?"

"I suppose not," said Charlie.

"Clifford's preparing the chauffeur's quarters for him. That ought to suffice." She was referring to the three-room apartment over the five-car garage.

"It should be fine," said Charlie, glancing at his watch. Gail Harris ought to be arriving with Frank Girouard at any moment.

"It will be nice to have it occupied again," said Elizabeth in a remote way. She cocked her head to listen. "Clifford's playing that atrocious music again. How can a man cook decently if he listens to heavy metal while he's doing it?"

"Does he cook decently?" Charlie asked, with a slight emphasis on the first word.

"Just decently. And that is not because I liked Henry's cooking better," she continued defensively. "Clifford has a knack with pastas and such, but it's all very trendy. I'd feel more confident if he'd ever turned out a really first-class beef Wellington or a crown roast of pork." Her expression changed. "There's the bell." She got to her feet at once. "Come along, Charles. You got me into this, and you're going to take full charge."

"Of course," said Charlie, putting his coffee aside and following Elizabeth down the long hallway toward the front of her house, hoping as he went that he had not taken too much of a gamble on behalf of Frank Girouard. It was too late to worry about it now.

"There is a Mister Girouard and a Miss Harris," said Clifford as Elizabeth came up to him.

"I told you to expect them," said Elizabeth before she smiled and extended her hand to Frank Girouard.

"Let me do the introductions," said Charlie as Frank and Elizabeth shook hands. He reminded himself to pick up the videos and pizza on the way home.

SIX

Monday afternoon and Tuesday morning

MOST OF THE morning had been taken up with pretrial motions on the Lewis Cornell case. Charlie returned to his office immediately after lunch, Lyle Hammond tagging along beside him carrying two large folders.

"Do you think you'll get the extra two weeks?" he asked as Charlie put his attaché case down on his desk.

"I've already said I don't know," said Charlie. "It all depends on how the judge decides. In this case, I can't call it."

"But it's not an unreasonable request," said Lyle.

"Not from our point of view; but maybe the judge will see it differently." He dropped into his chair. "God, I'm tired."

"The case getting to you?" Lyle suggested, tucking a legal-sized pad of paper into one of the folders.

Charlie smiled faintly. "Not really; we were up late watching TV," he said, his recollection of their fourth creepy movie very fuzzy; it was after two when it ended.

"Oh," said Lyle, obviously disappointed.

"It was fun," said Charlie, taking a stack of printouts from his attaché case. "Frank Girouard is supposed to be here tomorrow morning and I have to review this before we talk." He dropped his hand on top of the printouts Mickey Trang had delivered to the office first thing that morning. "I'll have the Cornell material ready in an hour or so; if you'll take care of filing your notes?"

"Sure," said Lyle, taking his things and heading for the door. "I was wondering if I could talk to you sometime today, though?"

"Oh? What about?" Charlie asked.

"This separate maintenance case I've got—the woman is

waffling about the restraining order. I think she's at risk. How do I make her believe it?"

"Have there been any threats in the past?" Charlie asked.

"Yes, but not like this time." Lyle spoke more briskly to disguise the revulsion he felt. "This time the threat is very specific. She says he'll change his mind, but I think a man who says he's going to get a knife and peel the skin off her hands and feet just might do it."

Charlie pursed his lips in a silent whistle. "I'm not an expert, but offhand I'd say your client has trouble. Get her to a family counselor as soon as she'll go and make sure you include this information when you appear—you know, 'Has your husband said anything to you that implied he might become violent?' or 'Do you have reason to believe that your husband might harm you?' Don't push it too hard or she'll probably deny it as a means to protect him."

"Okay," said Lyle. "What if she won't cooperate?"

"That's what the counselor is for. You might have to lean on her about it—from what you describe she'll resist the suggestion." He looked down at the printouts. "Lyle, I've got to get to this. I have three appointments this afternoon and I don't want to be up until midnight."

Lyle nodded. "I appreciate what you've said." He opened the door, then looked back at Charlie. "Does it bother you, defending a man like Girouard?"

Charlie looked startled. "Why should it?"

"Well, given the crime . . ." Lyle said uncomfortably.

"Which he didn't commit," Charlie reminded his associate.

"Well, that has to be the party line, doesn't it?" Lyle asked, his voice so cynical that Charlie stared. "I mean, you're defending him, so that's what you'd say no matter what."

It took Charlie a moment to work out his answer. "Listen to me. Frank Girouard is innocent. That's not what I'm being paid to say, it's what I truly believe to be the case. My job now is to find the evidence that will prove that."

"But guys who commit sex crimes always lie about them," Lyle protested. "Or almost always. If they boast about them, they make it sound normal and macho, most of the time."

"And innocent men say they didn't do it, which only confuses things," Charlie said for him. "Don't think I'm underestimating the problems we face: I agree that the testimony of the girls is convincing, and they are consistent in their accusation, but in this instance, I think they've picked Girouard to take the rap because they're afraid of the real criminal." He saw that Lyle still did not share his certainty. "And on the off-chance he is guilty, he still deserves the best defense he can get."

"Well, we're told in law school that an attorney has to support his client. I guess this is what they mean," said Lyle quietly.

"That's the least of it," said Charlie, and fingered the printouts on his desk.

"If he did it, I'd want to drop him in boiling oil." Lyle did not wait for Charlie to speak but closed the door with great finality.

Charlie looked at the door, wondering if everyone else in the office shared Lyle's feelings. Then he gave his attention to the papers in front of him.

Morgan listened to the opening remarks of the prosecutor and realized that John Morris was revving up for a vigorous contest.

"Not only will we prove that the defendant, Palmer Humphries, sold cocaine to other employees in the agency, but we will demonstrate beyond any reasonable doubt that he was supplying drugs to at least thirty men and women in the building. Don't be deceived by appearances. Not all drug dealers work the streets. Some of them, like Palmer Humphries, find their clientele in the skyscrapers of the financial district. It means nothing that his salary was well over a hundred thousand dollars a year; it means nothing that he was scheduled for a big promotion for his agency work. This man did not sell drugs to make money to live, he did it for the adventure, for the power, for the corruption!"

The defense attorney looked pained at this outburst and leaned over to whisper to his client. Morgan watched them and tried to decide if Drew Jacobson was very clever or very reckless. She waited while the Assistant District Attorney sat down, then said, "Mister Jacobson?"

The defense attorney nodded. "Sorry, Your Honor," he said as he rose. He adjusted his fashionable glasses and sighed. "Ladies and gentlemen, I know Mister Morris has impressed you. He's a skilled speaker, and he's upset. But we're all upset. My client has been accused of dealing in drugs; this is a very serious charge. Mister Morris tells you that it isn't important that my client makes very good money and has a lot to lose, because it is bad for his case to admit that he cannot find a real motive for Mister Humphries' alleged drug dealing. Most drug dealers want money, first and foremost. But my client has a great deal of money, earned and inherited. Of the three tests for a suspect—method, motive and opportunity—only opportunity applies to Mister Humphries, who has no motive, and no method, no means of conducting criminal activities, as we will show. We do not have to prove that the prosecution is wrong; we need only establish that a reasonable doubt exists, and that is what we intend to do, starting with the most obvious doubt—why a man so well off and with so much at risk would do something so incredibly stupid as dealing drugs, and would compound his stupidity by selling them in his place of work to people he knows. I ask you, ladies and gentlemen, to keep in mind that my client is not a fool. The prosecution will be reminding you that they assume my client was in this criminal activity for the thrill. The thrill. Ask yourselves why, ask yourselves *if* he would do such a stupid thing for so trivial a motive."

Morgan leaned back, still uncertain about Jacobson. She looked at the jury and tried to read their faces, but saw nothing more than cautious expectation in their eyes.

"She's here," Mickey Trang informed Charlie at a little after five. "With her aunt. The woman keeps a bed-and-breakfast place a little way outside of town, off Forest Hill Road. It's a real wedding cake. All the fans of Victorian architecture must love it."

"Where's here?" Charlie asked, staring down into a half-empty cup of cold coffee. He pulled his notepad closer.

"Auburn," said Mickey. "I've been up here for about three hours." He paused. "What do you want me to do?"

"Have you actually seen Missus Girouard?" Charlie asked, scribbling a few notes to himself.

"Yep. About fifteen minutes ago she and her aunt went food shopping. They're in the grocery store right now. I can see the station wagon from this phone booth. It's raining a little up here, by the way." He added the last with a touch of annoyance.

"Have you confirmed it's Missus Girouard or are you—" On his drawing pad he had written, "Auburn, Frank's wife," and was now drawing a duck in flight.

"I used the picture you gave me. I'm going to call the house later. If you like, I'll stay overnight at the place." He chuckled. "I'd like to do that. I hear the breakfast there is very good."

"Use your best judgment on that," said Charlie, fairly certain that Mickey could not resist staying at the bed-and-breakfast. "But don't spook her. We don't want her running again." He raised his head as he heard one of the office doors slam. "Make noises like a man taking a couple days off. No mention of the case, not even if there's something on the news. And whatever you do, don't speak with Missus Girouard directly. If you talk to anyone, talk to the aunt. You got that?"

"I got it," said Mickey with strong satisfaction. "You just wait for me to get back to you tomorrow. I should be in by two at the latest."

"Two?" Charlie echoed. "It's less than three hours from here to there."

Mickey made a derisive noise. "If you want me to look like a man taking a couple days off, you don't want me charging out of there before tenish, do you?"

"That puts you here at one," said Charlie.

"Not if I have lunch at the Nut Tree," Mickey said at once. "I'll try for one-thirty, how's that?"

"I've got a nine-thirty meeting with Girouard tomorrow. I'll need everything you can give me by then." The duck was turning into a monster with a long, undulating neck and taloned wings.

Mickey sighed. "Okay. I'll give you a call around seven-thirty. From a pay phone away from the house. I'll go out jogging or hiking or fishing or something. *Then* I'll have breakfast."

"And lunch at the Nut Tree, no doubt," Charlie added. "Good. I hope we can put Frank's mind at rest about his wife, at least."

"I'll do my best." There was a short pause. "Angel's Camp and now Auburn. It's fun, running around the Gold Country."

"Get everything you can about Missus Girouard and her aunt; that's what you're there for," said Charlie, trying to sound stern and not quite succeeding.

"Sure," said Mickey before he hung up.

Morgan was just clearing away their dinner dishes when the phone rang. Charlie glanced at her, gave a what-can-you-do shrug, then went to answer it. "Studevant and Moon," he said.

"Mister Moon? This is Leda Dawson? We met at your office?" In addition to her constantly rising inflections, she sounded nervous and upset. "Your receptionist gave me your number, in case I thought of anything?"

"And have you, Missus Dawson?" Charlie asked, a little surprised that the gym teacher was actually calling him.

There was a hesitation. "In a way. It's not directly related to your case, or I don't think it is, but it could be?" She was definitely nervous and Charlie was at a loss to know what to say to calm her.

"Something about Frank, is that it?" It was a guess, done more to say something than to prompt her.

"Not really. But you see, something's happened." She took three very quick breaths. "It'll be on the late news? On TV? But I thought I'd better tell you first."

"Tell me what, Missus Dawson?" asked Charlie, beginning to sense something very unpleasant in her faltering words.

"Well, there's another girl? She's . . . missing? She didn't get home and no one's seen her, not since two this afternoon. She cut her last class? At least, that's what everyone thought." Her voice broke. "But she's gone."

"Runaway?" Charlie suggested.

"A couple of the students saw her getting into a car a little after two." She was crying openly now. "On top of everything else, this."

Charlie looked up as Morgan stuck her nose into the hall. He made a gesture that meant he would explain later, and said, "Missus Dawson, please. Tell me whatever you know." He was not certain what—if anything—this could do to Frank Girouard's case, but he realized that more upset at the school would weaken what doubtful support Frank had.

"Her name is Susan Lake." She struggled to bring herself under control. "She is part of June Ryerson's synchronized-swim team, and when she wasn't at practice, at three-thirty, June tried to find her? And no one knew where she was? They called her parents at work, and neither of them had heard from her. So they . . . the principal's secretary and the Dean of Girls, that is? they called and . . ." As she wept she apologized. "I'm sorry. I tried to call Frank, to warn him, but there's just an answering machine."

"I'll take care of it, Missus Dawson," Charlie assured her.

"Yes. All right. Yes." She managed to keep from sobbing. "It's just that some people are saying . . . that the two things are connected? You know how that happens?"

"Yes," said Charlie quietly, who knew only too well.

"I mean, we know they're not, but it's all so . . . awful." Her hesitation did not last very long but it was eloquent. "I don't know what's going to happen now."

Charlie felt the same way but kept the weight of doubt and defeat out of his voice. "We'll get it straightened out, don't worry."

This time her question was barely above a whisper. "Mister Moon, do you know where Frank is? Do you know what he's been doing? There isn't any chance that he—"

"No chance. And, yes, I do know where he is and what he's doing," said Charlie, suddenly glad that he had insisted Frank go to Elizabeth's. "He's staying with friends."

There was relief in her tone now. "Oh. That's good to know," she said quietly. "I'll make sure everyone . . . hears about that."

"Thank you," said Charlie sincerely. "I would appreciate that."

"Well, I want to do something to help? I hate to think of Frank going through anything worse than what . . ." Her words faded. "The police officer put in charge of this is Sergeant Mitchell."

"Glen Mitchell?" Charlie asked, alert to the name; Glen Mitchell had handled several tricky abduction cases in the past.

"I . . . I think so," said Leda Dawson.

"Tall, hefty, long face, red hair going grey?" Charlie suggested.

"Yes. Yes, that's the man," said Leda Dawson in a sudden rush of confidence. "He came to the school, around five? All the teachers who were still there talked to him."

"That's a start," said Charlie. He rubbed his eyes, reminding himself that he ought to wear his reading glasses more often. "I'll see if I can reach him tomorrow." He gave her the chance to say something more, and when she did not, he thanked her again and hung up.

"So what's the matter now?" Morgan said, opening the kitchen door.

"It sounds like there's been an abduction from Frank's school," said Charlie as he dialed Elizabeth's number, trying to find the right way to tell Frank of the missing girl.

Sergeant Glen Mitchell frowned at Charlie. "To be blunt, counselor, I don't know what the fuck you're doing here." He indicated the corner of the restaurant where he usually had breakfast.

Charlie took the seat opposite. It was quarter after eight and he had just come from a long conversation with Mickey Trang. "Actually, I hope I'm establishing that there's no particular reason for me to be here." He consulted his watch. "I asked you for fifteen minutes."

"Yeah, and you got it if you need it," said Sergeant Mitchell. "It's about the Lake girl, I suppose? The abduction—we've classified it as an abduction now. Everything's been about her since last evening."

"Not exactly," said Charlie carefully, doing his best to focus on the man's worn face. "I have a client who—"

"The teacher who's supposed to have made sex slaves of those five girls?" He held up his hand. "I said supposed. The alleged sex offender—there; is that better?"

"It'll have to do," said Charlie, not wanting to cause Mitchell to become uncooperative.

"He was charged, right?" Mitchell asked.

"Yes," said Charlie. "And I would appreciate your assurance that your investigation at this time does not include my client. Notice I say at this time." He said it in a friendly tone but implied no concession.

"You got it," Mitchell said. "From everything I can find out, your man hasn't been near that school since the charges were filed. We have a partial description of the man who the girl might have been seen driving off with, and he doesn't fit your client at all."

"Thanks," said Charlie. "I can produce witnesses who can place my client on the other side of the city when the girl disappeared; these same witnesses can account for his actions for most of the day and all of the evening." He signaled to a passing waitress. "Will you bring me a pot of tea, please?"

"Sure," she said, scribbling on a slip of paper.

"Probably isn't up to your standard," said Mitchell, then smiled, transforming his face from haggard to Buddha-like. "I don't envy you having to defend that teacher. It doesn't look good for him."

"No, it doesn't," Charlie agreed. "But I don't want him saddled with anything else, and this new case—"

"I know, I know," said Mitchell. "It irks me, too. I'm trying to get a straight line on the man or men who kidnapped the girl, and I got half a dozen people trying to make your client the bogeyman. It's bad."

"That it is," said Charlie. He looked directly at Sergeant Mitchell. "Do you have any feelings about this case?" The policeman had the reputation of having very reliable instincts; Charlie respected that more than most attorneys did. "I really want to know, Glen."

"I'm . . ." He fell silent. "I got a sense that this is someone who's done this before. It's neat, too neat, if you get what I mean. Whoever got her just whisked her away."

Charlie nodded. "You've had other cases like this?"

"Not recently, and not here. But we're checking around, to see if we've got a traveler." He put his hands to his head. "I really hate these cases. I hate hearing that a kid's been taken, but when it's one of these, when you get that low-down cold feeling first thing, those are the ones I hate the most."

"And you have that feeling, the cold one?" Charlie asked, feeling an echo of it in himself.

"Yeah," said Sergeant Mitchell. "It's like it has a smell, like something dead a couple of days. Not too strong, but creeping."

"Searching?" Charlie suggested, using the word his grandfather would have chosen. "As if the smell is coming—somehow—to get you?"

Sergeant Mitchell looked a little surprised. "Yeah. It's something like that."

"Un-huh," said Charlie, recognizing it for the vile sign it was. "From the first?"

"Almost." He looked up as the waitress brought Charlie's tea. "I didn't know lawyers got that kind of feeling."

"Some do, sometimes." Charlie had never become comfortable talking about such things.

"And you're one of them," said Sergeant Mitchell in a tone that needed no confirmation. "I got that impression," he said with a touch of pride. "That case over a year ago; I remember what you did, and I know you didn't have to."

"I'm an officer of the court," said Charlie, as if that explained everything.

"That wasn't it." Sergeant Mitchell had the last of his english muffin, trying to keep the crumbs off his shirt. "You wanted to do the right thing. Not many people want that. And there was another thing, too."

"Oh?" Charlie said.

"Yeah, about eight months ago. I had to testify in your wife's court. I like her, by the way. She might not rule the way I want her to, but she's careful and she's thorough." He watched Charlie pour out pale tea. "Anyway, you were there at lunchtime, just coming from another trial, and you pulled her aside in the hallway. I didn't mean to eavesdrop, but . . . hey, cops are nosy."

Charlie concealed his minor annoyance. "What did you hear?"

"You said you wanted to take her to lunch because you knew it had been a rough morning. That was true. It'd been a bitch. But there was no way you could have known that, because it didn't start out that way and it wasn't the kind of trial you expected to turn nasty, the way this one did. But you knew, and you were there." He made a point of not looking at Charlie.

"I see," said Charlie after a minute. The tea was terrible, nothing more than hot water with a little bitter flavor.

"I didn't pay too much attention to it, but . . . well, you got a reputation, no doubt about it." He smoothed his tie. "You go the limit for your client, you aren't a news grabber and you don't have a huge ego. That's a bit unusual. Also you're an Ojibwa Indian, they tell me. That so?"

"Yes, I am."

"From Canada, I hear." He made note of Charlie's nod. "I was going to get ahold of you in a couple days, anyway. I'm relieved you called me. I wanted to straighten out this thing about your client, but . . ."

"But what?" Charlie asked, putting the dreadful tea aside.

"But I was hoping maybe in your investigation, maybe you might run across something that could help me out." He held up one square hand. "I don't want you doing anything to compromise your case, and I don't ask you to do my job for me. But you know what people are," he continued. "Sometimes they forget things, or don't mention them, or . . ."

Charlie was sympathetic. "I know. I had a case when a nurse went through all the pretrial period and never mentioned that the victim had been left-handed. That changed everything, but it didn't come up until she was on the stand and the prosecution asked it as a way to calm her down."

Sergeant Mitchell made a motion to show how helpless it made him feel. "So if you turn up anything you think would help us find the girl—"

"Susan Lake," Charlie supplied.

"Susan Lake, let me know if you can. It's irregular as hell, but in a case like this, with the whole faculty jumpy as sand fleas, I'm worried the whole thing'll turn into a pratfall." He looked at Charlie closely. "In a case like this one, that would hurt, and I don't mean the image of the SFPD."

"That's not the way your superiors would see it," said Charlie.

"Ah, the hell with them. Most of them are more politician than cop anyway. They're worried about the way it's going to look on the evening news." He raised his brows and narrowed his eyes. "And if this goes bad, it'll look like shit on the evening news."

"It sounds like you're expecting it to go bad." Charlie studied the Sergeant's face, watching for any sign of his feelings.

"I hope it won't," said Sergeant Mitchell in a tone that was eloquent.

Frank Girouard was rumpled and pale as if he had not slept. "Is there any news about Susan Lake?" he asked as he came through Charlie's door.

Charlie, who had arrived only a few minutes ago, was hanging up his coat. "Not so far. Was she a student of yours?"

"Last semester, yes, in my modern literature course." He walked restlessly around the room. "After you called, I wanted to call her parents, but . . . but I didn't."

"Good," said Charlie. "Sit down, won't you."

"Oh; yes." He dropped into the nearest chair. "They say she was kidnapped, this morning on the news. You told me she was missing."

"They weren't sure about the abduction until this morning," Charlie said. "Now it's official."

"They're sure? What does it mean, an abduction?" He leaned forward and braced his elbows on his knees. "That poor girl; God."

"It means that we're going to have to sort out some of the complications this morning, Frank," said Charlie crisply. "I've already told the cops to check with Elizabeth so that you're fully alabied for the time when the Lake girl disappeared."

He looked up at Charlie in disbelief. "What? Why should I need an alabi for . . ." His pale face became ashen. "Does someone think I did it?"

"It was one explanation offered," said Charlie very carefully. "But fortunately the cops have eliminated you as a suspect." He was sitting at his desk now, and he pulled Frank's file toward him. "First off, I want you to know that your wife is with her aunt in Auburn."

He nodded, some color returning to his cheeks. "Are you sure?"

"I have confirmation on this, and I will arrange for periodic checks on her. She's safe where she is and for the time being the press will leave her alone, I suspect." He hoped that Angelique Girouard would not be discovered until the trial was actually under way. "I am advising you not to call her or to write to her, not for a while. I can't force you to do this, but I'm very concerned what might happen if you contact her. Will you wait a little before you try to reach her, for me?"

"Not call her?" Frank said as if the request were unthinkable.

"That's right. Do not call her, do not write to her. Unless you want her picture in the tabloids." He said this with deliberate harshness, hoping that he could convince Frank to cooperate with him.

"I . . . I don't know." He stared down at the rug. "It's bad enough being gone from the house; to keep quiet now is . . . terrifying."

"Don't let it get to you, Frank," said Charlie. "I know it's hard, and I know that you're as worried about Angelique as you are about yourself. But you won't help either of you if you will not keep your distance from her, since that's what she seems to want." He paused. "One of the investigators who works for me has spoken with her. She told him her husband was dead." It had been the most disturbing thing Mickey Trang had told him, and he still flinched inwardly as he reported it.

"She . . . when did she say that?" Frank was stunned.

"My operative stayed at the bed-and-breakfast last night. He had breakfast there this morning. He talked with her over sausage and biscuits, just making conversation. He's very good at that," Charlie added as he saw the guarded look in Frank's face. "He noticed her wedding ring and asked if her husband would be joining them at breakfast. And she said that her husband had died recently, that she was staying with her aunt until she got back on her feet."

"She couldn't," said Frank.

"She did. If you like I'll supply you with a copy of the investigator's report." He hoped that Frank would listen to him. "She wants to keep away from you right now, Frank. Give her some time to . . . to figure out what she wants to do."

"She wants me to go to jail," said Frank with a sudden eruption of feeling. "That's why she said I'm dead; because if I go to jail, I will be, as far as she's concerned." He surged out of the chair and paced down the length of Charlie's office. "What chance have I got, when my own wife wants me locked up, or six feet under?"

Charlie remained behind his desk, making no move to stop Frank's prowling. "You have the same chance now that you had yesterday and the day before," he said. "Your case will be decided on the evidence"—if we can minimize the sensationalism, he added to himself—"by the jury, not by your wife." He indicated the file. "We've been provided more discovery documents. We need to discuss them, so that they can be handled properly in court."

"Discovery documents." Frank shook his head. "What they're going to use to hang me with. Why bother? You don't get it. We might as well throw in the towel now."

"And do what?" Charlie asked. "You're not guilty. What did you have in mind?"

"I could plead something like diminished capacity," said Frank. "I could say I was nuts, that I didn't remember doing it." He put his hand to his head. "That would end it. They'd lock me up, and that would—"

Charlie brought his hand down on the desk very hard. "First, it would not be ethical of me to do that. You'll have to find someone else to represent you if that's what you want to do. Second, you're leaving those girls with a lie, and that is going to be very damaging for them. And third, you are leaving someone who likes to abuse teenaged girls on the loose out there. You might think that's unimportant, but let me tell you, it bothers the hell out of me."

Frank glared at Charlie, his face darkening. "I don't want to go through any more of this."

"Do you think anyone else is enjoying it?" Charlie countered sharply. "Let me put your mind at ease: everyone *hates* sexual abuse cases. Everyone. The cops, the District Attorney and all his staff, the press, the public, the victims, defense attorneys like me, expert witnesses. All of us. You're not out on a limb by yourself." He moved his chair back from the desk. "It might not mean much to you right now, but I'm telling you the truth."

"But you're not accused of doing it," said Frank Girouard. "I can't tell you how it feels, being accused of something like this. I can't imagine anything worse than this. How could anyone think I would do something like that? How could they?" His hands were trembling; his fingers tightened. "I woke up this morning thinking that it was okay today. I wanted to believe it was over, that it was all nothing more than a misunderstanding. I wanted someone to tell me that the girls had changed their minds, or . . . or it hadn't happened at all."

"Frank woke up?" Charlie suggested. "It had all been a dream?"

"Yeah." Frank took a long, unsteady breath. "That's the one." He met Charlie's eyes, though it was an effort. "You're worried that if I start to bug Angelique she'll go to the press, aren't you?

You think that if my wife speaks out against me the jury will believe her and not me."

"Yes," said Charlie. "And my job is going to be hard enough without that." He had started to doodle again. "When you go home, I want you to take the time to go over everything you can think of about those five girls. I want you to write it all down for me. Everything, no matter how trivial, I want you to make note of it, do you understand."

"Why?" he asked.

"Because," said Charlie as steadily as he could, "these girls must have links. We need to know what they are. We need to know what is going on with them. Then we can find out what really happened."

Frank shook his head. "I don't want them to go through anything more than they've already gone through," he said in a determined voice. "They've been through too much shit already. Don't make it worse."

"I'll keep it as clean as I can," said Charlie. "But if they're lying, for whatever reason, we have to find out why." He could not make much sense of the squiggles he had on the page.

"If they're lying?" Frank challenged.

"Well, you tell me you didn't do it, and I accept that. But I am your attorney, and clients don't always tell the truth even when I ask them to." He paused. "For what it's worth to you, I believe you. And I believe that there is a man out there who is molesting schoolgirls."

"Okay," said Frank, nervous again.

"It might be that to get you off, we'll have to find him. That might be the only way to demonstrate a reasonable doubt to the jury. I don't know." Charlie tapped the file on his desk. "No more talk about plea bargaining, and no more fretting about your wife, not right now." He decided he might be able to turn the meandering lines on the paper into a skein of geese. "How do you like staying with Elizabeth."

Frank was startled by this abrupt change of subject. "I . . . I'm not sure. Under other circumstances I . . ."

When Frank did not go on, Charlie said, "Has she been hectoring you? She isn't supposed to."

"No," said Frank too quickly. "No, it's not that. She's just . . . imposing. She kept me in the library for hours yesterday. Not being bossy, you understand, just making sure I understood what she wants." He coughed. "In a way she's kind of sweet."

Charlie grinned. "Yes. I think so, too." He was certain now that Frank was in the right place. "Get to work on those lists about the kids, and call me tomorrow to set up your next appointment. I'm going to do some more interviews with people from the school."

"And the girls? What about them?" Frank asked, his mood darkening again.

"We'll decide that after I see your list. And Frank," he added as if it were an afterthought instead of the very deliberate instruction it was, "don't try to psych it out, okay? Just write down everything. Leave it to others to figure it out."

Frank did not quite nod. "All right," he said, going to the door. "What about practice for testifying? Don't we have to do that?"

"Yes, we do," said Charlie. "But first I need to see what the D.A.'s office has through discovery. Between that and the interviews, I'll find the best strategy I can, a way to demonstrate your innocence while doing as little to hurt the girls as possible."

"Does that mean you'll try to tear their stories apart on the witness stand?" Frank asked, his eyes livid.

"I'd rather not have to, but I will if I must," said Charlie, disliking the way the words sounded. Most of the time he took pride in the quality of the defense he could present, but not when it turned on how aggressively he could attack prosecution witnesses. He always abhorred the task of demolishing victims as part of a defense and he avoided it whenever it was possible. Five girls already abused deserved better at his hands than being methodically discredited.

"I hope you won't have to," said Frank.

Charlie responded with feeling, "So do I."

SEVEN

Wednesday, Thursday and Friday

"I'VE GOT SOMEONE I want to slip into the fringes of the school, into the hang-out crowd, not just around Sutro Glen, but the other schools near the Park, to keep a look out for our kiddie-porn crew. You know we can't send grown-ups in—the kids would clam up and the porno-honchos would just stay away," said Mickey Trang as he and Charlie shared *dim sum* at the Yank Sing on Battery; it was a luxury for Charlie, who rarely took the extra time to come to this part of the city where parking was so hard to find. "He can't pass for fourteen, but he can manage sixteen or seventeen, and there're places where kids always go to hang out near every school out in that part of the city."

"Who is this someone. You say he," said Charlie. The smell of the place delighted him.

"The one Gail told you about. Cadao Talbot." Mickey looked awkward, then grinned. "He's very good."

"So is lunch," said Charlie as he took a bite out of a fluffy pork bun. "Why do you want to do this?" The words were not distinct but Charlie waited for his answer, chewing.

"I think we've learned all we can from the teachers and the parents. Not that I think we should abandon that part of the investigation, not entirely, because I don't. But I think we need to take a wider approach. The kids hear things, see things, and they talk about it only among their friends." He selected another spring roll. "Cadao's done this kind of thing before."

"He's Vietnamese?" Charlie asked.

"And Latino. Most people think he's Mexican or South American because of his cheekbones; he lets them. He was adopted whe~ he was ten, by the way. That is where the Talbot comes from." He paused to summon the waiter for more food.

"Okay," said Charlie when Mickey had ordered more for both of them, "how important do you think this could be to the case?"

"I'm not sure, but if those kiddie-porn recruiters are out there—and it's a pretty good bet that they are—it could make one hell of a difference to some of those kids. And if we can find out what it is that the kids are keeping to themselves. Cadao knows the right way to do this. There are some high school guys who like their girls young; it makes them feel more grown-up. Cadao is five-four and slight, and he knows how to use it." Mickey laughed. "He's twenty-seven, but he's going to look like a kid until he's pushing forty. You know the type."

"Indeed I do," said Charlie. He picked up a wonton and popped it into his mouth, chewing well before saying, "All right, I tell you what." He reached for a pot sticker. "Put him in for a week. He'll need that long for the kids to talk to him, won't he?"

Mickey, who had his mouth very full, nodded.

"At the end of the week we'll see what he's got; if it looks worth following up, he stays on; if it doesn't, he's out." Charlie waited to hear Mickey's answer.

"That sounds pretty reasonable, so long as you're not going to pull the plug arbitrarily."

"Hey, I want to win this case. I don't want my client to go to prison. And I want whoever did those things to those girls strung up by his heels." This last was said quietly but with heat.

"Gosh," said Mickey in mock dismay, then added, "I was thinking of stringing him up by something more painful than his heels." He selected another pastry.

Morgan had recessed court at four-fifteen to allow both attorneys to present their closing arguments on the same day. She was growing heartily tired of the endless posturing of the defendant; Palmer Humphries was so busy trying to impress the jury with his affluence and business acumen that he seemed unaware that he was convincing them all of his guilt. While she waited for her coffee maker to finish perking she went over the case in her mind again. It always bothered her when the attorneys spent more time wrangling about the fine points of evidence than arguing the merits of the case. She knew her attitude was not sensible and was antithetical to her work, but it was one she could not rid herself of.

She was pouring her coffee when there was a knock at her door.

"Yes?" she called out, thinking it must be Drew Jacobson, who had requested a conference with her.

"I need to talk to you," said Ed Massie from the other side of the door.

"Sergeant Massie?" Morgan answered, feeling slightly apprehensive.

"Yeah." He paused. "Please. It's important."

Briefly Morgan wondered if she ought to ring for security, but the notion was gone as quickly as it came. "All right, Sergeant," she said, going back to her desk and sitting down. "What do you want to see me about?"

Ed Massie hung back, looking almost like a six-year-old who has come home to punishment. "I don't want to interrupt you, Your Honor."

"You're not. I have a conference in about ten minutes. We quit early so we can hear closing arguments tomorrow," she said, keeping her tone professional. "What's the matter?"

"Ben and I . . . we're being bound over for trial for perjury," he said with difficulty. "It isn't official yet, but we've been warned about it, so we can prepare."

"You mean so you can find a good attorney?" Morgan said. "You ought to know who the good ones are by now."

"I do." He shook his head slowly, as if he were dazed. "But that's not what I came to talk to you about. It's something else, something I want you to know. Ben's been saying that no one deserves to know about this if they're going to fuck us over. But I'm not sure he's right about this. I told him when we found it that we ought to turn it in. Ben was holding it back, in case something went wrong about the key, and we were ruled against for admissibility. I told him it wouldn't work. Shit, I told him none of it would work." He looked haggard, and when he came toward her desk his walk was hesitant.

"Really?" said Morgan. She wondered if Sergeant Massie was truly upset or if he was conning her.

"I'm not the cowboy you think I am." He looked down at her. "You got no reason to believe me, but it's true. I know I look like one. I know I've acted like a real turd, Your Honor. But you saw the tape we got. You know what Ferrand was doing. Doing things like that to kids so he could sell the tapes of it to guys as sick as he is! Can you blame us?" His voice rose a little. "We wanted to put him away. I know we did it the wrong way. But Ben was so sure we'd be believed."

"That was part of your error, thinking that you could get away with lying." Morgan braced her elbows on the desk. "We've been over this, Sergeant. I'm not going to change my position just because you come and ask me pretty-please-with-jam-and-sugar." She let this sink in. "I'm sorry things are going badly for you, but you brought in on yourself."

Although Morgan was prepared for an outburst, she was surprised when all that happened was Massie sighed deeply. "It's shitty. You need whipping boys and we're it. People bend the law all the time and this doesn't happen to them." He looked toward the window. "But it isn't right that Ferrand gets away because we . . . blew it. Your Honor, there was another tape. A real bad tape. We had no direct link to it, not to the case, and not to the key, that's the problem. But it's obviously Ferrand's work. It takes place in the same setting as the one you saw. It was filmed the same way. I know in my guts he did it. It has his marks all over as much as if we had a full set of fingerprints and one of those DNA matches."

"And? What is this about, Sergeant?" In spite of herself, Morgan wanted to know what Massie had withheld.

"The other tape." He folded his arm. "Look, we ran it, and Ben said we ought to find a way to link it up. We had no probable cause, no other trail to it. I don't know how Ben got ahold of it, but I suspect he stole it from Ferrand's safe. He said he was going to, so he could tie Ferrand up tight enough to choke. Through what was on the tape." His eyes met hers and then flicked away. "It was a snuff film."

"You mean . . . they killed someone on tape?" Morgan wanted to keep her manner distant; she could not suppress a sense of vertigo. "Is that what you're saying?"

"Yes," said Massie. "I saw it. Ben ran it after he . . . liberated it. He wanted me to watch it with him, so I could corroborate his testimony if he needed someone to back him up. He thought he could finesse it into evidence. It was worse than the others." His voice dropped. "They . . . there were two of them, doing it. One guy was pretty big and looked like a weight lifter. The other was skinnier and hung. They both were masks. I know one of them was in other Ferrand tapes, the skinny one. The girl was about thirteen, fourteen." His voice went flat. "They assaulted her sexually first, rape two at a time, hatpins through her nipples, all that shit. Then they started in on her with other things. They tore her up, sometime while they were jerking off. They put things inside her. They cut her so she couldn't fight back, so she just flopped around. It took almost an hour. It was all on the tape."

"I see," said Morgan, swallowing with difficulty. Her pulse was faster and it was hard to breathe. "And where is this tape?"

"Ben has it. He was holding it in reserve." He cleared his throat. "I warned him. I did."

"Your partner still has this tape?" Morgan asked incredulously.

"I think so. I think he's planning to use it as a bargaining chip to get out of the perjury charge. He said he wasn't going to turn it over without something in return." Massie wandered toward the window. "I'm a pretty good cop most of the time. You probably doubt it, though it's true. But I'm human. I get crazy about some things, and nothing more than this kind of sexual stuff, fucking kids." He looked back at Morgan. "I came here to tell you about the tape. I don't know what you can do about it, but I thought you ought to know."

Morgan stared at him. "Just like that? You're not going to tell your superiors?

"No. I gave Ben my word I wouldn't. He wanted me to promise I wouldn't tell anyone in the department or my lawyer. But he didn't say anything about judges." He took a couple steps toward her. "I think you're a ball-breaking bitch, Your Honor, but I think you're fair, by your lights. So I told you." He nodded to her once, then left her alone.

Her coffee grew cold; Morgan sat by herself, distantly wondering when Drew Jacobson would come to deliver her from the terrible things that had invaded her thoughts. Finally, very reluctantly, she called George Wycliff and told him that they had to talk, and fixed the time for tomorrow morning.

Sutro Glen Junior High School had begun as a neighborhood school in 1932, and had offered classes for grades one through eight, with a room and teacher for each grade. By 1956 the crowding had become intolerable and the building decrepit, and the school had been modernized, enlarged and limited to grades seven, eight and nine. It had not been converted to a middle school at the start of the seventies, for it and Kit Carson Junior High School were given over to the High Potential accelerated program begun a few years before.

Located in the narrow valley between Mount Sutro and Twin Peaks, it now boasted twenty-three classrooms including a small science lab, a theatrical auditorium and a gymnasium complete with swimming pool. The school drew students from the entire city west of Divisidero, as Kit Carson drew from the east. Most of the campus was surrounded by a chain link fence, except for the front entrance and the truck entrance on the south side of the gym.

David Covello had been principal of Sutro Glen for six years and nothing in his past experience had prepared him for the disruption that now shook his school. Before this, the worst he had had to endure was pressure from the public about the H.P. program. He was nervous as he met Charlie. His short brown hair was going grey and there were shadows under his eyes that Charlie suspected had not been there a month ago. "Mister Moon."

"Thank you for being willing to see me," said Charlie as he took Covello's hand, noticing how limp the handshake was.

Covello nodded. "The least I can do. Terrible business." He opened the door to his office. "We won't be disturbed. My secretary and the assistant principal are both gone for the day. The Journalism Club and the Spanish Heritage Club are still in the building, but otherwise there's nothing much going on. We've instituted a policy this last week—the building is to be empty by four every day. We have new security people to check the school out. I hate having to do it." He did not take his seat behind the desk but hitched his hip onto the edge and half-sat, half-leaned there. "You wanted to talk about the girls, I guess."

"Yes," said Charlie. "I don't want to have to subpoena their records for court, but I might have to. I trust you to understand my predicament, in which case you can help me find another way to handle this." He watched Covello narrowly.

"I'd prefer you find another way to get the material you need," said Covello uncomfortably.

"I will if it's possible, but that might mean putting the girls themselves on the stand, which I would prefer not to do." He felt awkward to say this because he knew that Isolde Aldred was very likely going to put the girls on the stand for the purpose of condemning Frank Girouard. "I'd like to make one thing clear: ordinarily for an interview like this, I would bring a colleague to sit in to take notes, but in this case, I have respected your request for confidentiality."

"I appreciate that," said Covello.

"But remember I am representing Frank Girouard and I have my primary obligation to my client. If serving his best interests under the law makes things unpleasant for you, then I must protect him." He opened his case and pulled out a pad. "I am going to make some notes while we talk. You're free to review them when we're through, and to add any corrections you feel are appropriate. I assure you that I don't want to cause you or the school embarrassment of any kind, but it may happen in spite of that."

Covello nodded. "I hope it won't come to that."

"So do I, Doctor Covello," said Charlie, knowing how important his degree was to David Covello. "But cases like this are distressing by their very nature. It is not easy to resolve them." He saw that some of the panic was gone out of Covello's eyes; his perch on the desk was less tenuous. "Are you willing still to answer some questions for me?"

"I'll do what I can. I want to help Frank out," he added. "He's been a very good teacher, and I can't believe he'd ever do anything like . . . what the girls say he did." He blushed, which only added to his discomfort.

"Neither can I, and not because it's my job," said Charlie, doing his best to convince Covello. "I've arranged for Frank to take a battery of psychological tests. I realize they're not conclusive, and the judge may not accept them as admissible, but it would help bolster his position." He held his pen at the ready. "Why do you think Frank didn't sexually abuse those girls?"

David Covello turned a brighter shade, bit his lower lip, then tried to answer the question. "I can't explain it, not really," he said. "I suppose you call it a hunch. It wouldn't be consistent with the other things I know about him. I've never seen him flirt with his students. I've never seen him treat them as anything other than kids. I've never known him to power-trip on his classes. I've never seen him play kids off against other kids. I've got teachers who do one or two of those things from time to time, but Frank's never been one of them. He's not all rigid, either. You don't get a strong sense of repression about him. And he's always been protective of his students, wanting to help them but backing them up all the way so they can build confidence. That doesn't seem to me to be the kind of man who would abuse kids the way these girls were abused." He took a deep breath. "I've had my differences with Frank, but never about anything that suggested he wasn't conducting himself properly. In fact, if anything, we clashed about his tendency to do his job every waking hour of the day. He was always available to his students, even at his home. I know his wife doesn't approve of that, but . . ." He wound down. "If Frank abused those girls, he's got to have a split personality, because the man I know isn't capable of that." The line of his jaw set to demonstrate his determination.

Charlie had written down a number of key phrases as well as two crucial sentences, though he was more interested in the manner in which Covello answered the questions than the words themselves. "Do you have any idea why these girls accused Frank if he didn't abuse them?"

"Not precisely. The school psychologist thinks they might have accused him because they liked him and thought he would sympathize with them. It could be. I can't begin to make a guess about that. It wouldn't be right. Young teenagers are so self-involved that they might come up with a scheme like that. But it's only a guess, and I don't know if it's any good or not." He had got hold of a paper clip and was studiously straightening it out. "I guess that isn't very useful."

"I won't know what's useful until the case is over," said Charlie, soothing the man. "Right now I'm just trying to get all the pieces to the puzzle before I try to put it together." He watched Covello while he wrote down his next question. "So far as you know, would any one of these girls have reason to be angry with Frank?"

"How can I be sure?" Covello answered. "Kids can get upset about anything. Tell them that their tan isn't even and they might fall apart on you. Tell them that a dozen people were killed when a fire truck hit a bus and they might think that's funny. They haven't got a sense of proportion yet; there's no way to anticipate their reactions. When the trouble is something this serious, who can say what's going to be hardest on them, not that I mean to imply that sexual abuse is ever easy, but it's not always a clear thing about the reactions. And now with Susan Lake disappearing, well, whatever the reactions are, they're going to be compounded." He lowered his head. "Look, Mister Moon, I want this case cleared up as much for the school as for Frank. Probably more, if I were to be candid. The school can't take something like this. We've already had parents apply to transfer their kids because the kids don't feel safe here. If that happens too often, who knows what the Board of Education might do." He got off the desk and walked over to his bookcase. "This is a good school, Mister Moon. We've brought our test scores up all across the board in the last five years, but I can bet that this year is going to look as bad as the scores were five years ago. All because the kids are nervous and can't concentrate because of what happened."

"Does that seem likely, Doctor Covello?" Charlie asked.

"Who can say? There're experts out there who insist that any disruption of school routine brings down test scores, and there are experts who say that only a few students are actually affected by disruptions. Most of the figures suggest it—schools where the students get traumatized because of a tragedy in the school do show a tendency to lower scores for a year or two. If the trial drags on and has a great deal of publicity, then it could affect the performance of more students." He wrapped his hands together. "Do you think I'll have to testify?"

"Probably, at least to establish that the girls are students here and that Frank has been their teacher at one time or another. I don't know what other questions might come up." Charlie felt the man's nervousness keenly.

"That's the prosecution, isn't it?" Covello asked.

"Yes. There's nothing unusual about such testimony. It's a little bit of an overkill, but since there's no guarantee that I will put Frank on the stand, the Assistant District Attorney will want all her bases covered." He scribbled a few more words. "Has your faculty been upset by Frank's case?"

Covello threw up his hands. "Are you kidding? Most of them are worse than the kids. I don't think there's a teacher in this school who feels safe. Every one of them is waiting for an accusation to be hurled in their direction. Half the time they threaten to quit or take sick-leave if anyone asks them questions. The rest of the time they get angry and indignant. Right now we have more substitutes teaching than we've had at any time since the flu epidemic four years ago. The faculty is scared. They think that Frank is being turned into a scapegoat and they don't like it. I don't know what to tell them."

"What about the parents? Do they think Frank is being made a scapegoat?" He saw uncertainty in Covello's eyes and did what he could to press an answer. "Not the ones who want to leave, the ones who want their kids to stay here. Do they have any sense of how this is going?"

"I don't know," said Covello testily. "I'm not speaking with the parents very much these days." He made a palms-up gesture of helplessness. "It wasn't that way before. A year ago I would have sworn we'd all stick together, parents, students and teachers, no matter what the trouble might be. But too much has happened, and I don't think that way any more."

"I see," said Charlie. "Was this the only reason?"

"Part of it, but not the only one. You know what's been happening in the schools. Everyone's terrified that we might get drugs on the campus, and then where would we be?" He finally sat behind his desk. "Last year a couple kids were caught smoking grass behind the gym. There wasn't much outcry at first. Everyone thought we were lucky because that was all that had happened. But then one of the swimmers began handing out pills— methamphetamines, for the most part—and that was another story. We got that cleaned up, but it cost us a lot of the confidence of the parents and solidarity of the students. School spirit took a beating."

"Why haven't I been told about this?" Charlie said.

"We make it a policy not to discuss it. At the weekly teachers' meeting, we bring it up sometimes, but never outside the meetings. It's hard to keep teachers from gossiping, but where something like the girls, or drugs, is concerned, we have to guard against it. Talking about it makes things worse, and it doesn't have anything to do with the girls, in any case." He set his jaw again, and Charlie was beginning to find Covello's obstinacy very annoying.

"It would have been helpful if I'd known about this," he said, and made a mental note to call Gail Harris that evening. "There could be a very good reason for Frank to inform me of the trouble you've had with drugs." He paused and regrouped his thoughts. "Were any of the girls involved with drugs, do you know?"

"I don't think I can talk about that," said David Covello.

"All right, but you may have to on the stand," said Charlie, doing his best to remain pleasant.

"I don't think it's appropriate." He pointedly glanced at his watch. "I'm afraid that's all the time I can spare, Mister Moon. If you'll let me glance over your notes before you leave?"

Charlie handed over his legal pad, saying, "I hope you can make out my handwriting."

"I'm used to what students do," said Covello, inspecting the three pages with the same attitude as he would use to review a paper. "I suppose that's satisfactory."

In spite of all his good intentions, Charlie said, "Only a C plus? Doctor Covello, you're a hard grader," before he gathered up his things and left the deserted school.

His office was handsome, wood-paneled and glowing from weekly polishing. The chairs were upholstered in a rich brown velvet and the draperies were a lighter version of the chairs. George Wycliff sat behind his desk, a Styrofoam cup of coffee open in front of him, a cream-cheese-smeared bagel beside it. "I hope you have some good reason to be here, Judge Studevant." Outside, unseasonable morning fog snarled traffic and frayed tempers as commuters made their way into the city.

"I do, George. I wouldn't have called you unless I was convinced it was urgent and necessary." She had to return to her chambers quickly, for court would be reconvening for closing arguments in under an hour; she knew that the District Attorney was aware of this, but did not mention it herself. "I had a visitor yesterday."

"And?" asked Wycliff, who was rarely cordial before ten.

"He said something to me. As an officer of the court, I am obliged to tell you about it. And you are obliged to listen." She did not change the level of her voice but her eyes grew more serious.

"Oh?" This was enough to catch Wycliff's attention. "Why's that?"

Morgan came two steps closer to his desk. "Ed Massie came to see me."

"That isn't very proper of him," said Wycliff with a shrug of dismissal. "About the perjury charge?"

"Are you going to listen to me?" Morgan asked as politely as she could. "Or do I have to do this in a more public way?"

Wycliff sighed. "All right. What is it?"

Quickly and directly Morgan related everything that Sergeant Massie had said to her. "I gather he wants someone to know about this. Because of what he says he promised his partner, I suppose I'm his only acceptable choice. The whole story is hearsay, of course, and I have only Massie's word that it means anything, and short of putting pressure on Ben Forbes, there's no way to test Massie's assertion, not that the tape would be admissible in any case, since it was obtained in a search that was more improper than the one that brought them the other tapes. But under the circumstances, since I had to throw the case out of court, I would be failing in my office if I didn't tell you about this."

"Snuff films." George Wycliff pursed his mouth in disgust. "Wasn't kiddie-porn bad enough?"

"Apparently not, if what Massie says is true, and if the tapes were in fact made by Scooter Ferrand." She shook her head. "And aside from notifying Towne, I don't know what more you can do, George."

"Well, I have to do that much; if I don't it might lead to new exclusions if we get our hands on Ferrand in the future." He took a bite of his meager breakfast. "I'll see what I can find out, and I'll pass the word along to Harding Towne. God, I hate it when that bastard's right."

"Sorry," said Morgan. She was about to wish him good morning when Wycliff glared at her.

"Send me a letter about this. I want some paper in my files. And it wouldn't hurt you to have some in yours. You don't want Towne claiming a conspiracy against his client, do you?" He sipped noisily at his coffee. "I'll make sure you get a memo back from me, just in case."

"You don't think Towne would really . . ." She did not go on.

"Better get back to court, Your Honor," said the District Attorney.

Mickey Trang pulled his Stanza into a parking place half a block from the front steps of Sutro Glen Junior High School. Beside him, Cadao Talbot scribbled notes, half in Vietnamese, half in a mix of French and English; he was dressed in a good-quality tweed jacket, dark flannel slacks, oxford-cloth shirt with a regimental tie. His dark hair was slicked and sculpted into place and looked about as grown-up as his disastrously young face would allow. Mickey approved. "This is the school. Two open entrances: the main one and then another open gate back by the gyms. You'll have to get familiar with it, but be careful how you go about it. They're pretty paranoid these days." Students streamed by the Stanza, and dozens of cars lined up in the loop at the front of the school to let off young passengers. "Last week, most of the kids who lived within a mile of the place walked here. They bus from further away. But now they all get dropped off and picked up, or almost all."

"So they're scared. They've got good reason for it," said Talbot. He watched the kids, noticing how they hurried.

"And then some. The local hangout is down toward Seventh Avenue, the usual kind of thing, a place that does pizzas and burgers," Mickey went on. "The kids from this school and the local high school hang out there. We're getting together a list of other places like this throughout the city, in case this one doesn't pan out. Incidentally, the Sutro Glen kids are razzed a lot for being intellectuals. You know how that goes. The hangout doesn't have many high school seniors, by the way—most of them won't go near so many young, bright kids."

"Hey, I want you to know that makes it tough," said Talbot in mock dismay. "I can pass for a senior, but younger's harder. I warned you."

"So you were kept back a grade because your English wasn't good enough, or you were having trouble in class or something. It happens. You can come up with something credible, can't you?" said Mickey, taking care of that problem. "And most of these kids aren't as good at guessing ages as they think they are; they judge by height and the books you carry. Have you worked that out yet?"

"I did my homework last night," said Talbot proudly. "I go to Parkside High, a junior"—he emphasized this—"with a low B average, which I'm trying to get up for my senior year so I can go to college. I take geometry from Miss Siddings, French from Mister Baxter, chemistry from Missus Martinez, English from Ms. Ridge, mechanical drawing from Mister Ordway, my P.E. instructor is Mister Fitzwilliam, who coaches the diving team, and my reading coach is one of the part-time librarians, Ms. Hill. I've got clearance with all but Missus Martinez, and she's supposed to call me tonight. You said the schools will cooperate."

"So fudge a little on the chemistry for the time being," said Mickey. "Just to be on the safe side."

"I'll try," said Cadao Talbot, whose minor had been organic chemistry.

"Say you don't like to talk about it," Mickey recommended. "You know how kids are about things they don't do well, especially at that age." He paused, and added, "Kind of like the way you don't talk about Gail."

"That's not the same thing," said Talbot, reaching for the door handle. "I'll check this place out. I've got my ID, and I'll use the cover we arranged—that one of the parents hired me to tell them how secure the school is."

"Missus Linda Berringer hired you. She has a daughter and son in school here. She's been pretty vocal about school issues."

"And I've got her letter in my case," said Talbot, tapping the valise he carried. "It's not going to take me very long to check this place out." He looked up as a loud buzzer sounded. "First period?"

"Actually, there's a twenty-minute home room at the start of the day. That's for announcements and attendance and all the usual checks. They start regular classes at nine-thirty; five minutes between classes. Most of the kids are gone at two-thirty, but a few of the classes go on until three-thirty: third-year French, second-year Spanish and German, beginning Chinese and Latin, also elective astronomy and physics. All part of the H.P. program." Mickey had been over this with Talbot yesterday evening, but this last check often revealed weaknesses before they became risks, and he did not apologize for the review.

"Special classes and electives, right?" He ticked off on his fingers. "Third-year French, second-year Spanish and German, elective biology, current events, world history and ecology, remedial math and reading in the main building. The other classes are in building D."

"And they include contemporary literature and journalism," Mickey added with a warning look.

"Oh, yeah. Our guy did the contemporary literature class, didn't he?" Talbot nodded. "Okay. I'll check back after lunch and we can work out how you want me to slip into the group."

Mickey gave a thumbs-up sign, then said, "Don't let the kids get too good a look at you. You don't want someone recognizing you later on."

"All they're going to see is the tweed jacket," said Talbot with confidence. "Right now I look like an adult, maybe a teacher or a cop or something. Very few of them will remember my face, except that it might be Mexican."

"All right, so I get twitchy," said Mickey as Talbot opened the door.

"Good thing you do. It's easier for those of us out in the nowhere." He hesitated, then slammed the door closed and started away toward the shallow front steps of the junior high school.

By six-thirty Morgan dismissed the jury for the day and reminded them not to discuss their deliberations or watch anything on the news about the case. That process had taken more than ten minutes, and she knew that most of the jury members were hungry and restive. She was a little puzzled about the delay in reaching a verdict, for the jury had begun deliberations at eleven that morning, and so far as she was concerned, it was not so complicated that it justified more than an hour or two of debate. Perhaps by tomorrow morning they would reach agreement.

The morning fog, instead of burning off, had thickened steadily all day so that now there was mizzle to make the fifteen-minute drive home almost ten minutes longer. As she pulled into the driveway and thumbed the garage-door opener, she did her best to put the whole day out of her mind. It was now a little after seven-thirty; she had missed the national news. She pulled into her place and shut off the engine, signaling the garage door to close behind her. She had had no further word from George Wycliff, which dragged on her more than all the rest.

"You okay?" Charlie asked as Morgan came from the basement into the kitchen. "I was getting worried."

"Instructions to the jury," said Morgan shortly.

"No verdict yet?" Charlie asked with some surprise. "I assumed it would be over by now."

"So had I," said Morgan. "Is there any chardonnay in the fridge?"

"I put some in half an hour ago," said Charlie. "And I fed the dogs."

"So I guessed," said Morgan, feeling guilty that she had not until that instant missed their pets.

"And I brought home some brie, stuffed it into a hollowed-out stubby French loaf after putting chopped garlic in it, and it is now warming in the oven. I reckon another ten minutes should do it." He smiled at her, knowing that she loved that appetizer. "Go on. Get your coat off and find something proverbially more comfortable."

"I don't think I *have* anything proverbially more comfortable," she said.

"What about that soft knit thing—sort of curry color, loose tunic top and pants? Won't that do in a pinch?" He indicated the door to the hall. "Go on. The brie's going to be melting soon."

As Morgan started toward the door, she asked over her shoulder, "Are we celebrating anything?"

"No; but I figure we both need a break and this will help, won't it?" He shooed her out of the kitchen.

"That we do," she admitted, and went down the hall, still puzzling about the delay in verdict. As she hung up her suit she noticed that the bottle-green wool had a coin-sized stain on the lapel. "Damn," she whispered as she set it aside to go to the cleaner's. She got into the outfit Charlie had suggested—it was cashmere, a terrible luxury—and paused to run a comb through her hair and change into soft-, low-heeled shoes before going back downstairs.

"You look very comfortable," said Charlie, handing her a glass of white wine. "Here. Taste."

"I gather it's too much to ask what you've planned for dinner?" she inquired archly as she took the wineglass.

"Not too much, but a little impractical. It won't be here for another hour. I've arranged for a delivery from *Ganesha*," he said grandly.

"Oh, yummie, but dear Lord, the calories," she exclaimed. The smell of garlic and melting cheese was much stronger, and she took a sip of wine to hold her sudden hunger at bay.

"Tonight I have banished calories. It's a shamanistic trick." He laughed at himself. "If I could, think of the fortune we'd have."

"True," said Morgan. She leaned against one of the two tall barstools that served them at their breakfast counter. "Why this extravagance? Did you get a break on the Girouard case?"

"No, but we got Durkheim a very good out-of-court settlement. We really didn't think they were going to give in so quickly, that they'd resist a lot more, but Watson called and said they were prepared to negotiate a reasonable settlement. Nially was spitting nails, but he admitted that he couldn't win, so . . ." He picked up his own wineglass. "So I said, 'What the hell,' and splurged. It isn't every day you get your client a tidy seven point five million dollars."

"What were you asking?" Morgan inquired.

"We'd asked twelve-five, just for negotiating room." He reached over and turned off the oven. "Come on; I'll bring this into the living room."

As they went through the dining room, Morgan noticed that the table was already set and the candles ready to be lit. "Very elegant."

Charlie leaned over and kissed her cheek. "That's the idea."

"That client of yours had the effrontery to call me nice!" Elizabeth informed Charlie as he arrived for Friday lunch; she had summoned him the day before, with a choice of seven times over three days. Charlie, knowing he was outmaneuvered, took the earliest.

"Did he call you cute as well?" Charlie asked sweetly, refusing to take part in her fallacious indignation.

"Luckily I was spared that." She summoned Clifford, motioning him to take Charlie's coat. "Charlie doesn't take wine at this time of day. See that a pot of Earl Grey is brought to us. That's all for right now; spend your time getting the lunch on the table."

Clifford fought a snarl. "Of course, Missus Kendrie."

"I don't know what it is about him," said Elizabeth as she watched Clifford make his way down the hall that led to the kitchen. "I do try to be pleasant to him, but it always sticks in my throat. And it's not because he's not Henry—not entirely, in any case." She folded her arms. "I must tell you, Charlie, that I think your Mister Girouard is not in very good shape. He's very seriously depressed, and I know what I'm talking about."

"I appreciate that," said Charlie, who had long been aware of Elizabeth's sponsoring a half-way house for depressed people, a place where she volunteered two mornings a month.

"It's bad enough that his wife is out of the picture. Though I gather she's not as much of a loss as that poor man thinks she is." She had led him to the lanai. "Have a seat. I understand he's going to take some tests soon. I'd like to recommend you postpone them a week or two. They aren't so crucial that you can't do that." She looked out the vast windows into an arm of her garden. "I think he ought to be seeing someone. Professionally."

"Are you suggesting that we give him another high-priced, high-pressure concern right now?" Charlie asked, a bit startled that she would not be aware of how difficult it would be.

"Not exactly. I may be old, but I haven't lost my wits yet, Charlie. No. I know Kevin Blackwell somewhat. And I'm sure I can arrange for a few appointments for Mister Girouard in exchange for a few needed additions to his clinic. Not unreasonable, is it?" She smiled, her eyes brightening. "What do you think, Charlie?"

"I think Frank might feel very beholden to you. Possibly more than he does already, and that might be hard on him." He said it as gently as he could. "Where is Frank, by the way? Will he be joining us?"

"Well, no. He won't." She looked up toward the ceiling, her expression supposedly angelic, which alerted Charlie all the more. "He's having a first discussion with Kevin Blackwell. Incidentally, I think Kevin might be willing to serve as expert witness where Frank is concerned. His word carries some weight in a courtroom. I know that sexual abuse is not exactly his line, but he's done enough with dysfunctional—I hate that term, don't you? It's being overused for everything from sports teams to governmental departments—families and the rest of it, I am sure he will have a few cogent remarks." She gave Charlie another one of her smiles.

"Outflanking me, Elizabeth?" Charlie asked.

"No, only saving a little time. I'm sure you'll come around to see this in a more reasonable light, but this way, Frank doesn't have to be pulled in one more direction. He's got quite enough of that already." She looked up as Clifford came into the room. "Is lunch prepared?"

"It's in the morning parlor, Missus Kendrie," he answered in a forbidding way.

"Very good," said Elizabeth. "We'll get ourselves there. You can take care of the shopping now, and I'll clear the table for you." She waved him away. "He's going to quit one of these days soon." She sighed. "And how are you coming in your search for his replacement?"

"Nothing so far," said Charlie, who had barely thought of it at all since he made the bargain.

"Better get on it," she said as she made her way toward the morning parlor. "I don't want Clifford to have to endure one day more of me than he can bear."

"Surely it's not that bad," said Charlie, aware as he spoke that Elizabeth rarely spoke so critically of anyone who worked for her.

"It's growing worse every day, and if there is a way to change it, I cannot see it, and," she added emphatically, "at this stage I don't want to."

"Well, that does make salvage a little hard," said Charlie. He held the chair at the head of the small, oval table for Elizabeth, then took the other chair himself. Outside, the rhododendrons waited for spring; in another six weeks they would be glorious.

Elizabeth picked up her soupspoon and tasted the contents of her bowl. "Well, it's good, but I'm growing very tired of Southwest cuisine, and I don't care how trendy it is. I am not a trendy person."

Charlie agreed that the soup was excellent. "Tell me what you promised Kevin Blackwell," he said.

"Oh, he's been after the Kendrie Foundation to shift funds his way for that battered wives' shelter the city won't put up for him. He has a location—it's a good one, and the security plans are very sensible—and about half the funding to put it up. You know how I am, Charlie. I do think we need such places, and we haven't enough of them, and those that we do have cannot begin to handle the problem. So when Kevin said he wanted the place built and funded, I told him it sounded quite reasonable to me." She had a little more of the soup, then set it aside. As she reached for the salad bowl, she said, "If I find one hot pepper or one sun-dried tomato in here, I will go into strong hysterics."

Charlie finished his soup.

As she helped herself to a bit more salad—no hot peppers or sun-dried tomatoes—Elizabeth made one last observation. "You know, Charlie, there must be something those girls are holding back. Whatever it is, you're going to have to find it out, or this case will follow Frank for the rest of his life."

Charlie put down his salad fork. "I know. And it bothers me. I don't want to make it seem that the girls are making it up. Society's been saying that about women's pain—all of it—for the last five thousand years; denying it, trivializing it. I won't do that. But if I press them, force them to deny it, or belittle what happened, I . . . I don't know if . . . if I can . . ." He drank some of his tea.

Elizabeth gave him a faint, understanding smile. "Damned if you do and damned if you don't. The trouble with you, Charlie Spotted Moon, is that you think it is possible to have justice in this life. Real justice."

"I know better than that," said Charlie, avoiding her penetrating gaze.

"Maybe. But you don't believe it, not in your heart of hearts." She put more salad on his plate. "It's one of your most endearing characteristics."

EIGHT

Saturday

CAESAR AND POMPEI were less exhausted from their run in Golden Gate Park than Charlie and Morgan were. The dogs pranced ahead of them, straining on their leashes, and only hesitated when it was apparent they were leaving the Park. As they waited for the light at Fulton to change, Caesar leaned against Charlie's leg and Charlie scratched his head.

"It was fun," said Morgan as they crossed the street and headed up toward Third Avenue. "But I'm not going to say we ought to do it more often. That's ridiculous."

"Why?" Charlie asked, though he agreed with her. "We're not so old and crotchety as all that."

"Because I can't get up this early every morning, head out for a fast walk for the better part of an hour and then be worth anything in court. It's fine for weekends, but we'd better stick to the end-of-day walks during the week." She watched Pompei pulling on the leash, and gave a complicated little sigh. "They could use a lot more of this."

"Well, when we retire, we'll get up at seven every morning and take the dogs for a long, fast hike," said Charlie, so glibly that Morgan laughed.

"Retire? And when were you planning to retire? A day after you're buried?" She patted his arm affectionately with her free hand, and then drew back. "Sorry, I didn't mean—"

"It's fine," said Charlie, not quite truthfully, for the bullet scar was aching, as it ached at the start of each day. "It's not worth bothering about. I'll soak it in that tincture you hate so much this evening."

"You mean that stuff that smells like rotting asparagus?" She made a face. "How can you bear it?"

"It works," said Charlie. "You'll admit that, won't you? It fixed that sprain you had year before last."

"Conceded," she said. "But what a price to pay." Her laughter pleased him, though he still felt a little defensive.

"You knew that I have special methods," he said quietly.

"And I think they're wonderful," she said, turning to look directly at him. "I have nothing but respect for what you can do with those herbal preparations. But that doesn't change the fact that some of your concoctions aren't very . . . savory."

He nodded, capitulating. "I can't disagree." He reached over and slipped her hand through the bend of his elbow. "What're your plans for the rest of the day?"

She gave it a little thought. "I have to do some shopping— shoes and a suit—so I'll probably have lunch downtown, take care of the shopping and pick up the groceries on the way home. How does that sound?"

"Sure you don't want me to get the groceries?" he offered. "I've got some work to do, but I can do the groceries if you like."

Once again she laughed. "Maybe you'd better. You are the cook in the house, after all." They turned the corner and started down the street toward their house. "More on the Girouard case?"

"Yeah. I'm going to talk with Glen Mitchell, the guy who's investigating the Susan Lake disappearance. He told me he'll give me all his reasons to demonstrate that this disappearance is in no way connected with Frank and he said he'd let me have any information that could be useful to the case." He released her hand and reached into his jacket pocket. "I'm grateful to him. He doesn't have to do this. And I wish it was all so easy."

"Talking with a cop is easy?" Morgan said, remembering her horrid interview with Ed Massie.

"With this one. He doesn't want this case cluttering up his investigation, any more than I want his case cluttering up mine. The last thing we need is for that kind of speculation to get going. You know what the press would do. It's worth taking time now to make a clean line between the cases." They climbed the steps, the dogs coming to heel as they did. Charlie used his key and opened the door, standing aside to let his wife enter first.

"What if there isn't a clean line? What if they are connected, after all?" she asked as she pulled off her anorak. "It's chilly in here. I'm going to turn on the heat."

Charlie was hanging his jacket in the closet under the stairs. "What do you mean?"

"Well, you might not be cold, but I sure as hell am," she said, and there was the distinct sound of the furnace coming on.

"No," he said, wanting to banish her annoyance, "not about the heat, about the cases. You're implying they might have a connection."

"Well, they could." She came back around the wide living room door, holding out her anorak to him. "It's my innate distrust of coincidences. This strikes me as too much of one: this girl disappearing right after Frank Girouard is accused of molesting five of his students looks pretty fishy to me. If I were in charge of investigating the case, I'd be very careful to check out the remotest connections before I ruled them out. That's all I'm saying."

Charlie nodded. "Yes. It's tempting to say that it's more of the same thing, though there's no proof of a link. Mitchell hasn't turned up a lead tieing one to the other. And assuming there is one with any proof isn't going to help his case or ours. He's very worried that if the press makes that connection—and you can bet your booties that some of them are going to try—he'll never be able to conduct a proper investigation, and they'll never find anything." He hung up her anorak and closed the closet door.

"There's a little coffee left. Do you want me to heat it up, or would you like a fresh pot?" She was past him and heading toward the kitchen, the dogs trailing after her expectantly.

"Let's have a fresh pot. After that settlement, we can splurge a little." He wandered into the living room, thinking that he ought to do the breakfast dishes before he started on his work. He glanced toward the dining room, realizing it was more than two months since he and Morgan had entertained. He ought to have Lydia and Anthony over. As soon as things were a little more settled with Frank's case, he would. He picked up the Sunday paper—available throughout the Bay Area early on Saturday morning—and thumbed through it looking for the pink section, in case he and Morgan might decide to go to the movies that night.

"Coffee," said Morgan a few minutes later, holding out a large white mug. "Black." She sank down on the sofa. "I think I'll try Union Square first, and if that doesn't turn up the right suit and the right shoes, then I'll go down to Market Street."

"Where are you going to have lunch?" Charlie was mildly preoccupied, going over the list of new films.

"I suppose one of the stores. I'll get something. Probably a salad." She put her hand to her waist. "It never gets any easier."

"I've told you that you don't have to stay a perfect size eight for me," Charlie said, hoping that she might come to believe him.

"Maybe not for you, but it helps on the job. We all say that it makes no difference if the judge is male or female, tall or short, fat or thin. But every psychological study proves otherwise." She stared down toward the fireplace grate. "I want to make sure I keep the edge I need."

Charlie nodded. "Well, at least find a place that does a tasty salad," he recommended.

Morgan had not been gone more than a quarter of an hour when Charlie received a call. "Moon? This is Sergeant Mitchell. Look, something's come up and I have to roll on it. Can we talk later."

"Sure," said Charlie at once, hearing an urgency in the man's voice that held his attention. "What is it, if you don't mind my asking?"

"We think we've found the Lake girl. We've found the body of a teenaged girl, in any case." He coughed. "I'm going out there now."

"Out where?" Charlie asked.

"Below the Palace of the Legion of Honor. Someone dumped her. She's in pretty bad shape. We figure it had to have been late yesterday evening." He paused. "I'll tell you more when I know more."

"Have you closed off the area?" Charlie asked.

"Diverted traffic on the road; hikers and bikers are being turned back on the paths and trails. But I'm not kidding myself; the scene isn't pristine." He sounded very tired. "I was afraid this was going to happen. It had that smell about it."

"I know," said Charlie, and hung up, his thoughts crowded with unpleasant possibilities.

Morgan had returned to the house an hour ago, later than she had anticipated, and had retired to her study to go over a few notes; Charlie was slicing green peppers in the kitchen, setting them out beside the shallots and Japanese eggplants he had already done, getting ready to add them to the diced turkey and rice in the casserole pot by his elbow. Dinner would be ready in less than an hour, he thought, which wasn't much time to walk the dogs.

The doorbell rang, and the sound chilled him.

"I'll get it," Morgan called from her study, which was at the front of the house. She hurried to the door as the bell sounded again.

A uniformed policeman stood in the doorway. The name on his pocket pin was K. Jaffrey. "Is Charles Moon here?" he asked, his voice gravelly with fatigue.

"Charlie," said Morgan carefully, "there's someone to see you."

The officer took off his cap. "Sergeant Mitchell sent me." He did not cross the threshold.

In the kitchen, Charlie put down his knife and went to wash his hands.

"Mitchell sent—" Morgan called.

"Yes," Charlie answered as he reached for a towel. "I heard." He looked over his half-finished dinner preparations, shook his head once and went to the front door. "Good evening," he said to the policeman. "Sorry to keep you waiting."

The officer did not hold out his hand. "I'm here for Sergeant Mitchell. He would like you to come down to headquarters at once, if that's acceptable. I'll provide transportation."

There had been no mention of convenience, which was more ominous than the rest. Charlie nodded once. "I'll get my jacket and be with you in a moment." As he started back down the hall to the coat closet, he said to Morgan, "Look, this may take a while. I've got everything ready for dinner. All you have to do is layer the veggies on top of the turkey, add a couple cups of white wine, put the lid on and stick it in the oven at three twenty-five for forty-five minutes. Everything's laid out. There's no trick to it."

She frowned. "What's this about?"

"The Lake girl," said Charlie. "They found her body earlier today. Don't ask me why Mitchell wants to see me, but you can bet it's important if he's pulling this kind of end run." He lowered his eyes. "I don't mean to stick you with this, but I don't want you to starve while I'm out."

"What if I just put everything in the fridge until you get back?" she asked. "Okay with you?"

"It could be late," he said as he pulled on his tweed jacket.

"So we'll have a fashionable midnight supper," she said, her flippant suggestion unable to disguise the worry in her eyes.

"I guess we will," he said, giving in. "I'll call you when I find out how long I might be. If you want to change your mind then, you can."

"Thanks, but I won't," she said, and leaned over to kiss him on the cheek. "Take care of yourself, Charlie."

"I'll do what I can," Charlie said, knowing he was dodging an answer. He went out to the policeman waiting on the porch.

Glen Mitchell looked as if he had been sleeping in his clothes. His eyes were red-rimmed and he needed a shave; he had a mild case of coffee-jitters. He indicated the mess on his desk. "We can't talk here," he announced as he looked around the squad room. "There's some interrogation rooms open. We'll use one of those. No one will disturb us. Things don't pick up around here until a little later, and we'll be through by then." He shoved himself out of his chair, straining against bulk and fatigue. "Down the hall."

"I know where they are," said Charlie.

"Of course, counselor," said Mitchell as he trundled along beside Charlie. "I got the preliminary medical on the Lake girl," he went on, changing the subject without apology. "It's pretty bad."

"And that's why I'm here?" Charlie asked, certain of the answer.

"Kind of, yeah." He tapped on the door of one room, waited, and when there was no response, stepped inside, motioning for Charlie to follow him. The room was small, the walls and ceiling covered with acoustical tiles. A single, small table jutted out from the wall, and there were four plastic chairs pushed against it. "Have a seat."

"All right," said Charlie a bit guardedly. He pulled one of the chairs out and sat in it, doing his best to ignore how uncomfortable it was.

Mitchell sighed deeply, then sat down. "I told you before that there was no connection between the two cases. When I told you that, I was certain it was true." He put his elbows on the table and dropped his chin into his hands. "I'm not as sure of that now as I was yesterday, not now that we've found the body."

"Meaning?" said Charlie, taking care to volunteer nothing.

"Meaning that the girl was used pretty hard before they killed her. They . . . well . . . shit, they tortured her to death." His face, already pale, was pasty now. "There's a lot of damage, but it looks like they started out with sexual things before graduating to mayhem." His eyes were blank, set on a distant horizon. "They actually washed her before dumping her. Apparently they did a good job of it, really thorough. It's going to wreck most evidence, though they're trying to find traces of blood, semen, anything that we could use in court. If we could get a DNA type on one or more of the men who did this to her . . ."

"Are you certain there were more than one?" Charlie asked, appalled at what he had heard.

"The medical examiner seems to think so," said Mitchell. "That's what this first report says, but he could change his mind later, I guess. But he's got reasons. Something about bruise patterns showing two separate knuckle shapes. He'll explain it to me later, when he has more information." He shuddered. "Christ! the things they did to that girl." He rubbed at his face as if to rid it of lingering contamination. "You think you've seen everything. You think that you're a cop and nothing can get to you like that. But that girl."

Charlie felt deep sympathy for Glen Mitchell, but he could not afford to reveal it. Instead, he kept his tone carefully neutral. "Why did you want me to come here, Sergeant? How do you think this concerns my client?"

It took a few seconds for Mitchell to respond. "If he is guilty—I said *if*, counselor—then he has to have an accomplice, if he's mixed up in this. And you can bet that his accomplice is tied up in this somehow."

"None of the girls accused him of having an accomplice," said Charlie very carefully. "They have all said Mister Girouard was the only one who abused them. There is no indication that whatever was done to them was done by more than one man."

"Yeah, I know," said Mitchell. "But I can't get it out of my head that the girls who are after your client were part of some kind of . . . audition. And they were lucky enough not to get cast. Someone's been after the girls at Sutro Glen Junior High, and that's all there is to it, at least that's how it reads to me." He lowered his hands and spread out his fingers on the Formica surface of the table. "There's no reason to think I'm right. You don't have to put any credence in this, but if your man is guilty, he's guilty because he's part of a ring. I'd stake my pension on it." His eyes met Charlie's, and this time he was fully present. "I've been over the complaints against Girouard. Whatever the reason, whoever molested the girls did almost identical things to them, and their responses were similar. If the Lake girl had gone to another school, I wouldn't insist on a connection, but I've got to assume there is. Wouldn't you do that, if you were in my position?"

Reluctantly Charlie nodded. "In your position, yes, I would probably assume a connection. Or I would assume that the girls had made it up between them."

"That's something," said Mitchell. "So those girls could have been killed the way the Lake girl was."

"I can't see my client being any part of such a thing," said Charlie very cautiously.

"Even if you could, you won't tell me about it, anyway," said Mitchell. "I know the rules. I even approve of them, most of the time. But I think you better have a heart-to-heart with your client, because if there is any link at all, he will not only be up on his current charges, he might find himself an accessory to murder."

"That's stretching a point," said Charlie.

"Maybe, but I'll stretch points and anything else to get Susan Lake's killers." He slapped the table. "I want your help, Moon. I want to know everything you can tell me about what's going on at that school. I know you don't have to do anything for me; you'd be within your rights to tell me to fuck off. But I don't want to find another corpse like that again, and unless the killers are stopped, I know in my guts I will."

Charlie said nothing for a short while. "I'll have to see what I can do. My client might know something that will help you. I'll need to speak with him and abide by his decision."

"Sure, sure." He stared down at the tabletop. "Officially, I can't show you the medical report, you know that."

"Yes," said Charlie.

"But if you stopped by here on Monday, sometime in the afternoon, the report ought to be on my desk. If you happened to read it accidentally, I couldn't be responsible for that, could I?" He directed his gaze at Charlie. "So you'll know what the stakes are."

"How do you mean?" Charlie asked, very curious in spite of himself.

"I mean that I think this is going to happen again, unless we stop it. Another girl will disappear and we'll find her like Susan Lake, or worse. I mean, counselor, that if your man is involved, that you talk to him about immunity in exchange for blowing the whistle on the others. I mean that if he's covering up for anybody, it isn't going to be worth spit for him to keep on. I mean that if this happens again, and your guy has been part of it, no matter how small that part, I will not rest until he answers for it, all the way." He let out the last of his breath in an uneven sigh.

Charlie rose. "I'll talk to my client, Mitchell. But I ought to warn you that he is innocent, and if you decide to go after him instead of the men who killed Susan Lake, you, not my client, will be responsible for anything that happens afterward." He paused, and went on more gently. "I'm very sorry about the Lake girl. And I'm sorry you have to deal with it."

The ferocity was gone from Mitchell now. "Yeah. Well."

As he reached to open the door, Charlie said, "I'll see you Monday afternoon?"

Mitchell said, "Jaffrey'll give you a lift home. Sorry to cut into your Saturday night."

"Dinner in twenty minutes," Charlie called to Morgan from the kitchen. The casserole was in the oven and he was putting thin-sliced lemon cucumbers into vinegar.

"Fine," she answered. "What do you want to watch?" There were three videotapes beside her. "*Last Emperor, Tootsie* or *Wicker Man*?"

"Let's save *Last Emperor* for tomorrow. You can put on whichever one of the other two you want first," Charlie suggested as he put the cucumbers in the fridge. He took a bottle of Sutter Home White Zinfandel out and got two glasses and the corkscrew. "I'm coming in. The timer's set."

"Okay. We start with *Tootsie*." There was a pause while Morgan loaded the tape in, and as Charlie came through the dining room arch, the copyright warning appeared on the television screen. "Just in time."

Charlie put the wine down on the coffee table and went to work on the cork. As he pulled it out, he said, "Hold your glass out, will you?"

She did, her attention more on the screen than the wine, and allowed herself more in the glass than usual. "I should have watched more closely," she said as she realized what he had poured for her.

"The casserole will soak it up for you," said Charlie, pouring his own. He watched the temperamental Michael Dorsey's antics, and though he smiled, he did not feel the humor of the actor's plight as he had the last time he had watched the movie some five months ago. He leaned back against the sofa cushions, trying to blot out something that came unbidden to his mind—the death of Susan Lake.

"Charlie?" Morgan said a little later as Dorothy Michaels began her rise to stardom. "The timer went off."

He gave himself a mental shake. "Oh. Sorry. I was woolgathering." He made himself move vigorously as he got to his feet. He had not touched his wine and he felt as if it were much later than it was. "I'll be back in a couple of minutes."

"I'll put it on hold," Morgan offered, thumbing the control.

The casserole smelled good, and the salad was tangy. Charlie set up two plates, then called the dogs in from the back and gave them their evening meal in the enclosed back porch. Everything he did was automatic, and the sense of the dead girl never left him.

The movie was more than half over, Morgan's plate was empty and Charlie's half-finished and abandoned when she put the film on hold again.

"All right, tell me what's wrong." She turned on the sofa to face him, her eyes serious. "You've been in outer space most of the evening. What did Mitchell tell you that got to you?"

Charlie shook his head. "It's . . . not that important."

"If it can take your mind off relaxing, it *is* that important." She took his hands in hers. "You're caught up in something. I'll bet it's that missing girl, the one whose body they just found. That's it."

He did not respond at once. "They're beginning to look for ties to Frank, after all. They think he might have something to do with it."

"Because of the coincidence?" asked Morgan, being as kind as she could.

"In part." Little as he wanted to discuss it, he made himself go on. "I gather that Mitchell thinks there's some kind of . . . ring operating out there, and that the other five girls got away because they weren't what the ring was looking for. Reading between the lines, Mitchell thinks that Frank's been a kind of . . . talent scout for the ring."

"You mean kiddie-porn?" Morgan asked, shocked. Everything in the last few weeks seemed always to come back to kiddie-porn, she thought, and despised the notion.

"I think that was what he was implying. It's too complicated, too full of maybes and what-ifs and possiblys, so I can't say for sure." He nodded toward the television. "Let's watch the movie."

"If that's what you want," said Morgan skeptically. "But as long as this is bothering you, I think it would help to get it out of your system."

"I've got a call in to Frank; he's doing something with Elizabeth tonight. After we get together tomorrow, I might have a better idea where we stand." He touched her cheek and managed part of a smile. "I don't know how we're going to sort this out, but until I know where Frank stands, I better not talk about it until then."

Morgan hesitated, then said, "This might not be anything." She set her wineglass aside. "But if it's connected, you'll need to know about it. Something happened to me a couple days ago, something I haven't mentioned. It wasn't in confidence, exactly, but ordinarily I wouldn't bring it up, because of how the information was given. But maybe it's important." And painstakingly, she described to Charlie what Edmund Massie had told her about the videotape Ben Forbes claimed to have pilfered from Scooter Ferrand.

Tootsie was forgotten

Sunday

HIS DISCUSSION WITH Frank Girouard had gone pretty much the way that Charlie had anticipated it would: Frank had listened to the new information, aghast at the death of Susan Lake, and terrified at its implication for him. "But I wasn't anywhere near the school when it happened," he protested when Charlie had finished telling him about it. "I had Susan in a class, but I never did—"

"Neither was she," said Charlie, "near the school."

"I was here. There are witnesses," said Frank, his voice rising.

"I know," said Charlie. "And that's why I'm not pressing you. If there were holes in your alabi, then I'd handle this differently. But I know you could not have done it. Elizabeth vouches for you, and there's nothing stronger than that. What I am beginning to wonder is if you have some sense of who might have done it." It was a leading statement, designed to get a reaction out of Frank.

"That's ridiculous," he said.

"Is it?" Charlie countered. He listened to Frank's protestations and was satisfied that the teacher was not a willing scapegoat for anyone at the school. "What about other adults—administration? parents? outside advisors?"

"If any of them were up to something, I never heard even a rumor," said Frank, his tone contemptuous. "There's no reason I should assume that any of my colleagues were aware of . . . any of this." He stopped. "The case is getting awfully complicated, isn't it?"

Charlie knew better than to lie about it. "Yes."

"And that makes it harder on me." This was no longer a question but a surety for Frank.

"It does; it makes it harder on everyone," Charlie agreed. "And that's why I want to be able to find those responsible as well as establish your innocence. You don't want those doubts tagging after you." He did not discuss how he planned to do this, for he still did not know himself.

"But I might as well give up teaching right now," said Frank, depression returning. "Bob Nettles was right. He said that you never get away from charges like this no matter what you do. He said that Wilson Harness did the only sensible thing. I guess I'd better start thinking of alternatives, too."

"You don't have to do that," said Charlie. "If we can find out who is the real criminal, you'll be fine."

Frank shook his head twice. "You don't know schools, if you believe that."

By the time Charlie left, he had convinced Frank that there was still a chance to prove him completely innocent, and that no matter how slim, it was worth pursuing. He went across town to the house near the zoo where Mickey Trang lived, thinking as he drove that he needed something to show Frank, something Frank could accept as real help. While he looked for a parking place, he reviewed his position once again, and liked it no better than he had before.

Mickey had converted the garage into a home office consisting of one large room with six five-drawer file cabinets and two computers. Mickey himself had a leather sling chair in one corner where he could sit back and watch TV while his machines were busy. Today he made no pretense of doing anything more than watching figure-skating competitions from Europe.

"I thought you said you wanted to talk to me," said Charlie as he hesitated, his attention caught by Brian Boitano doing something beautiful and dangerous at high speed.

"I do, but let's wait until this is over." Mickey dropped back into his sling chair. "I love that guy; he skates like he's doing a martial arts demonstration."

When the announcer came on, followed by a string of commercials, Mickey reached over and turned the TV off. "Cadao Talbot stopped by last night. After spending about five hours at the hangout joints. He said that there is a very strong rumor going around that someone has a standing offer to the girls to take their pictures in the nude. The word is that the girl would get ten dollars per picture. There are a few girls who are supposed to have done it, but no specific names or examples. And since this thing with Girouard, speculation is rife." He looked over his shoulder. "You want a beer?"

"No, thanks," said Charlie. "Tell me some more of what Talbot's come up with."

"Well," said Mickey, reaching over and picking up his notebook and flipping it open. "Cadao's been checking out the middle school and high school hangout joints. He didn't turn up anything at the place on Seventh Avenue. He didn't expect to. It's a pretty safe bet that the photographers have backed off from there, but there's a good chance they're pulling the same shit somewhere else. Cadao tells me that as far as he's been able to trace it, the rumors of the photographers have been around for more than a year. According to one of the boys, the guy offering the money used to work a couple of high schools in San Jose, but moved up here when things got too hot. I haven't tried the San Jose police yet; you might get better results than I could. A teenagers' rumor isn't much cause for an investigation, but it could lead to something, if you can find some way to back it up and make it official. Cadao's going to keep looking. Not obviously; he said he'd try to make it sound like the average inexperienced and horny high school boy wanting to get in on the excitement."

"All right," said Charlie, thinking that they could have done most of this on the telephone. "What more is there?"

"A couple of things." Mickey held out a Polaroid photograph. It showed a skinny teenaged girl lying naked on lace pillows, her face averted. "Cadao paid fifty dollars for this; he got it from a guy who was there to sell them. According to the boys Cadao talked to, the guy comes by about twice a month, usually on weekends, and has other Polaroids to sell, usually of four or five different girls. Apparently he's been doing this for more than a year. Cadao guesses him to be in his mid-twenties, lean and cocky, with crazy eyes. Those are Cadao's exact words—crazy eyes."

"And the other thing?" asked Charlie, his neck going cold.

"Judging by the snapshots they're selling, Cadao thinks they're looking for young girls, innocent-looking, not the fourteen-going-on-twenty-two kind. The girls in the photos were all like this one—young, inexperienced and scared."

Charlie handed the picture back to Mickey. "Keep that for now. And tell Talbot that he may have to testify how he came to have it." Even after Mickey took the picture, Charlie felt it on his fingers, like a slimy residue. "And I want to know how long those things have been sold, and maybe how many of them, too."

"What does it do for your client?" Mickey asked as he made a note of the request.

"I don't know," said Charlie, recognizing the confusion that threatened to overtake him. "That's the hell of it. The way things are going, I really don't know."

"Technically I suppose I should tell the D.A. or the cops about the guy selling the pictures," said Charlie as he and Morgan finished up with the dishes. "But it could have bearing on Frank's case, and I can't turn it over until I'm certain that it isn't part of the defense."

"It gets worse and worse, doesn't it?" Morgan said as she wiped their large glass salad bowl.

"It sure seems that way," said Charlie. "And that's starting to scare me. I suppose we have enough questions now that we might be able to try for a dismissal, but I doubt we'd get it in a case like this."

"And it wouldn't settle anything, would it?" Morgan said, pausing to put the salad bowl in its place on the open shelves. "Frank would continue to have a cloud over him."

"The way things are going, I might not be able to stop it, not completely." He went to work on his omelette pan, determined to get out the burned cheese. "I'm almost afraid to continue our investigation; considering what's been turned up already, I don't want to think about what else may be out there to find."

"Including a guilty client?" Morgan suggested.

"No," Charlie said with heat as he scrubbed at the cheese. "Not that. I'm still convinced that he's been set up, though I can't figure out who did it, or why. But if it gets more complicated or there's more levels of trouble than we have now, this could take a long time to handle." He finally had the cheese off. "It's a little like the way you felt when you had to throw the Ferrand case out—the law is upheld—and I have no argument with that. But in this case, it works against itself. That doesn't mean that we need to get rid of the law, but it needs to be enforced properly, and the trouble is sometimes, it isn't easy to know exactly how to do that." He gave the pan a last going-over, then dunked it in the rinse water.

Morgan had been drying flatware and now she dropped the pieces into their drawer. "I wish there was a way to get the cops to see that."

"I'd like to give a few lessons to the press, too," said Charlie, reaching to drain the wash water. "I don't want to endanger the First Amendment, but I don't want my client's rights—" He broke off as the phone rang. "I'll get it," he said, starting for the telephone before Morgan could put down the omelette pan.

"Charles Moon here," he said as he picked up the receiver.

"Mister Moon," said a voice that was vaguely familiar. "I . . . this is Melissa Budge. We spoke a couple weeks ago—"

"I remember you, Ms. Budge," said Charlie, deeply curious what this woman might want with him.

"I need to see you again." She seemed genuinely distressed. "It is fairly urgent. I've been trying to reach Frank Girouard, but there's only an answering machine and—"

"That's all right," said Charlie. "Tell me what it is and I'll see that Frank is informed." He frowned as he listened, trying to anticipate what the psychologist might have to tell him.

"Well, I hate to say this . . . and you understand that ordinarily I would not speak out this way . . . but this is a criminal issue, and . . . and I am fairly certain that at least one of the girls . . . isn't telling the truth about Frank Girouard." She took a deep breath and plunged on. "You see, her story keeps changing. And the changes aren't the kind you see in abuse cases. She isn't denying the abuse, or taking it on herself, none of those things."

"How do you mean, Ms. Budge?" Charlie prompted, sensing the discomfort increasing in his caller. He could hear Morgan in the kitchen finishing the last of the dish drying; she was whistling occasional scraps of a tune he could not quite recognize.

"Well, I have no other way to put this: I have come to the conclusion that in the case of Wendy Maple, the man who abused her was very large and muscular. Four of her . . . well, the various descriptions she has offered indicate that her assailant was much bigger than Mister Girouard. And I am very concerned about it, Mister Moon."

Charlie did not often suffer from headaches but he had one now. "I don't blame you, Ms. Budge," he said. "In your position, I would be concerned, too." He rubbed his eyes. "When are you available to meet with me?"

"I am free Tuesday morning," she said promptly. "And I will try to obtain the permission of the Maples to reveal some of what Wendy has told me, verbatim, so you can have an idea of the scope of the problem. They have said they will speak with me tomorrow morning." She paused. "I've never had to do anything like this, Mister Moon, not in all my years with the school system. It bothers me to have to do it now."

"I can understand that, Ms. Budge," said Charlie quietly. "In your position, I would be bothered, too."

She paused again, this time with more apprehension. "I can't make any statements about the other girls, but I believe I will have to listen to their sessions more critically than I have. But now that I am looking for this other man, I must take care not to project him onto what they say."

"It's a very difficult thing," said Charlie, meaning it.

"I appreciate your understanding." She coughed once. "I think it was the death of the Lake girl that shook Wendy's story. I don't know why. But she changed how she spoke about her molestation when Susan Lake disappeared. All the children at Sutro Glen heard about the car; that seemed to trigger something in Wendy." She broke off abruptly. "I shouldn't say anything more now. I'll have to speak to Wendy's family tonight. Wendy has already said she wants me to do this, so . . ."

"I'm certain you'll be able to make it clear to them," said Charlie. His headache was sharper, more insistent.

"I certainly hope so," said Melissa Budge. "Thank you so much for hearing me out. I'll plan to see you on Tuesday."

"My office will leave a message about the time, if that's all right," said Charlie, who could not bring to mind what his schedule was for the next week. The headache dug in spurs.

"That will be fine. I'm very grateful to you for—"

Charlie cut her off, both because of his own aversion to thanks and because his headache was claiming all his attention. "I'm the one who ought to be grateful, Ms. Budge. I'll see you on Tuesday."

"Oh," she said. "Yes," she said. "Well, good night."

NINE

Monday and Tuesday

"SO TELL ME," said Nathaniel Wong to Charlie as he got off the elevator, "how are you making out on this client my sister brought to you?" He looked especially sleek this morning, preparing to go to court. "She told me at dinner last night that it's going to be hard going."

"She's right," said Charlie, wishing he did not have to speak to Nathaniel just now. "The case is very difficult, more complex than it seemed at first." He paused by the door to Nathaniel's office. "Frankly, I haven't a clue how it's going to turn out."

Nathaniel shook his head once. His mellifluous voice lent a spurious sympathy to his next observation. "Cases with sex in them—they're always more trouble than they're worth."

"Is that what you told Lydia?" Charlie inquired.

"It's what I *would* have told her," said Nathaniel, "had she bothered to ask me. But she decided you had more experience in the area, and went to you first."

"Does that bother you?" Charlie asked, aware that it did.

"Under the circumstances, no," said Nathaniel. "But I wish she'd talked to me before she brought the thing to this firm. It doesn't look good when we get caught up in one of these messes. Leave it to the specialists and the hotshots who like dealing in perversions. Every time you get a mix of kids and sex, it's poison." He adjusted his unnecessary glasses. "But I'm just her brother. I worry about things like family reputation." He started to open his door, then looked back at Charlie. "I don't envy you the case, and that's the truth."

"It's not pretty," said Charlie, "but I do think our client is innocent."

"Fat chance of proving it," said Nathaniel with a long, measured look.

"Yeah," said Charlie as Nathaniel went into his office.

Walking to his own office, Charlie pondered the impact the Girouard case might have on the firm. It was too much to assume it could damage MacCurrey, Moon, Nelson and Wong, but it could prove divisive for a time. He stepped through the door and noticed that there were message tags on his desk already. A few had come in over the weekend, but two were urgent for that morning, including one from Glen Mitchell. He sat down and picked up the receiver.

Sergeant Mitchell was not at his desk, but a note would be left for him to call as soon as possible.

"Great," said Charlie to the ceiling. "Phone tag." He looked at the next tag and made another call, this one to Gail Harris.

"Morning, Charlie," Gail said brightly. "I don't mean to start off the week with bad news, but I checked on Missus Girouard over the weekend, to see how she's doing, and she's being courted by a tabloid reporter to give them an exclusive on what it was like being married to a child rapist. If Girouard is convicted, they want the rights to her story for a TV movie. She's tending to say yes."

Although he had been expecting just such a development, Charlie ground his teeth. "All right," he said, "I'll see what we can do to get a stop to that, since the case has not yet been brought to trial, let alone a verdict. I might need you or one of your people to deliver a couple of documents to her, in person."

"A pleasure," said Gail at once. "I like the Gold Country. And I don't like the way she's behaving. I'll do it myself, for a change. Mickey can run things while I'm away." She laughed easily. "Next on the list: we've continued our watch on Girouard, and we can account for every hour he was not actually in Elizabeth Kendrie's house. We have records for all of it, and we're prepared to go into court with it any time you say. I think you could move for a dismissal on what you've got, in spite of the girls. There are too many factors that point to someone other than Girouard."

"It might work," said Charlie, "if it weren't the kind of case it is. But we can't leave a hint of doubt lingering. And we're not in any position to do that yet. So let's keep at it, all right?"

"You're the boss," said Gail, still cheerful. "We'll try to find something that will clear him, or at least act as hard evidence against the accusation. Maybe," she said enthusiastically, "we'll find out who really did it."

"Good," said Charlie. "But for the time being, we'll make sure Frank's movements are all documented, just in case. That'll take the pressure off for the Lake girl's death. It doesn't do much about the original complaint, but at least we'll have something to show for his time at Elizabeth's." He scribbled a note to himself. "When Mickey gets in, tell him I want to know more about those snapshots. I want to know where they were taken, if Talbot can find it out."

"All right. Anything else?" She had a voice that smiled on the telephone, a skill that often worked to her advantage when she was trying to worm information out of reluctant people.

"I don't know yet. Let me call you in the afternoon, all right?" He hoped that he and Mitchell would have talked by then. "If anything interesting turns up, let me know about it."

"Of course," said Gail. "By the way, we're hunting down a missing witness for Jocelyn Nelson; the guy's down in San Diego, so if there's anything you need done in the southern part of California, let us know and we can do both at once. Saves us and M.M.N. and W. time and money."

"Okay; I'll keep that in mind." Charlie wondered which of Jocelyn's cases had taken such a turn. He would have to ask her later. "You'll hear from me before four-thirty."

"Fine," she said. "I'll be here. Or Mickey will."

Though he did not say so, Charlie was relieved it was so.

There was a shine in Harding Towne's eyes as he faced Morgan in her chambers. "Your Honor," he said, making the title sarcastic, "I thought I should warn you that I am about to file a harassment suit against the police department, the District Attorney's office and you, for the damage you are doing to the reputation of Stanhope Ferrand. Secondarily, I will be lodging a protest with the Judicial Review Board."

"I don't see how anything we can do can damage Scooter's reputation more than he has himself," said Morgan, unwilling to get caught up in Towne's dramatic presentation. "Your present case aside, he has been convicted of contributing to the delinquency of a minor and drug possession already. That may have no direct bearing on the current issue, but it does indicate a trend and an attitude that trouble me. And since I had to dismiss the case because of illegal search and seizure, I can't imagine what your grounds for complaint would be. The law is very specific and I did what is required. But I appreciate being informed."

Towne did not warm to her reasonableness. "I received word that there has been a *second* illegal seizure, supposedly unauthorized—"

"Since there was no warrant issued, and no record of the seizure either from the police or your client, you know damn well it was unauthorized. In fact, since there has been no complaint, there is no indication that such a seizure ever took place," said Morgan sharply. "Stop all this posing, Towne. You aren't in front of a jury and histrionics don't impress me."

"This isn't histrionics," he protested.

"Well, it sure as hell isn't righteous indignation," she said, her words blunt and deliberate. "You are milking this, Mister Towne, and I don't want to have to make a countercomplaint against you, but I will if you force me to it." Her eyes and her voice were steady, which surprised her, for she could feel herself trembling as she spoke.

Towne shook his head. "You must take me for a total novice, Your Honor. I know what I'm doing, and it's time you realized it."

"I know that you're good at what you do," said Morgan, taking care not to let her temper get the better of her. "That was never disputed. But I am questioning your judgment now."

"A little high-handed, don't you think?" He came as close to her as her desk would allow. "The tide's turning, Your Honor. You can't hide behind your civil-rights-and-radical-chic pose forever, not while you are abrogating Ferrand's First Amendment rights."

"I didn't know I had a pose, Mister Towne," said Morgan with utmost politeness. "Thank you for informing me of it. And my proceedings have nothing to do with the First Amendment, and you know it; we've already cleared that up. Your client is free to express his artistic urges any way that is appropriate—"

"Not likely," said Towne.

"—until that expression breaks the law. Sexual abuse of minors, for any purposes whatsoever, is against the law. Let him use young-looking adults if it is his intention to film such acts. Sexual acts between consenting adults can be filmed and the films distributed; that's what the law says, and I believe it is a good law. But there must be no harm done to the actors or . . . models, or the charge is apt to be assault, not because of the sexual acts but because of the physical damage done." Morgan made herself stop.

"I don't want to hear anything more about Scooter Ferrand and the First Amendment in regard to this case. Is that clear."

"Making the law up as you go along?" he challenged, trying to throw her off-guard.

Her face set. "If there were any means to do it legally, I would hold you as responsible for the abuse of those children as Ferrand is, Mister Towne." She watched him. "According to the records introduced, you were the one who helped him establish his . . . studio. I suppose you knew its purpose."

He sensed that he had somehow overstepped the mark. "I came here out of respect for your position, Your Honor, so that—"

"So that I could be stampeded into making concessions to you in return for your assurance that you would withdraw or mitigate your complaint," she finished for him. "Sorry; no sale. You came to the wrong judge, Mister Towne. And if you try anything like this again, I am putting you on notice that I will express my feelings not to you but to the California Bar Association." She gave him a short, feral smile. "Don't linger, Mister Towne. I am sure you have other errands to run."

This was not what he had anticipated when he came to her chambers, and now he faltered. "I will be heard."

"If you insist. But not right now." She made a show of looking at her watch, then addressed him briskly, without emotion. "I have to be in court; my bailiff will be here shortly."

Harding Towne glared at her, some of his sleekness missing. "Your Honor, you're a bitch."

"Be glad you didn't say that in court, or I'd hold you in contempt," said Morgan affably. "You've worn out your welcome, Mister Towne." She indicated the door. "Don't let me keep you."

For several seconds Towne was silent; then he did his best to salvage his dignity. "You'll hear from me, Your Honor."

Morgan was already on her feet, going to the closet for her robe. She did not turn as she said, "I have no doubt of that, Mister Towne."

From three-thirty until five, the Space Station was busier than any other time of day. Kids from Parkside High, Richmond Middle School, the private Sea Cliff Day School and the Catholic Saint Clair's High School streamed in for pizzas, burgers, hot dogs, cherry Cokes and flirtation. On Fridays, the activity went on until almost nine.

As was the case in most establishments like the Space Station, there were very strict unwritten rules about who was permitted to sit where. The kids from the Middle School, being the youngest, were relegated to the tables along the dark west wall and the back of the main room. The Richmond and Saint Clair's students had most of the rest of the tables in the main room. The Sea Cliff Day School students isolated themselves on the covered patio in the back. Then there was a kind of no-man's-land in the smaller dining room, where newcomers usually went until they figured out where they fit in.

Edgar Elton, the owner and manager of the Space Station, noticed the kid immediately. It was only the second or third time the boy had come to his place, and never this early in the day. Asians were not unusual at the Space Station, but this new kid was not obviously Asian, which piqued Elton's curiosity. Only his name—Cadao Luong—which he grudgingly gave to the waiter when he placed his order, caught Elton's attention. The slightly built newcomer was probably one of those Vietnamese, Elton decided—half some kind of American.

"We'll call you when your pizza's done," said the waiter, paying little attention to the kid, though he remembered to say, "Welcome back to the Space Station."

"Who's the guy?" Elton asked from his place by the grill where patties and onion slices sizzled. "He hasn't been here very much."

"From Parkside. He's got new covers on all his books. Probably a transfer student," said the waiter. "Name's Vietnamese."

"Um." Elton flipped two of the burgers. He glanced toward Cadao. "He looks . . . I don't know."

"You know what Asians are like—you're never sure how old they are," said Tim as he drew two mugs of Coke. "This is for the kids at table six. I'll take care of them and you do the pizzas. We got three ordered."

"Fine, fine," said Elton, giving one last glance in Cadao's direction before he turned his mind back to the burgers.

Cadao had opened one of his books and went through the motions of taking notes. He did not want to appear overeager to make conversation. He was still unfamiliar to the regulars here and knew it would be folly to press acquaintance with them. He knew that the Polaroid had been a fluke and he could not assume he would have such an advantage again.

"Cadao," called Tim from behind the tall counter. "Pizza's ready."

"Coming." He left his books and went to collect the pizza, fumbling for his cash. "I hope you remembered the extra cheese."

"Double portion," said Tim as he handed over the pizza. "That's eight seventy-five." He made change and watched as Cadao stuffed it back in his pocket before grabbing the pizza. He looked around as the door opened and a group of teenaged boys came in, all of them in tight, faded jeans and bomber jackets over bright tee-shirts; they jostled their way to the center table, claiming their territory noisily. "It's going to get really busy around here, Cadao. If you want something to drink, better order it now. I don't think I'll have time for another half hour."

Cadao longed for a dark beer, but knew better than that. "You have any V-8? My mom won't let us have Coke."

"And you do what your mom says?" Tim chided.

"Sometimes," said Cadao. "What about the V-8?"

"We got some. Small, medium or large?"

The door opened again and this time the group was girls, many of them giggling nervously. Not one of them was older than fifteen.

"Large." It would be easier to nurse a large drink than a small one. "Mom won't mind about the pizza if she knows I had this."

"If you say so." Tim gave him a glass and a can. "There you are. That's one twenty-five."

Cadao went through the process of taking out his money again, and gave Tim the money, adding a fifty-cent tip, which was about right for a kid in high school, he thought. "Thanks."

"You'll get to know 'em in a couple weeks," said Tim, aware that Cadao was staring at the girls. "They need a little time to warm up. Especially since that girl got killed."

"I heard about that," said Cadao, shaking his head as he claimed his meal. Then he retreated to his table to eat the medium-sized pizza as slowly as possible and eavesdrop. The Space Station was filling up quickly and he wanted to be certain he missed as little as possible.

By six-thirty most of the kids had vanished; only a few boys remained in the main room, clustered around two of the central tables. Cadao was about to call it a night and head for home when he saw a slender man come through the door, the same one who had had the Polaroid photos. He remained still, watching the newcomer approach the group of boys.

"Hey, Paco," one of the boys called out, "you got anything new to show us? You're over a week early."

"Not exactly," said the lean man, "not yet." He sauntered up to the boys, amused and confident, aware of how eager they were. He was olive-skinned and had dark, reddish hair; his eyes were grey-green. "No, I'm here because you might be able to help me out."

"What's up, Paco?" asked the most respected of the lot. He had his elbows on the table and there was a smudge of tomato sauce on his sleeve.

Paco grinned and his crazy eyes glinted. "Well, it's kind of tricky. You know the kind of things I'm into. You know what it's like, with the magazines and things out there for competition. I can't afford to stick with the same old like, know what I mean? I'm trying to find some fresh talent. You know how things are. You don't want to see the same old girls, do you?"

"How do you mean, talent?" asked the oldest boy.

"You know," said Paco.

"You mean, girls we know?" one of the boys asked uneasily.

"Maybe," said Paco, then slung his weight into his hip and went on. "You hear things, guys like you. So you can help us. You find us a girl who wants to pick up a couple extra bucks doing this, I'll give you a discount on the pictures we take." He beamed.

"But most girls don't—" said one of the younger boys at the table. He blushed, which only added to his shame.

"Well, that's why I'm here talking to you," said Paco. "We know that most girls don't do things like this. But there are a few who get a kick out of it, aren't there? Hell, you guys are the cream of the crop; you know which girls are in the mood and which aren't."

"Sometimes," said one of the boys darkly, and sniggered.

Paco was undaunted by this response. "It's something you can do to help me out, that's all. We all get what we want. Know what I mean? You find me more girls, I get you more pictures, that's all." He drew up a stool and sat down. "They get a little extra change, you get the discount, I get the pictures, everybody's happy."

"You mean, you'd be selling pictures like you showed us of girls we know?" asked the youngest boy, managing this time to keep his blushing under control.

"Sure," said Paco, his eagerness tinged with something that was not quite contempt. "Why not?"

"But if we know the girls, and we see pictures like . . . like yours, the girl's not going to have any reputation left," said one of the older boys. "They'll have to move away to get over it."

"Well," said Paco with a shrug. "If they're the kind of girl that takes pictures like this, what kind of reputation can she have, anyway?" He showed his teeth. "If you know that kind of girl, ask her first."

"Yeah," said one of the boys slyly. "Well, if we do, what about it?"

"Share the wealth, man," said Paco.

"How?" asked one of the boys. "How do you get a girl to do those kinds of pictures?"

"I don't know about this," said a boy with freckles.

"Jesus," said Paco. "You get them to do this the same way you get them to do everything else. Get 'em to like you. Give 'em a little present so they're grateful. Then you ask 'em real nice. You get someone to tell them it's okay. Make it a dare, or get a couple of them to do it as a joke. You tell them how pretty they are and you'll break their necks if they don't let you. Do anything you want. And they get paid. It's not like they're being ripped off. It's a good deal."

"For who?" The boy who asked was staring at the tabletop, unwilling to look at Paco, his shoulders tense.

Cadao took a last piece of pizza and pretended to be puzzling over something in one of his schoolbooks. He hoped that no one had noticed him, or if they had, that they supposed he was still studying. He knew Paco would not like being watched.

"Hey, for everyone. You can get more photos, too. It'll cost you forty instead of fifty for any picture I got on hand. It's a good deal," said Paco with a great show of patience. "The girls'll get money for posing. You'll all come out ahead."

"But if you let the pictures . . ." said a boy with white-streaked dark hair. He nudged the leader of their group. "We don't want our girls shown that way, do we, Grady?"

"What's the matter, Grady?" Paco goaded. "Greedy? Selfish?"

"Well," said Grady, taking his time in answering, "I don't want anybody taking pictures like that of Nicole but me." He did not laugh easily. "And I don't want her knowing about the offer."

One of the other boys looked surprised. "Why not?"

"Because she'd be pissed if she knew I'd had an offer like this. And she might do something to prove she could handle herself, and it might be worse than have her picture taken. Use your head,

Perkins." Grady stared at Paco. "They say some of the other schools have girls who are easier."

Paco continued his ferocious smile. "What about Richmond Middle School?"

"Kids!" one of the boys scoffed.

"They got new little breasts and you can get them to do anything, between sweet talk and the back of your hand," said Paco, determined to convince these boys.

Grady growled. "He's right; they're kids."

"You aren't looking real close if you think that," said Paco, his chuckle full of menace. "They got some real prime cuts over there, and being young makes it better."

The boys exchanged uneasy glances and Grady shook his head. "They're just kids," he reiterated. "They don't know anything."

"They know enough to lie back and show off their goodies," said the youngest of the boys with sudden vehemence. "They do that, some of them. And then they run and tell." His blush returned and three of the older boys gave him a long, hard look. "Well, they do," he muttered.

Paco seized on this. "Who does this?" He tried to make light of his interest. "Hell, I've got to find talent somewhere. Who does this? Do you think the girls would talk to me?"

"I don't know," the youngest boy muttered.

"Well, you think it over, and you talk to me when you got something to tell," said Paco. His gaze was frenzied and insolent, but he spoke calmly enough. "I don't want to have any hassle because of this. If you guys get chicken and go to the school or the cops, I'll know who did it and I'll make sure you regret it."

"Hey," said Grady, not quite frightened.

"It's because Susan Lake got killed," said Perkins. "I don't think any of the girls'll do this right now. Maybe in a little while, but Susan Lake has them all scared."

"Yeah, that's right," said Grady hastily, as if he ought to have made the point himself. "Nicole's jumpy all the time because of Susan Lake."

Paco's laugh raised the hackles on Cadao's neck. "Aw, shit, you guys are wimps! It's good when a girl's jumpy like that. It makes them remember who's in charge. Don't you know they're best when they're scared? What's the matter with you chickenshit kids?"

Grady rose. "That's out of line, Paco."

"You gonna do something about it?" Paco taunted. "You can't

keep a girl in line, and you think you can put muscle on me?" He laughed again, and it was worse than the last time. "You get straight about who calls the shots and then we can talk. Maybe. In the meantime, the price on the pictures just went up ten bucks." He gave an ironic little bow and strolled away to the door.

Cadao waited until all the boys had left, some forty minutes later, before he went to telephone Mickey Trang.

Isolde Aldred hated her name as only a child who has been teased can hate. She answered to it only professionally, and even then she preferred Sally. She was deceptively mild-looking, with soft brown hair and schoolmarmish glasses. Her styles, conservative and businesslike tended toward the preppy and favored her scholarly look. She faced Charlie across her office. "By all rights you shouldn't be here, Moon," she reminded him as she had when he had called her the night before and asked to see her first thing in the morning.

"Maybe," said Charlie, refusing to be flustered. "But I think we ought to go over a few ground rules, just to be sure we understand each other." Since he had not been invited to sit down, he contented himself with pacing. "I want to reassure you that I do not want to get caught in a morass of technicalities. For my client, to be let off a matter of legalistic procedure would be no advantage. I am not going to try to finesse a lesser charge." He saw that he had her attention. "He's a teacher, and a teacher cannot have this sort of cloud over him."

"Granted," said Sally, taking care to give nothing away, either in the tone of her voice or her posture.

"So it is in our interest to pursue the case to an acceptable conclusion. Which in this case means to determine who actually abused those girls." Charlie reached the window and swung around, headed toward the center bookcase.

"That's supposing it wasn't your client? Just for the sake of argument?" Sally said.

"Yes. My client did not abuse those girls. He did not do the things to them they claim he did. I am confident of that." He saw skepticism in her eyes. "Oh, I know that's my job, but in this case, it's also my considered opinion."

"And you'll be bringing expert testimony to prove that he is not psychologically capable of such acts," said Sally, ticking the options off on her fingers. "And you'll go after the girls on the stand until they modify their accusations, and—"

"Wait a minute," said Charlie, turning at the bookcase. "You make it sound as if there's no reason to question what those girls have sworn to. But I know you're talking to one of them today who wants to change her story."

"Oh, come on, Moon," said Sally, "you know the pattern. Women are forever trying to change the charges they bring against men. Look at the domestic-violence cases that never make it into court because the woman withdraws the complaint before the law can act. It's textbook standard. You know the statistics on convictions, too. Most of the time the offenders get off. So tell your teacher that he doesn't have much to worry about."

"You don't get it," said Charlie. "This teacher wants the one who abused those girls caught. He wants the man punished. And he wants to be free of any taint from this case. He does not want to be the object of whispers and stares for the rest of his life. And you can't blame him."

"I sure as hell can, if he's guilty," said Sally with sudden emotion. "You've done your bit. Now get out of here. You might stop and pick up the most recent discovery material—save us having to messenger it over to your office." She consulted her watch. "I've got a very full day, and I'm sure you do, too."

Charlie stopped pacing. "Okay. I wanted to straighten a few things out. I'll talk to you later, Sally."

"Up yours, Charlie," she said as she pointed him out the door.

Melissa Budge had just arrived when Charlie walked into his office. He paused to order tea from Merek and pick up his messages before hurrying down the hall, saying, "I'm sorry, Ms. Budge. I didn't mean to leave you by yourself like this." He put his case down beside his desk but did not sit.

"That's all right; I've been here no more than two minutes." She smiled a little but her expression was distracted. "You have no idea how difficult this is for me."

"Oh, I think I can imagine," said Charlie, remembering times when clients had suddenly pulled a complete turnaround with him. "And I'm grateful you're willing to talk to me."

"Well, I feel I have to, for poor Mister Girouard's case, you see." She gave an apologetic little cough. "I hope I'm doing the right thing."

"You are," said Charlie at once. "Please believe that, Ms. Budge."

"I suppose you have to say that, don't you?" she asked, her face forlorn.

"It's the truth, Ms. Budge," said Charlie, trying to find some way to ease her sense of betrayal. He walked over to her and took the chair beside hers. He hoped she would feel less apprehensive if he did not barricade himself behind his desk. "And wouldn't you rather we discuss this now than have to deal with it in court."

"You mean that we won't?" she asked, her face brightening.

"I really don't know, Ms. Budge. I would like to think we can avoid this, but it may be necessary to introduce the Maple girl's change of accusation into the testimony in court, and very likely you'll be the one called upon to do it." He knew she did not want to hear that; she winced as he told her.

She nodded, still flustered. "What troubles me the most is how plausible Wendy's explanation is. She told me that she and the others had agreed that Frank Girouard was the one they would accuse because he was the most understanding, and he wouldn't get mad." She bit her lower lip. "Oh, dear, it's so distressing, speaking this way about the girls. It sounds as if I don't believe them, and I do."

Charlie nodded. "So do I, Ms. Budge. And I want to know who really did those things to them so we can stop him." He shifted in the chair so that he faced her more easily. "That's why it's so important that we know they were using Frank Girouard to protect themselves. We need to have something that the court can recognize. Wendy Maple is being a very courageous girl, coming forward this way."

"Well, she's a little more . . . self-examining than the others. And I think this whole experience was very hard on her, because of her . . . sexual orientation. She's already gone through so much, and then this . . ." Large tears formed in her eyes and she pulled off her glasses, then reached for her leather tote handbag. "I knew I was going to do this. I'm very sorry, Mister Moon. Most of the time, in my work, I can control it, but sometimes, it builds up, and then . . ." She found a packet of tissues and pulled three out. "I feel so badly for these girls. The trouble is, I know what things like this can do to kids. It isn't going to be over this year or next year. Wendy's family's trying to help her face it as best they can. The Hawkinses are not doing well, but that's because they're in the middle of a divorce and each parent is blaming the other, which makes Michelle feel responsible for everything."

"Ms. Budge," said Charlie, "you don't have to tell me this."

"Do you mean I shouldn't?" She looked directly at him, her eyes not quite focused without her glasses, her hand still lifted to dab at her tears.

"No," Charlie answered very gently. "No, I mean that if you don't want to tell me, you don't have to."

"You'll find it out, anyway, won't you?" she asked, her tone sensible while she continued to weep.

"Probably," said Charlie. "But I don't want you to think you . . . that you did not behave properly."

She nodded. "Yes. I can see what you mean." She wiped her eyes again. "Oh, gracious, this is difficult. I want the girls to tell the truth, but I don't want to make their ordeal any worse than it has been. But I see what's happening to them, and I'm afraid for them." She was crying again, without sobbing. "The Twayns are all seeing a therapist, and that seems to be working pretty well. The Westfords . . . they're convinced that Emma being so intelligent can put this into perspective—that is their phrase—without any more unpleasantness. They've said they don't want her dwelling on it. I dread thinking what could happen to that girl. The Camberwells are having trouble; Ruth's father is not very mature, and Ruth, and her mother, big-sister him. In a situation like this . . ." She had used up her tissues and rummaged in her bag for another. "I trust this will remain confidential, Mister Moon?"

"If it is possible, yes," said Charlie. "If I must use what you tell me to defend my client, then I may have to ask you questions on the stand about what you've said. But I would have to ask you similar questions in any case, if it comes to that."

She considered the answer. "I do understand. Yes. I accept your caveat, Mister Moon." Her hands trembled as she held her fresh tissues. "But if I don't tell you, it could mean that Frank will remain under suspicion. That would be as bad as letting him go free if he were guilty."

Merek tapped on the door. "Coffee and tea," he called out.

"Come in," said Charlie, glad for the mild distraction he supplied. "And thanks."

Merek put the tray down on the side table, diplomatically paying no attention to Melissa Budge's distress. "A call came from Mickey Trang," he said as he set out the milk and sugar packets. "It's fairly urgent."

"Ask him if he's free for lunch," said Charlie. "That's the first hole in my schedule this morning. And let me know what the answer is."

"My pleasure," said Merek as he headed out of the room.

Melissa Budge held up her cup gratefully. "It's so warm," she said inconsequently. "Thank goodness."

Charlie did not press her. He picked up his cup, pleased that Merek had provided Earl Grey, stirred it, then set the spoon aside. "Tell me about Wendy again." At least, he knew, he was getting somewhere in Frank Girouard's case. He was prepared to take all the time necessary to hear what Melissa Budge had to say. He sat back and listened as she began to speak.

"Charlie Moon, this is Cadao Talbot," said Mickey Trang as Charlie finally reached their table at the back of the crowded Greek restaurant.

"Moon," said Cadao as he shook Charlie's hand. He was dressed in dark slacks, turtleneck and jacket; he did not look like a teenager now.

"Mister Talbot," said Charlie, sliding into the chair. "What's so urgent?"

"Remember that picture I showed you?" Mickey asked, his expression somber. "Well, Cadao bought it—I told you about that? And there's been some new developments along those lines."

Cadao Talbot nodded. "I've been going to the Space Station, that hangout on Balboa with all the *Star Trek* posters, both generations. Most of the kids come from Parkside High, Richmond Middle School and Saint Clair's High. I was there yesterday afternoon and stayed late. Something happened." Quickly and succinctly he recounted the details of Paco's visit to the Space Station. "He had a lot of Polaroids with him, and he's trying to get more. This guy's a serious recruiter. He was doing a sell job on the boys, but I'd wager he's already courting a few of the girls on his own. The boys turned him down, at least for the time being, but I don't know what they might decide to do in a day or two. Who knows, some of them might think it's macho to get a girl to do that." He looked directly at Charlie. "Those boys have been buying pictures and who-knows-what-else from Paco. I think it's part of a pattern."

"And you think it has something to do with Frank Girouard," said Charlie, recalling everything Melissa Budge had told him that morning.

"Yes. I think your man's been set up. I think the whole thing comes back to this Paco, and whoever's working with him." Cadao hesitated, doing his best to remain calm.

"You think Paco isn't working alone?" Charlie prompted.

"That's right," said Cadao. "I thought about it all last night, and the more I went over it, the more it seemed to me that he had to have a partner of some kind. He's some kind of front man, I think. He's the one who sells the pictures and scouts the girls. But he's the wrong type. Kids . . . girls are wary of guys like Paco, most of them, anyway. I figure that someone else takes the pictures. That way Paco can do his job without worrying that someone is going to come after him." He made a quick, condemning gesture. "He's slime."

Charlie listened with interest. "All right. Let's say you're right. It means that you're talking about a ring of some kind."

"Maybe, or just a small operation." He looked at Mickey. "I want to follow the guy—Paco—if I can find him again. I want to know the kind of setup he's got."

"And you want to find out who else is involved," Charlie added, certain he was right.

"That's part of it," said Cadao. "The rest is that . . . I get a very bad feeling about Paco. It's his eyes. He's got the maddest— insane mad—eyes I've ever seen."

"We've been arguing about this," said Mickey impatiently. "Gail says no, absolutely not, no following. It's not directly connected to the case and if Paco is a wholesale crazy, the last thing you want to do is get on his tail. I mean it, Cadao," he went on, addressing his associate. "You're asking for trouble if you try."

"Hey," Cadao protested, "I'm not an amateur. I know how to go after guys like that. He won't see me. And maybe it has everything to do with this case."

Mickey shook his head emphatically, but glanced at Charlie. "What do you think?"

"I think it might have some bearing on the case," he said slowly. "But not enough to take chances over. If this guy is selling pictures, inform the cops. It doesn't violate client confidentiality, and the cops could put more men on it."

The restaurant noise grew louder as a group of reporters from the *Chronicle* came in, calling greetings to other regulars.

"Cops," Cadao scoffed, raising his voice as much to be heard as to express his scorn. "Sure. And they could screw it up, and then our hands would really be tied." He slapped at the table. "I'm not going to do anything stupid, Mickey. I just want to get something real worthwhile on this Paco so we'll have something more than a misdemeanor to put on him." He looked at Charlie. "I teach martial arts. I can take care of myself."

"He's the best we've got," Mickey confirmed. "Which is why I don't want anything to happen to you," he added to Cadao.

"Hold off awhile," Charlie recommended. "It might not be necessary, and why take chances when you don't have to."

"Shit!" said Cadao, and Mickey stared at him. "You saw that picture. You should have heard how that guy was talking. He's poison clear through."

The waiter was threading his way toward their table, and belatedly Mickey handed Charlie a menu. "Get anything that has lamb, eggplant or spinach in it," he recommended.

"Order for me," said Charlie, and gave his attention to Cadao again. "If I thought we needed to get more on Paco, I'd say so. I accept that he's wrong clear through, I won't argue about that. I respect hunches and all the rest of it. All the more reason to keep your distance unless you have to check him out."

"I don't like it," Cadao said before ordering the lamb, onions and rice special. He glowered at Mickey. "It's not responsible, letting him get away with taking those pictures."

"It's not our job to stop him," Mickey said. "Get that through your head, okay?" He placed an order for Charlie and himself.

"I don't like it," said Cadao very quietly.

"Let it go," Mickey told him. "Enjoy your lunch. You did a good job."

Cadao repeated, "I don't like it."

Hearing the determination in Cadao's words, Charlie felt a pinprick of inner chill, and though it faded quickly, he worried.

TEN

FOR THE FIRST time in over a week Frank Girouard looked as if he could dare to hope. "Wendy says it wasn't me?" he repeated, staring at Charlie across the bridge table in Elizabeth's television-cum-game room. Elizabeth herself was at the theater with friends and was not expected for another two hours.

"According to what Melissa Budge told me; I gather that the prosecution is going over the statements of the other girls." Charlie braced his elbows on the table. "If the other girls decide to . . . change their stories, then you're clear."

"Not completely," said Frank quietly. "Not so long as the man gets away with it." Some of his doubts returned. "And how likely is that?"

"A lot more likely now than it was two days ago," said Charlie, determined to keep Frank from sinking back into depression. "There's a very good chance that we'll never go to trial on this, not if just one other girl agrees that they chose you because they thought you were their most sympathetic teacher." He paused. "And probably at least one of them had a crush on you at some time. That happens in junior high, doesn't it?"

"Sure," said Frank with a faint smile. "But it doesn't mean anything most of the time. It fades quickly."

"Most of the time," Charlie reiterated. "My guess is that a crush would make it easier to say you were the one. Not only would you be understanding, it was more tolerable for the girl to think you had done something pleasant to her instead of what actually took place." He went on with some emphasis, "We're rapidly getting into the area of reasonable doubt, and that makes your position much stronger."

"I suppose it could be like that; that the girls thought I wouldn't mind. Kids have strange reasons for some of the things they do. Why not?" said Frank a little distantly. He looked up and shook his head once, his eyes clouded with apprehension. "I've got to tell you, though, when I think of going back into a classroom, I get so scared . . ."

Charlie had anticipated something of the sort, and he did his best to counteract the worries that possessed Frank. "Remember the old saw about being thrown by a horse? You need to teach again, Frank, just so you know that you can." He patted the table. "You'll manage it, Frank. I know you can manage it."

"Maybe. The trouble is, I don't know for sure that I want to," he admitted, feeling ashamed of himself. "I don't know that I'd ever trust my students, not the way I used to. And the way the school's acted—" He sighed heavily.

"And your wife as well." Charlie knew better than to try to excuse Angelique Girouard to Frank; not only did he have little sympathy for her himself, he realized Frank was changing his mind about her. "You haven't had very much support, have you?"

"No." He looked away from Charlie. "I thought she was just scared. Maybe it was because she's pregnant, I thought it was okay because she needed protection. I was wrong. I had a letter from her, from Angelique. She says she's going to stay with her aunt."

Charlie had been prepared for this, but he still felt deep sympathy for Frank. "I'm sorry," he said.

"She's not asking for a divorce. She doesn't believe in divorce. She wants a separate maintenance or something like that. She wants our child to grow up away from me, but she insists I support him or her." He tried to smile and failed dismally. "She's convinced the kid's going to be a boy and she'll have the chance to raise him right, better than his father."

"She'll change her mind," Charlie said, not at all certain she would. "And she can't refuse you reasonable visitation."

"If she still thinks I'm a child molester, she'll do everything she can to keep me away from her and the child." His face crumbled and he turned around in his chair so that Charlie could not see his tears.

"There's no reason for her to think that. If she does, and you're in the clear, then there are legal remedies you can seek." He spoke steadily, soothingly. "You don't know if she's going to do anything so drastic. Give her a little time. Let's get you cleared first, and then we'll go to work on your wife."

Bringing himself under control, he swung round again. "The trouble is, I'm beginning to wonder if I want to bother. Oh, not about the kid, that's not what I mean. But I don't know if I want to be married to a woman who actually thinks I'm capable of sexually abusing children. Maybe it's just as well she stay in Auburn. Maybe I ought to stop fighting."

Although Charlie thought that this was the most sensible thing Frank had said about his marriage, he held his tongue. "Wait awhile, until the case is resolved, and then you can decide about your wife. Really, Frank, one hurdle at a time. It's easier that way." He had seen the pattern before: a client faced with two or three legal problems would elect to concentrate on the least pressing one as a means to escape the demands of the most pressing one. "You need to have this case behind you."

"That's the truth," said Frank, now sounding exhausted. "Was that just bullshit, about not going to trial?"

"No, not bullshit," said Charlie. "It's up to the District Attorney, of course, but if Wendy's statement convinces them, I think it's pretty unlikely that we'll have to do much beyond pretrial motions for dismissal."

"And then what?" Frank asked.

"And then it's over," said Charlie, knowing that was not entirely the case. "You can resume your work—"

"If they let me," he said darkly. "I talked to Covello the other day and he was saying something about waiting until next semester before coming back. He said it has to do with continuity."

Charlie's eyes hardened. "I'll have a little discussion with Doctor Covello. He might want to rethink his position."

Frank got up and wandered toward the thirty-eight-inch TV. "What if he's right? What if it really would be too upsetting to the kids for me to come back now? It could be he's right, and that's asking too much of them. They have the sexual abuse thing and Susan Lake's death to deal with. Maybe having me back would be more than they can handle."

"Cut it out," said Charlie mildly. "That's ludicrous."

"I doubt it," said Frank. "But it doesn't matter." He tried to stand a little straighter. "First thing is to get rid of the charge against me, right? And then I worry about this other stuff, like my marriage and earning a living and what's been in the papers? Isn't that what you've been telling me all evening?"

"That's about it," said Charlie, relieved that Frank had at last accepted his priorities.

Gail Harris and Cadao Talbot had not been sleeping together long enough for them to know each other's rhythm, or where to put their elbows, and as a result often woke one another during the night. Tonight was worse than usual, for Cadao had been uneasy and restless for several hours.

She propped herself on her elbow and yawned. "Not again."

He thrashed his upper body out of the covers. "Sorry." He leaned over to kiss her cheek and got her eyebrow instead. "I can't stay asleep."

"You've been tossing for hours." She leaned a little nearer to him, seeking to balance against his upper arm. After a first miss, she found his shoulder. "What's the matter? Something bothering you?"

He gave her a quick, rueful smile. "You won't believe me if I say no, will you?"

"Probably not," she said, one hand tentatively brushing his chest. She had not yet learned if he liked being seduced out of melancholy.

He nodded. "And you'll keep at it, right?"

"This?" she asked, moving her hand more boldly.

"Not just that," he said, catching her fingers in his own. "Not right now."

"You mean being awake," she said, hesitating to settle beside him just yet. "Well, as long as you keep waking me up, I guess it's only fair." She tried to read his expression in the dark but without success. "Besides, Cadao, I love you. I don't like to see you worried and upset."

For her sake he smiled a little. "Okay. Sure. What the hell." He moved so that they were both more comfortable, but he held her as if she could shield him from what he said. "It's the case we're doing for Charlie Moon. It's getting to me."

"The sexual abuse thing, about the teacher?" Gail asked. "That kind of thing gets to me, too." She took a chance. "Do you want off the case?"

"Christ, no! I don't . . ." He released her and rolled onto his back. "When I spend all day trying to find the guys who do the things those guys have done, I . . . I don't know. I want you, and at the same time, I don't want to do anything that's like what they do. I . . . I can't explain it."

She took a chance and put her head on his arm. Like him, she stared up at the ceiling. "I do understand. I think I do. I know how I feel when we investigate rape cases. More than anything I want someone to hold me, and it's also the last thing I want."

"Un-huh," he said, some of the tension fading from his voice. "I've got to get those guys, Gail." He reached out for her hand, and after two tries, caught it in his. "Not for that teacher or for Moon, but for me. I can't stand it. It makes me sick, what that guy Paco was selling, the way he sold it, and the way he conned those high school boys to get girls for him, so he could take more of those damned pictures!" His voice had risen, but he forced himself to speak more softly. "I can't give you . . . as long as they're taking those pictures, it's in the way, between us."

She heard something in his tone that alarmed her. "Cadao, you can't take it on yourself. That's not what we do. You get the information, but no direct action, no following. You promised me," said Gail, the first line of worry firming between her brows. "I don't want you taking risks for something the cops could do." She rolled toward him, her words growing softer. "I don't want you taking risks, period."

"Yeah," he said, releasing her hand and pulling her closer. "But it makes me nuts, Gail. That creep out there, walking around with those Polaroid shots in his pockets and . . ." He kissed her, but in a distracted way. "I want to stop him. Shit, I want to break him in pieces."

"You're helping a lot, Cadao. You're making a difference." She was baffled by his state of mind.

"I know. But it's not enough." He kissed her with more attention this time, and was silent as he touched her face. "When I met you last year, I never thought—"

"Well, I did," she said, hoping her candor would reach him.

"I didn't think someone like you—"

"We've been all through this. So you're part Asian and I'm not. Why does that have to be a problem?" She realized that if she had to argue this as well, she was likely to cry.

"People stare," he said remotely.

"In San Francisco?" She drove her fist into her pillow. "The only reason they'd stare is because you're so good-looking."

"That must be it." He rested his hand against her face, then once again drew back. "It's not enough. Someone has to stop that guy."

"Someone isn't you," said Gail, the first edge of irritation in her words. "This one we leave to the cops. And don't disparage the cops. They're not all yahoos," she added in an attempt to forestall his complaint.

"But they'll fuck it up," said Cadao darkly. "They'll do something wrong, the way that Sergeant did, and they'll blow it." He grabbed her and held her tightly. "And they'll get off."

"Don't worry about it, Cadao," she whispered. "It'll work out. They'll get stopped."

"How?" He looked away from her, though he did not release her. "The guy's still out there. Oh, I can identify Paco and say I heard him asking high school boys to get their girls to pose for him, but what's that worth in court, without something real?"

"You've got that Polaroid shot. That's real," she said, doing her best to mask her distaste.

He slapped the pillow with his far hand. "Gail, oh, God, I'm sorry. I've got no business doing this to you. I shouldn't bring this home."

She found a way to brace herself over him. "Hey. We're almost *living* together. You let me bitch about the clients all through dinner." She smiled as she moved closer. "Cadao. Please."

"I shouldn't do this to you," he muttered, not quite shoving her off him, but trying to get away from her. He made himself relax. "See what I mean? I shouldn't do this to you."

Her voice was so soft he could barely hear it. "If it bothers you, it matters to me. Cadao, I take you seriously. Don't you get that yet?"

This time his manner was different, gentler, more tender. "I guess I don't. Not yet. More fool me." The anger went out of him. "But I wish I could—"

"It's not your responsibility. It's not your fault," she said, coaxing him away from his preoccupation with quick, light caresses.

"Not there; I'm ticklish," he said, stopping her as she reached the top of his hip. He rolled her off him once more, but did not move away from her. "Even if they catch him, he won't have to answer for what he's done. Something will happen and he'll find a reporter to defend him and a lawyer who'll bring up a technicality or some old statute that gets him off." Abruptly he tangled his free hand in her hair, relishing the texture of it, the lightness of it. "God, you feel good."

"You've finally noticed," she said, only half joking.

"You feel good all over, don't you?" He reached to pull her leg over his thigh.

"So do you," she whispered, taking care not to touch his ticklish places.

He guided her hand lower, hardening as her fingers closed around him. "Right there," he sighed, falling silent as she stroked him. His body arched. "How'd I get lucky enough to sleep with the boss?"

"You got lucky enough to sleep with Gail Harris; nobody's boss here, not here," she corrected him as she felt him shiver in anticipation. The first time they had made love, she had been so nervous that she could not feel those little tremors pass through him; now she was learning to evoke them. "What about me? I got lucky enough to sleep with Cadao Talbot."

"Not that we sleep all that much," he murmured as he bent to tongue her nipples; she responded more quickly now than she had two weeks ago. Her excitement increased his own.

They ran out of words then, and left understanding to their bodies.

Victor Lovejoy and George Wycliff were already waiting in the conference room when Morgan arrived. She looked at the two men and was immediately on her guard. "I wasn't expecting to see you here, Victor; this must be more important than your message indicated," she said, her manner just cordial enough to be professional. "You're busy most mornings, aren't you."

"George thought it would be a good idea if I came along, since it concerns the Ferrand farrago." He smiled, and Morgan could not help but wonder how long he had labored to come up with that quip, or how often she would hear it before he grew tired of it.

"Is that what this is about?" Morgan asked as she tried to decide which of the remaining three chairs to take. "Who else are we expecting?" she asked, curious to know why they were having this meeting at all."

"Forbes and his attorney," said George Wycliff, so elaborately casually that Morgan realized he was acting beyond his authority.

"Why?" she asked.

It was Victor Lovejoy who answered. "It's about that videotape—the one we've heard so much speculation about. Since you were the one Massie talked to about it, we assumed you would want to be present for this . . . informal interview."

"How do you define informal?" Morgan inquired, deciding on the seat that was furthest from Wycliff and Lovejoy.

"No notes, no official record," said Wycliff. "We want to find out as much as we can about this videotape."

"I can just imagine," said Morgan, smoothing her skirt. In the hard, cold glare of the fluorescent lights, her new teal suit appeared dull brackish green. "Does Forbes know what he's getting into?"

"He's bringing his attorney," said Wycliff with a downward turn of his mouth. "He must suspect something."

"But if the material was improperly seized, it isn't usable," Morgan reminded them. "And you know it."

"Yes," said Lovejoy, and something changed in his face. "But we want the tape. Sergeant Mitchell has said that he might be able to identify the victim if the tape is . . . what Massie told you it was. There is a missing person report." He looked quickly away from Morgan. "There is reason to suppose it might—"

"You mean it might have some bearing on a different case?" Morgan said. "It's still improperly taken. It can't be used in evidence. If you're planning to hang something else on Ferrand, you can't use contaminated evidence to do it, Victor."

"Not in evidence, perhaps, but it could . . . identify the missing girl Mitchell is . . ." Lovejoy was pale about the mouth. "It would mean her family wouldn't have to wonder."

Morgan shook her head. "Do you think they'll be relieved, knowing she was sexually tortured to death?" It was difficult for her to contain her outrage, though she recognized the pragmatism of these men.

There was a discreet knock on the door, then two men came into the room. Even without an introduction, Morgan knew that the tall young man in the sports jacket and jeans, dark-haired and blue-eyed, who bore himself with Byronic stoicism was Bennet Forbes, Ed Massie's former partner. His attorney was Neal Lester, a fussy, balding fellow in an expensive but ill-fitting suit who did not often stray from civil into criminal court.

"Good morning, Mister Lovejoy, Mister Wycliff, Your Honor," said Lester nervously.

There were a few muttered responses; Forbes watched it all with what he presented as cool contempt.

"Please sit down," said Wycliff, indicating the two remaining chairs.

Forbes chose the one nearest Morgan, taking time to slouch into the chair, deliberately insolent. He looked over at her, favoring her with a slow smile. "Morning, Your Honor."

"We're here," said Wycliff with a disapproving glower at Forbes, "to discuss a certain . . . item that is of interest in an ongoing missing person case, a case we have reason to believe was an abduction."

Lester looked uneasily from Wycliff to Lovejoy, not yet sitting down. "Does this have any bearing on my client's current—"

"Of course it does," said Forbes.

"Not directly, and this is in reference to the . . . item in question, not to the manner in which the item was obtained," said Lovejoy. "And we are willing to consider his cooperation as mitigating in any final decisions in that case."

Forbes whistled softly and shook his fingers, giving a sly glance at Morgan. "Fancy, fancy."

"Stop it, Forbes," said Lester in an undervoice.

"Pay attention to your attorney, Mister Forbes," Wycliff cautioned him. "We need not continue this discussion if you would prefer not to."

Forbes shrugged. "What the fuck." He put his hand to his mouth. "Oops. Naughty me."

"Mister Forbes," said Wycliff coldly.

Lester put his hand on Forbes' shoulder. "Ben, please. You know what we talked about on the way over." He looked at Morgan. "Sorry, Your Honor." He increased the pressure on Forbes' shoulder.

Forbes folded his hands in his lap. "Yessir," he said in mendacious contrition.

This was not promising: Morgan looked at Wycliff, giving him a little time to recover. "Is there some point to this meeting, or is it merely a gesture?" she asked when she was certain she would have the attention of the District Attorney.

"I was hoping we could learn something," said Wycliff.

Lester was fully cognizant of the warning inherent in that exchange. He sat down nervously. "I'm sure my client does not mean to . . . to interfere with your inquiry, since it is not official."

"Really," said Lovejoy, unable to conceal his skepticism.

"Shall we try again, Mister Forbes?" he inquired, looking at the former cop.

Forbes started to say something, then stopped. He looked down at his folded hands. "Sure."

Wycliff sighed. "Mister Forbes, I am not asking you to say that you broke into Scooter Ferrand's house and stole a videotape of two men sexually torturing a young woman to death. That would be an admission, and it would compromise your case. I am going to ask you, however, if you have such a videotape in your possession?"

"It's possible," said Forbes, his eyes wary though he spoke laconically.

"If it is possible that you have such a videotape, is it also possible you would permit Sergeant Glen Mitchell to examine that videotape, pursuant to the missing person case we have already indicated may be an abduction?" Wycliff looked from Forbes to Lester.

"What purpose would this serve, again?" asked Lester, his manner revealing how nervous he was.

"It could provide identification," said Wycliff shortly. "You understand that the girl in question has been missing for some time; an identification would close the investigation. And that would be much appreciated."

Some of his irritating pose faded. "You mean that Mitchell is after Ferrand, too?"

"No," said Wycliff quickly. "There is no evidence whatsoever to link Mister Ferrand to this missing person. We ask you to show the tape to Sergeant Mitchell to permit identification of the victim only."

Morgan, who had deliberately kept silent, now said, "And if Sergeant Mitchell were after Ferrand, as you put it, your seizure of the tape, as your illegal seizure of other evidence, would render the prosecution's use of the tape impossible. You would be responsible for letting Ferrand go free a second time, Mister Forbes."

He rounded on her, no longer lazy. "That's pure shit, lady. Ferrand's guilty as sin, and everyone in this room knows it."

"Mister Forbes!" Wycliff admonished as Lester put his hand on Forbes' arm to restrain him.

"Ben, please."

Morgan refused to be distracted. "This is the truth, Mister Forbes, whether you like it or not. You have ignored procedure not once but very likely twice, and both those actions may well serve to guarantee Ferrand his freedom. That isn't the work of a good cop, Forbes, it's the work of a bent one." She met his irate gaze coolly. "If you will not observe the law, you are no different than any other criminal. The fact that you wrap your illegal actions in the name of justice only serves to make your illegal crime more reprehensible." She stood up. "Do you mind, gentlemen, if I leave?"

"Your Honor . . ." said Lester, acutely embarrassed by his client. "I'm certain there'll be no repeat of what—"

"If you wish, Your Honor," said George Wycliff. "Since you have been so good as to clarify our position for us. It might be easier if Mister Forbes is given the chance to consider his answer."

Morgan shook her head. "Whatever deal you cut, I hope it does something to helping Mitchell. To be candid, I think Forbes has no business in any branch of law enforcement, and I hope you will insist he answer for some of what he has done. However, if you must trade Forbes' conviction for an opportunity to lock Ferrand up a good long time, well—" She shrugged. "I've seen worse."

Ben Forbes laughed. "They're not going to put me away, Your Honor. I've already got a job lined up doing research-site security for one of the Silicon Valley giants. I'll take my slap on the wrist and get out of your hair."

Her voice was soft, and for that reason the men in the room listened to her closely. "Mister Forbes, if you were in my court, I give you my word you would receive more than a slap on the wrist. If you were in my court, I would require you to serve the greatest amount of time permissible under law. Whether cops or storm troopers, when the police do not obey the law, then justice is dead."

Forbes lifted his hands as if he intended to applaud, but saw the warning in Lester's eyes, and changed the motion to an offhand salute. "Yessir, Your Honor, sir," he called after Morgan as she left the little conference room.

It was after five when Mickey Trang showed up at Charlie Moon's office unannounced and upset. "I don't like what I'm thinking," he declared as soon as Charlie closed his office door.

"And that is?" asked Charlie, who had not been able to make much sense out of anything Mickey had said since he arrived. "What's going on that you're prowling around this way?"

"Gail's in San Diego today and tonight. It's for another client. We've got three more trips down there the next couple of weeks. She left word that she wanted me to put Cadao on something that would keep him busy." His hands had been deep in his jacket pockets, but now he thrust them into the air to express his frustration. "She's going to have my hide."

"What's wrong?" Charlie asked with unaccountable apprehension.

"I gave him an assignment I thought would keep him out of trouble." He did not so much pace as wander forcibly about the room. "We've been hired to find some heirs. They were flower children back in the sixties, dropped out and went heaven-knows-where. I should have figured he'd pull a stunt like this. I don't know what I'm going to tell Gail."

"Why do you have to tell her?" Charlie sat down at his desk hoping that perhaps Mickey would light, too.

His hands slapped down at his sides, and behind his exasperation there was something darker and more desperate. "They're lovers, that's why. They've been edging toward living together for the last three months. She's not going to like it if anything happens to him."

After a first startled blink, Charlie nodded. "I see."

"You don't know how . . ." He held himself back. "That part isn't your business." Belatedly he added, "No offense, Charlie."

"None taken," Charlie said honestly. "But perhaps you'd better explain this to me, all of it, if you please. What's Cadao done?"

"He's disappeared," said Mickey, and sat down, as if that admission had used up all his strength. "He went on the heir-hunt this morning, called me at noon to update his progress. I saw him over at the Hall of Records about three, when he gave me a couple of pages of information on one of the heirs. It shouldn't be hard to locate the guy now. He was supposed to go home—back to Gail's flat, that is—but when I called there half an hour ago, he'd left a message for Gail. He said he thinks he has to try one more time. Whatever that means. I don't like it."

"Which means you have some idea what he's up to," said Charlie with deep certainty that he could sense Cadao's intentions.

Mickey nodded heavily. "Yeah. I think it's still the Girouard case, in a way. I think it's the guy with the pictures. He came up with another name—Mal—and that, along with Paco, is what he's got to go on. Or so I think."

"You're implying that he held something back," Charlie said.

"That Paco guy's been under Cadao's skin for days." Mickey

made a gesture of resignation and aggravation. "I'll bet our entire fee for the case that Cadao's got more information than he admitted, and now that he has two names, he's after those guys—Paco and Mal. Cadao's the kind of man who'd pull a stupid stunt like this." In those last condemning words there was tremendous respect.

"Are you wishing he'd asked you along?" Charlie ventured, aware that Mickey was damning himself as much as Cadao Talbot.

"No." He paused. "Yes. I don't like that stuff any better than he does. And shit, he knows better than to go off this way, winging it, without some kind of check-in or backup in place. It's a dangerous, foolish trick."

"It could be worse than that," said Charlie in a neutral tone. "That's what's really bothering you: you're afraid that Cadao's got in over his head and you don't know how to get him out."

"That's part of it," Mickey said grudgingly, the droop of his shoulders a greater admission than his words.

"You think he might have taken on more than he can handle. And you're afraid that there's a chance the guy with the pictures could be dangerous," Charlie finished for him.

"Yeah," said Mickey. "Yeah, that's the worst part of it. I know it isn't usual for someone in . . . that line of work to be violent. That's not what they do. But I keep coming back to something Cadao said, about the man's eyes."

"Mad eyes," Charlie supplied.

"That's it," said Mickey. "And Cadao's convinced that the man isn't working alone. In that case, if he's following Paco, he could—" He stopped abruptly.

"He certainly could," said Charlie, reaching for his telephone.

"What are you doing?" Mickey was alarmed; he got to his feet at once.

"I'm calling Sergeant Mitchell, to let him know about this." He looked at Mickey before he punched in the number. "That's all right with you, isn't it? He's working on the Susan Lake case."

Mickey hesitated, then nodded. "Okay. Go ahead." He stared up at the ceiling. "How'm I going to tell Gail? She's calling me tonight. If she calls home and gets Cadao's message, she'll . . ." He could not express what she would do.

But Charlie understood. "All the more reason to—" He stopped as his call was answered. "Sergeant Mitchell, please. This is Charlie Moon calling." He waited. "Thank you. I'll hold."

"Do you really think he can help?" Mickey asked, his voice forlorn. "I don't think Cadao wants help from the cops."

"If he's in trouble"—and in that place within him that was wholly Ojibwa, he knew that Cadao was in desperate trouble— "he won't care if the cops or the cavalry help him," he said.

"I guess you're right," said Mickey. He turned toward the window and looked out. "We're supposed to get rain tonight."

"Don't you believe it," said Charlie, the ache in his shoulder a far more accurate forecaster than the weather reporters on the evening news. "No rain until tomorrow, and maybe not then. It could pass over us and go snow on the Sierra." He heard the operator transfer his call.

"Mitchell here. Moon?"

"Good afternoon, Sergeant Mitchell," said Charlie in his best brisk manner. "I'm sorry to disturb you, but I need some information. Are you busy with the Lake case still?"

"We don't have anyone in custody," said Glen Mitchell, his voice a little ragged. "We're working."

"Yes," said Charlie. "So is a private investigator retained by me for the Girouard case." He was no longer certain he agreed with what he said next. "I realize the cases are unrelated, but some of the investigation we've conducted has been over territory more closely tied to your case than to ours."

"Does that mean you've come up with something?" Mitchell asked with the first spark of real interest.

"Not exactly," said Charlie, choosing his words very carefully. "But the investigator seems to have disappeared. He was following a man who he had seen peddling pornographic photos to high school students. The man may be connected to your case as well as mine. The investigator was supposed to report in before now, and we've been unable to reach him."

Mitchell no longer sounded tired. "What else can you tell me?"

Charlie looked inquiringly at Mickey, and was relieved when Mickey nodded. "The investigator works for the Bay Area Investigation Agency. The offices are on—"

"I know the outfit," said Mitchell. "Who's missing?"

"Cadao Talbot, aged twenty-seven, though you wouldn't believe it to look at him. He's small, about five-four, maybe one hundred twenty-five pounds. He's Vietnamese and Latino, according to his boss," Charlie added, remembering what Mickey had told him when he had brought Cadao into the investigation.

"Okay, we'll keep an eye out for him. Do you have any idea where he might be?" Mitchell added the last automatically.

"If we did," Charlie pointed out, "I wouldn't be making this call."

"Ri-i-i-ight," said Mitchell. "How official do you want this to be?"

"For the moment, regard it as a request. If Talbot stays missing, we'll make it formal," said Charlie, ignoring the dark look Mickey shot him.

"You got it," said Mitchell. "Talbot, Cadao; twenty-seven, five four, one twenty-five. Brown and brown, I guess?"

"That's right," said Charlie.

"I'll keep him in mind. Anything else?" He was brusque now, wanting to resume his work.

"That's it. Thanks," said Charlie, and heard Mitchell hang up. "Well, he's got the description."

"Somehow," said Mickey slowly, "that doesn't make me feel any better."

"No," Charlie agreed. "Nor me."

High thin clouds wrapped the sky in white paper. Morgan was still in the shower and Charlie was finishing shaving when the phone rang. "I'll get it," he called out to his wife before he stumbled into the bedroom. "Charles Moon," he said as he lifted the receiver.

"Charlie," said Sergeant Mitchell. "Sorry to call so early, but I think you better get down here."

Cold engulfed him. "Where's here?" he asked very quietly.

In the bathroom the shower was suddenly quiet. There was the sound of the stall door opening and then the burr of a hair dryer.

Mitchell gave him an address. "It's behind that old pink-fronted church off of Potrero. There's crime-scene tape all over the place. Ask for me."

He knew the answer even as he asked, "Talbot?"

"That's what you've got to tell me," said Mitchell.

"Dead?" The cold grew deeper. He swallowed hard against it.

"The forensic team is on their way. We've closed everything off. It'll take them a little while to get everything they need." Mitchell coughed. "I tried to reach Harris."

"She's out of town," said Charlie. "I'll call Trang, if you like. He's a better choice for . . . identification than I am."

"Thanks," said Mitchell. "I don't like breaking bad news more than once in a day." He faltered. "You better warn him, Moon. You, too. It's pretty bad. You won't like what you see."

"Thanks," Charlie said quietly. "I'll get there in . . . forty minutes." It was an optimistic estimate, but he was determined to adhere to it. He hung up, his thoughts moving quickly, keeping to practical things, avoiding what he had been warned of. He could be dressed and out of the house in ten minutes if he skipped breakfast, and right now he knew that would be the wisest course.

The hair dryer was silent. "Charlie?" Morgan called from the bathroom.

He closed his eyes to concentrate. "Yes?"

"What's wrong?" Morgan asked. She had come to the doorway and stood with her towel still around her. "What is it?"

"I have to leave. I've got to make two calls right now. I'm sorry, love. It's urgent." He touched her arm, taking comfort in her aliveness.

"What is it?" She could see the dismay in his eyes and hear it in his voice. "What's wrong?"

"I've got to call Mickey Trang right now. Listen in. Then I've got to let Frank know I'll be late for our meeting this morning." He kissed her quickly, before he lifted the receiver and dialed Mickey Trang's home number, hoping that he would not have to leave this message on a machine.

To his surprise, Mickey answered on the second ring, and admitted he had been up most of the night, hoping Cadao would call.

When he was through with his brief, terrible conversation, he hurried into his clothes while Morgan watched him, her quiet expressing her concern. "I'll call you when I'm out. If you're in court, I'll leave a message."

"All right," she said, setting her towel aside and opening her underwear drawer. "If you like, I'll call Frank Girouard for you. And your office."

Charlie paused in tucking in his shirt. "Would you? I don't like to ask, but it would make things easier."

"Go ahead. You're going to have to hurry to get there when you're expected." She opened her closet and took out a peach-colored silk blouse. "Frank will understand."

"I hope so." He finished dressing and combed his hair, admitting as he did that he needed a haircut. "I'd better call Frank," he said, and picked up the telephone, pressing out Elizabeth's number quickly, as if that would speed the whole process.

Five minutes later he backed the Camry out of the garage and headed toward Fulton, glad he was a little ahead of the morning rush.

ELEVEN

Thursday and Friday

A UNIFORMED OFFICER lifted the yellow tape as Charlie identified himself. "Mitchell's over there, by the dumpster," he indicated. "He's expecting you. Watch out where you walk."

Four black-and-whites were parked in the street, serving as barriers as well as protecting the crime scene. A large, modified van from the medical examiner's office was drawn up near the dumpster, a stretcher with a folded body bag waiting beside its open rear doors, two assistants from the medical examiner's office waiting to claim the body. Half a dozen policemen were standing about the area while the forensic team measured, gathered evidence and took pictures.

Charlie saw Mitchell standing behind the dumpster, his jaw stubbled and his eyes pink with fatigue. As he approached, he raised his hand. "Sergeant," he said, coming up to Mitchell.

"You made good time," said Mitchell while they shook hands briefly.

"I tried," said Charlie, then added awkwardly, "Mickey Trang should be here shortly—fifteen minutes at most. I called him before I left the house. He was up already."

"Thanks," said Mitchell. He was in no hurry to turn around. "Look, I don't know how to say this to you, but you better prepare yourself. Take it slow." He folded his arms, using them as a shield. "I don't like asking you to go through this, but . . . before Trang gets here, will you tell me if this is your man?"

The chill that had taken hold of Charlie grew more severe. "All right. If you think it's necessary."

"Yeah. I wish it wasn't." He hunched his shoulders for more protection. "In there. In the dumpster. Get up on that box and have a look. Make sure you got a good hold. It'll help." He turned around and yelled, "Freiberg, let Moon have that box."

A pale man with an expensive camera nodded gratefully. "Sure, Sergeant." He stepped down with alacrity. "Hang on to your innards," he recommended as Charlie put his foot on the box.

The dumpster was half full, most of its contents trash: a broken chair, plastic sacks of unknown content, magazines, bottles, papers. But on top of those things, flung against the metal side, was human refuse.

There were long cuts running from his thighs to his neck, most of them superficial, three of them deep; large patches of blood had dried on his body, showing that he had died in some other position; his shoulders were massively bruised, the right one dislocated; his tongue had been cut out and his mouth slashed; he had been mutilated and partially castrated.

Charlie hung on to the side of the dumpster, determined not to vomit, though his throat burned. He closed his eyes, which only served to intensify the presence of violent death. For a moment he swayed on the box, and then he had enough control to step down. "I can't be official," he said, his voice rough. "I'm not a close enough associate, but that's Cadao Talbot." His recognition came from more than knowing his face; it was a deeper and more painful knowledge. He gathered his thoughts. "Does Mickey have . . . Christ! can't you wait until he's ready to go to the medical examiner before he has to identify him?"

"I'll do what I can," said Mitchell in a subdued tone. "They'll be getting him out of there in a little while. If Trang isn't here before then, we can work it out." His face was grim. "It's hard to ask someone to look at him. You saw the damage. You know what it means. They took their time about it. That's the worst part."

Charlie could only nod. He turned his back on the dumpster, aware that it was a futile thing to do. Cadao's death had touched him and he would not be rid of it so easily. "When was he found?"

"About six-fifteen; the call came a couple minutes afterward. A guy in the neighborhood was tossing some trash out before he left for work. We've got his preliminary statement. He's pretty shaken up." Mitchell cocked his head in the direction of the nearest squad car. "Want to sit down? You're looking a little green around the gills."

"You don't look too good yourself," said Charlie, permitting

Mitchell to draw him away from the dumpster. His hands were icy; he shoved them deep into his pockets, though he was certain that would not warm them.

"Lack of sleep. My wife had a fit. I didn't get in until close to three. I had a lead on the Lake case that fizzled. I didn't get a chance to change or shower or anything. I had dinner and turned on the TV, and the call came." He opened the squad car door. "Want to sit in the back?"

"Not if there aren't handles on the doors," said Charlie, only half in jest. He leaned on the black-and-white. "You must have called me shortly after you got here."

"About ten minutes, yeah. As soon as I was sure we didn't have any other major surprises around, if you get me." He slipped into the passenger seat, looking out the open door at Charlie. "I'm sorry if I woke you up."

"You didn't. We get up early." He was silent, watching the forensic team finish their preliminary work. "Did anyone notice anything?" God, he thought, what am I going to say to Gail? She's been sleeping with Cadao. How can I tell her what happened?

"What is it?" Mitchell asked, his expression sympathetic.

Charlie steadied himself. "You know the answer to that."

Mitchell folded his arms again. "I don't know if anyone noticed anything. We haven't started asking questions. If he was . . . left there before five, I don't think anyone was up, or if they were, they're not going to reveal what they saw. People around here are pretty careful."

"Um-hum," said Charlie, the clammy presence of death holding on to him, algid tendrils clinging to him . . . He forced himself to speak. "How long do you think he's been dead?"

"Five, six hours. It's hard to tell, the shape he's in. Postmortem lividity only tells us he didn't die in that dumpster, that he probably hasn't been dead very long, though with the amount of blood he's lost, it makes a difference. We'll know more later." His jaw was tight and square. "We got to get this guy, these guys."

"You think it's more than one?" Charlie would not look toward the dumpster as the medical examiner's assistants climbed in to bring out the body.

"Yeah. It's a question of styles. One of them's a real slasher, goes hard and deep. The other teases, gives lots of little cuts in lots of places." His eyes were dark with raw hatred.

"But couldn't that be one man?" Charlie asked, the image of Cadao's body strong in his mind. "One crazy man?"

"It could be, but it isn't." He stared down at his sturdy, scuffed shoes. "You get so you recognize signatures. Whoever did this, it was the same two who killed Susan Lake. I know it. For sure."

"Is there any evidence to support you?" Charlie asked. "I don't doubt your feeling, but . . . in court you need more."

Mitchell looked at him. "They washed her body? I told you about that. But not all of it. Just the outside. We found semen— two men. They're getting the DNA typing on the samples." He looked at Charlie. "That's part of what we're withholding. Keep that to yourself."

"Fine with me."

The corpse was out of the dumpster now, being eased into a body bag. The rigor had made it stiff enough that this was a difficult task.

"They'll be leaving as soon as Trang gives them a proper identification," said Mitchell, doing his best to sound disinterested.

"At least he didn't have to see—" Charlie offered no more complete description.

"Yeah. That's something." He put his hand to his head. "We're going to be here a while with Homicide. Them and Forensics. Because of the possible connection to the Lake case." He rubbed at his stubbled face. "I'm going to try to get home by noon. My wife'll probably be waiting with a meat cleaver. I'm going to clean up, take a nap. Maybe I'll give you a call later on. You going to be in court today?"

"Not today," said Charlie. "I'll be at the office in the afternoon, and at home in the evening, unless I have to—"

"Mickey Trang's here," said Mitchell, getting out of the squad car. He stretched and ran his hand over his fading ginger hair. "I hate this part. It's always worse than . . . God, the poor guy, having to do this. You want to talk to him, or shall I?"

"Both," said Charlie, and started toward the edge of the cordoned area, raising his hand so that Mickey would see him and stop arguing with the uniformed police officer who blocked his way.

It took a much greater effort than usual for Charlie to concentrate on what Frank Girouard was saying. "How did the tests go?" he asked, determined to pay attention to Frank's answer.

"Well enough, I suppose," was Frank's careful reply. "The trouble with being a teacher, I guess, is you get test-wise. I kept trying to psych out the questions that were psyching *me* out. And some of the interpretation stuff was pretty wild."

"But generally you felt that you got through them all right?" Charlie persisted. "You didn't get too frightened?"

"I suppose. I don't really know what 'all right' is in a case like this. I've got more tests tomorrow, including that vocal-stress thing. I don't know what good that will do—I'm stressed out now." He put his hands together, fingertips to heels. "Elizabeth's been wonderful."

"She's like that," said Charlie absently. "There isn't a better ally in the world."

"She's real fond of you, too," said Frank, a little amusement in his voice. "She sure roars a lot."

"That she does," Charlie agreed, thinking he could use a dose of her staunch good sense about now. "I've got to ask you some more questions about Sutro Glen. And I don't want any punches pulled, no evasions, no watering-down, no excuses."

Frank's eyes changed, flattened. "Sure," he said without emotion.

"Stop that," said Charlie. "I'm not after you. But this morning a private investigator who was working on your case was found dead." He said it bluntly, hoping the shock would jar Frank out of his resentment. "He was murdered."

"Murdered," Frank repeated as if he had never heard the term before and did not know what it meant.

"So we need to know what can of worms we've opened here." He put his icy hand to his forehead. "I want to know about rumors, things the kids were saying that might have had bearing on this case. I want to know about any rumors about someone having girls pose for pictures in the nude. I don't mean what happened to Harness, I mean something more recent."

Frank lifted his hands. "I never heard anything."

"Oh, come on," said Charlie, his patience running short. "From what we've learned, there had to be something going on, something the kids knew about. The investigator who was killed discovered a man selling pictures to high school boys. We think he was following the salesman when he was killed. Someone must know something. There had to be some kind of talking going around."

It took a short while for Frank to speak. "You see, after Wilson Harness got into trouble, we all—well, we all wanted to get away from it. None of us wanted to be caught with it." His face darkened. "It was pretty cowardly. But we were scared it could happen to us. And it *did* happen to me, didn't it?" This last was particularly hard for him to say.

"Then there were rumors?" Charlie asked.

"Some," he admitted. "I don't know for sure. None of us knew. I didn't pay attention—deliberately."

"Tell me," said Charlie, leaning forward at the desk.

There was a longer wait for this response. "The end of last semester, one of the boys was boasting that he'd been given a hundred dollars for taking pictures of his girlfriend."

"Who gave him the money?" Charlie demanded.

"I don't know. I didn't ask. I . . . I didn't want any part of it. I told you how we all shied off from anything . . . that might turn out like Harness did."

"Go on," Charlie said.

Frank studied his hands. "I've always tried to be there for my students, to listen to them, pay attention to what they say. I really have tried, Charlie. But it's hard, doing that when you know that it could go against you. I was more willing to listen to problems at home, or conflicts with other teachers, than I was to hear what the kids had to say about . . . that kind of exploitation. And the trouble is," he went on with difficulty, "I think that once one of my students wanted to talk about something like this. It was a year ago last Christmas. Just before the holiday break one of the girls in my modern literature elective tried to tell me about a guy her boyfriend knew, someone who had wanted her to strip for him. That was the word she used. A friend of her boyfriend's wanted her to strip for him. I didn't let her go any further. I said she needed to see the Dean of Girls about it." His voice dropped. "I didn't want to get involved, not in that."

Charlie had started to doodle on his legal pad, letting the pen make its own patterns and sworls. "Wasn't that unusual?" He saw Frank nod. "Did you mention this to anyone at the time?"

"Only to Angelique. I told you, it was right before Christmas break. By the time I got back, I'd pretty much put it out of my mind, and the girl didn't bring it up again."

"Too bad," said Charlie, doing his best not to sound critical.

"It was," said Frank with a heavy sigh. "And I know it. But at the time I thought I was being sensible. And it wasn't as if I were shutting all my students out—I was willing to listen to most of their problems and do what I could to help. It seemed like enough."

"But now you don't think so," said Charlie for him.

"Yeah." Frank shrugged. "I don't know what else to tell you, Charlie. I keep thinking I can come up with a reasonable excuse, but I can't. I made a decision not to turn out like Harness, and I did. That's the way it was for me." He shook his head. "I did a pretty good job with the other stuff, but I couldn't manage this. I just couldn't."

"What did you say to the girl, other than she should go to the Dean of Girls?" Charlie asked.

"That was about it. I don't know if she did. The Dean never brought it up if she did." He paused. "You could talk to her—the Dean, that is. She might be able to tell you something."

"I could," said Charlie, "but it might be better if you speak with her first, assuming you two are on reasonable terms." He added this last with some apprehension. He was acutely aware of how awkward Frank's colleagues felt about his situation.

"I can't tell you how we stand. She and I usually get along, but we're not buddies, if that's what you mean." He rubbed his face as if forcing himself to remain awake. "I rub her the wrong way, sometimes. That's not unusual between teachers and deans."

"Do you think she'll talk to me?" Charlie asked.

"I hope so. It depends on how much she's going along with Covello about me. If she thinks I really am a bad influence and all the rest of it, then she might not want to say anything."

"What would you expect her to do?" Charlie noticed that he had drawn a lion-headed knocker in his doodles.

He shrugged. "I don't know."

Charlie tried another tack. "What was the girl's name? The one who told you about the stripping?" He emphasized the lion's mane and lengthened the ring-knocker in his mouth.

"I don't know that I should tell you that. She spoke to me in confidence and she wanted our talk to remain private." He watched Charlie's pen move.

Charlie sighed. "Frank, I understand your position, but think it over, okay? I respect your desire to keep a confidence. That's commendable. But we're trying to establish a pattern here, something that will demonstrate that there is a reasonable doubt in suspecting that you are the one who sexually abused those girls. The more we can show that something very kinky was going on at that school, the more we can protect you. There's something else to think about. The Lake girl was killed, possibly by the same man or men who assaulted the five girls. And the investigator was killed, too. Someone is playing for very big stakes, much bigger than ours."

"I don't know what to do," said Frank. "I'm sorry, Charlie."

"Well, think about it, Frank," Charlie told him, his patience all but exhausted. "How the hell am I supposed to defend you if you won't help me?"

"But she's a kid, Charlie," said Frank, growing more upset, "and who knows what's happened to her since then?"

"Is that it?" Charlie asked, jumping on this admission as if he had Frank in the witness seat. "You're afraid that she might have done it? You don't want to know what the outcome was because you might not like it?"

"That's part of it," Frank allowed. "Not all, but part."

Charlie shook his head slowly. "Let's get the test results," he said after a short, thoughtful pause. "Let's see how conclusive they are. In the meantime I'll find out if the Dean of Girls at Sutro Glen ever had a complaint last year about a girl who was being pressured to strip for a friend of her boyfriend's, and if there was such a complaint, what, if anything, was done about it."

"I feel like a total coward." Frank spoke so softly that Charlie almost did not hear what he said.

"You can't afford to think that way," Charlie pointed out, more caustically than he had intended. "You can indulge in self-pity after we get this case dismissed. But not until then." He put his pen down. "Sorry, Frank. I shouldn't have said that. I was out of line. The only excuse I can offer is that I was up early to identify the body. It's still bothering me."

Curiosity and repugnance warred in Frank; curiosity won. "Was it bad? I've never had to do that, identify a body."

This time Charlie took care to weigh his answer. "They hadn't removed it from where it was found when I got there. Dead bodies can be . . . pretty pitiful like that." A lingering chill of the presence of death gripped him, reminding him that Cadao Talbot was dead through him.

"Hey," said Frank, seeing something in Charlie's expression that troubled him. "I didn't mean to bring it up, not if it's that bad."

"I hope you never have to go through something like that," said Charlie with feeling. Then he made himself tend to business. "That voice-stress test is very important. More than a standard lie detector, in a way. We've got one of the best independent technicians doing the job. He's done consulting work for the security departments of half the guys with defense contracts down in Silicon Valley. His expert testimony will make a big difference."

"That's assuming I pass," said Frank. "I'm pretty stressed out about this whole thing."

"It won't make that much of a difference; the voice-stress patterns work differently when you are lying and when you are telling the truth. It doesn't change that much just because you're upset. Besides, that's why we're going to an expert like Jock. He knows all the ways stress can show in the voice, and he can indicate which is which." Charlie pushed his chair back and got up. "I want this case cleared up as soon as we can do it. I don't want it hanging around to haunt you. You need to be able to put it behind you. And I want to find out why my investigator was killed."

"Put it behind me." He shook his head. "There's going to be people who believe I'm guilty, no matter what happens. I've resigned myself to that," said Frank. "It's going to follow me around."

"Probably," Charlie admitted.

"I can handle that, if I know for sure the guy who did it pays for it." He stood. "I know I've said that before, but I mean it now. I have a better sense of . . . how these things work."

"Good," said Charlie. "Did that come out of the tests?"

"A little. And Elizabeth has me going to Kevin Blackwell twice a week. I've only been three times, but I think it's helping me. I don't think I'm being as unrealistic about this as I was for a while. I think I've got a better understanding of what's been happening to me. He's been helping me get rid of my fantasies about having all this wash off, like mud. I know why I wanted to be rid of the whole case, completely shut of it. But people aren't like that. I'll always know I was accused, and there are people out there who will know it, and suppose that the accusations were justified. You can get a direct and specific confession that completely exonerates me and someone will think that the confession was bought in some way. That's how people are."

"Yes," Charlie said quietly. "That is how people are."

Gail Harris was terribly pale but her eyes were dry. She moved as if her joints did not fit, and when she spoke, her voice had less emotion than the synthesized speech of computers.

"I can't tell you how sorry I am," Charlie told her as he came into her office. He had grown used to saying these things, though they made no sense to him. There were other ways to deal with mourning, ways he found more familiar and workable. He would much rather have told her that it was all right to tear her clothes in pieces and cover her head with ashes and bark, but that would seem as if he were mocking her grief instead of honoring it.

"Yes," she said.

"I wish there were something I could do," Charlie told her, hating her remoteness, her unacknowledged pain, because she was his friend.

"He's dead," she said as if she were discussing grapefruit.

Charlie did not sit down. He came a few steps nearer, but kept a certain distance between them. Apparently that was what Gail wanted because she looked at him briefly. "I feel partially responsible."

"It wasn't you. He was obsessed." She was so far away.

"He shouldn't have died," Charlie said, and saw tears in her eyes for the first time.

"No," she whispered.

"I want to do something about it," Charlie said, hoping Gail would cry at last.

"What? Unless you can raise the dead." She turned away from him and covered her eyes.

"Yeah," said Charlie, making up his mind. He could not raise the dead, but he could discover the truth of Cadao's death. He owed the young investigator that much. "If there's anything you need, will you call me?"

Gail only motioned him away.

Charlie spent two hours in his basement steamroom, chanting now and then as he strove to focus his mind on the task ahead of him. He was grateful to Morgan for saying nothing, for he knew that she was aware of how he felt. He made himself recall in minute detail everything he noticed about the body. His thoughts took him back to the dumpster, to the look and smell of Cadao, dead, to the damage that had been done.

By the time he came to bed, Morgan was half asleep. She reached over and put her hand on his shoulder. "You okay?" she murmured.

"I will be," Charlie promised her.

Mickey Trang had not slept; there were circles under his eyes and his face was pale. "What do you want?" he asked when Charlie knocked on the door of his home office. "It's not even eight."

"That's two days in a row I've got you working early," said Charlie in a voice too serious to make the words amusing. "I need something from you."

"What are you talking about." Mickey had gone to his desk, using it to isolate himself.

"I need to know everything Cadao had in his records, his notes, his files, everything." He sensed Mickey's need to argue and forestalled it as best he could. "I don't want to do anything that will compromise him. That's not my intention at all, Mickey. I want to see if I can . . . reconstruct his investigation. If you'll let me go over his files, I might be able to find enough to go to work on his case for him."

"You're not an investigator," said Mickey, his attitude openly slighting.

"Not the way you are, but I've got a few . . . skills," said Charlie, uncertain how to go on, how much to reveal.

"Sorry, Charlie. This isn't your concern." He made no excuse for the bluntness of his words.

"But it is," Charlie said with purpose. "It is my concern because he was working on a case for me when he was killed. I share responsibility for that."

"Not the way I look at it. You're off the hook, counselor." His eyes hardened. "I don't mean to tell you to go fuck yourself, but I'm not up to much more than that. I've got a funeral to arrange."

Charlie stood his ground. "I know. I don't want to interfere with that. But I do want to . . . retrace his steps. Really." He leaned a little closer. "I've canceled all my appointments for today, and I'll cancel them tomorrow if I have to. Let me do this."

"Let you do what? Spend a little time filling in blanks?" His eyes were hot and cold at once, unforgiving. "They found his car. Did you know that? They let me go over it, with a cop watching. They haven't towed it to the impound yet. I didn't want Gail to have to do that."

"Where did they find the car?" Charlie asked, seizing on the information.

"At the Great Highway, near the zoo. There was some blood on the carpet; the cops said it was dry. They suspect it was the killer who drove the car and left it there. They want to get prints and everything from it. They're going to type the blood, to find out whose it is. To be sure." Mickey shrugged as if none of this were important to him.

"Did you find anything worthwhile in the car? Notes? Anything?" Charlie pursued.

"Nothing much. There was a map Cadao was using. He'd marked a few addresses on it. I memorized them. The rest of the stuff, if there was anything, is gone." He made a quick, futile gesture.

"I'd like to know the addresses. I'll get a map," said Charlie, refusing to be put off. "Maybe I can fill in enough of the blanks you mentioned that I'll be able to help you get the guys who did it." He waited, unwilling to be defeated by Mickey Trang's sense of responsibility. "I can be of help, Mickey, if you'll let me."

"Gail's coming over in half an hour," said Mickey, making the announcement a gauntlet to fling at Charlie. "We've got a lot to do. I don't have time to help you with anything."

"I understand that," said Charlie. Then he added, "Besides the map, I'd like to take something of his with me."

"What?" Mickey's expression was outraged. "Where do you get off saying something like that?"

Charlie did not bristle in response. "Something that belonged to him, preferably something he wore, something metal."

"Jesus Christ, you're a real ghoul, aren't you?" He used each question to batter at Charlie, to drive him away. "What is it? You need more of a thrill? Seeing the corpse wasn't kick enough for you? You've got to find something more to wallow in?"

"It will help my concentration," said Charlie, undaunted by the ferocity of Mickey's attack. "It could make a difference."

"In *what*? What kind of difference? Cadao's *dead*, Charlie. Someone tortured him to death. What good is going over his records going to be?" His hostility faded as he spoke. "Hey, I know you mean well, but man, this is only making the pain worse. Let it go. Just let it go."

Charlie did not answer at once. "I don't expect you to believe me. I don't know how to explain why I want this from you. I'm not trying to con you or do anything to make it worse for you and Gail. But if you'll allow me this chance, I may be able to find out who killed him, and why."

"I'm telling you, Charlie, the answer isn't in his records. Don't you think I looked? Don't you think I tried to find out already?"

"My methods aren't quite the same as yours," said Charlie, recognizing the despair that Mickey was attempting to keep from overwhelming him. "I have other resources, other means of gaining information. Let me have the map, his files and something that belonged to him, please. I'll return them to you before he is buried, you have my word on it. I won't disgrace his memory, and I'll do everything I can to find his murderers."

"Oh, yeah," said Mickey in patent doubt. "Sure."

"*Please*, Mickey," Charlie insisted.

Mickey folded his arms, but a glimmer of hope was in his eyes, a hope that he strove relentlessly to subdue. "What the hell do you think you can do?"

"If I'm lucky, I can find out what happened," said Charlie very deliberately.

"What are you?" Mickey scoffed. "Some kind of medicine man?"

Charlie did not laugh with him. "Yes," he said. "That's exactly what I am."

"Here you are," said Glen Mitchell as Charlie reached out for the folder, "It's just the preliminary examination, but the medical examiner clearly established that there were two men involved. One right-handed, one left-handed. It has something to do with angles of penetration. I don't follow all that stuff too well."

Charlie looked over the report, finding the specific, clinical language ironic, a denial of the terrible death Cadao had suffered. He noticed how specific the medical examiner had been about his reason for determining the left- and right-handedness of the killers. "How long before you get the final report?"

"Depends on what they find. If we can do any DNA typing we might have to wait a week or more, but it would be worth it. That stuff's pretty damn conclusive." Mitchell was much neater than he had been yesterday morning. His sports jacket was a blue-and-brown Harris tweed, his slacks were slate blue, his tie was a conservative brown stripe. He looked neat and very presentable, not at all like a man who was caught up in terrorism and violence.

"How much more would you need for identification and conviction?" Charlie asked. He turned the page and looked at the diagram where the nature and extent of Cadao Talbot's injuries had been catalogued.

"Well, a signed confession in the presence of a defense attorney would be nice, but I'm not losing sleep waiting for it," said Mitchell, then went on, "Realistically, we need the usual kinds of evidence: things that place the suspects at the scene of the crime at or about the time the crime was taking place. We need some link that establishes motive, or at least capacity for committing the crime. If these suspects are anything like I think they are, motive is going to be off the wall. And we need the specific talents or knowledge that would give us reason to suppose that the suspects would know how to do the things they did." His mouth grew tight. "Physical evidence is best, of course, but convincing circumstantial might be good enough if the suspects turn out to have a history of sadism."

Charlie looked at Mitchell. "Do you mean literal sadism or only cruelty?"

"I mean that apparently, according to the medical examiner, we are dealing with two men who get sexually aroused when inflicting pain on others. Classic sadists." He lowered his eyes. "Nasty."

"Yes," Charlie agreed. "Thanks for showing this to me."

"I didn't show you anything," said Glen Mitchell. "You came in here and while we were talking, you happened to glance at some papers on my desk. You shouldn't have done that, but I probably shouldn't have left them where you could see them." He glanced toward the back of the squad room. "I don't want to tell you your business, counselor, but I think you ought to keep in mind that vengeance isn't part of the deal."

"Isn't it?" Charlie asked.

"Not according to the law, and you're the lawyer around here," said Mitchell with care. "In case you'd forgotten."

Charlie stood up. "Thanks for giving me a little of your time, Sergeant," he said.

One of the things Mickey had given Charlie was a map of the city. There were a number of neon-pink marks Cadao Talbot had made, some of them at locations Charlie already knew: Sutro Glen Junior High School, The Space Station, the Greek restaurant where they had had lunch. But there were four others that were not as familiar, and Charlie climbed into the Camry, determined to find the places. Somewhere he would pick up the trail.

The first location turned out to be a film-processing lab near China Basin. The hefty woman behind the counter thought she remembered Cadao from Monday but was not absolutely certain.

"I seem to remember he wanted to know about the repro we do on Polaroid shots. I gave him a price list and he said something about ordering in bulk was sure a better deal than just one or two dupes." She smiled. "That's the way this business is. I explained it to him, if that's the guy you're checking up on. Nice kid."

"Thanks," said Charlie, and went back to his car.

The second mark was at a video store. It was big and bright, with three TV screens showing the latest hot rental items. In one corner of the shop was a number of video games; in another there were the X-rated videos. The whole place had the patina of success.

"Yep," said the man with prematurely thinning hair. "We're doing a real good business in this location. We're near enough to Parkside High that we get a lot of the kids coming in here. And we're just close enough to the Safeway that we get people stopping in for something to go with their groceries. I sank an entire insurance settlement into the place. It was the smartest thing I ever did."

Charlie asked him about Cadao, though he didn't have much hope.

The owner scowled, then said, "Well, last Tuesday there was a kid in here, looked a little like an Indian—you know, not quite Chinese, not quite Chicano?—who wanted to rent the X-rated stuff. I told him if it was up to me, I'd be glad to let him have one. But we got laws about minors. He made some comment about being twenty-seven and showed me a driver's license. I told him he'd better choose a more realistic age if he was going to carry fake ID. Anyway, he did ask if one of those tapes was made locally, since the studio had a San Francisco address. I told him that was probably just the distributor. I don't know if he bought that, but it was true. You know what kids are like—most of them have a thing for movies."

"Do you remember the name of the tape?" Charlie asked, knowing the question was futile.

The man shook his head. "Nope. I used to try to remember all that shit, but no more. There's too damn much of it, know what I mean?"

"If you say so," Charlie told him as he left the shop.

At the third mark, Charlie found a rather seedy office for Dunnigan Escorts and Models/a professional agency. Neither the receptionist nor the manager Charlie requested to see had any memory of Cadao Talbot's visit.

"We don't do much work with Asians, except the Japanese," said the manager, raising his brows provocatively. "Very few of our models are Asian."

"Do you have a policy against Asians?" Charlie asked, deliberately goading the man.

"Of course not. That's against the law," snapped the manager. "We don't attract that part of the trade is all. Personally, I think the Chinese are very beautiful people."

"What about the Vietnamese?" Charlie could not resist the opportunity.

"We've never had any Vietnamese ask for a position, and we haven't had any that I know of as clients." He was getting huffy now, trying to force Charlie to leave without actually making such a request.

"What about film or television work? Do any of your clients do jobs of that sort?" Charlie asked.

"We don't . . . have many requests from those sources, except occasionally for commercials. We've done quite well for some of our models with commercials. They pay quite well, you know, and they get your face and bod out there." His pride was evident.

"How much of the bod, can you tell me that?" Charlie inquired.

"That's not very funny," said the manager.

The fourth was an address at the edge of the industrial area near the foot of Army Street. It was little more than a tremendous warehouse, with a few of the windows broken. A chain link fence surrounded it, both gates secured with imposing padlocks.

Charlie stood outside the larger gate and saw a weathered sign over the main door: Connoisseur Studios. Near the door there were the fading tracks of two vehicles. The place had a presence that seemed alive with malice. Charlie nodded to himself. "Bingo."

TWELVE

Thursday night and Friday

BY NIGHT THE warehouse loomed larger than it did in the day. The broken windows were not visible and the general air of neglect gave an impression of brooding hostility as real as the hate in the eyes of mistreated animals. Charlie stood beside the gate, dressed in severely simple clothes. On his right wrist he wore the watch Cadao had left with Gail when he went out on his last search. He had rubbed his body with a special tincture and now he smelled of resin and juniper berries. He had heightened his senses with a ritual learned from his grandfather; the air, the night, the ground spoke to him, and he listened.

He had brought bolt-cutters along, and used them now to get through the chain link fence; he clipped an entrance where the fence bowed, and opened the way by pulling part of the fence in the direction opposite to the bow. With luck, he thought, he would be able to press the two sections back together so that his break-in would not be obvious to the casual glance.

Once he was through the fence, he went toward the door under the sign. He hoped he would not have to break the window or the lock to get in. "Connoisseur Studios," he read on the door, "films for the discriminating palate."

"Charlie, I wish you wouldn't do this." Morgan was standing in the kitchen at the head of the basement stairs. *"Or if you've got to, find someone to go with you, to guard your back."*

"And to witness me breaking-and-entering? Share the blame with me if I happen to get caught?" he answered her. *"This way, I'm the only one at risk. You have to let me do this, Morgan."*

"There's another way," said Morgan.

"What? Search warrants? What acceptable probable cause do I have, can you tell me that? What cop would act on what I tell him, if it's about this." He was wrapped in a bath sheet and in his hand he carried a small basket containing three little jars. *"You know what I do isn't acceptable to the cops or the law, not our law here."*

"But Charlie—" she protested, her eyes large with worry. *"If you do this, you could be hurt."*

"Yes. And if I don't, Cadao Talbot's murder might not ever be solved." He was about to close the door between them.

"There's physical evidence," Morgan reminded him desperately.

"Yes," said Charlie. *"But that's not enough when there are no real suspects. We're back to probable cause, aren't we? And when and if they're able to do a DNA match with someone taken into custody, they ought to be able to link the suspect to the crime, if they can demonstrate probable cause. How can they do that? Let's suppose they do, somehow, and the evidence is allowed, and it looks like they've got the real bad guys. But you know how juries are. Technology is voodoo to most of them—hell, half the time I think it's voodoo—and a clever attorney can cause them to question such evidence, no matter what the cops say or the judge instructs. Am I right?"* His expression softened, and he looked at her with the depth of his love. *"If you want to help me, go get into a hot bath with some of the tincture we keep in the bathroom. Use about half a cup, in very hot water. And stay there about an hour. Just let your mind drift, nice and easy. That will help me, not gambling on probable cause."*

She watched as he pulled the door closed.

The lock was a simple one, easy to jimmy. He worked steadily, not rushing, for he sensed that there was no one about—no one alive. His one worry was a possible burglar alarm, but there were no wires, no special fittings, no bells sounding as the wards of the lock gave way.

The front office looked more like the ordering counter for a printing company than the headquarters for a film studio. The walls were in need of paint, the ceiling fixtures had broken bulbs, and the one vinyl-covered sofa was missing an arm. In one corner two file cabinets stood; in another a medium-sized bookcase was filled with videotapes, more than half of them probably blank because no labels identified them. Charlie went and ran his fingers over the tapes.

"Say, boss, what did you think of the last one we did? Mal kept it together, right to the end. We clocked it at over an hour. Not too shabby. You wanted us to take our time."

Charlie flinched at the loathsome excitement that surged through him from the tape.

"It's pretty good. You got to be more careful, though. You almost lost her twice. That's getting careless, Paco, and you can't blame it all on Mal. This treatment is only for special clients. They expect a lot from us. Don't forget it."

Grateful to be away from the miasmic sensation of the tapes, Charlie approached the file cabinets. He pulled on the top drawer of the nearest one, only to discover it was locked. Very carefully he began to work on the lock, taking his time.

Four minutes later the drawer was open and Charlie was holding an open file folder in his hands. According to the lease agreement and a business contract, Connoisseur Studios was owned by three men: quarter shares were held by Pacholos Aksander Kirim Orestes Hambal and Ryffial Malkuros; the controlling half was the property of Stanhope Theodore "Scooter" Ferrand.

Mickey Trang left Gail Harris at his place, understanding her dread of going home. "I need to see Charlie," he explained for the third time. "I wouldn't go otherwise. Are you sure you don't want someone to come and stay with you while I'm out?"

"That's all right," said Gail listlessly. "You've got some tapes. I'll watch TV. And there's food in the kitchen, isn't there?"

"Help yourself," said Mickey to his partner. "I shouldn't be too long. But he's got to see the things I found. I wouldn't go if I didn't know it's important." He hovered over her, knowing that there was something more he ought to do and unable to think of what it was. "I'd call, but he's got to see this."

"The things from under the floor carpet in Cadao's car," said Gail as if reciting a lesson she did not understand. "I guess you better."

"I should have looked there before now," Mickey told her, edging toward the door, still watching her closely as if he expected her to burst or crumble if he were not near. "You *sure* you're going to be okay?"

"Not sure, but close enough," she said, leaning her head back against the roll of the upholstery. "I'll find a way to handle things. It takes time, though." Her hand came up to her eyes. "I wish I could stop crying. This is ridiculous."

"You go ahead and cry," said Mickey, wishing he could weep with her. "You cry as much as you want."

She shook her head slowly, looking away from him. "Get out of here. Get your errand done. Then come back and we'll eat something fattening and have too much wine so we can sleep."

Reluctantly, urgently, he headed for his car.

In the file cabinet there were boxed and rubber-banded photographs. The nearest bundle of photos was labeled "Debutantes." Before he touched them, he could feel what they were.

"Lord, lord, you're a pretty little thing. You don't have to be ashamed, sweetlips. You just lie back the way I told you. No, no, don't cover anything up. Stop fussing. Just let me see everything you got.

"I don't like this very much."

"You'll get into it if you don't fight it. Don't you like the way it feels, having someone look at you like you're better than a chocolate sundae? You leave your hands where they are. Don't cover up. You're mighty nice to look at, all new and fresh."

"This is scary."

"Scary? Oh, no, sweetlips, don't say that. That's . . . why, that's just silly. Let me see your nice little cunt. That's not so bad, is it? Now, that's real sweet. You stay just like that. Just like that."

"I don't want to do this. I changed my mind."

"Now, don't say that, sweet thing. I don't like it when a girl pulls that kind of shit. It tells me she's mean. You got me all ready for you, all revved up, and now you're telling me you changed your mind. That makes you a tease, little baby, and teases make me real mad, you know? I can't help it. I get turned on—you try to turn me off, I'll have to hurt you."

Revulsion swept through Charlie; he almost dropped the pack of photographs.

He tried to clear his mind of what he had sensed. He opened his secret ear, listening for Cadao Talbot, but there was nothing here that suggested him. Charlie put his hand on Cadao's watch, and felt a faint, ill-defined echo, but nothing that he could hook on to.

A very old typewriter was on a flimsy table next to the filing cabinets. Charlie ran his hands over it, more from curiosity than from any conviction he would learn anything worthwhile.

"The man called again, the one who wants the ultimate film. God, what a phony phrase. Just like him, though. He wants to see somebody die, that's all, so long as it's someone young and pretty

with beesting tits, and no hair on her twat. He's upped the price he's willing to pay. I think you could get him up to twenty-five thousand if you push him."

The secretary's voice was bored, slightly quarrelsome.

"That's not a lot of money for what the old fuck-head wants. Tell him we haven't found the right . . . ingenue yet. We're looking. But the trouble is, he likes them so young. There's not many girls who'll hold still for a real audition with Paco. And we can't use just anybody. She's got to get into it or it won't work. We can't get into real production if the girl won't cooperate. Fucking pervert. Jerking off while Paco and Mal work her over. The guy thinks he's a fucking patron of the arts."

"Don't let him know you laugh at him. Old guys like him, with a lot of money, they can get even. You better be respectful when you talk to him. If he thinks you're laughing at him, you'll get your legs broken."

"Shit, he's three hundred miles away. What can he do? He won't break my legs because I'll blow him out of the water. If he's going to do anything to me, he better take out a contract, and do it right. But who else is going to make movies for him? Tell him the price is thirty thousand, because he wants the . . . actress to be so young. I got Paco working on it. He'll find the right one. In the meantime the old fart can keep his pants up and his hands around a beer can."

Charlie stumbled back, away from the typewriter. The tremendous rage in the two voices he heard almost overwhelmed him. His eyes ached and he gagged on bile. He had been inside the office nine minutes.

The pounding on the front door continued, and finally Morgan sighed and got out of the steamy bath. The air was redolent with the scent of pine and other things. She pulled her Turkish robe on and headed down for the door, prepared to be very rude to whoever had interrupted her.

Mickey Trang was on the porch, his face dark with a strange emotion. "I've got to talk to Charlie," he announced, then noticed how Morgan was dressed. "Oh. Sorry, Your Honor."

She could not bring herself to argue with Mickey—he looked too haggard and too desperate. "Please come in, Mister Trang. I'm sorry, but Charlie isn't here right now. I don't expect him back for . . . several hours." Her frown was slight, but Mickey saw it.

"Where is he?" He pushed the door a little wider. "I've got to see him. It's very important. I've got something he tried to find."

This time Morgan's hesitation lasted longer. "Is it really very urgent?"

"I think it probably is. I wish the cops had found it, and that's the truth. That's why I have to reach Charlie." Mickey looked hard into Morgan's eyes. "He told me he wanted to check out Cadao's movements the last day. Is that where he is?"

"I think so," said Morgan very carefully.

Mickey jumped on that. "Do you know where he is? Cadao went several places the day he was killed. We know that. Do you know which one Charlie is going to?"

She sighed. "I don't think I ought to be telling you about this."

"Did Charlie tell you not to?" Mickey asked.

"Not as such, no," she admitted.

"I have to find him. I have to talk to him." Mickey put one hand on the doorsill, leaning toward Morgan. "I don't want to intrude on you. I'm embarrassed to be here. I never wanted to disturb you. But I've got to see Charlie."

Morgan studied him, looking at the expression in his eyes, the tension in how he stood. "Will it make a difference right now, do you think?"

"It might, it could, if he's really after—" He stopped abruptly. "He's chasing murderers, if he's really trying to retrace Cadao's last day. I have good reason to think so, anyway." His eyes grew hard. "I don't want to see him at risk the way Cadao was at risk. I don't think I could handle it if someone else I like ends up dead."

Morgan studied his face, feeling doubt and the first certainty that Charlie would need help. "Do you think there's a chance of that?" she asked, trying to conceal the shock that was going through her; she hoped that Mickey Trang would say something that would end her apprehension. "He has ways to handle himself that . . ." She was not able to continue.

"Where is he?" Mickey demanded.

"I don't know," said Morgan, feeling a grue slide down her spine. "Honestly. I think he may be at some kind of film studio. He said it was a warehouse, that no one was on the premises. I offered to go with him, but he wouldn't let me. He wanted to protect me, if he gets caught." Her face turned ashen. "You mean that there may be someone there? that the place isn't empty?"

"I don't know." Mickey looked away from her, eyes hooded. "I have no way to be sure, but what I found really scares me. If I don't get a chance to warn him, he could get caught."

"And you say that the parties in question are murderers?" The word sounded unreal, as if she had stumbled upon an alien concept. "Are you certain?"

"About that part? Yes, I'm certain. Whoever has that studio is the person who ordered Cadao killed." He held out an envelope. "I've got material in here that indicates that Cadao had enough information to make sure he was headed in the right direction."

Morgan looked at the envelope. "I don't suppose it would be right for you to show the contents to me, would it?"

"No, Your Honor, it would not," said Mickey emphatically. "And it could compromise the Girouard case."

"I've had enough of compromised cases, Mickey."

He nodded. "I understand."

She made up her mind. "He's gone to that studio. He said he was going inside. But, Mickey, he's not going there for quite the reasons you think." She gave this warning sharply. "And any interruption could . . . be harmful."

"Tell that to the guys he's trying to find," said Mickey, then added, "How do you mean, he's not going there for the reason I think?"

She frowned. "He's not interested in gathering . . ."

"You mean it's something witchy," said Mickey, clearly not quite believing it.

"Yes," said Morgan quietly.

Mickey stared at her, recognizing her sincerity and worry. "It's for real?"

"Yes," she repeated. She drew her robe more tightly around her as if the thick terry cloth could keep out the chill that held her.

"Oh, shit," said Mickey with an emotion perilously close to awe.

Beyond the office there was a narrow hallway with several small rooms, each with tremendous mirrors, all fly-specked; they were supposed to be dressing rooms, Charlie decided as he looked at the rank of lights flanking the mirror in room number 3, then noticed the stack of discarded tissues, many with smears of makeup still clinging to them, a few made stiff with dried blood.

I told you I don't like that kind of thing, Paco. Not when both of you do it.

The voice was querulous, shaking a little.

"Don't be so squeamish, girl. You knew what we wanted, Mal and me. We told you about it. And you've posed for us before. Okay, we did some different stuff, but it doesn't make it that different from last time."

"There was just you last time. There was no one else. The camera was bad enough, but doing things with that other guy . . . he's so big, and all those muscles. Guys like Mal can get scary. I feel kind of sick, Paco. I've never done those things before. And two guys—"

"Most people are afraid to do what we do. But they want to. They don't have the guts to do it, but they want it bad. They wouldn't buy our pictures if they didn't want to do these things themselves. But they're chicken. They piddle around, straddle their bored wives once a week, and the rest of the time, they want to see the real thing, the things they don't have the nerve to do. All the real things. That's what we can give 'em, sweetlips, the real thing."

"I don't like it, Paco. I don't know if I want to do any more tapes with you."

"Not ever? Not for a hundred bucks a pop? Hey, didn't I tell you about that? We're raising your wages, from sixty to a hundred. A hundred bucks for a couple of hours with me and my friend Mal. Scooter doing the camera, just like today. Think it over. It's not like we'd expect you to sell yourself on the street corner. The money's yours, free and clear. There's no paperwork so you don't have to pay any taxes on it. What's a couple bruises for that kind of money? If you do right, we might give you more than the hundred. That's not too bad wages for someone who's only fifteen."

Charlie flinched and tossed the tissue away. There was a lingering pain in his back that was an echo of what the girl had felt. What had they done to her, that she hurt so badly? He looked around the dressing room for something else that might provide an answer, but all he could see was a tin of cold cream. Not enough personal substance for his purposes. He shut the door, feeling as if he were closing it on a scream.

At the end of the row of dressing rooms there was a door that opened on the main part of the warehouse, the studio. Tall windows on the south wall had been partially screened to keep out sunlight. There were lightstands clustered at one end and a number of props—a bed, now without sheets or blankets; a large pile of pillows in front of a paisley drape; an old-fashioned settee with two dark, rust-brown stains on it; a group of chairs and small tables stacked at the far end of the room—were set up at various points in the cavernous room. Near the back wall was an iron cot covered in a rubber sheet. Charlie stared at it, repelled and fascinated with the intensity of sensation that clung to the place.

At the settee, he examined the marks, finding what he expected—blood.

"Wait. Wait. I'm not ready for you to do that. Oh, God, I'm not ready yet."

"I'm all ready now. Stop doing that. Stupid bitch. You'll only make it worse."

"It hurts. Stop! No. No more. STOP!"

"Hold still, damn you."

"A-a-a-a-u-u-gh."

"Shut up. Stop that noise. Shit, what do I have to do, hit you again? Lie still. There. Shut up."

"No. Don't do that again. I'll try. I'll try."

The desperation in the girl's voice was so all-encompassing that Charlie sank to his knees beside the settee. He trembled with her presence, his arms crossed over his abdomen in sympathy for what she had felt. He was faintly aware of how the lights had been set up, at the two video cameras on stands, of someone behind them, directing one of the cameras as the girl struggled with her assailant. His eyes closed, so that he could concentrate on the impressions that were still in the blood.

"You said you wouldn't hurt me any more. Please. Please."

"This isn't anything much. You get hurt worse in sports all the time. It'll give the audience a real kick. It's no big thing, girl. It's just like piercing your ears. You got pierced ears, don't you? And then you'll have two gold rings through your nipples. It'll get you excited, just moving the rings. Your nipples will stand up, like there was a man between your legs. It makes the whole thing lots better."

"It hurts."

"It's gonna be worse if you don't cooperate. I'll just pound 'em through with a leather punch. It'll take longer, too, doing it that way, so think about it. No more squirming. Just lie back and let me do it. You got such pretty little boobs. Just enough, not like some older girls."

"Please. I'm bleeding!"

"Don't block the camera, Paco; this is good stuff you're getting."

"PLEASE!"

This last degenerated into a shriek and then changed to sobs.

Charlie broke away from the settee, scrabbling to stay on his feet. The room had felt cold a moment ago, now it was hot and clammy at once. He had rarely experienced anything so deliberate, so horrible. The man on the settee had been Paco, that much he was sure of. But who was behind the camera, and what did they have to do with Cadao Talbot's death? He forced himself to search for videotapes, for Polaroid shots, or the peel-offs. Think sensibly, he told himself, and was not certain what that meant.

There was a traffic snarl on the freeway; Mickey Trang decided to take the surface streets, heading by zigs and zags along one-way streets toward that part of the industrial area where Cadao's records indicated the film studio was located. He hoped now that all the notations were correct, that he had the right address. He knew it would take at least twenty minutes to get there, and he chafed at the time.

There were other drivers who had decided on the same tactics as Mickey and were filling up the streets. At the second stoplight, Mickey spotted a man in the lane next to his in full tails with a big, black case for a musical instrument—he supposed it must be a tuba to be so large—in the passenger seat beside him. Was there a concert this evening? Mickey had no idea. But why else would a man drive about in such clothes and with the huge case? He made himself concentrate on his own mission.

At the next major intersection a Taurus had been rammed by a Mazda, and the cars were inching around the wreck, directed by impatient policemen. Mickey swore and resigned himself to waiting for the next change of light, or the one after, to get through. He could not spare time for such minor things as traffic accidents. "And you can't afford to have one of your own," he told himself aloud as he moved forward another foot.

What was it about this case, that it had mushroomed so unpredictably? He had told Gail that it kept getting more confusing, and now he was also convinced that it grew steadily more hazardous. He was used to cases going off on odd tangents, but this was something else, and it made him worry, not only for himself and Charlie but for the girls who had been photographed. The men taking those pictures were more than pedophilic panderers, they were selling more obscene things than the abuse of underage girls; the material in the envelope showed other stills of two men in various stages of increasingly sadistic depravity that culminated in the death of their victim. The girl, Mickey realized as he looked at the photographs, could not be more than fifteen or sixteen.

As he made his way past the wreck, Mickey checked the road ahead, trying to decide which route was likely to be the fastest. He begrudged every minute, for he was increasingly certain that Charlie was in danger.

His hunt, rapid and disorganized, turned up little of interest. He discovered a drop cloth with paint and bloodstains on it, but they were too old to have strong images. He suspected that the cloth had been used somewhere else and had been brought here recently, for what few impressions he garnered were of a place much different from this warehouse with the grandiose name. He shoved it aside and started for the bed, realizing then that what he had thought was mosquito netting was instead a tangle of cords, all secured to the frame of the bed. Whoever had lain here had been thoroughly confined. Charlie reached out and touched the heavy, soft cords, hoping that the material was dense enough to hold some memory of what had taken place.

"*You didn't tie me up before, Paco. Why do you have to do it now?*"

"*It makes it better, darlin'. You're not supposed to do anything but feel good. You leave everything to me, and all you have to do is lie there and let me do it.*"

"*You don't have to tie me up for that, silly.*"

"*Sometimes you do. Don't fight with me about this, Diane. You're just starting to get good at this. You're not the expert yet I still know more than you do. And you gotta let me show you how it all happens. Don't fight about this.*"

"*I don't like being tied up. Paco, don't do it. It doesn't turn me on.*"

"*Why, sure it does, honey. You haven't given it enough time. You're not getting into it. You need to relax, not fight it. You can let everything out, because you're tied up, see? You can let yourself go because you're tied up. You're safe, you can't lose it.*"

"*I don't like it. I want out.*"

"*You're making it real hard, girl. That's not smart. You're trying to make me your toy. You said you'd do anything I wanted if it made you feel better. Well, this is what I want. I want you to lie there and let me do all the things that turn you on.*"

"I don't want to."

"You kick me again and I'll tie you up for real, with wire, not these soft velvet ropes. I don't want to hear anything more out of you until you come. You got that? I want you to lie there like a corpse until you come."

"I'm not going to come, all tied up."

"Shit, stop kicking that way."

"Untie me and I'll stop. You better not try to get that other rope, or I'll kick harder. And lower."

"Maybe you better stop for now, Paco. Maybe this isn't the time."

"Hell, you're filming this. You like to see her fight this way?"

"Not for this tape. Let her go. We don't need her acting that way. Maybe she's not the kind of girl we need. Maybe you better find someone else."

"Yeah, Paco. maybe you better untie me and find someone else."

"Okay, you bitch. You probably can't come, anyway, no matter what I do to you."

Charlie was shuddering as he released the ropes. Only by clamping his jaw shut did he keep his teeth from chattering. If that girl had not been so angry, if she had not fought, he knew that she would have died on this bed, tied to it, at the mercy of Paco and the man operating the camera. His breath came painfully, and his eyes were sore. He pushed himself free of the bed and made himself stand upright. There had to be copies of those tapes somewhere. He had to find them before he left this hellish place.

Morgan had returned to the bathroom, but now the hot water and the pungent scent of the tincture irritated her, making her skin feel tender, and her thoughts no longer drifted as Charlie had instructed her. Again and again she thought of the things Mickey Trang had said, and with every review of the information, she felt herself become less certain that she had done enough to help her husband. As the water cooled, the odor of the tincture turned musty, almost repulsive. She reached for a bath sheet and stepped out of the tub.

There were so many times she had tried to sense him as he so clearly could sense her; she had not been able to, her own innate skepticism insisting that what she sought could not be found because it was not real. Now that she worried for Charlie, she wanted to suspend her doubts and open her mind as he had wanted to teach her, but did not have the knack of it.

She sat on the edge of the tub as the water drained and wished she could reach Charlie, warn him. Her inner voice said *Try the telephone,* a notion she dismissed as soon as it occurred. She did not know the name of the place, and she was fairly certain that the number would not be listed, anyway. Charlie, Charlie, Charlie, she thought, and tried to picture him in the next room, safe.

So caught up was Morgan in this reverie that she did not hear the first two rings of the telephone. When she did realize it was ringing, she hurried into the bedroom to answer it. She wanted the voice to be Charlie's, and when it was not, she was disoriented, stammering, "Wh-who did you s-say this is?"

"Sally Aldred, Your Honor," said the Assistant District Attorney politely but firmly. "Is your husband there?"

Morgan gathered her thoughts. "No, not right now. Is it urgent?" It was a strange hour for such a call, and Morgan had to resist the urge to ask why opposing counsel was calling.

"I think so," said Sally Aldred.

"About the Girouard case?" She stopped at once. "Better not answer that, Sally. Just in case."

"Will you tell him that there is a meeting in my office at one-thirty tomorrow afternoon and I would appreciate it if he could attend?" She was very businesslike, but there was a faint sound of contrition in her tone, a hesitation that was not characteristic of her. Morgan listened with sharpened interest. "It would be very helpful to his client as well as the case if he could be there."

"I'll give him the message," said Morgan, more intrigued than ever.

"Thank you, Your Honor." There was a quality of relief in her tone now, a note of gratitude that made Morgan suspect that whatever the reason for the meeting, it would materially change the nature of the case.

"Any time, counselor." Her bath sheet was damp and turning cold. As Morgan hung up the telephone she looked around for her warmest nightshirt, pulling it on with alacrity as soon as she laid her hand on it. If only she weren't so cold. She pulled the fleece garment on, snuggling into it, her need for heat increasing. If only she weren't so cold, she thought, and realized that the gelid air was not the true cause of the chill that held her. If only she could tell Charlie about Sally's call. If only she knew where Charlie had gone. If only she weren't so cold. If only she could believe that Charlie was truly safe. If only she weren't so cold.

He could no longer avoid the cot at the end of the room. Charlie approached it with care, as if the object itself had the power to ensnare him. He saw that the rubber pad was new, with packing creases still in it. This did not bring him any sense of relief, for he was already aware that something hideous clung to that cot, and nothing less than fire would eradicate the repellent presence of agony that permeated the metal frame.

He dreaded what he would feel if he touched it, though he knew he must. He chanted a short charm for protection, providing himself a little extra armor against the impact of violent death. He could feel his ribs turn steely within his chest, his hands taking on the protection of invisible gauntlets to keep him from having to take all the pain into himself.

More than one person had died here, he realized as he came up beside the cot. The rubber sheet had been placed there in anticipation of more death. He fingered the rubber, searching for the men who had put it there.

"I still say it's too soon; cops aren't that stupid. They're in the middle of the investigation on Lake, and that means they could figure out the—"

"Paco, Paco, they haven't figured it out before, have they? You and Mal leave that part to me. I know what I'm doing. Besides, who's gonna hassle me? Who's gonna risk a suit? No cops'll come here, not after the judge came down on those two pricks. It's safe, man, I tell you."

"But the Lake girl's not the same as the others. I don't think you ought to have let that tape go while the cops are still so hot on the case. The buyer could get nervous, and what happens then?"

"Hey, Paco, we're getting thirty thou for it, and we kept the client waiting for more than two months to deliver. He was not real happy about that. We don't want him finding another source because he thinks we can't deliver. Next time we'll up it to forty thou. He'll pay it if he likes the Lake tape, and he will. You guys did good with the girl. Mal didn't lose it, not till the end. Three hours is long enough for that old pervert. Probably the only time he gets his blood pressure above freezing is watching those tapes."

"You keep a copy?"

"I always keep a copy. You know that. And this one'll be for

that guy in Texas. He wants to see lots of sex and not so much blood. He said he wants to see the girl have a prick up her cunt and her ass and both coming out her mouth."

"Another real sicko."

"It pays the bills. At least we're not dealing dope."

"Yeah."

"Tomorrow night, late. You bring your stuff here about two, after the bars are closed. And make sure that this girl's real eager, you know what I mean? I won't want to have to show the rough stuff."

"It's better for me if it gets rough. I don't get much out of these ritual sacrifice things. I'd rather do some things with knives before we cut her throat."

"Not this time, Paco. Maybe later."

"Just the sex and the killing now?"

"That's right; just the sex and the killing."

It took all of Charlie's will not to vomit. The casualness of it, he thought. The simplicity of it all. As if neither man had any inkling of the enormity of their acts. He took several long, deep breaths, then knelt beside the cot. He had to brace himself for what he was certain was to come. He lowered his head, his eyes closed, and let his mind open to what was in the metal.

shrieks screams whimpers

He jerked back. That was too . . . frenzied. He steadied himself and concentrated on Cadao Talbot.

"You're all bastards."

"But you're the one tied up."

"You're proud of that, are you? You're scum."

"You shouldn't talk to us like that. You'll make us mad."

His cry was more from shock than from hurt. That came a heartbeat later and sucked away his breath for most of a minute while the two men laughed. Their laughter sounded in Charlie's ears as Cadao had heard it.

"That's just a start, Mister Talbot. It's a little taste, in case you want to change your mind or go along with us."

"Fuck your grandmother."

"He's not getting the point. Let's help him get the point."

The pain came this time with immediacy—deep and enormous. He doubled over, as Cadao would have done if he had not been bound to the cot. His hands clenched to fists and pressed against the base of his ribs.

"Who sent you here to find us? You want to tell us that?"

Cadao's answer was garbled, little more than a few half-syllables. Charlie put his knuckles to his mouth, biting hard to bring himself back to the present. His body shook with agony that faded a little as he focused his eyes on the far side of the room, away from the cot. He drew his knees up to his chest and rolled a little way toward the bed.

Traffic had thinned out, but now Mickey Trang was unsure of the way. He pulled to the side of the road under a streetlight and checked the address again. He memorized the numbers and tried to remember which cross street would bring him the closest to the warehouse without making him pass in front of it. He wanted to be able to check the building out, examine the premises before he ventured inside. He did not want to walk into a trap or something worse. If someone had already found Charlie, he would have to be doubly careful, or his presence could make their investigation more risky than it already was.

He decided to be cautious, approaching the area where the warehouse had to be by using the rutted street where the train tracks stretched down the middle. Here there were loading bays and storage facilities, and Mickey knew that his presence would not be remarked if he did not appear too interested. As he went through the intersection, he glanced toward the warehouse where Connoisseur Studios was located. He spotted Charlie's car parked some distance away. He cursed in English, French and Vietnamese as he hung a sharp left and pulled in behind the Camry.

"What the fuck do you think you're doing?" he demanded of the car, in order to be furious with something.

He pulled on a dark sweater and took leather gloves and a high-tech flashlight from what he called his gumshoe kit. He set the various alarms in his car, then got out, trying not to hurry, hoping he would attract no notice as he made his way toward Connoisseur Studios.

More than one person had died on that iron cot. Cadao Talbot had been the most recent, and his suffering was the strongest presence, but there were others as well. Charlie shivered violently as each new atrocity arose.

"Don't do that yet. She's been screaming too much. Take it easy, both of you. If she dies, we lose the tape, and the commission."

"But look at her. Jesus! She can't even talk any more."

"Well, no more screams. The client doesn't like too much noise."

"Well, shit, you want us to gag her?"

"Make it interesting."

Something unspeakable juddered through Charlie; his eyes, his head burned and there was no way to get enough air into his lungs. He was panting now, but it did not seem to do any good.

"If you're going to cut her there, let me reposition the number two camera. I want to get a good, close shot while you do it."

"I read that they still do this in parts of Africa; some of the Arabs, too. Just cut out the clit and these things. They say it makes for faithful wives."

"Sure takes the fun out of it."

"Very funny. One of you help me with the focus."

He could see them now, as well as feel them. The three men who had killed Cadao Talbot and at least four girls in the last year. There would never be a time when those faces would fade from his memory now, and he would never be able to regard them with anything other than abhorrence. He struggled to get to his knees, but the images still came, consuming his thought in their anguish.

"What the fuck—"

"You must've cut an artery. Look at that."

"Hey, roll her over; I don't want to have to paint the walls."

"She's going out."

"Make sure you keep her on the rubber sheet. Don't get sloppy on me."

"The blood's wrecking my clothes, man."

"She's almost gone."

"Try to keep her going a little longer. The client wants forty-five minutes and this isn't much more than thirty. And you haven't cut off everything he wants off yet."

"Sorry. Nothing to do."

Charlie smelled the coppery blood, saw it steam as it spurted from the underarm wound, the last stage of cutting off her breast. The girl had been insane with shock and pain, but she knew that much blood meant it was over, and she welcomed the death that filled her as her veins emptied.

It was more of an effort than Charlie could make to crawl away from the cot. He knew that he must put distance between himself and the forces of the dead, but it took too much strength. He collapsed on his side, lying half under the cot.

* * *

Mickey Trang found the cuts Charlie had made in the fence, and while he called Charlie twenty kinds of a fool, he went through the improvised door, his growing determination revealed in every movement.

The office was deserted, and Mickey could not conceal the relief that filled him. He made a quick inspection of the room, his flashlight set on its narrowest beam and left on for as short a time as possible. He resisted the urge to call out to Charlie, for if the owners of the studio had arrived, he would alert them to his presence. With a stern reminder to himself to be sensible and do it right, he went through into the dressing room hall.

He made his way carefully, checking each of the numbered rooms, apprehensive and satisfied at once. At least Charlie had made it this far. He wanted to take comfort in that, though he did not manage to. It was even possible, he suggested inwardly, that Charlie had come and gone. That required a somewhat greater leap of faith, for his car was outside; while Mickey was coming in, Charlie might well have left the warehouse. He doubted very much that this had happened. He feared that Charlie had been discovered, and that he was in the hands of the men who worked in this place. He shied away from what that could mean. It was not to be thought about, not given the chance to make him afraid. He had almost rallied his spirits enough to investigate further, chiding himself for lacking the guts to finish the job he started.

Very few times had he ever felt the hair raise on his neck, but as he stepped into the main part of the warehouse, he heard a sound that etched itself in his memory and filled him with the greatest misgivings. It was impossible to believe that such a sound was entirely human.

He was caught. The voices of the dead had taken hold of him. He dimly realized how bad this was; it had nothing to do with him. But it could possess him, sapping his strength and his soul until nothing could hold him together.

His grandfather had been stern in his warning; his blind eyes were fixed on a place where his blindness meant nothing. "The land of the dead is cold, and the cold is greater than the heat of blood. While you are listening to the voices of the dead, you must keep warm, Charlie, or they will have you."

Charlie, fourteen years old, all skinny legs and elbows, nodded, his face solemn. "I will keep warm, Grandfather."

"You will draw them, call them from where they are, but you will not give them anything more than your attention." He scowled, shifting his stance to increase the impact of what he said next. *"If you cannot keep from giving them more, or if their voices are very demanding, be sure you are not alone."*

"Not alone," Charlie murmured, and heard the voices of the dead all around him, heard their intolerable deaths. He jerked like a gaffed fish.

"When the dead cry out, listen. Open your mind to their voices. For those who have the magic, it is what we must do. But do not welcome them, or claim them, or take up their cries. The dead endure in stillness, Charlie, and it is not the stillness of the living. To take that stillness and breathe is beyond any knowledge I have, or anyone else has had. There is not heat and movement enough in all the living to end the stillness of the dead. That is more than any man can do, Charlie." He had bent down, resting his hand on Charlie's shoulder. *"Do not allow them to command you. Do not let them take your hand.*

Was his grandfather's voice one he heard now, or had he conjured up the memory. He wanted to feel himself there, in his grandfather's house at the Iron River Reservation, where he had been taught the lore of his family. He, Charles Spotted Moon, the boy who had come from California, who many in the tribe regarded as a stranger when his father returned home. Was he still a pupil at his grandfather's knee? Had any of the rest of it—the return to California, law school, Lois, Elizabeth, Morgan—been more than a vision? And were these dead voices anything more than a warning of what could happen?

It was very cold on the warehouse floor.

Mickey Trang raced through the warehouse, dread giving him a swiftness he had never known before. His shoulder knocked one of the camera stands aside as he ran. He was not thinking. There was one goal consuming him: to stop the sound that abraded and shattered the fabric of the night.

THIRTEEN

Friday until four P.M.

THE TWO MEN in the Lincoln were arguing as they came up to the rear warehouse gate. The driver did not change his mulish expression as he stopped. "Well, you going to open that fucker, or what?"

Paco slapped the dashboard. "Man, you haven't heard a word I said. I tell you, they're getting onto us. Ever since that cop broke in—"

"How many times do I got to explain it to you? They can't use the tape. Not that First Amendment crap, this is about the way they got it. The judge already threw that stuff out. No warrant, remember? The cop did it on his own, so it's just like any other thief ripping me off." Scooter Ferrand took a firm grip of the steering wheel. "It isn't good business to move again. It makes us look unreliable. We haven't been here all that long; just over a year. I don't want to shift addresses again, not after what we went through the last time. That fool Cloony took all his business to Jack!" His indignation was as fresh as when he had learned of this perfidy. "That guy was spending twenty thousand a month on private movies. I figure Jack owes me for that. And I'm gonna get it back."

"I still say it won't do us any good if the cops get on our case. You know what they're like if they take a notion to squeeze you." Paco reached over for the door handle. "I say we got to get out of here. If we don't, we're going to have the cops all over us everytime a kid runs away, or someone gets a little too friendly with the neighbor's daughter."

"Dream on, nightmare," said Scooter with contempt. "We can stop all that with one call to the lawyer."

"We need to be somewhere more private," Paco insisted, sticking to his original argument. "Maybe we ought to look for a place out in the Valley; Fresno or Bakersfield, maybe."

"Too hot. Too close to L.A." He gestured toward the gate. "Go on. Open it up."

"Well, shit," Paco grumbled as he got out of the Lincoln.

Mickey knelt beside Charlie; he slipped his flashlight—which he had been holding like a bludgeon—back into the clip on his belt. Luckily Charlie was no longer making the banshee howl. Not only did the sound pick at his sanity, it made hearing anything else impossible; Mickey would have missed the distant slamming of a heavy car door.

"Hey," he whispered, reaching out to grasp Charlie's upper arm and drawing back as Charlie pulled into a tight fetal ball.

There was the sound of a chain now, and the shriek of the rear gate opening.

"Fine time to zone out on me, Charlie," Mickey said with as much bravado as he could muster. How was he supposed to deal with this? What was going on here? Was there any danger in waking Charlie? Could he wake him at all? What was wrong with him, that he lay that way, huddled and vacant? What was he supposed to do, drag him out of here by main force? Charlie had three inches and twenty-five pounds on him. There was no certainty that he could move him. And he might start making that hideous sound again. If only he'd gone against his agency's rules and brought a pistol with him. Or better yet, he added bitterly to himself, an Uzi.

Charlie was keening softly, a high thin sound, cold as steel. He pushed his forehead down against his knees.

"What's wrong with you? Paco! One decent snuff in over three months! One! How're we supposed to make a living this way? All the rest of this crap is feel-thie peek-churs. Not much market for them, with what's on cable. Underage beaver to kids at fifty a pic won't get us very far. We have to deliver the real thing. That's what people want."

"Okay, Scooter. But you tell me how I'm supposed to look at a room full of high school kids and figure out which of the girls will be right? How'm I supposed to tell the ones that'll be right? It's one thing to get their boyfriends to bring them, or to get two or

three girls to pose at once. But for the heavy stuff, it takes a little finesse, you know? I can't leave it to someone else to turn on the old magic, you know? I need to spend time with the girl, to get her eager and scared all at once, and that won't happen if it's her boyfriend's idea. Look, we can't exactly hold auditions for what we do, know what I mean?"

"You can't shit me, man. It's not my job to think of that stuff. And you can't use Mal at first. Gorillas like him are too scary for white-bread girls."

"I'll do what I can, but it's gonna take time."

"We gotta do something about that body. Another day or two and it'll start to stink. Make sure you clean her up real good. Don't leave things for the cops to find, you know?"

"Yeah, I know about that. Don't worry. She'll get washed. Maybe the way things are going, we'd better hold off on more bodies. At least for a little while."

"What's that supposed to mean?"

"It means that when girls turn up dead, and it's all over the news, then the other girls get skittish. They're not so willing to go along with what I want. They're afraid that something could happen to them."

"It's the girls who want something to happen to them you ought to be bringing in. They're the ones who're the best."

"Hey, I know what I'm doing. I've done okay before."

"It could be you're losing your touch. Ever think of that? You're making a lot of excuses, but it all comes down to the fact that we can't deliver. And we can't deliver because you're not getting the kind of girls we need. We need better girls than the last two before Susie. She was pretty good, but those others! Tightest twats in San Francisco. They're never going to let go all the way. That Diane bitched the whole time, and the kid you said could do gymnastics never did more than the splits for you. Think about it, Paco—we need better quality. You don't take every kid with an itch to undress. You've got to be more careful, take more time."

"Well, Jesus-fucking-Christ, what am I supposed to do? It's hard enough to get girls this young to pose for pictures. Most of them don't know about anything; they think they've lost their cherries if you take off their underpants. If you'd let me get older girls—"

"The clients like kids. We give 'em kids."

"Then it'll take a while to find the right one."

There was something beyond the voices of the dead and the

echoes of those who had killed them. Charlie stove to shut it out, to surrender to the voices of the dead. But behind that cold, rapacious clamor, there was something else, something that was warm. There was the warning of his grandfather and there was another thing. Something reached through the tremendous gulf and caught a tiny part of his mind, a remote island of himself.

"Charlie!" Mickey hissed, shaking him harder.

He wanted to retreat, beyond the voices into the cold.

The sound of the car approaching gave urgency to Mickey's efforts. He grabbed Charlie with both hands—one on his arm, the other at the sharp bend of his knee—and rocked him vigorously from side to side, not caring that a cut opened up on the ridge of his cheek.

"If you let the dead deceive you, you will be lost to them," his grandfather had said as he showed Charlie how to bring himself back from the voices of the dead. "Especially if there is great badness in the dying, for such death is unclean and unaccepted, and the spirit is not relinquished as it must be. Many of those who die that way will seek your life so that they will not have to know their own death."

"Is that what happened to my father?" Charlie had asked, older now, spending the summer in Canada when his law education permitted. "Is he trying not to die?"

His grandfather's sigh had been full of many things: regret, affection, bafflement, reluctant disapproval, resignation. "No. That was not the way it is with your father. Daniel . . . Daniel is an invalid because he never learned how to live with himself, with what he is. This suffering is what he . . . thought he must have."

"He just lies there. They say he understands, but it never shows. He hasn't spoken since it happened." It took courage for him to go on. "Sometimes I hear his voice." He had been flustered by his own admission.

His grandfather was not. "Sometimes so do I."

"Wake up! Snap out of it, damn you!" Mickey whispered as he heard the car stop outside the loading door.

The cut on his face seered him like a brand. He slapped his hand against it, and winced as he was rolled again, this time pressing his fingers against the concrete.

Someone was working the padlock on the loading door.

"Charlie!"

He coughed twice, groggy. He tried to say something but could not make the words come. Everything felt so used and rusty. He was like something misassembled from unmatching parts.

"Aw, Charlie," Mickey whispered as the lock was taken off the hasp. He looked around desperately. No way out now. They would have to hide and hope for the best. He decided the bed might be the safest place; it was closer than any other hiding place he might consider. With a muscle-wrenching shove he started Charlie moving in that direction.

The cut on his face was getting worse, and that sharpened his attention even more. Charlie listened to the cacophony of screams and words and stillness, no longer able to discern individual voices.

"Help me!" Mickey muttered, as much to himself as to Charlie. The door was starting to rise.

A little of Mickey's desperation touched Charlie, and as much from reflex as from understanding, he started to pull himself forward with his arms. The movement was sluggish and weak but it was better than leaving it all to Mickey. He heard the rattle of the loading door, and it was enough to goad him into more action. In a lurching roll, he reached the shelter of the bed, and was shoved over as Mickey Trang slid along beside him.

The Lincoln drove in and was parked, idling, a little way inside the door.

"What do you need out of here, anyway?"

"Towne said we'd better get the tapes. You do the office, I'll get the cameras. Take anything you think might get us into trouble. It's just for the time being. Like I got 'em out of my house. Not the soft stuff, but the ones that—"

"Yeah, I could've guessed," said Paco, ambling off toward the dressing room hall and the front office.

Mickey hated enclosed places, and it was all he could do to keep from leaving the hiding place. It was one of the things he dreaded about investigations—the way they sometimes landed you in small, enclosed places. He touched the underside of the mattress, less than three inches from his nose.

"I won't forget, I won't forget, I won't forget . . ."

Charlie swallowed hard, as if he were trying to make his ears pop. There were only remnants now.

". . . don't. Please don't . . . I'll do what you . . ."

The driver was walking around the settee, whistling a little through his teeth. He put his hand on the lightstand, flipping the little klieg on for a few seconds, then turned it off again.

". . . you're killing . . . MAMA! . . ."
". . . no . . ."

Very slowly Charlie opened his eyes. He was jammed under a bed, on his side, his face was bleeding and he was colder than he had ever been in his life. He tried to move and felt Mickey poke him. He wanted to ask why they were under the bed. He kept silent.

Paco called from the office, his voice echoing off the dressing room hallway, "What about the photos in the files?"

"Lock 'em and leave 'em for now. I'll have the files cleaned out by the weekend." He walked around the settee again, this time pausing to check the video camera mounted there. "You bring the ledger, too. I want to hand that over to Towne, all sealed, for safekeeping."

"You're sure that's a good idea?" Paco asked.

"Right now it is." He went to the camera by the cot. "You did a shitty job of cleaning this place up, man. It looks like somebody got dragged through the war backward."

"We didn't have much time. Like now!" Paco sounded irate as he rummaged in the shelves.

"It's a bad job, that's all," said Scooter quietly.

"What?" Paco hollered, deliberately more loudly than necessary.

"Nothing," came the answer. "Just get the tapes. And shut up."

"Why?" Paco asked, still very loud. "Who's going to hear us? The nearest apartment is two hundred yards away."

"Keep it down, anyway. In case someone's around." He giggled softly to himself.

Under the bed, Mickey Trang was starting to feel nauseated. His throat burned with every breath.

Charlie could sense Mickey's distress but there was nothing he could do to alleviate it. The cold held him, ruthless as time. Concentrate, he told himself. You've got to concentrate. He tried to shift his posture to something less uncomfortable and felt the frame start to move. He froze.

Morgan had wrapped herself in her heaviest robe and still she could not get warm. She sat huddled in the living room, her thoughts oddly disoriented. She studied the mantelpiece clock, making out the numbers with difficulty. Charlie should have been home before now, she decided. He was late. Mickey Trang had been right, and that terrified her.

But what could she do? She balked at calling the police. Charlie was very likely breaking the law, Morgan knew. More than that, interrupting him at his task could do more harm than good, both legally and in less well defined ways. She would not allow herself to call the cops. But she had to do something. In sudden impatience she got up and went to the kitchen. Hot tea, she told herself. That will warm me up. Hot tea and a little brandy in it, and the chill is behind me. As she stepped into the kitchen she realized that Pompei and Caesar were still out in the backyard. She upbraided herself for this oversight as she put the kettle on the flame, then took the basement stairs and pulled open the door, calling the dogs.

Most of the time the two malamutes would come bounding at the first call, but tonight they faltered, circling in front of the door before coming, whining, into the basement and their spacious kennel. Morgan had never seen them like this apprehensive, fretting. Caesar carried his tail down, almost between his legs, and Pompei stopped every few steps to bite nervously at a spot on his flank.

"Sorry, guys," said Morgan as she made sure they had dry food and plenty of water for the night.

As she reached the kitchen once again, she heard the teakettle shrill. Rubbing at her arms through the thick velour, she went to heat the pot and measure out the tea, finding such mundane things more comforting than a devoted servant would have been. As she set the tea to steep, she decided that she would wait another hour and then she would call Gail Harris. At least, she decided, they could worry together.

Mickey had been sweating the last few minutes, and the scent was sharp and skunkish with fear. In spite of everything he attempted, he felt his clothes grow damper. He felt Charlie next to him, and was angry and ashamed that there should be any witness to his cowardice.

"I think this is them," said Paco, coming down the dressing room hall at a brisk pace. "Where do you want them?"

"In the trunk. In the boxes labeled 'Business Records.' That way, even if they stop us, they'll have to have a warrant to search those boxes in the trunk or they can't touch us." He giggled. "Towne is always finding the angles. He said that they're going to have to be extra careful about me because of the way the cops blew it before."

"So will you open the trunk?" Paco asked, clearly unimpressed.

Mickey had a few hideous seconds when he feared he would sneeze. The open loading door had brought dust and chill with it.

"Oh. Sure. On the driver's side, the lever with the picture of the trunk lid up. Go ahead and do it yourself." He started to whistle, then stopped. "You did arrange for the storage unit in your name, right?"

"My full legal name, with all three middle names," said Paco with emphasis. "No one's going to get their hands on this shit."

"That's good. Say, do you remember where we put the tape that was in the second camera? I checked it out, and it's empty."

Paco had opened the driver's door of the Lincoln. "I thought that was with the stuff you took over to Stelle's place."

"I don't think so," said Scooter, then gave it brief consideration. "But maybe I did." He snapped his fingers. "Load up and we'll get out of here. We'll come back to do a better cleanup come afternoon."

The trunk lid popped. "Is that all you can think of?"

"Evidence is all I can think of right now. And making sure we can get rid of it." He paced back over to the settee. "We got to get some good tapes going, Paco. We don't improve our product, we're down the tubes for sure."

Paco was busy putting the videotapes in the boxes. "You want me to seal these lids?"

"That's what the tape's for."

Although the breeze through the open door was cold, now Mickey was glad of it, for it made him alert. Even the smell of exhaust from the idling Lincoln served to hold his attention more than his hiding place. He had passed the urge to sneeze but now he felt panicky, and he had to ignore the sound of his pulse as his heart beat faster.

Beside him, Charlie brought his senses back, but the cold did not disperse. He remembered how he came to be at the warehouse, and what he had done there. The voices of the dead lingered faintly, but there was less allure and compulsion in them than there had been only minutes before. His face hurt and he welcomed it for its immediacy.

"You finished up back there?" Scooter called as Paco continued at the back of the Lincoln.

"Not quite yet." There was a loud crash and Paco let out a stream of obscenities.

"What the fuck was that?" Scooter asked sharply.

"I dropped the jack. Why don't you put it back where it belongs? Shit, it's scraping my hand." Paco came around the car. "Okay, let's get out of here."

"Yeah," said Scooter. "You close the door. I'll back out."

The Lincoln door slammed, and it hiccoughed as it was put into reverse.

With a whine of protest the loading door clanked closed.

"Don't move yet," whispered Charlie, so very quietly that Mickey almost could not hear him.

"But—"

"Paco's inside," Charlie warned in the same soft voice.

As if in confirmation, the loading door groaned upward again, the counterweight cable moaning, then slammed down tight. Both Charlie and Mickey heard the padlock snick back into place.

The Lincoln's door opened and closed, the engine raced and then it was gone.

Mickey rolled free of the bed and sat up, his head almost between his knees. He took several long, deep breaths, making himself let the air out slowly, steadying himself.

For Charlie, moving took longer, demanded more concentration. He felt as if his bones were unfamiliar to him, and that the cold was slowing him to a glacial pace. He did not try to stand up until he had sat beside Mickey for several minutes. "Thanks," he said at last.

"What for?" Mickey asked.

"For coming," said Charlie. "I didn't think I'd get quite so . . . drawn in. I've never been exposed to anything so deliberate as this. I didn't know what it would be like." He had a fleeting, appalling thought of what might have happened to him if Mickey Trang had not followed him, if he had been discovered alone in this warehouse when Paco arrived. He had experienced enough of Cadao Talbot's death to shudder at what could have been done to him at the hands of those two men.

"What now?" Mickey asked when he was sure he could speak without having his voice break.

Charlie hitched his shoulders. "I guess it's time to go home."

The fright and tension of the last hour gathered in him. "Is that all?" he demanded with elaborate politeness, knowing his behavior was shameful, yet unable to stop. "Now that you're through breaking the law you're going home? What was all this about, anyway?"

"It was about finding out what happened to Cadao. I know now," said Charlie quietly.

"So do I," Mickey countered with heat. "And I didn't need to pull some damnfool stunt like coming down here the way you did. All I needed to do was look at his corpse."

Cold beckoned, offering distance and quiet. Charlie did not quite shrug but he made a concession of sorts to Mickey. "If all I wanted to know was that he was dead, that's all I needed to do, too." He got to his feet slowly and laboriously. "That wasn't all there was to it."

"Sure," said Mickey with cutting sarcasm.

Charlie stood very still. "You can believe what you want. And you can be angry if that will let you mourn. But don't disdain what I tell you, Mickey."

"I thought all that 'heap big medicine' crap was supposed to be demeaning to Indians," he said, refusing to be mollified, intending to wound.

"I won't answer that," said Charlie. "At least not now. Later, if you decide you want to talk about this sensibly, let me know." It was a major effort to walk. He put his mind to the formidable task of coordinating his legs to get him into the hall. "Did you—"

"Hear them? Oh, you can bet I did that," said Mickey Trang with the kind of obduracy that made Charlie nod in sympathy. "If the court needs someone to impeach the testimony of either of those guys, you can bet I'll do it."

"Un-hum," said Charlie, his legs aching with his labor. "How do you figure that?"

"What do you mean?'' Mickey asked, reaching for his flashlight to show them the way down the dressing room hall.

"I mean, while I agree with you completely, I know that you are not going to be able to do much in court." He could feel more than see the resistance in Mickey's demeanor. "You didn't actually see these men, did you."

"I heard them. I would recognize their voices again." He sounded so committed that Charlie had to resist his inclination to laugh.

"And how long do you think it would take Harding Towne to shoot you down in court? He's not going to accept you as a witness in terms of what you've heard unless you're a voice teacher or blind. You're neither of those things. Neither of us is here legally, and that would make anything we say questionable. I doubt we'd be given immunity under the circumstances." Charlie recited his objections as he made his way with great care from dressing room door to dressing room door. "You want this man in jail. You have a colleague dead because of what these two men might have done—"

"Might?" Mickey challenged.

"That's right; might have done," said Charlie, stopping and turning back, grateful for the chance to lean on the door and recover a very little of his remaining strength. "Harding Towne can make tatters of your assertion in less than five minutes, guaranteed."

"Not if there's a good cross-examination," said Mickey.

"And if the questions are allowed and the answers don't confuse the jury too much, and all the rest of it." He put his hand to his head, not entirely satisfied that his brains were back in his skull. "Pay attention to what I'm telling you, Mickey. We both know that Scooter Ferrand and Paco are part of the same group and that they're making kiddie-porn films, some of them very violent and perhaps deadly. But our testimony—assuming they would permit me on the stand, which isn't likely—could well be worthless because it might be viewed as still being fruit of the poisonous tree. If that is the case, nothing we can do will change what has already happened." He sounded more like himself now, and he was able to stand a little straighter. The cold continued to permeate his body, but not with the ferocity of ten minutes ago. He looked directly at Mickey. "I could probably try to get my testimony in via amicus curiae, but that might be excluded from the first."

"So you're telling me all this—Cadao's death and whatever it was you were doing here, and the rest of it—was for nothing." Mickey let his anger have full range as he confronted Charlie. "That's a lot of help."

"No, it isn't," said Charlie very bluntly, "but it does give us a place to start."

"That's a great comfort," Mickey said nastily.

"There could be one more thing." He turned away from the main room of the warehouse so he would not have to look as he spoke. "There's a video camera back by . . . by that iron cot. You go check it out. It might have a tape in it. If you take it with you, there might be something on it that would be helpful, even if it's blocked as evidence. Go get the tape, if it's there. Neither man went back to that camera." He said it quickly, attempting to stave off the vertigo-like sensation that iron cot created in him.

"You sure it's a good idea?" Mickey asked. "If it's disallowed, what good does it do?"

"I don't know," Charlie admitted, "but it could make a difference."

With a great show of reluctance, Mickey made his way to the iron cot. He inspected the video camera in a perfunctory sort of way, then stopped, opened the side and removed a tape. "What's on it?"

"I hope with all my heart I don't know," said Charlie, taking two involuntary steps backward, moving to the next dressing room door.

"What do you mean?" Mickey asked, annoyed with himself that he had bothered to question Charlie at all, though he pocketed the videotape as he said it.

"I mean," said Charlie with full deliberation, "that we may have to come at this business sideways. And when I figure out what I mean by—" Without warning, Charlie collapsed in the doorway of dressing room number 2.

Morgan held the receiver with both hands as if she were afraid she might break it. "Does that mean you intend to leave his car where it is?"

"Well, I wouldn't trust him to drive, not the shape he's in," said Mickey. "I'm calling from my own car. I hope half of San Francisco isn't listening."

"I doubt it, not at this hour," said Morgan, reminding herself that the right to privacy did not extend to conversations on cellular telephones. This isn't a case, she reminded herself, and it isn't being presented in court. No one is checking you out right now, no reporter, no lawyers, no one. You're entitled to your own opinion. She did her best to sound confident. "I was waiting for your call. I hope everything went well."

"You can ask Charlie about it, when he's a little more himself." He hesitated. "Tell you what though, Your Honor: I've never seen anyone so cold as he is right now. If it was me, I'd get something going in the kitchen or the bathroom or both that would warm him up. I swear he's only a couple of degrees warmer than marble."

It was an effort not to scream at Mickey for tactlessness. "Have you put something around his shoulders?"

"Not yet. I always carry a blanket in the back." Once more he faltered. "I don't want to sound crazy, but I think that Charlie really did something witchy tonight. I can't stop thinking that he managed to make it all . . . real." There was another pause. "When I found him—it was like he was somewhere else, somewhere far away from here."

"Well, bring him back to me, Mickey, will you?" Morgan hung up before her voice broke.

Mickey was limp with fatigue, his muscles as useless as deflated balloons. As he parked in Charlie's driveway—there were no places available at the curb for more than two blocks—he hung over the wheel, having no idea how he was going to get Charlie out of his car and himself home.

"I'm grateful," Charlie said in an undervoice. This was about the fifth time he had mentioned it.

"No big thing," said Mickey, not wanting to go into the matter again. He was already regarding their time in Connoisseur Studios as a shared nightmare, not part of the real world at all. He wanted it behind him. The weight of the tape in his pocket was immense.

"I . . . I'll talk to you tomorrow. Later today," he corrected himself as he reached to open the door.

"Okay," said Mickey, wanting Charlie to leave him alone.

Charlie managed to get the door open and swing one leg out. He had forgot how cold he was. He did not know if he could make it up the stairs. "We'll work out how to get this to the police. I'll . . . think of something," he promised vaguely.

"Good night, counselor." Mickey reached over and pulled the passenger door closed, preparing to back out of the driveway just as Charlie reached the bottom step. He resisted the urge to tap the horn as he drove off into the misty night.

Before Charlie could drag himself up the first three steps, Morgan opened the door and rushed down to him.

Again the bath was filled, and at Charlie's instruction certain herbs—rosemary, winter savory, pansy, others unknown to her—were added.

"Charlie," she admitted with consternation, "I'd rather you saw a doctor. You're much too cold."

"If I'm still cold when I wake up, you can call one for me. But I won't be." The smile he offered her was ghastly. He dropped his clothes as he removed them and he left them where they fell. When Morgan bent to pick them up, he stopped her. "No. No, don't touch them. They aren't fit for touching any more. There are—"

"It's part of what you did?" she asked, though it was not a question.

"Yes." He looked at the oversized green bathtub. "Let me clean the worst off first, will you? Then get in with me?"

"If that's what you want," said Morgan, still watching him, her robe clutched tight around her.

He was starting into the tub when he remembered something. "I have an appointment at nine-thirty tomorrow. Will you let them know I won't be able to keep it?" His foot seemed to scald as he touched it to the water. He knew it was not nearly as hot as he usually insisted it be, but that meant little.

"All right," she said in her most neutral tone.

He looked around at her. "Oh, Morgan, don't let it frighten you."

"It doesn't," she said, and then she qualified her answer. "Most of the time it doesn't. But when you . . . the first time I went to work at Ogilvie, Tallant and Moon, you did something like this. About that malpractice case."

He nodded.

"Well, that scared the shit out of me. And I hardly knew you then." To her astonishment, she began to cry. "And tonight, I was sick with worry about you the whole time you were gone. I was afraid you'd never come back to me. Or you'd come back damaged." She looked away from him, not wanting him to have the burden of her tears.

He reached out and touched her arm. "Morgan. Morgan, Morgan."

"You were in danger like that, weren't you?" She dared not look around for fear of what she might see in his eyes.

"Yes," he told her simply.

"Oh, God." Her shoulders were shaking; she pressed the cuff of her robe against her open mouth to keep from sobbing.

"Morgan. Would you rather I lie?" The tone of his voice made her turn; he did not often reveal so much of his love in how he said her name. "You know I would not put myself at risk for no reason. You know that I would not do anything that would harm you, not knowingly. Then trust me, Morgan. I won't do anything that would endanger what we have together unless not acting would endanger it more."

She caught hold of his hand. "You couldn't do that."

"Couldn't I? Would you feel I was the man you want to live with if I could know about men who rape and kill teenaged girls in order to provide video entertainment for their . . . clients? Know about them and do nothing?" His eyes, dark and unyielding as slate, fixed on her. "How could I ignore that, and still be the man you want to love?"

"But if something happened to you . . ." It was all she could bring herself to venture.

"Death is going to happen to both of us eventually." He had to harden himself against the scattered echoes of dead voices. "When it comes, I hope it isn't cruel. That's the best deal available." His hand tightened on hers.

She made herself wipe her eyes. "Take your bath. Call me when you're ready."

He gave her two little nods. "When I'm warm enough," he said.

Morning came and went before Charlie Moon woke up. His deep, restless sleep turned calmer after the sun rose, and he slumbered easily. Eventually a car passing in the street honked twice, and jarred him out of a fragmented dream. He had a brief sense of disorientation as he opened his eyes, then he recalled everything that had taken place. He brought his hand to his forehead, astonished that he had no headache, no protesting muscles beyond the usual. He stretched out, testing himself to be certain that the gelid lassitude of the previous night was entirely gone. Then he sat up. There was a note on Morgan's pillow:

Charlie love,
I was here at noon; you were still asleep. I'll be late this evening: expect me around eight after the Mayor delivers his annual harangue to the judges.
Call me if you need anything. In fact, call me. I'll take a recess to find out how you are.

I love you,
Morgan

A quick glance at the bedside clock informed him that it was two-eleven. He stood up, dumbfounded that he had actually slept so long. He read over Morgan's note again and reached for the telephone.

"I'd like to speak to Judge Studevant. I know she's in court," said Charlie when he reached the courthouse switchboard, "but her instructions are to interrupt her."

"May I say who is calling?" the operator asked, sounding more like a machine than most of the women on the staff.

"Yes. This is Charles Moon." He waited while the call was put through to her bailiff, and waited again until Morgan herself picked up the line. "How are you?" he asked her.

"More to the point," she said, "how are you? You were out in the ether when I saw you a couple hours ago."

"I wasn't out in the ether, actually. I was asleep," he corrected her, his voice tender. "I miss having you beside me." He went on before she could speak. "And no, that is not a suggestion that you should compromise your position as a judge and give up everything you've worked for so I can have a few extra moments of security."

"You are better," said Morgan, halfway between aggravation and joy. "I'm glad."

"Thank you," he said, with more ease than he generally showed with the words. "It'll take a day or so before I'm back to speed, but the worst is over. It's time for me to start catching up. I've got to call Elizabeth, and after I speak with Frank, I'm going to have a conversation with Glen Mitchell. Did Mickey Trang call while you were home?" He tried to keep his voice light, his attitude brisk so that he would be less of an intrusion for her.

"No, but there was a message from him. He said he'd watched as much of the tape as he could stand." She paused. "From what he told me, I gather it was pretty rough."

"That's likely, I'm afraid," said Charlie, shuddering at the recollection of the iron cot.

"His message said he'd be with Gail Harris this afternoon, if you wanted to talk to him." She had a dozen questions she wanted to ask, but not on the telephone during a ten-minute recess.

"What's up for court today?" Charlie asked, as if to head her off.

She hesitated. "Oh, a really smarmy custody case. The dead mother's parents versus the father. The whole thing stinks. I don't like the idea of giving either of them the child. But I suppose that's what it will have to be in the end, unless someone comes up with a different, workable proposal. I'm having a meeting with the attorneys this afternoon, before the Mayor's annual pep talk."

"Do you want me to come down for that?" Charlie offered.

"The pep talk, that is?" He would not be welcome at the meeting in her chambers.

Morgan knew how much he hated such functions; she disliked them intensely herself. "I might want it, but I'm not going to ask. I can't stand the thought of you going through two crises in less than twenty-four hours. You stay home and think up something good for dinner."

"Yes, Your Honor," he said, speaking very precisely.

"I've got to get back to this dismal suit. I'll see you later." She was about to hang up, but added, "I love you more than anything, Charlie."

"And I you," said Charlie as she put down the receiver.

Gail Harris answered the telephone on the fifth ring, much slower than her usual response time. Instead of her customary greeting, she said, "Hello?" as if she did not want to speak at all.

"Gail, this is Charlie. How are you?" He asked with genuine concern, wishing he could offer her something other than condolences.

"I'm managing, most of the time; occasionally I lose it," she answered, her tone cool. "I suppose this is for Mickey, though."

"I would like to talk to him, yes, but I want to know if there's anything I can do. For you." He waited, anticipating nothing, neither anger nor contrition.

"You can put the scum who killed him six feet under," she answered in a brittle voice.

He did not known how to answer her, sharing her feelings and knowing that she was still in the first rage of mourning. He tried to make his response appropriate. "I'll do what I can."

"I'll get Mickey. Don't keep him too long. He's a wreck." She hurried away, and Charlie listened to her footsteps as they receded.

When Mickey came on the line, he said, "I left a message for you."

"So I understand," said Charlie. "The videotape?"

"I watched about ten minutes of it. It's not Cadao, thank God, but I think it might be that girl who was killed recently, the one whose body was found by the Palace of the Legion of Honor."

"Susan Lake?" Charlie asked, surprised.

"Yeah. I think. It was late in the . . . proceedings. And I think this was a number two camera. It shows mainly distance shots, the camera holding still for long periods, no zooms, just pictures and . . . and sounds." He coughed. "What am I supposed to do with it?"

"Well," said Charlie, choosing his words very precisely, "I have a few suggestions. Mind you, I am not advising you as your attorney, merely telling you the law as I understand it in answer to a theoretical question or two. You're not supposed to conceal knowledge of a crime from the law. I think it very likely that you have a civic duty to present this tape to the police."

"And then what? Confess to breaking-and-entering?" Mickey asked.

"Of course not. You did not break-and-enter. I did. You followed after me, though you were not specifically instructed to do so. Because you were afraid that something might have gone wrong in my attempt to gain information on this particular operation, you came after me, not knowing that I had not gained access to the building in a legal fashion—and I'll thank you to keep that much to yourself. Your evidence on that is only hearsay—you did not see me enter the building, did you?—but I don't want to put ideas in the cops' heads." This warning was delivered with a trace of humor but not enough for either man to smile. "If there're any questions about the hole in the fence, we'll have to think of a plausible reason for one to exist, that we have only taken advantage of. Perhaps one of the boys buying Polaroids from Paco followed him and wanted to find out what was going on inside."

"I could make a pretty good case for that," said Mickey, warming to the subject in spite of himself.

"Yes. As could I. Not that I am suggesting that you lie to the police. I would be most remiss in my responsibilities if I did that." Charlie was slightly more amused now. "But if our suppositions run along similar lines, I think it likely that the police would not challenge us too closely, considering what we are bringing to them."

"You mean what I am bringing to them," said Mickey.

"Yes. That's accurate enough." Charlie hesitated. "If you can, arrange to give the information to Sergeant Glen Mitchell. He's in Missing Persons and specializes in abductions. Since we have reason to think that the videotape is part of his ongoing investigation, let him have it and turn it over to Homicide in his own way. He knows how to get around the SFPD."

"Okay, so I stumbled into the warehouse by accident, afraid that you were in nonspecific danger. What other lies would you like me to tell in court?" Mickey inquired, then said, "Sorry. That was a cheap shot. My tongue gets sharp when I'm upset."

"So I've noticed," said Charlie drily. "I don't expect you to tell any lies in court. But if you want the cops to take that tape, you have to make sure that they keep their minds on what matters—that videotape. My guess is that neither you nor I will ever be called as a witnesses, just as I suspect that this tape will not be allowed as evidence. But I reckon that it will point the cops in the right direction, and they will make sure that their case is boulder-steady when they go to trial this time."

"I hope you're right," said Mickey.

"I'm reasonably certain that's how it will go." He put his fingers to the cut on his cheek and felt the reassuring presence of a scab. In time it would be a small, trangular scar, looking a little like an arrowhead. "When you talk to Mitchell, you can say that you were not looking to find this tape, but that after the two men came to the warehouse and took some of the records there, you wanted to be certain that one of the tapes they left behind did not fall into the wrong hands."

"That sounds pretty thin to me, Charlie," said Mickey.

"It won't hold very much water, but I think there will be enough, especially if you tell Mitchell that you have been worried that Susan Lake's death might be connected to Cadao Talbot's."

Mickey hesitated. "I think what bothers me most is . . . whatever it was you were really doing in there."

Charlie became more remote. "It's an old discipline. I learned it long ago." He was not ready to tell Mickey any more, given his earnest skepticism of the night before. "We'll discuss it some-day," said Charlie in another tone, very polite though not inviting.

"Pardon me, counselor, but I'm not going to make a bet on that," said Mickey, and was able to chuckle. "Okay. I'll go to the cops."

"Today," said Charlie, preparing to make a call.

"All right; an hour," said Mickey, and sighed as he hung up.

FOURTEEN

Friday evening, Saturday and Sunday

ELIZABETH HERSELF OPENED the door as Charlie approached. She was dressed in a neat suit of tan silk broadcloth and she had put on her necklace of baroque pearls for the occasion. "Not that I think women over fifty should wear only pearls. That's a ridiculous notion. But faceted stones for a casual tea-and-cocktails is too self-indulgent." She came a step or two nearer. "I've told Frank that you would—" She stopped and stared long and critically at Charlie. "Please don't take offense, but you look quite dreadful, Charlie."

He was able to smile at her as she linked arms with him. "Not bad enough to scare small children and the mentally bewildered, I hope." He wanted to discuss something else, but knew that the more he resisted her chosen topic, the more doggedly Elizabeth would pursue it. And it was true that he looked as if he was recovering from a long, wasting illness. He had been shocked when he looked in the mirror to shave before he called Mickey Trang two hours ago. "Morgan didn't say a word about it."

"That's because she's besotted with you," said Elizabeth, making it clear she would accept no excuses from Charlie's wife. "And no doubt she wanted to keep from adding to your state." She peered up at him in the fading light. "What on earth did you do?"

"I did a little investigating," said Charlie in a tone intended to dismiss the matter.

She shook his arm. "Which is your very polite Canadian way of telling me to mind my own business, I suppose." She pushed the front door open a little wider and dropped his arm long enough to precede him through jt. "I trust that whatever it was you were doing got the results you wanted."

"I think it will turn out to. I'll need to make a telephone call in a short while, to be sure." For the first time he had no awkwardness at the prospect of meeting Frank Girouard. "After the call, we can celebrate."

"We'll begin celebrating right now, if you please. There's time enough to make the call a little later. You look like a sip of sherry is in order," said Elizabeth. "I trust that Frank will appreciate what you've done for him. Not that he will, of course." She indicated the hallway and the door to the library. "Incidentally, I've been having some conversation with Frank the last few days."

"Have you?" said Charlie, wishing that Elizabeth would not move quite so energetically. In general he admired her indefatigable spirit, but today it was a bit much for him.

As they entered the library, Elizabeth indicated the chairs that flanked the fireplace. "Sit down, for heaven's sake. You're weak as a cat. Not that cats are often weak." She sat down opposite him. "As I was saying," she resumed as soon as she was satisfied that Charlie was comfortable, "I've been speaking with Frank. About his future. And while I'm sure he'll want to return to teaching, it might be best if he waited a short while. That's what his therapist has been saying, in any case. Frank's become gun-shy—small wonder—and he needs a little time to steady his nerves, reestablish his perspective. So," she continued emphatically, slapping the arms of the chair, "I have suggested to him that he might like to work for me, at least through the summer. I won't stand to have that Clifford around another month. Frank can't cook, but I can find someone who can to tend to such chores. I think Frank might enjoy running my household while he and that wife of his work something out and he makes a few decisions about his job. I think he should return to teaching, but not just yet."

Charlie shook his head in amusement. "You are the most ruthless old woman I've ever known in my life, Elizabeth. What you really mean is that you've decided that this would be good for Frank and you've badgered and bullied him into it." He could not quite laugh, but there were glints in his eyes.

Elizabeth Kendrie did her best to look affronted. "I'm not ruthless at all." She folded her hands primly in her lap. "I can't help but notice that Frank would do better if he had a little more time to . . . to revive. In fact, you appear to need it more than he, but I won't mention that."

"That's an apophasis, Elizabeth," Charlie murmured, hoping to get her off-track.

"And me using rhetoric, at my age," she declared, pretending much shock. "And *that* was an antiphrasis, as I recall." She reached for the small bell that stood on the low table in front of her. "Clifford hates it when I ring this. He says it makes him feel like something out of *Upstairs/Downstairs*." She rang it, anyway, a wicked little smile at the corners of her mouth. She leaned back and returned to her question. "Now, tell me briefly what you have been doing to yourself. Doubtless it was something to do with—"

"The dead," said Charlie, who had learned in the last four years not to mince words when Elizabeth was this insistent.

"Which dead?" she inquired, not turning a hair.

It was Charlie who hesitated. "Children, mostly. It was bad." He looked at her. "There are ways to learn from the dead, to go with them, or to listen to them, to how they died. To go with them is a spirit walk, to listen is to call up their voices. The voices of the dead, the voices of their killers."

"Like a séance?" Elizabeth asked, then held up her hand to keep him quiet while Clifford came into the room. "Clifford, we'd both like sherry and something light to eat. And ask Mister Girouard to join us in ten minutes, please."

Clifford made a slight nod to indicate he understood, then left them alone once more.

"No," said Charlie as Elizabeth motioned to him to go on. "It's not quite like that. At least, I hope that mediums don't go through—" He made himself break off. "They died of torture, most of them. I could hear their deaths, and what they heard, the men who were killing them. I took on what they had left of their pain so I could know how it happened."

"And what did that achieve?" asked Elizabeth, for once in a neutral tone.

"It told me how they died and what had made them die." He knew he had not answered her question.

"That sounds quite harrowing," said Elizabeth, apparently willing to accept what little he had told her. Then she turned toward him. "Does this change anything for Frank?"

"I'm not certain, not yet," said Charlie carefully. "That is one of the reasons I have to make a phone call."

She gave him a satisfied smile. "And I've waylaid you. Well, while Clifford tries to decide which sherry is appropriate—shooting sherry would be my choice—I think it might be best if you slipped out to the lanai and used the extension there."

Charlie rose. "You're being very cooperative, Elizabeth," he said. "That fills me with apprehension."

She laughed. "Now, what could an old lady like me do to you?"

"I daren't speculate," he said, thinking as he moved away from her that she had the knack of bringing him back to himself. As he left the library, he had the impression that Elizabeth had risen behind him, and was up to something. He was tempted to linger, but instead went down the hallway into the lanai and placed his call to Glen Mitchell, hoping as he did that the Sergeant was still at his desk.

"Yeah," said Mitchell as he came on the line.

"Good afternoon, Sergeant," said Charlie mildly. "I expect you're waiting for this call."

"Moon!" said Mitchell. "You're damned right." He took a deep breath and launched into their conversation. "I thought you might call earlier. That investigator you work with—Trang?—was here half an hour ago. He brought me a present. A videotape. He's good at his job; at least he was good at it here. He kept his mouth shut about where he got the tape, just answered the most basic questions. He didn't exactly say it came from you, but he didn't deny it, either."

Charlie kept his tone even, though a cold finger touched him. "What did you find on the tape? Anything interesting?"

"We found Susan Lake, is what we found," said Mitchell, his words so abrupt that Charlie knew how grisly the tape must be. "In pieces. I haven't seen the end of it yet. I can't stomach it. We have the voices of both men, for voiceprints, and we have something we might not be able to use in court, given how we got the tape. We'll refer to it as a tip, I guess. But we got those two perps cold."

"Can you establish a link to Cadao Talbot?" Charlie asked, wanting to know as much for Mickey and Gail as for himself.

"Probably. We have semen types from Susan Lake, and we found . . . more of the same in Talbot. We have a match on them." He did not speak for a moment. "I think the D. A. will accept that."

"Pretty hard not to," said Charlie, then asked, "What bearing could this have on other cases?"

"You mean your case with that schoolteacher?" Mitchell sounded tired now.

"I didn't say that," Charlie pointed out.

"No, you didn't. You were real careful about that." He made a ponderous sigh. "I think there are more than enough grounds for reasonable doubt, all things considered. We're going to get a composite drawing of that guy Paco—after a certain point on the tape, he took off his mask. He probably didn't think he needed it any more—and we're going to turn it over to Ms. Aldred. She's planning to see what happens if she shows it to the girls in your case."

"It could be very hard on them," said Charlie, remembering what the dead experienced at Paco's hands.

"Paco. We're trying to get a make on him now," Mitchell went on. "We're pretty sure he isn't Hispanic. He doesn't look real Hispanic, and that accent of his isn't Hispanic, either."

"He has an accent?" Charlie interjected, thinking he had not noticed one.

"Faint, but it's there. It's not the kind of accent you expect a guy called Paco to have, so because it isn't strong, you don't really hear it." He cleared his throat. "We might have to call Trang to the stand."

"That's all right with me, if it's about how the tape came into his hands, so long as he's not required to discuss his cases," said Charlie. "What he was doing at that location could be regarded as a matter of client confidentiality, but the circumstances—"

"He said he was following you," Mitchell cut in.

"So I understand," said Charlie, offering nothing.

Mitchell was losing patience. "Aw, come on, counselor, tell me what this is all about."

"Client confidentiality," Charlie reminded him. His hands were feeling cold again. He looked out the wall of windows to the rhododendrons in the garden, thinking that in another month they would bloom. Some of them were already starting to show first ferrules of pink and salmon and amethyst.

Mitchell said, "What you mean is you aren't going to give me squat."

"You know I can't, so let's stop tap dancing," Charlie said, not wanting to keep up the game. He sensed a breeze from the huge sliding glass door; on most occasions he would have enjoyed it, but at present the goose flesh it raised was unpleasant. "I haven't seen the contents of the tape, but I saw the still photography—

some of it, anyway—that they had on file. I'd guess that a good seventy percent of it was of underage girls. They've moved a lot of their goods to a storage site. I don't know where."

"This is the fucking weirdest tip you're giving me," Mitchell complained. "Go on."

"The space where the tapes and photos are stored is rented in Paco's real name—" Charlie began.

"Oh, great. We don't know who the bastard really is, and—"

"Just out of curiosity, how many storage spaces in San Francisco do you suppose have been rented in, say, the last two months by someone with three middle names?" Charlie interrupted.

Mitchell grunted with surprise. "Three middle names?" he repeated.

"That's what he said."

"You talked to him?" Mitchell asked, startled afresh.

"No." Charlie watched twilight take hold of the garden, softening it until it gradually disappeared. "You might try South San Francisco, Colma and Daly City, while you're at it. Call San Mateo County and see if they'll cooperate."

"Okay," said Mitchell, his defeat of an hour ago gone. "There aren't going to be many with three middle names, no matter what they are."

"And, just so the search warrant will be accurate, the tapes and pictures are in packing boxes for office supplies." He added the one thing that rankled with him, the thing he had not mentioned yet to Morgan. "I think this guy may be doing business with Scooter Ferrand."

"Shit!" Mitchell burst out. "Shitshitshitshit."

"Be very careful to mind the fine details," Charlie warned him.

"Four guys in this department saw part of that tape. It's on its way to Homicide. We're not going to let those . . . those *alleged criminals* get away with it." He made himself calm down. "Don't worry. No hotdogs on it this time."

"Good," said Charlie.

"I suppose you're not to be mentioned," said Mitchell with a trace of amusement. "Especially if we get Ferrand back in front of your wife."

"No, I'm not," Charlie said, adding, "And neither is Mickey, if you can avoid it."

"Bad for business," Mitchell agreed. "I'll do what I can. But I might not be able to keep him out of court."

"I know that, and so does he," Charlie said. "Be careful, Sergeant. Those are very dangerous men."

"I figured that out, watching the tape," said Mitchell. He paused, making a decision. "I appreciate the call, Moon; I don't want to say I owe you one, but . . . maybe I do."

Charlie was glad that Mitchell had not thanked him; he was not anxious to be under ritual obligation to the police officer. "Good hunting, Sergeant," he said as he hung up. He did not linger in the lanai where that fickle, thin breeze could find him.

Frank Girouard was in the library with Elizabeth when Charlie returned. He was sitting on the short sofa, a glass of sherry in one hand, a bacon-wrapped broiled shrimp in the other. He rose as Charlie came into the room. Apparently Elizabeth had warned him about how Charlie looked; aside from an uneasy shifting of his eyes, Frank said nothing more than, "It's good to see you again, Moon."

"Good to see you, Frank," Charlie said, coming nearer and holding out his hand. While he had the man's hand in his, he said, "I never asked. Do you know someone named Paco?" His hand remained unchanged. Charlie dropped it.

"Paco?" Frank thought it over. "No, I don't think so. Not anyone at the school, unless maybe someone on the kitchen staff or maintenance, or someone like that . . ." He shrugged. "I can't place it."

"Did you ever hear any of your students talking about a Paco—any of the girls, especially?" Charlie went on deliberately. His tone was light but his eyes were piercing. "It's important, Frank."

"Paco. Paco." Frank glowered. "The trouble is, half the time you don't know what they're talking about, anyway." He regarded Charlie with puzzlement. "What is it? What's this all about?"

Charlie answered very carefully. "We think there may be a break in your case. We need to find out who this Paco is, and then what he has been doing." Out of the corner of his eye he saw Elizabeth nod vigorously. "Try to remember, Frank. I need to know everything you can tell me about a man named Paco."

Frank put his sherry down and stared toward the hearth, at the laid fire waiting to be lit. After a long silence, he said, "I can't be sure. But I think I heard a couple of my composition-and-grammar students talking about a Paco. It was last semester. I wasn't really listening, but I think that was the name. One of them said he was sexy. The other one blushed and looked embarrassed. I thought they were discussing a rock star. You know how girls that age are."

"Actually, no, I don't. Not very well." Charlie sat down in the chair he had vacated to make his telephone call. He picked up the single glass of sherry waiting on the lacquer tray, but did not drink. "How long ago was this? Which girl said Paco was sexy, do you remember?"

"God, that was months ago," said Frank, doing his best to cooperate. "I think it was right after class. I think one of the girls was talking to the other about the way Paco made her feel. Girls that age gush a lot. It was the usual sort of enthusiasm. The one who was silent wasn't jealous or petulant, just . . . embarrassed, like I said." He shook his head, frowned, then opened his free hand, palm up. "Sorry. I really don't remember anything more."

"If you should think of something, would you let me know about it?" Charlie asked.

"Certainly," said Frank, taking another taste of his sherry. "Is what Elizabeth told me true? Is the case almost over?" The questions came out of him in a rush.

"I think so," Charlie said. "Probably. Unless something else turns up. The way things are going now, all charges will be dropped against you."

"That's wonderful, Frank. But how sad. Oh, those poor girls," said Elizabeth at once. "To have to go through whatever was done to them and then to have to answer for their lie." She was on her feet abruptly, pacing in her strange, straight-legged way. "No child should have to go through what they have gone through."

Charlie watched her. "And the fact that they did their best to ruin Frank Girouard's reputation? What about that, Elizabeth?"

"That's reprehensible, of course. It was wholly . . . it is a very wrong thing to blame Frank as they have done. I don't think it can be excused without any remark. On the other hand, I believe they intended no malice, not from what I've been told. And it's understandable, in its way. We're not speaking of grown women, but girls, who are just beginning to enter the realm of women. No one prepared them for something like this. They didn't comprehend the repercussions of what they reported; they only knew that they wanted to report the crime and remain safe. From what I've learned, they felt safer with Frank than they did with the man who abused them. It was an attempt at self-protection. You can't hold them responsible the way you would a woman of twenty-five."

She stopped and looked at Charlie. "Naturally you can't condone what they've done, but you won't do anything to them, will you? They've been through enough already."

"No more than I must," said Charlie, aware that Frank would not act against his former students. "Wendy Maple has helped a lot. If we can get the cooperation of two of the others, or better yet, if they are willing to identify the man or men who abused them, the whole thing ought to go very well." The last was deliberately optimistic, and he used it to set up his next statement. "I should think you could return to the classroom—"

"In a couple of years," Frank finished for him. "Elizabeth told me she talked to you already."

Charlie nodded. "She did. But I've known Elizabeth a long time and I know she's a little like a volcano—proud as you are of her spirit, you can't stop the lava if it comes your way. I don't want you to feel you must go along with her Plan B unless you want to."

"I want to," said Frank with purpose, then more tentatively, "I called Angelique today. I know you told me not to talk to her, but I had to. I wanted to tell her that the case was almost over, that the charges would be dropped, that I'd be cleared. I wanted her to know that she'd been wrong. I wanted to hear her admit it."

Charlie saw Elizabeth give a little frown and a tiny shake of her head. "And what did she say?" he asked Frank.

"She's certain that I did it. She thinks the school or someone is covering up for me. I tried to explain to her that she was wrong, but she wouldn't listen. She's made up her mind, and that's that." Frank downed half of his sherry. "It's a funny feeling, when you realize that someone could believe that about you, in the face of the evidence. It made me think that maybe there isn't a way to fix the marriage."

"It happens," said Charlie, recalling his own divorce well over a decade ago. At the time he fretted about what he could have done differently.

"I talked to her aunt for a while. She says she'll be happy to have Angelique with her for as long as she wants to stay." He stared down at the appetizers. "She said she thought it was too hard for Angelique, living in the city. She comes from a small town. Her only notion of how you do things in a city comes from watching carefully selected programs on television. She said that Angelique hadn't a notion of how to manage in San Francisco. There was too much of everything for her."

"Do you agree with her?" Charlie asked.

"Sometimes. Sometimes I don't." He shrugged a little. "That's why I'm in therapy." He looked over at Elizabeth. "Being here is going to help me. I know it. I can do the work Elizabeth needs and I can get my life back together. I won't jump if a student stays after class with a question. I won't feel that the entire administration is waiting to see if the law fucked up and let a bad guy get away." He covered a cough. "I think I want to rent the house out, at least until Angelique makes up her mind, or I make up mine. If she comes back, she'll want to live there. I don't want to sell it if we'll have a use for it. If we get through this. But if we don't, then . . ."

"Have another shrimp, Charlie," Elizabeth ordered, aware that Frank was about to get lost in a tangle. "And try the mustard. It's quite superb."

Obediently, Charlie took a shrimp, and gave Elizabeth his attention while she outlined her plans for bringing Frank into the household. At the end of it, she said, "As soon as you have the formal dismissal, we'll do a proper champagne dinner. You and Morgan will come, and if I'm annoyed with Victor, I'll ask him along, too. He's such a stuffy fool when he's disgruntled." She had the last shrimp herself. "That's the kind of advantage you have when you're my age. Even your oafish nephews have to pretend to respect you."

Charlie raised his brows. "You mean Victor Lovejoy?"

"He's my only nephew named Victor, and well you know it. And he wouldn't be where he is in the District Attorney's office if he hadn't begged me to use my clout for him. Now, of course, he resents me for doing it. Very full of himself, our Victor. So he might as well face the music." With a gesture of triumph, she put her hand on Frank's arm. "I'll cater the whole thing. You and Frank will be my honored guests." Her little eyes were bright and sly. "You know you'll both have a delightful time. Morgan, too, I shouldn't wonder."

Charlie had the last of his sherry, lifting his glass to Elizabeth in ironic acknowledgment. "Whatever you say, Elizabeth."

It was warm and breezy on Saturday, a day when laziness was acceptable. They had breakfast, then lounged around the living room, reading the paper and playing with the dogs. Around noon, Morgan suggested impulsively they get a picnic from the deli and spend the afternoon at the Marin Headlands. "We haven't been over there in months. The dogs'll love it."

Charlie's energy was still low, and he slid in and out of depression, but he considered it, recognizing the good sense her suggestion made. "Sure," he said after a short hesitation. "It sounds good." It sounded like earth and wind and sky, he told himself, all the things that heal. It sounded like woods and water and sandpipers at the edge of the waves.

As they gathered up the pages of the weekend paper, Charlie said, "Do you realize we've done something we never intended to do?"

She stared at him, the Travel section slipping from her fingers. "What?" She felt quite vulnerable; his question unnerved her but she no longer answered with a sharp challenge as she would have five years ago. She waited, not quite holding her breath. "What have we done, Charlie?"

"I think it's going to turn out that you and I have been working on the same case," he said as he rolled the papers into a tube. "Classic conflict of interest."

"Well, not intentionally," said Morgan, laughing as much from the absurdity of what he said as from respite. "And there's no real conflict of interest, is there? I was off the case before you were on."

"Not if they get Scooter Ferrand," said Charlie. "And Paco, and the rest of the slime."

She was almost as tall as he in her Romicas. She leaned over and kissed his cheek. "Tell you what: we won't do it again."

"Not intentionally," Charlie concurred.

By one-thirty they had picked up a lavish lunch at the most outrageous deli on Clement, had crossed the Golden Gate Bridge and were waiting for the light to change on the long tunnel leading through the mountain to Fort Barry and the northern part of the Golden Gate National Recreation Area.

"How is it, then?" Morgan asked a few hours later as the sun declined and the first line of fog blurred the horizon. Most of the picnic things had been put back in the basket but a few remained for occasional picking.

Charlie had been lying on his back on their blanket, his eyes half shaded against the increasing glare. He squinted up at her. "Pretty good and getting better."

Caesar and Pompei, for once tired enough to lie quietly, tongues lolling over their paws, yawned and sniffed at the few scraps remaining of lunch.

Morgan let them take turns finishing off the last of the quiche. "You guys are such beggars," she said, adding to Charlie, "You know, I never thought I'd come to like dogs. But I love these two."

"Looks like it's mutual," said Charlie, lying back down, his forearm sheltering his eyes. He remained quite still for some time; Morgan sat beside him, content to listen to the Pacific Ocean strum the shore. A while later Charlie said, "Thursday night, while I was listening to the dead, I remembered something my grandfather said. I'd forgot completely, but it came back to me. About the years my father was—"

"In the hospital," said Morgan, knowing how painful the topic was for Charlie. "What about it?"

"I always thought it was because he didn't want to be Indian. He knew he thought he had disappointed his father when he was born without medicine, but he magnified that until he . . ." Charlie rolled onto his side. "At least, that's what I assumed. He came to California before I was born, to build ships in World War II, but he was also getting away from Iron River. There was always something eating at him, and I thought it was being Ojibwa. But there was something my grandfather said, Thursday night, that . . ."

When he did not go on, Morgan looked over at him. "That what?"

"That made me think maybe it wasn't about being an Indian at all. All those years, going from Canada to California to Canada and then back to California again. Maybe it had nothing to do with race. Maybe it was something else entirely." He sat up and moved next to her. When he kissed her it was with comfortable passion and friendly desire. "You've made the difference for me, Morgan. Thursday night. Last year. Since we met."

She put her head on his shoulder. "You've done it for me, too."

He brushed her hair back from her brow; the wind caught it and messed it up again. "I'll do that proper, later."

This time she kissed him. "Promises, promises."

"I thought you'd like to know we have Scooter Ferrand in custody, Your Honor," George Wycliff told Morgan over the phone late on Sunday morning. He spoke with his usual zest and Morgan had to resist the urge to remind him he was not addressing a jury. "I was leaving for golf when the call came. I assumed you'd want to know, after what happened."

"What charges are being filed, and how were they established?" Morgan asked. She held up her hand to Charlie, signaling him to wait. They had decided to have brunch out and take in a matinee.

"Harding Towne can't quash this warrant, if that's what's worrying you. I've been told that the cops were tipped to a cache of Ferrand's . . . work. They traced the tapes to a storage place in Pacifica. We arranged the warrant through San Mateo as well as San Francisco, and the police executed the warrant first thing this morning. The storage unit wasn't Ferrand's, but his name was all over the boxes and the labels on the tapes. There are also files with letters bearing his signature, some of the receipts for specific tapes. The subject descriptions are making interesting reading." He was all but crowing now. "And according to what I was told by Lieutenant Palmerston of Homicide, this ties in with the murder of Susan Lake. We're now investigating other disappearances of teenaged girls who might also have been the victims of this pornography ring."

"That's excellent news, George," said Morgan sincerely. "You've taken quite a load off my mind."

"I can see how. No judge wants the release of a pervert like Ferrand on his . . . or her conscience." He did his best fulsome chuckle. "With what we've been told, an associate of his is willing to roll over on Ferrand for a reduced sentence. He's the man who actually rented the space and I gather he's afraid that Scooter will try to put all the blame on him. He's been very talkative, with his attorney present, so everything's kosher—not Harding Towne, naturally, but Jonah Warren. We can't let him off all the way, but we can reduce the charges significantly, and he's promised to be helpful." The chuckle came again, rotund and plummy.

"Thanks for letting me know about this, George," said Morgan. "I really appreciate your concern."

"Nice to give good news for a change," said Wycliff. "And now, if you will excuse me, the greens are calling."

"Have a good game, George, and watch your slice," said Morgan, and hung up and noticed that her hands were shaking. Until that instant she had not known how tense she was. She turned to look at Charlie, who stood by the door, jacket in hand. "Did you get the gist of that?"

"Not precisely, no. But it was about Scooter Ferrand?" There was a look of real satisfaction in his eyes.

"In custody," said Morgan. "It just could stick this time."

Charlie smiled.

Morgan studied him. "So." She waited for him to speak. When he said nothing, she asked, "Was it worth it?"

"You mean the other night?" He put his jacket on the newel-post and walked down the hall to her. "It's not a question of worth, it's a question of necessity."

She tried to find the right thing to say. When she spoke again, she startled Charlie. "Then let's make sure we know it happened. What if we call Mickey and Gail. We'll do a movie some other time, or bring home a videotape."

"No videotape," said Charlie softly. "Not for a while." He shook off his sudden melancholy. "You mean you want to tell them about Ferrand?"

"And all the rest of it. Including how much good Mickey did, turning over that information to the cops. Come on, Charlie. We'll buy us all brunch." She did not give him a chance to object. "I know it's hard on Gail, losing Cadao Talbot. You don't want to make light of her loss. That's not what this is about. This is about his living. And at least his killers aren't going to walk, not this time. He died—"

"A hero?" Charlie suggested, no trace of sarcasm in his voice.

Morgan nodded, her throat feeling tight. "It might not bring him back, but it takes a burden from her."

"I suppose," said Charlie carefully, then made up his mind. "All right. But if they don't want to, then the movie's still on?" He saw her nod, grinning. "Give me the phone. I'll call them."

Monday midmorning

LORNA BALLINGER SAT in her chambers, a stack of files on her very neat desk, her robe open to reveal a tailored business suit of hunter green beneath. Her hair was white and swept back from her lean, aristocratic features. Behind her a portable screen had been pulled down. She indicated the many chairs that had been crowded into the room, saying to the first arrivals, "Mister Maple, Missus Maple, if you will sit here in the front, please? And Wendy. Come here, girl." She held out her hand.

Cowed by her surroundings, Wendy Maple did as she was asked. "Good morning, Judge Ballinger."

"And to you, Wendy," said Judge Ballinger. "I'm afraid this meeting is going to have a larger attendance than I would have liked, but it appears that more than one investigation was on-going in this matter. Wendy, your courage in telling the truth was crucial. If you hadn't come forward, an innocent man might have been convicted and guilty men have gone free." She nodded to the chair by her desk. "We are expecting another one of your classmates this morning, another girl who has refuted her first charges. Diane Twayn."

"She went along with Emma and Ruth, just like the rest of us," said Wendy, so quietly that she could hardly be heard. "Emma and Ruth said it would be okay with Mister Girouard."

"Speak up, honey," said her mother.

Judge Ballinger intervened. "I can hear her very well, Missus Maple, and I will repeat whatever is required." She motioned to Wendy to sit down. "There will be someone from the District Attorney's office here, and a few men from the police department. Another judge will attend, Judge Studevant, who sat on a case . . . related to this one."

Each new person seemed to weigh down the girl. "Will Mister Girouard be here?"

"Yes," said Judge Ballinger kindly. "He and his attorney will both be here. This is an informal meeting, Wendy, and ordinarily we do not do this. But since these cases involve many minors— like yourself and Diane Twayn—we have decided that such a preliminary meeting would be useful to everyone."

Oliver Maple, Wendy's father, leaned forward as if to speak to the judge in confidence. "I was told that Doctor Covello will be here."

"Yes, he will, as will Melissa Budge, the school psychologist, and Ms. Tarrington, the Dean of Girls at Sutro Glen," said Judge Ballinger, not dropping her voice at all. "I have said already that this is a most unusual situation and—"

The door opened and Diane Twayn with her mother and her oldest sister entered the room.

"Missus Twayn?" said Judge Ballinger, indicating the other chairs in the front row. "I've just been explaining to the Maples how we will handle this meeting."

"I apologize for being late, Your Honor," said Mary Twayn. "We had trouble finding a place to park. I'm sorry my husband isn't with me, but he's out of town on business. My daughter Holly's with me," she added, indicating the tall, thin college student beside her. "This is Diane."

"Will you come up beside me, Diane?" asked Judge Ballinger, although she meant it as an order.

From the other side of the desk Wendy stared. "Hello, Diane."

"Hi," came the shy answer.

"The purpose of this meeting is to establish a few ground-rules for the upcoming trials you've been informed of." Judge Ballinger waved the Twayns to chairs next to the Maples. "It is also to clear up a question of identification. That is what the slide projector is doing here. We are going to conduct an informal lineup. Is that all right with you two girls?" She looked from Wendy to Diane.

"Yeah," said Diane.

"I guess so," said Wendy.

"All you have to do is tell the truth, which is why it is so important that you do. There are no tricks in any of this. No one is trying to catch you or mislead you or shame you. We don't want you to do anything but tell the truth," said Judge Ballinger with great patience.

"Excuse me, Your Honor," said Helene Maple, "but we were assured that the identity of our girls would be protected. If they have to appear in court, how can we be sure that—"

Judge Ballinger turned her blue, basilisk stare on Helene Maple. "We will not expose either of these young women nor any of the others to public attention. We are all agreed that in cases like these public focus is undesirable for most of the witnesses. You have my assurance on that point. The District Attorney's office and the police have already agreed to this, or we would not be here." She waited until she saw Missus Maple settle back in her chair. "I do not approve of any court that exposes children to the attention of the news media, especially in cases of sexual abuse. I will not tolerate it in my court. I suppose I have made myself clear enough."

"Yes, Your Honor," said Oliver Maple for his whole family.

Again the door opened and Sergeant Glen Mitchell came in with Lieutenant Hugo Palmerston of Homicide. Both of them exchanged brief greetings with the judge and took seats toward the back.

"I have the slides you wanted, Your Honor," said Palmerston, who had the right by rank to present them.

"Bring them here, if you will. And ask my bailiff to step in to set up the machine." She gave both girls an encouraging smile. "It won't take long, and then you can put the worst of it behind you."

"I don't like this," said Diane.

"It's real scary," said Wendy.

"Yes, I'm sure it is," Judge Ballinger said in a rallying way. "But it won't take more than an hour and a half, and you will have the satisfaction of contributing to the conviction of two men who have been abusing young women like yourselves for the last year at least." She motioned to the two cops to keep quiet; she was aware that mentioning Susan Lake would renew the two girls' terror. "Try to relax, if you can."

"What are we going to say to Mister Girouard?" Wendy asked.

"Well," said Judge Ballinger in her usual brisk way, "you might apologize. He'll probably accept your apology if you make one."

Victor Lovejoy was the next arrival, and this morning he was very nervous. As soon as he was through the door, Sally Aldred arrived, frowning at Lovejoy as if she wanted to continue an argument. He took his place near the back of the room away from the police officers.

After him came Melissa Budge, who went up to speak with the two girls before finding a seat behind the parents, one seat away from Sally Aldred. She looked preoccupied and once or twice referred to the notebook she carried.

Charlie and Morgan came in next; Morgan had a few words with Lorna Ballinger, Charlie with Glen Mitchell. Then they sat down near the windows, leaving a seat on the end for Frank Girouard.

The bailiff arrived and set up the slide projector. No one in the room said much of anything now; several of them fidgeted. The rush of the heater clicked off.

When Frank Girouard walked through the door, Wendy Maple nodded to him; Diane Twayn could not look at him at all.

"Good morning, Mister Girouard," said Judge Ballinger.

"Your Honor," said Frank, taking his seat beside Charlie.

Last to arrive was Doctor David Covello with his Dean of Girls, Delphinia Tarrington, in his wake. He bustled importantly, greeting the parents in the room while ignoring the two girls. "I was told this wouldn't take long. I hope it doesn't. We're having a fire drill right after lunch. Your Honor." This last was an afterthought.

"We will conclude it as soon as possible, Doctor Covello," said Judge Ballinger in a tone that was not promising. "If everyone will sit down?" she went on, clearly speaking to the two last arrivals, since everyone else was seated. She braced her elbows on the desk and steepled her fingers. "Now then, this is an informal inquiry. Nevertheless there is a tape recording being made of these proceedings, which is technically off the record. Only in the question of identification will the comments be considered binding. We are attempting to minimize the amount of attention given the victims by the news media. I am afraid this is going to be a very juicy story for them, and I, for one, am anxious to see that the victims are not victimized again. I include you as a victim, Mister Girouard."

Frank looked up in surprise.

"To begin with, we are going to show some slides." Judge Ballinger motioned to her bailiff. "In just a moment we are going to show you a series of slides of men, both their faces and their full bodies. If either of you girls recognizes any of the men, I want you to speak up at once. All right?" At her nod the bailiff turned out the lights and flipped on the slide projector.

The first man was bearded and dark-haired. He had hazel eyes and wore a blue shirt. When the second slide flipped on, showing him full-body, he was more than six feet tall, running a little to fat.

No one in the room said anything, although Hugo Palmerston thought that his brother had done a pretty good job of looking sleazy.

The second man was a light-skinned black, older than the first, and bigger framed. The silence continued.

The third man was crucial, for if the girls were going to make a mistake, it would be this one. Witnesses who were guessing tended to choose number 3 or number 7, and as a result the SFPD was at pains to put the actual suspects in other positions. This time the third man was a San Jose attorney, in San Francisco on a fraud case. He had fixed his normally expertly coiffed hair into a greasy pompadour, darkened his eyebrows and taken off his horn-rim glasses. In the gardening clothes he had in his trunk, he looked appropriately gungy. Four of the people in the room had to keep from chuckling, for they knew the man and found his disguise amusing.

The fourth man had a wedge-shaped face. His skin was olive, his hair a dark red shade and curly. Pale, grey-green eyes stared at the camera lens, glittering.

Diane Twayn shrieked and started to cry.

Wendy Maple stood up, her face stark in the projector's light. "That's Paco," she said in a soft, determined voice. "That's Paco."

Mary Twayn was already on her feet, rushing to comfort her child.

Charlie sat still, his eyes fixed on the face on the screen. The warm room went cold, and he felt the corruption of the man even at this remove. "That's Paco," he echoed, seconding Wendy Maple very quietly.

Morgan put her hand in his. "Charlie," she whispered. "Charlie."

"The man identified as Paco is Pacholos Aksander Khlm Orestes Hambai," said Judge Ballinger crisply. "He and a Ryffial Malkuros have been identified as business partners of Scooter Ferrand."

Charlie held Morgan's hand, glad that there was a sudden outbreak of consternation in Judge Ballinger's chambers; aside from Morgan, no one noticed his response. "I saw him. Thursday night."

"How did you see him?" Morgan asked softly.

"Through the dead. And I saw his living feet. From where Mickey and I were hiding." He admitted the last ruefully. "We were under the bed. It could have been funny, if Paco and Scooter hadn't been there."

"Don't make light of it," she said. "I saw how you looked afterward." The tightening of her fingers on his revealed how much affected she was; she made herself let go.

Judge Ballinger rapped on her desk, using the flat of her hand instead of a gavel. "If you would all calm down?" she said in a tone that cut through the outburst. When some order was restored, she turned to Missus Twayn. "Your daughter has been very brave to do this. If you will, I'd like you to go with Ms. Budge where Sergeant Mitchell is waiting. He will take you to a more private conference room."

"But I don't have an attorney," wailed Mary Twayn.

Judge Ballinger smiled a little. "You don't need one, Missus

Twayn, and neither does your daughter. Neither of you is accused of any crime. We want a statement about that man—the one your daughter called Paco—for the District Attorney's office and the police. Everything Diane can remember about him will help."

Diane was still crying, but not as violently as at first. "He . . . he said I was a bitch. He and that . . . that Mal wanted to hurt me."

"Sergeant Mitchell will listen to everything you tell him, Diane," said Judge Ballinger, gesturing for Mitchell to come and retrieve his charges.

"We'll take care of everything, Your Honor," said Sergeant Mitchell as he came to Mary Twayn's side. "Come on. Ms. Budge, if you will?"

Melissa Budge at once came to his assistance. "Certainly. Come along, Diane," she said, putting her arm around the girl's shoulder. "You will feel very much better once you start talking about it."

When they were gone from the room, Judge Ballinger said, "We already have a very complete statement from Wendy." She looked at Victor Lovejoy. "I want the District Attorney's office and the police to be very careful in this case. There is to be no repeat of the farrago that required Judge Studevant to dismiss the Ferrand case. These men are extremely dangerous, and I expect the bail being asked to reflect that." She leaned back in her chair. "Doctor Covello, I hope you will be willing to permit Sergeant Mitchell to speak to your student body? I am sorry to say that the history of these kinds of cases shows that for every one instance reported, five to ten are not. You have five known cases and a related homicide at your school. Under the circumstances, I believe it would be best if you would permit him to address a general assembly and with Ms. Budge's assistance, listen to any students who have something to tell."

"But, Your Honor," David Covello objected, standing to make his point, "the students are upset already. If we have a cop come and threaten them—"

"I beg your pardon, Doctor Covello, but nothing was said about threatening them," said Judge Ballinger. "In fact, I think that some of your students might find the presence of the police reassuring. They have been through more than children their age should have to endure, and we do not yet know the extent of what that may be. The sooner we know the magnitude of the trouble, the sooner your school will cease to be upset." She looked at the woman seated beside Covello. "I am curious, Ms. Tarrington. How is it that you had no inkling of these abuses?"

The woman's face darkened. "Your Honor, we try to get kids with problems to see the psychologist, or their counselors. We try to keep home and school problems separate." She lifted her chin. "Most of the parents say they prefer it that way."

"They do? Nevertheless, I recommend you alter your policy, Ms. Tarrington," said Judge Ballinger with comprehensive scorn. "From what I have seen, that policy contributed significantly to the charges brought against Mister Girouard. He might have grounds for a complaint against you for that policy. Keep that in mind. Speaking of Mister Girouard," she went on, paying no notice to the stricken look on David Covello's face and addressing Victory Lovejoy directly, "how is your office coming on those charges, Mister Lovejoy?" she inquired.

Victor Lovejoy cleared his throat. "Mister Wycliff will announce the dismissal of all charges against Mister Girouard at a press conference at three this afternoon. Lieutenant Palmerston will make an announcement about the arrest of Hambai and Ferrand. He's going to make it very clear that the charges against Mister Girouard were entirely groundless."

"Your Honor," said David Covello, raising his hand.

She ignored him. "See that he does, Mister Lovejoy," warned Judge Ballinger. "Mister Moon, Mister Girouard, you are free to leave. Doctor Covello, Ms. Tarrington, I suggest you retain counsel. I suspect you have only seen the tip of the iceberg in this case. Judge Studeveant, if you will join me? I think we can wrap up this business in short order."

Morgan kissed Charlie's cheek before she went up to the desk. "See you tonight," she said.

"I'll take you to dinner. Some nice place, not too caloric, very classy." He smiled at her, warmth spreading through him. "In the meantime, go serve up some belated justice."

Morgan grinned. "My pleasure," she told him.